# THE EARTH CHRONICLES

## SHADOWS OF THE VOID SERIES

### BOOK TWO

## J.J. GREEN

# BOOKS OF SHADOWS OF THE VOID

# CONTENTS

# PREQUEL

Sign up to my reader group for a free copy of *Starbound*, the Shadows of the Void prequel that tells the story of what happened to Jas Harrington in Antarctica, and for discounts on new releases, advanced reader opportunities and other interesting stuff:

https://jjgreenauthor.com/free-books/

# SHADOWRISE

# ONE

Lifting his duffle bag onto his shoulder, Carl Lingiari took a final look at his cabin before preparing to disembark the *Galathea*. He wasn't usually so sentimental, but the prospecting mission he'd just finished had been eventful. Hostile aliens called Shadows had killed the ship's officers and appeared as perfect copies of their victims, and Carl had fought alongside Harrington, the chief security officer, to save the ship. The menace of the Shadows had followed them to the colony planet, Dawn, which was supposed to have been free of the hostile aliens. It had turned out to be anything but.

The original pilot of the *Galathea* had been among the fatal casualties of the alien attack. For Carl, this meant that he'd gained precious flight hours piloting a starship, though it was the worst way for the opportunity to occur. He intended to put the experience to good use. He would pay his folks at home in Australia a brief visit, then he would apply for a full pilot's position and go touring the stars again.

"You all right in there, mate?" He directed the question to his duffle bag. A pair of bright eyes peeked through the half-open zip.

"Yeah, but get a move on," Carl's friend, Flux, replied. "It's stuffy in here. And your socks smell. Have you washed them?" An alien resembling a cross between a sugar glider and a bat, Flux was hiding, ready for the disembarkation inspection. Pets were banned aboard ship—not that Flux considered himself a pet—and prospecting crews weren't allowed to bring anything back that they hadn't taken with them when they departed Earth territory, especially not any alien life forms.

Strictly speaking, this meant Flux should have been safe from confiscation because Carl had smuggled him aboard when they'd set off, but the higher-ups in Deep Space Customs wouldn't see it that way. Flux would have to hide, and Carl would employ a special signal an old girlfriend who worked in Customs had taught him. The signal would guarantee that his bag wouldn't be inspected.

His door chime sounded. Harrington was waiting outside, looking stormy.

"What's up?" asked Carl as he left his cabin and closed the door for the final time.

"Haven't you received Haggardy's message yet?" Harrington replied. "Check your interface."

Carl unzipped his bag, lifted a disgruntled Flux off of his screen, and pulled it out. The alert light was flashing, indicating a message had arrived. Flux must have been sitting on the speaker when it beeped.

Haggardy had taken over as the *Galathea's* master when Akabe Loba had died, and had avoided as much responsibility as was possible in his new position. Carl wondered what the man had to say now that was suddenly so important.

Harrington supplied the answer before he could even open the message.

"He wants us to lie about what happened," she said. "He's sent us a 'report' to repeat to the investigators so he doesn't get into trouble for not helping to save the officers from the Shadows. Kratting misborn. I'm damned well not lying for him."

"Crew to departure hatch," came a voice over the comm system. "Prepare to disembark."

Carl and Harrington set off, joining the crowds of shipmates heading in the same direction.

Carl wasn't surprised that Haggardy wanted to cover up his role in the events of the last few weeks. If Polestar or the Global Government found out the extent of his inaction, he would be dismissed and his pension withdrawn at the very least. At worst, he could be charged with criminal negligence and involuntary manslaughter.

"Does he really think he can brush everything under the carpet that easily?" Carl asked. "There's gotta be security vids of it all, and he can't expect the whole crew to lie for him."

"He doesn't need *everyone* to lie. The rest of the crew don't know what actually happened. All they saw was a bunch of officers fighting. They only had our word for it that the officers were alien imposters, and I'm sure some of them didn't believe us.

If we told the investigators Haggardy's side of the story, they'd buy it, I think. But there's no way in hell I'm lying for him."

"We don't have to lie," said Carl. He thumbed the interface screen. "If he's telling us we have to stick to his report, we've got the evidence right here." The screen brightened with the acting master's message.

"He isn't that dumb, Lingiari."

Carl scanned the writing for a moment. "Yeah, I see what you mean." Haggardy's report on the incident on K. 67092d was addressed to Carl, Harrington, and Sayen Lee. Navigator Lee had been seriously injured when the *Galathea* had crash-landed. Carl had heard she was at that moment being transferred from the ship's stasis room to the nearest genetic hospital, where doctors could assess the extent of her brain damage and grow her a clone if necessary.

The subject line of the message simply read FYI. Only the people addressed in Haggardy's message would understand its true meaning: that was the story, and they were expected to stick to it, or else...what?

"You aren't considering covering up for him, are you?" asked Harrington.

"No, 'course not," replied Carl, but he wondered what Haggardy would do when they didn't. The man had decades of service under his belt, and he probably had stacks of influential friends.

"Do you think they're going to use the same tests for Shadows that they had on Dawn?" asked Harrington. "Krat, I hope not. I mean, they say the testing's foolproof, and that a Shadow must have got onto Dawn another way, but I don't see how they can be so sure. I'd swear we brought one with us."

"What I don't get is, if they could test us here on Earth, why did they send us all the way to Dawn?" Carl said. "Unless the problem's bigger than we thought and they can't process everyone who arrives here? Anyway, we'll have to go along with it. They seem to think they know what they're doing, and it's out of our hands now. The only alternatives are to refuse us permission to disembark or to go right ahead and destroy the ship. That'd reduce the risk all right."

"Urgh, don't say that," said Harrington.

"Anyway, let's collect Makey on our way out. We can show him where to go and vouch for him while he claims refugee status."

"Good idea," Harrington replied.

"By the way, what's happening with the Paths?"

"They've been transferred to a quarantine ship. None of the xenobiologists seem to have heard of them. It'll be a while before they're cleared to go planetside. And Karrev and the others were taken down by police transport this morning. They've all been charged with mutiny."

When they reached Makey's cabin, they found the Dawn native cleaning the shower room, which was already spotless.

"Hey, mate, you don't need to do that," said Carl. "They're gonna go through this ship and sterilize it top to bottom once everyone's off. Come on, we've got to disembark. We've got heaps of testing to get through once we're planetside."

The skinny young man straightened up and put down a face cloth he'd been using to wipe the surfaces. "If you're sure. I don't want to seem ungrateful for the cabin and free passage to Earth."

"No one thinks you're ungrateful for the chance to come with us," said Harrington. "I just wish Haggardy had agreed to bring some of Dawn's inhabitants."

"Me too," said Makey. "I'll get my stuff."

As the kid quickly packed his bag, Carl wondered what he would think of Earth. It was very different from the poor farming community he'd left behind. The kid would see luxuries and lifestyles that he'd probably never dreamed of, and a big gap between those who could and couldn't afford them.

The three joined the stragglers leaving the ship to board the shuttle that would take them to a spaceport in London, UK. From there, they could catch shuttles that would take them to the other side of the planet within a few hours, or airplanes that would get them to their destination much slower, but much cheaper.

At the departure hatch, a ginger-haired woman—the engineer-in-training MacAdam—was waiting for them. She was smiling like all her birthdays had come at once.

"You haven't disembarked yet?" asked Harrington.

"No, not yet," MacAdam replied. "I wanted to take this last chance to thank you. I might not see you again once we all go our separate ways."

"How come? You hanging up your wrench?" Carl asked. Prospecting crews often encountered old shipmates in the course of their work.

"I might be." The engineer grinned. "I sent a request to visit my kids, and I just heard that I've got an appointment. If I manage to stay clean for another six months, they said I stand a good chance of getting them back."

"Great news," said Carl. He had a feeling that Harrington's mail to the relevant authorities about MacAdam turning over a new leaf might have had something to do with the favorable response to her request.

"Yeah, great news," Harrington said, followed by, "Krat."

Haggardy was striding toward them. They'd nearly made it onto the shuttle without meeting the brown-noser.

"Lingiari, Harrington, just the people I wanted to see. MacAdam, and..." The acting master's eyebrows rose. "I remember you," he spluttered as he recognized Makey. "I gave instructions that you were *not* to board the ship."

"Not a lot you can do about it now, is there?" said Carl. "Makey, wait for us when you're through the testing. We'll point you to the refugee office."

As the kid went away, Haggardy followed him with his gaze, then turned his narrowed eyes to Carl and Harrington. MacAdam made herself scarce, mouthing 'goodbye'.

Haggardy said, "I gave explicit instructions—"

"What's done is done," said Harrington. "The kid's here now, and he can claim refugee status. It's going to be a long afternoon, so we'll be on our way."

"No you don't," Haggardy said. "Until you leave the ship, you two are still under my command, and I *order* you to remain. I have something to tell you."

Folding his arms over his chest, Carl waited with the grim-faced Harrington.

After checking that the rest of the crew were out of hearing range, Haggardy said, "I sent you both a report detailing what happened when we first encountered the Shadows. You are to memorize and repeat the facts as I stated them. There is to be no mention of your versions of the events, no interpretations, twisting, or embellishments of the truth as I have laid it out. Is that clear?"

"No way, Haggardy," Harrington said through her teeth. "No way am I lying for you. Forget it."

"Yeah," said Carl, "that's not happening, mate. You didn't do your job. That's the truth, and that's what I'm telling anyone who asks. Let's go," he added to Harrington.

The two walked away, and Haggardy shouted after them, "If you know what's good for you, you'll tell *my* truth. Or I'll make things very difficult for you. Very difficult indeed."

As they went through the exit hatch and boarded the shuttle, Carl wondered what Haggardy meant.

# Two

By the time Carl had passed through the Shadow testing and then Customs, it was late evening. He stepped out of the spaceport and into the heat, humidity, noise, and bright lights of London. Flux had long ago fallen asleep in his bag. When Carl checked on him, the animal's closed eyes and half-open mouth with its double row of needle-sharp teeth showed through the transparent wings he'd wrapped over his face.

Carl yawned. He had an appointment the next day with Polestar's investigators. He needed to find somewhere to stay the night.

Even at that hour, the multi-lane road that skirted the spaceport was busy with traffic, both at street level and just above as cars passed slower-moving vehicles by flying briefly over them. Carl wondered how long it would be before constant hover-driving was legal, and the traffic would split into road- and just-above-road level, and after that, maybe a third level? He didn't spend enough time on Earth to bother with buying a hovercar of his own, and driving had become all computer-automated, which took the fun out of it. He would have liked to drive/fly, dodging up and down and around the other cars.

He felt a tug on his sleeve. A dero had appeared beside him, unnoticed while Carl was watching the traffic. The man was barefoot, and from his overgrown toenails to his matted hair, he was grimy. A nauseating smell infiltrated Carl's nostrils.

"Just off a prospector, ain't ya?" the dero said. "You must be rolling in creds. I used to work the prospectors, too, till I caught thermatic plague. They cured me, but I'll never work again. Not like you. You look like a healthy bloke. Got years in you. Spare us some cred, eh?" The man was cradling a reader. The machine was old and cracked, but the display still glowed.

Carl didn't believe the man's story. No one survived thermatic plague. The dero probably lived from one run to the next. Carl didn't like the idea of supplying the man's habit, but for some, that was as much as their lives would ever hold.

"All right, give it to me," he said, taking the ancient reader from the man. He pressed the credchip embedded in his wrist to the scanner before typing in a nominal amount. When it registered the deduction from his account, he returned the reader.

The dero squinted at the display. "That's all you're giving me?" he said.

"Hey, if you don't want it..." Carl held out his hand to take the reader back, but the man clutched it to his chest and shuffled off without looking back.

"Thanks," Carl called out after him. He was beginning to remember why he spent so much of his time in deep space. The realization arrived quicker each time he touched down.

He yawned again. He needed to find a bed before he fell asleep on his feet. After checking on Flux a second time, he zipped up his bag and headed toward the autocab station. He wished he had someone to carry him around in a bag while he slept.

At the station, no autocabs were available and, according to the screen, none were due to return for another half an hour. *Krat.* He sat on the bench and pulled out his personal interface. He'd handed over his ship's one to the investigators of the incidents on K. 67092d. He hoped they would let him leave in enough time to catch the shuttle to Sydney the next day. He didn't want to wake his folks up with his surprise arrival in the early hours of the morning.

He tried to contact another autocab service, but they were all busy. He would just have to wait for a spaceport autocab to return. He started to look up local hotels on his interface to book a room. He found a place that didn't look like too much of dive but wasn't too pricey either. He was about to pay for it when the bright lights of an autocab caught his attention. One had returned earlier than the system had predicted. It drew up in front of him.

As he got up, the door opened. Harrington was inside. She leaned over the seat and smiled at him.

"Can I give you a lift?"

Carl laughed, put his bag on the back seat carefully to avoid disturbing Flux, and got in.

"I thought I'd return your favor," Harrington said as the door closed and the vehicle moved away. "Though I'm not exactly saving your life."

She'd been referring to the time he'd picked her up in a shuttle when she was under attack on Dawn. He said, "Thanks, but you would've got yourself out of that scrape if I hadn't happened along."

"I don't think so."

"I appreciate it anyway. How'd you know I was waiting?"

"I was hanging about, just in case. I saw all the autocabs got taken fast. Thought you might need a ride."

"Thanks a lot. I'm going here." He showed her the hotel he'd picked.

"Hmmm...well..." Harrington gave him a sidelong look. "My place isn't far. How about you save some creds and stay with me tonight?"

"That'd be great." The evening was getting better and better.

After Carl's agreement, a slight awkwardness invaded the atmosphere in the autocab. He wasn't sure what Harrington's intentions were. Maybe she was only offering him a place to sleep, or maybe she had more in mind. He was confused about how she felt toward him, and his feelings about her weren't yet clear to him.

When he'd first known her, she'd been a crush of his, but the woman had been so wrapped up in doing her job, she'd barely seemed to register that he existed. Dealing with the Shadow officers aboard the *Galathea* had brought them closer together, and he'd felt like he was getting to know the inner Harrington a bit better.

But then she'd grown close to a lieutenant stationed on Dawn. He'd backed off, assuming that he'd imagined her increasing feelings toward him. After she'd killed the Shadow of the lieutenant, however, it had been *him* she'd turned to in her confusion and grief.

The truth was, he had no idea where he stood with her.

The autocab was turning off the street, and a wide garage door lifted up, revealing the entrance to an underground carpark. Carl leaned back as the vehicle's nose dipped and it went down into the dark space. The cab halted abruptly next to an elevator and the doors popped open.

"This is it," Harrington said. "Don't forget your stuff."

"You do live close to the spaceport."

The woman shrugged as they went into the elevator. "It's convenient. I usually signup again pretty quick after finishing a mission."

The conversation lapsed and the awkwardness continued as they went up thirty floors.

After getting off the elevator, Harrington pressed her wrist to the door scanner, and the door opened. "It's small, but I don't need much," she said as they went in.

She wasn't joking that it was small, Carl thought. He put down his bag. He'd heard that space was at a premium in London, but Harrington's apartment was so small it would have fitted into his parents' living room. The place reminded him of a starship cabin. The bed, kitchen, and living area were combined, and a single door led to the shower room. The place was clean and tidy, and it didn't look poor, but it had an institutional feel to it. Someone had told him once that Harrington had grown up in a government orphanage, and the gossip rang true now that he saw how she lived.

"Are you hungry?" asked Harrington. "We can order something."

"No, I'm not. How about you?"

"No." She sat on the bed.

"So...I'm pretty bushed," Carl said. "I'll take the couch."

"Oh, okay."

Did she sound disappointed?

"I'm going to freshen up," Harrington said. She went into the shower room.

Carl got Flux out of his bag. The creature remained sound asleep. He put him on the end of the couch and covered him with a throw. While waiting for Harrington to finish, he looked out of her window and across the cityscape. Rivers of light marked the roads and freeways. No stars were visible due to their glow.

At the nearby spaceport, a shuttle was arriving from a starship, and Carl squinted in its glare as it landed. When the engines had been shut off, he recognized it was the latest model. He'd never flown one, but that no longer mattered. His eyes were on higher stakes. He was looking forward to his first starship commission.

Behind him, the door to the shower room opened, and Harrington appeared. She'd changed into loose pajamas and her hair was damp and messy from towel drying. Her sleepwear was typical Harrington—more functional than feminine—yet his long-time attraction to her remained the same.

"Your turn," she said.

He went into the shower room and mulled over what he should do as he got ready for bed. He was confused. Should he make a move? Was that why she'd brought him home? Or was she only doing a shipmate a favor? Harrington wasn't the flirtatious type. He found her hard to read.

If he tried something and the timing wasn't right, he might kill any chance he had of getting closer to her. He recalled again how shaken up she'd been by killing the Shadow of the soldier she'd got close to on Dawn. That decided it. He would wait for a crystal-clear signal before he would try to take things any further. She had to still be pretty upset by that incident.

Carl returned to the living room. Harrington was already in bed. They said goodnight, and after she'd turned out the light and dimmed the window to near darkness, he lay awake for a while, watching the faint trails of light from incoming and outgoing space shuttles shining through the glass. Memories of their encounters with Shadows played in his mind, as well as thoughts about the possible repercussions of the upcoming investigation. Concerns about Haggardy's possible methods for getting revenge also nagged at him.

From the sound of her breathing, he could tell Harrington was still awake.

"Have you thought about what you're going to tell them at the investigation tomorrow?" he asked.

"No. What's to think about? I'll tell them what happened of course."

"Yeah, but...I've been thinking about what Haggardy said. Do you think he can really do something serious if we don't go along with his story?"

"I don't know. Does it matter?" Harrington asked.

"It matters to me. Flying's my life. I dunno what I'd do if he got my license revoked."

Harrington's soft sigh breathed out into the night. "We don't have a choice. We have to tell the truth, no matter what. Haggardy's a real misborn. We can't let him get away with it. It wouldn't be right. If he'd done something when I warned him about Loba, maybe none of those officers would have died."

"I'm not disagreeing, but what's done's done. And that was his last mission. He's retiring now. He's not a danger to anyone anymore."

"Krat, Lingiari," Harrington replied, her voice rising, "I can't believe you're even saying that. You were with me there on the *Galathea*, right? You did know all those officers too?"

"All right, calm down. I was just thinking out loud. Geez."

Harrington mumbled something inaudible, and her sheets rustled. She didn't speak again. After a while, her breathing became deep and regular as she fell asleep.

# THREE

"Thank you for your time, Pilot Lingiari," said the chief investigator, extending his hand.

Carl sat up from his slouched position and reached to take the man's hand. He was in front of a team of five investigators, and he'd been there so long he'd lost track of time. "That's it? I can go?" His throat ached from answering the men and women's questions, and his head buzzed from going over the events on K. 67092d again and again.

The questioning had felt more like an interrogation than an investigation. He was glad he'd told them nothing but the truth according to his memory of the events. He would never have been able to keep track of Haggardy's lies if he'd decided to go along with the man's story.

"Yes, we have no more questions for you at the moment," said the investigator. He glanced at his colleagues on his right and left as he spoke. All of them shook their heads.

"Great." Carl stood and stretched.

"But, until the investigation is concluded, you are not to leave Earth," added the man.

"What?" Carl stopped mid-stretch and deflated a little. "How long's it gonna take? I mean, I'm a deep space pilot. I've gotta leave Earth to work."

"We understand. The investigation shouldn't take too long. I'm afraid I can't promise you anything more than that, however. We'll notify you when we reach our final conclusions."

"Great," Carl repeated with less enthusiasm. He took his jacket from the back of his chair and made his way out of the Global Security Headquarters. It was nighttime. He'd been answering questions the whole day. He checked the time and realized that he might make the last shuttle to Sydney if he hurried.

He requested an autocab on his interface and waited for it to arrive. It would be a close thing to make the shuttle flight, but after a day of talking about Shadows, fighting, and death, he had a strong urge to set eyes on his aging parents and his childhood home again.

The shuttle would be worth the extra expense to feel the hot Australian sun on his back again the next day. Outback New South Wales was worlds better than muggy, humid, polluted London.

He opened his bag. "We're going home, mate," he said to Flux, who was inside, eating a cracker.

"About bloody time," replied the creature. "I've been in this kratting bag nearly two days. I need to stretch my wings."

Flux wasn't the friendliest of aliens at the best of times, but he'd only had an hour or so of flying outside Harrington's window that morning, and the creature's grumpiness was only to be expected.

Carl jumped into the autocab that arrived, and he jumped out of it again at the spaceport. He ran through the terminal to make the shuttle, and soon he was strapped in and waiting to take off.

Night changed to dawn as he flew to Australia. The sun was coming up over Bondi when the shuttle touched down. Carl had managed a short nap on the flight, but his eyes were heavy and gritty by the time he hired a car at Sydney spaceport. He told the car the address of his parents' farm beyond the Blue Mountains and settled down to catch up on his sleep while it took him there.

As his eyes closed, he imagined his parents' surprise when he turned up months earlier than expected. His mum wouldn't have cooked his favorite meal, as had become a homecoming tradition since he'd first left home to go to flight school, but it didn't matter. He was smiling as he fell asleep imagining the happiness on his mum's face when she set eyes on him.

The pinging of the rental car door opening awakened him. On the adjoining seat, Flux had unzipped Carl's bag from the inside. His brown button nose poked out first, followed by black, beady eyes and large, tufted ears.

"Wake up, idiot, we're home," he said as he climbed out of the bag and spread his wings. "Ah, that's better," he said before jumping over Carl and through the open door. "I'm off to catch some breakfast. Say hi to your folks. I'll see you guys later." The alien flew off, gaining height to fly over the eucalypts that edged Carl's parents' farm.

Carl grabbed his bag and closed the car door. He would leave it in the road. The farm was in an area that saw little more than local traffic. He went toward the farmhouse, which stood at the end of a driveway. Though it was still early morning, he was a little surprised his folks hadn't come out to greet him. His mum and dad were usually up with the sun. Maybe they were already out in the yard or working in the fields.

He went up the driveway and around the back of the house. Only delivery drones used the front door. No one was in the yard. He tried the back door, but it was locked. Carl's hand dropped in surprise. The back door was never locked. He stepped backward and peered at the upper floors of the house. His parents' bedroom window glass was clear, which meant they were up.

Returning to the house, he looked in the downstairs windows, cupping his hands around his eyes. All the downstairs rooms at the back were empty, and in the kitchen there were no signs that breakfast had taken place. He knocked on the back door. No one answered. After three or four more tries, he went out into the yard again and shouted up, "Mum, Dad."

He ran around the house to the front, but that door was locked too.

Carl decided to investigate the barn. If his parents were out working in the fields, equipment would be missing. But when he checked, everything seemed to be in its place. He wondered if they could have gone for a walk around the farm. It was possible, but why would they lock the door?

A terrible fear rose in Carl. He tried to quell it with reasoning. He tried to tell himself that his parents might have gone away to visit a relative, or they might have had another reason for leaving their cherished farm, but he couldn't convince himself that something wasn't very wrong.

He needed some help. Carl tilted back his head, put his hands to his mouth and shouted, "Cooee." The sound echoed back from the farmhouse and surrounding trees. A few minutes later, Flux appeared over a wattle tree and glided down to land on Carl's head before hopping onto his shoulder.

"Something's up, right?" Flux asked.

"You noticed?" said Carl. "I was gonna ask if you'd seen Mum or Dad about the place."

"Nope. Haven't seen them anywhere, and what's more, look around you, mate."

Carl went up a low rise, and gazed at the fields, the yard, and the house. His alien friend was right. The farm looked as though no one had been there in weeks. In his concern over his missing parents, he hadn't noticed that the house windows were grimy with red dust—something his dad would never have tolerated—and that the yard was thick with dead leaves and other plant debris that had blown in from the fields.

And the fields themselves—where was that year's crop? The ground should have been filled with green shoots at that time of year, but it looked as though it hadn't even been sown. A hard crust covered the land. The soil hadn't been tilled since the previous season's harvest. How long had his parents been away?

Carl's legs felt weak. He sat down right there in the cobbled yard, fear gripping him. He took his interface from his bag, and with trembling fingers he called the nearest neighbor. Mrs. Jesson had been friends with his parents all his life. If anyone would know where they were it would be her.

The neighbor answered, and her voice became full of sorrow and concern the second she recognized Carl's voice.

"Oh, love, I'm sorry. I thought you might know where they are."

"What? Have they gone missing? How long has it been?"

"Come over, Carl, and I'll tell you everything I know. It isn't right to talk about it over the phone."

"All right. I'll be there in a minute."

Carl jogged the kilometer over the fields to the neighbor's house, dreading to hear what she had to say. She was standing at her open door, waiting for him.

"What's going on, Mrs. Jesson?" asked Carl as he wiped his feet on her doormat. Flux was perched on his shoulder. As Carl went inside, the creature took off and circled the room twice before settling on the top of a display cabinet holding the woman's prized blue heeler ornaments collection. Flux was never normally allowed inside Mrs. Jesson's home as he'd never quite embraced house training, but she must have felt the occasion warranted an exception.

"Carl, dear, please sit down. You really don't have any idea where Bernard and Joyce have gone? We searched high and low for them. We told the police, and we locked the place up so nothing got stolen. It was lucky they gave up raising horses. It looked like they'd been gone two or three days before anyone realized." Reading Carl's expression, the older woman began to weep. "I'm so sorry. You were our last hope."

"Mrs. Jesson, what's happened to my parents?"

"Dearie, I don't know how to tell you this. Your mum and dad have been missing for three months. The police sent a message to your company to pass on. Didn't it get through?"

# FOUR

When Sayen Lee woke up, she knew something was wrong. She tried to make sense of the feeling. Then, as always, the realization hit as her memory returned. She'd been injured in the crash-landing on K. 67092d, and now all that remained of her mind was trapped within a brain that no longer controlled her body. Machines were keeping her heart beating and her lungs breathing. She was in stasis, and though she could think, hear, and speak, she was otherwise entirely cut off from the world.

Except...except...Sayen could feel. She was lying on sheets, and air moved gently on her skin. Her heart began to race. A beeping sounded.

"She's coming around," said an unfamiliar voice.

"Sayen, oh, Sayen," said another voice. Her mama. It was her mother speaking. The events of the last few days came flooding back to her. Could she...move? Was it possible...? Sayen had grown so used to not being able to open her eyes that she had to make a conscious effort to do it. She willed her eyelids to lift. A blur of indistinguishable shapes and light came into her view.

Footsteps sounded beside her, moving away. A door opened. "Craven," her mother called. "Get in here. She's woken up. Our baby's awake."

The footsteps returned.

Sayen forced her lips and voice box to work. "M...mama?" Her voice was no more than a whisper.

"Oh, sweetheart." Her mother's voice broke. The door opened again. More footsteps sounded, heavier and firmer than her mother's.

"Sayen, darlin'," said her father, "now don't you try to move or say a thing. The nurse has called the doctor, and she'll be here any minute. It's a miracle, Carleen, a miracle."

The shapes Sayen saw were becoming more defined by the second. They were multi-colored tiles, lined with thin light strips. But the lights weren't on. Her vision was filled with sunlight. The sound of her mother's sniffles was coming from her right-hand side, and the window was to her left.

Sayen felt like crying herself. The operation had been a success. The genetics team had grown her a new body, and they'd taken all the knowledge, memories, and personality contained in her old brain and transferred it to the new one. She'd survived. She would move, eat, speak, live again.

After Dr. Sparks had told her about her accident, and that it would be a long time before the *Galathea* could return to Earth, if ever, she'd thought she was living a kind of half-death, and that her real demise was only delayed a little. It had been good, of course, to talk to Carl and Jas and others aboard the ship, and to help out with their problems, but she'd given up on any chance that she might be saved.

Yet here she was, in a brand new body. And not only was it brand new, but it was also enhanced. She'd been fitted with the latest in organic-synthetic technology. She didn't only have a new body, she had a *better* one.

The door opened again. "Hi, Sayen. I'm Doctor Evans, and I'm in charge of your treatment. Do you remember me? We had a long talk before we attempted the transfer. Now, I don't want you to say a thing. Just close your eyes once for yes, twice for no, okay?

"So, how're you feeling, sugar? You feeling okay?"

Sayen closed her eyes once.

"Great. Do you have any pain anywhere?"

Sayen blinked twice.

"Even better. Well..." A shadow crossed Sayen's vision as the doctor moved past, blocking the sunlight. "All your vitals are looking great, honey. I don't like to be too optimistic—there's plenty that could go wrong even at this stage—but I think you're gonna be fine. Mr. and Mrs. Lee, could you join me outside, please?"

Her parents and the doctor left the room, but Sayen remembered one of her new enhancements. She strained her hearing hard, and through the closed door, she could clearly make out the conversation the doctor was having with her parents. Had the doctor under-estimated the quality of the hearing the cloning service had supplied, or did she intend for Sayen to hear what she said?

"Mr. and Mrs. Lee, I know I already told you this, but I wanted to emphasize that it's very, very early days with Sayen. She's got her new body, but you have to remember that she's spent quite a while trapped in her mind. It'll take her some time to get used to controlling her movements. She'll be like a little baby learning to walk. She'll learn faster than a child because she's done it before, but she will have to learn."

"I understand, Doctor," said her mother. "We're prepared to pay for the very best in therapy to get her back to normal."

"Yup," added her father. "Whatever it takes."

"I know you are. You've both been very generous, and we all appreciate your kind donation to the hospital. But the real reason I wanted to speak to you was so I can be totally sure you understand she might not have all the mental capabilities she once had. Even without the death of brain tissue, there's no guarantee we can recover *everything* from the old mind, and after Sayen's accident..."

"We do understand," came her father's deep voice.

"We know, Doctor, we know. But it doesn't matter. You brought our baby girl back, and we can never thank you enough..." Her mother began to weep again.

"Just doing our jobs, Mr. and Mrs. Lee," said the doctor, "but it's a pleasure. A real pleasure. Now, why don't you go spend some time with your daughter? Just an hour or so. Please continue to resist the urge to hold or touch her, however tempting I know that must be. Her body is very, very fresh. We were forced to push the envelope on getting her transferred into it, in consideration of the conditions she'd been stored in. If we'd waited any longer, well, let's just say it might have been a very different Sayen you would be taking home."

"We'll be careful," said her mother. "Don't you worry." She blew her nose. "We won't let anything bad happen to her ever again."

———

Three days later, Sayen could sit up, and she was eating, drinking, and speaking normally. She was still experiencing the sheer joy of being alive. She would spend hours looking out the window, studying every feature of the hospital's lavish garden. Each flower, plant, insect, and bird delighted her. She felt like she'd never truly appreciated how beautiful the world was until she'd been nearly taken from it.

The hospital was wonderful too. Everything was so clean. She couldn't have wished for a neater or more dirt- and germ-free room.

Her doctor had told her that the next day she could begin learning to walk, and that to pass the time, she was allowed to start having one or two visitors. She'd known exactly who she'd wanted to see and she'd made a couple of calls before pleading with her parents to take a break and have some time to themselves when her visitors arrived. Her real reason for asking them to leave her alone was so that they wouldn't overhear upsetting details about what had happened aboard the *Galathea*.

The next day, a face appeared at the small window in her door. Sayen grinned and waved Harrington into the room.

"You get sick in style," were the security officer's first words as she came in.

"Thanks for coming. I'm not sick. I'm here to get better."

Harrington perched on the edge of her bed, squashing the mattress.

"Is Lingiari coming too?" she asked Sayen.

"No, I can't contact him."

"Must be busy with his parents." The woman studied her. "You look...totally the same."

Sayen laughed. "What were you expecting?"

"I don't know. I thought you could choose what you wanted for your new body? Like, height, size, shape, hair, eye, and skin color. Everything."

"I suppose I could have, but I didn't want to. I just asked for a clone. Are you saying there's something wrong with how I look?" She laughed again. "Seriously, why change anything? I like the way I am. And so do my parents. They've gotten used to the old Sayen. If I looked any different, it would be weird."

"I guess so," said Harrington. "But...are you sure you wouldn't rather be a little taller?"

The security officer maintained a deadpan expression long enough for Sayen to begin to look outraged, then both women burst into giggles.

As their laughter subsided, Sayen said, "I'm not totally the same, you know."

"Really? What's different?"

"Well, for one thing...I, er...I know, I'll show you. Let's arm wrestle."

"Sure," said Harrington, her eyebrows rising. She pushed her sleeve up to her elbow and rested it on the bed tray. Sayen did the same and grabbed the woman's hand. In a matter of moments, Harrington's forearm was flat against the tray.

"Woah," she said. "Let's try again. Maybe you caught me by surprise."

Harrington lasted a few moments longer the second time, but the victory was just as decisive.

"That's amazing. Is it just your arms that are stronger, or are you like that all over?"

"My muscles are enhanced with synthetic fibers," Sayen said. "And that's not all." She paused dramatically.

"Go on, tell me what else you've had done."

"Enhanced hearing *and* sight. And my skin can withstand freezing and boiling temperatures."

"Wow, that's impressive. It sounds like you didn't come too badly out of nearly dying."

"Huh, yeah, well, I'd rather that hadn't happened, but I'm not complaining about the end result. Though I think my parents' accountant might be. You know, Jas, I used to be so afraid of everything. I wouldn't even set foot on an alien planet."

"I remember."

"Something's changed in me. When I came so close to dying, I realized I'd never really lived. Do you know what I mean?"

"I guess so."

"After I get my strength back, I'm not going to hide away anymore. I'm going to take risks. I'm going to live my life to the full, even if it means a little danger now and then."

"That's great. I'm happy for you. Just...take things easy at first, okay?"

"Of course I will. But what's been happening? What are the results of the investigation? Have they arrested Haggardy yet?"

"No, not yet. I told them everything that happened, and they said they'd let me know the verdict, but I haven't heard anything so far, and there's been nothing on the news. I wish they'd hurry up. I just want to move on, you know? It's been longer than a week. I'm ready to sign up for another mission."

# FIVE

J as couldn't believe it. She was at home in her apartment, and she'd been standing when the message appeared on her interface, but her knees buckled and she sat on her bed as she read it.

*All individuals involved in the attempted capture by unknown aliens of the prospecting starship Galathea while it was in orbit around K. 67092d are found to be innocent of any dereliction of duty or other criminal or civil culpability in the resultant loss of life. No legal wrongdoing on behalf of any Polestar employees involved, living or dead, has been found.*

How could it be true? She'd told them all of it, beginning to end, and her story would have been totally different from Haggardy's. The investigation committee *must* have known one of them had to be lying. How could they have found no one guilty? Didn't they even suspect that something wasn't right? People had died. Margret Statton and nineteen officers had lost their lives. Even Loba deserved some kind of justice for his death. Haggardy shouldn't be able to get away with his cowardly and negligent behavior.

After staring at the screen for several more moments, and resisting the urge to throw the interface across the room, Jas released a groan of frustration. She would never, never understand the workings of governments, or human beings in general.

She got up and went to her window. Looking out across the spaceport, she went over the events of the last few days. It looked like the investigation into the events with the Shadows was over, and despite what she'd thought was a growing closeness with Lingiari after what had happened with the Shadows on Dawn, he didn't seem that interested in her.

She'd messaged him once or twice, but she hadn't received a reply. She suspected that now that Sayen was better, the two of them would get together. The pilot had spent a lot of time with her while she was in stasis. She wished the couple well, but she couldn't help but feel a little sad. The more she'd gotten to know the pilot, the more she'd liked him, even though he'd wavered over telling the truth about Haggardy. She understood how important his job was to him. Her career was important to her too.

A shuttle was taking off. Her gaze followed its glowing path into the hazy blue sky. Somewhere up there, out of sight, a space vessel awaited its passengers. Maybe it was a prospector like the *Galathea*, or a transport to Mars, Europa, Titan, Callisto, or Ganymede, or maybe it was an alien vessel belonging to one of the Transgalactic Council allies.

Jas's heart yearned for the simplicity of space, far from the complex and bewildering machinations of humankind. It was time for her to return to the stars and her job working with the predictable, comprehensible defense units. She knew it was crazy, but she liked the fighting androids better than some people she knew. She'd even said goodbye to them before disembarking the *Galathea*. They hadn't replied, but she'd felt like they were a little bit sorry to be parted from her too. It had probably been her imagination.

Scouting for danger, protecting, and defending—these were concepts she could wrap her head around, even though they weren't easy in practice. Still, she could understand them. Yes, it was time to get back to work.

She reached for her interface and searched for current deep space security job openings, filtering the results for prospecting ships leaving within the next week. She didn't anticipate too many problems finding another berth. Her qualifications and experience counted heavily in her favor. Most people in her line of work switched to another profession within their first few years, assuming they survived. And she wasn't fussy about pay. Her bank account was already stacked with more creds than she would ever spend. A life in government institutions had left her uncomfortable with frivolity and luxury.

Five positions popped up on the screen. One was a two-year mission to a far-distant, little-explored section of the galaxy. It was another Polestar job. They weren't the best employers, but they weren't the worst either. Jas applied. With luck, she would be off the planet the day after tomorrow.

She composed a final mail to Lingiari, telling him she'd enjoyed working with him and wishing him well. Next, she wrote to Sayen and told her she hoped her recovery was going well, and that maybe they might meet on a starship somewhere if the navigator decided to return to work. From what she'd understood as the cost of Lee's treatment, it looked like she didn't have to worry about never working again.

Getting up, Jas went to put on a light jacket. She wanted to head out for a final meal at a local noodle shop before she embarked on another mission. Her favorite restaurants were about the only thing she missed of Earth.

Her interface pinged. Had Lingiari finally replied? She checked the screen. No. It was a mail from Polestar. Thinking the reply was suspiciously quick, she opened it. The position had been filled. *Krat.* She would have to apply for the shorter missions. They were all pretty much the same—one-year trips to planets that had been passed over in the first prospecting rush. Usually, this was because they were too high or low gravity, or had some other feature that made the potential profits from resource extraction marginal.

Whatever. A longer assignment would have been better, but Jas didn't really mind what kind of planets she worked on. She applied to all four positions, put on her jacket and went out.

In the basement of a department store, she went to one of the many small restaurants that lined the walls. She took a seat and spoke her request into the ordering mic. As always, her height and coloring made her stand out. The rest of the patrons in the basic restaurant watched her for a few moments before returning to their meals. She didn't have to wait long before a bowl of noodles appeared on a serving cart and trundled over to her.

She'd barely begun eating before her interface pinged again, twice, in her pocket. She took it out and propped it up against the condiment containers on the table. She'd received two mails replying to her job applications. That was fast. She opened the messages and read that both positions were no longer open. Her stomach began to sink. Three jobs filled as soon as she applied for them? It was too much of a coincidence.

With a sense of foreboding, she continued to eat. Sure enough, a few minutes later, a third mail arrived. The company was very sorry, but her application had been unsuccessful. *Krat. Krat. Krat.* She'd finished her meal, paid, and was leaving the restaurant when the fourth mail arrived. She almost didn't bother opening it. The security officer position had been posted in error, the message said, and the company was not accepting applications.

It had to be Haggardy's doing. He hadn't only got off scot-free, he'd called on all the contacts he'd built up over his long career and managed to get her blacklisted. *Damn the misborn.* He'd followed through on his threat to her and Lingiari. She stopped in her tracks. Lingiari. If Haggardy had punished her for refusing to cover up for him, had he punished the pilot too?

Did Lingiari already know he'd been blacklisted, and did he blame her for pushing him to tell the truth? Was that why he hadn't been answering her mails?

Jas continued on her way back to her apartment. When she arrived, she threw herself on her bed. Her plans to get away from Earth were falling through, and it looked like a good friend now hated her. Could the day get any worse?

As she lay thinking about what other spacework she could apply for and wondering how far Haggardy's reach stretched, her interface pinged again. Lifting her arm from across her eyes, she peered at the screen. She blinked away the blurriness of her vision. Someone was calling her on a live vidmail.

She sat up and squinted at the name. When she recognized it, she smiled. Finally, she had something to be happy about. She thumbed the icon to open the vid.

"Jas," exclaimed Makey as soon as he saw her.

"Hi, what's up, kid? How are you doing?"

The young man looked much better than he had when Jas had last seen him. His face had filled out, and his skin was a healthy color.

"I'm all right. I'm living in a holding center while they process my refugee application. Some of the people here say I shouldn't have any problems because Dawn's being invaded at the moment. Did you hear they're sending in extra troops?"

"Yeah, I did. I hope they win back the planet soon, Makey."

"So do I." He paused and screwed up his face as if he found it difficult to say his following words. "I'm worried about my da. I know he wasn't good to me, but…"

"I understand. He's still your father. Try not to worry. I'm sure the army's doing everything they can to protect Dawn's inhabitants."

"And I miss Mam and Neeve. When they got taken by the Shadows…and I left so fast…what had happened to them didn't really sink in. Now I've had time to think about it…" The kid's expression fell.

"I'm sorry, Makey," Jas said. "But, you know, I think they would have been happy to know that you got away, and that you're going to have a chance at a new life."

Makey smiled sadly. "Yeah, maybe."

"So, what's the plan when your application's approved?" Jas asked.

"I haven't decided. There's so much I don't know, and so much I want to do. But I was…I was thinking about becoming a security officer like you. I want to fight the Shadows, Jas. I want to get them back for what they did to my family and my friends. It might help me feel better about leaving them on Dawn if I could work at protecting other people."

"Makey, you've got nothing to feel bad about—"

"I know. I know. I understand what you and Carl said about me being just a kid and everything. But it doesn't change how I feel. Jas, could you help me? I don't know anyone here, and I need someone to help me apply for courses, or maybe apply to the military. I haven't decided yet exactly what I want to do."

She arranged to go and see him at the refugee center. It would be good to see him again, and it would give her something to occupy her while she figured out what she was going to do with the rest of her life, too.

# Six

Carl sat in the kitchen of his parents' farmhouse. Though the weather was as hot as an oven outside, the room felt cold to him. It was twilight, but he hadn't turned on the lights. He preferred the dark. It matched his feelings, and artificial illumination only seemed to drive home the fact that his parents weren't there. From outside came a kookaburra's laughter and the songs of cicadas, driving away the unwelcome silence.

Carl's eyes were sandy and sore, and his head throbbed. He couldn't remember the last time he'd slept properly since finding out that his parents had gone missing. After the initial shock and visits to the police, as well as anyone else who might provide a clue as to what had happened, his sleep had been invaded by dreams of his mum and dad.

His sleeping mind jumbled up his parents with the events of his time aboard the *Galathea*. He would dream of fighting to get over to the Shadow of Grantwise, the former pilot, and take over the flight controls before the starship crashed. But when the Shadow turned around, it was his father. Or he would see Makey take aim at the Shadow that had been about to kill Harrington on Dawn, but the Shadow would transform into his mother. Whenever he woke, sweating, from the nightmares, he would always ask himself the same questions:

Had his parents been taken by Shadows? Was Earth being invaded?

He didn't have any evidence for his fears, and all that he knew about Shadows contradicted the idea. If Shadows had taken his parents, he would have expected to find replicants in their place. And if Shadows were on the farm, he would have expected to find their traps. But he'd checked every meter of the familiar soil and found nothing but weeds and the remains of unharvested crops.

The only explanation for his parents' disappearance the police could offer was that they'd gone for a walk—their car was in the garage—and they'd had an accident. It was also remotely possible that they'd been attacked or abducted, though crimes like that were unheard of in the area.

Carl couldn't accept the police's conclusions. His parents knew their surroundings too well to go anywhere unsafe or do anything dangerous. And they were fit and healthy for their ages. The idea that both of them could suddenly collapse, with neither of them able to get help, just wasn't credible.

Over the last few days, Carl hadn't paused in his search for them. He'd tramped the landscape, calling them both by name, and flown his dad's old plane over the whole farm. He'd spoken to everyone who could possibly have seen them before they disappeared. He'd read everything he could on what had been happening in the area at the time, hoping to find something—anything—that might be remotely related.

Nothing. He'd found nothing that might lead him to the two people who meant the most in the world to him. It was as though they'd eaten breakfast, tidied up the kitchen, gone out, and stepped off a cliff into a sea that swept them away, leaving no trace.

As he sat in the dark, a deep fatigue came over Carl. He put his head on the table, resting it on his folded arms, and fell asleep.

In the middle of the night, a pinging awakened him. It was coming from the interface he'd fallen asleep on. Wincing from a crick in his neck, he sat up and checked the screen. It was an advertisement. *Great.* He was about to try to go back to sleep when he saw a message below the ad. It had arrived that morning from Harrington.

It had to have been the fourth or fifth time she'd mailed him. He'd put off replying because it felt like the moment he talked to someone who didn't know his parents were missing, and told them the news, it would make it all real. He'd hoped that when he finally answered her messages, it would be to tell her about the crisis in the past tense, with his mum and dad safe and sound beside him.

But he couldn't put off answering her any longer. He swiped the screen. As he read the message, his face fell. She was leaving already, going off on another mission. Between the lines, he read her frustration about the findings of the investigation into the *Galathea* incident. He'd barely registered the information when it had arrived, being too preoccupied with his parents' disappearance, but he could imagine how disappointing the result would be to the security officer.

He was sad that he hadn't had the chance to speak to her again before she left. He would miss her, and it would have been good to have someone to talk to about his fears for his parents. And though it hardly seemed important at that moment, he also hadn't completely given up on the idea that she might one day be something more than a friend.

But maybe it wasn't too late to speak to her. She'd only sent the mail the previous morning. She might not have left yet. He spoke a quick reply into his interface, asking if she could talk. After checking the message on the screen, he hit send.

Almost immediately, he got a vidmail request. As he read the sender, he understood that it hadn't been too late. He accepted the request, and Harrington's face appeared on the screen. He didn't think he'd ever felt happier to see her.

"Woah. Is something wrong?" was the first thing she said. "Sorry, Lingiari, but you look kratting terrible."

"It's a long story, Harrington. I'd tell you all about it, but I dunno if you have time. Are you shipping out soon?"

"Huh. No, I'm not. And you might not be either, sorry. But tell me what's happened there first. Are your folks okay?"

"No, they're...they're..." He fought to control himself.

"Krat, Lingiari. What's wrong?"

He passed a hand over his eyes. "If you aren't going anywhere soon, do you think you could come out here? Something's happened, and I can't make any sense of it."

"Of course. I'll be there on the next shuttle."

# Seven

Jas had never been to Australia. As the shuttle descended to the spaceport, she realized that she'd seen more of other planets than she'd seen of Earth. Most of her childhood had been spent on Mars. It was only when she'd reached puberty that it had occurred to the orphanage director that if she didn't go to Earth soon, she would grow too tall and weak to ever go there. A few more years in a government institution in Chicago had passed, then she'd gone directly to security training and as soon as she'd graduated, she left on her first mission aboard a prospector.

At the time, she'd seen no reason not to start work immediately. She had no family nor any particularly close friends to leave behind, but as she looked out of the shuttle window at the bright blue of Botany Bay and the thin, white-yellow line of the beaches along the New South Wales coast, she wondered if she should have spent more time exploring the home planet of humankind. Maybe it wasn't such a bad thing that she'd been forced to stay a while. At least she could help Carl search for his missing parents. Their disappearance was very odd, and he was naturally out of his mind with worry.

Jas grabbed the cabin bag that held the few things she'd brought with her and went directly out to meet her friend. He was easy to spot among the happy faces of the people waiting to meet other passengers. He was smiling like them, but he had dark shadows under his eyes, and he'd lost so much weight he looked positively gaunt.

"Thanks for coming," he said as she approached. After a welcoming hug, he pulled something out from his jacket. "These are for you." It was a pair of flight goggles.

Jas took them from his hand. "Don't tell me we're going to—"

"The family plane's the fastest way to get home. Unless you're tired of flying after your trip?"

"No, I'd love to have a ride in your plane."

"Great. Let's go over to the airport," Carl said. "The place is a lot quieter than it used to be. More and more people take the shuttle these days."

Carl's plane looked out of place among the expensive, gleaming hobby aircraft at the airport. Jas was no expert on airplanes, but she would have bet money that it was from the previous century. A simple two-seater, its paint was dull, and the fuselage was patched in places. But she liked the look of it. There was something about it that explained a lot about Carl.

He helped her up into the passenger seat. As he got in, she stowed her bag in the footwell, fastened her safety harness, and put on her goggles. Carl checked over his shoulder that she was ready, and he started the engine.

What followed was one of the most memorable experiences of Jas's life. As they soared up into the cloudless sky, she understood why Carl loved flying so much. She'd never felt so free or exhilarated. The roar of the engine and the wind made it impossible to speak, but when her friend looked over his shoulder again, they shared a smile. Jas relaxed in her seat and gazed at the mountains at the edge of Sydney, content to be carried along in the plane.

A little while later but too soon, it seemed, they were descending. She could see fields, a narrow road edged with trees, a house, and a flat, open place that she supposed served as an airstrip. Her bones were rattled as they landed on the bare dirt.

Carl took her over to his family home: a two-story, wide, wooden house. Once they were inside the cool interior, he showed her to the guest bedroom and left her to freshen up after her journey. She went to the bathroom and washed off the dirt that had accumulated on her face around the goggles before returning to the bedroom to unpack.

The room was simple, old fashioned, and cozy. On the wall hung a photograph of a tall, part-Aboriginal man and a blonde, fair-skinned woman with their arms around a gawky, teenage Carl. Jas's heart ached at the thought of how her friend had to be feeling about his parents' disappearance. She also ached for the normal, loving childhood that she'd never known.

Downstairs, she found Carl in the large kitchen, his fingers sweeping an interface on the table. He looked up as she came in.

"Found any leads?" she asked.

He shook his head. "I've looked everywhere and so have their friends and the police. It's completely unlike them to just go off without telling someone, and they would never willingly let the farm fall into the state it's in. I can't help but think something terrible's happened."

Jas sat down opposite him and reached over to put her hand on his. "I'm so sorry. I'll do everything I can to help. What was the place like when you got here? Did it look like there'd been a fight?"

"No. Everything looked normal. Like they'd just gone out for a walk and hadn't come back."

They talked on, discussing each possible reason for the disappearance and dismissing each in turn. Outside, the sky darkened as evening began to fall. Carl turned on the light and made them both dinner. As they ate, they continued to discuss the problem. What could persuade an older couple who had busy lives including daily duties to keep their farm going, to simply up and leave?

An answer, based on her and Carl's experiences aboard the *Galathea*, nagged at the back of Jas's mind. She didn't name it, though. She didn't want to make the suggestion to her friend.

They had both been silent for some time, Jas realized, when Carl asked if she would like to take a walk with him around the farm before it got too dark.

"I'd love to," she replied.

The air felt thick and warm as they stepped out into the twilight. Cicadas sang loudly. All color had left with the setting of the sun, and the farm looked mysterious and other-worldly in shades of gray and black. They went through the yard and up a short slope that led to the fields. Trees rose tall and slim at their edges, and they followed a track toward them.

"This leads to the upper paddock," Carl said, "where Mum taught me to ride."

"You can ride horses too? That's amazing. I can't even drive a car."

"Yeah, I can. Though I learned so long ago I can't really remember. But I've seen the pictures of Mum teaching me. They don't keep horses any more. They sold them all when I left to go to flight school. I think they must have only been keeping them for my benefit."

"They sound like great parents."

"Yeah, they're good people. No one had anything but good to say about them when I went around the neighborhood making inquiries. Some people said how much they would be missed, like they didn't expect to see them again." Carl's voice dried up. Jas touched his upper arm.

They were under the trees, walking through the leaf litter and fallen bark. The rustle their steps made echoed the sound of the breeze in the long, thin branches and leaves above them.

Carl stopped, his head hung low, as if he hadn't the will to go farther. Jas waited beside him, her hand still gently touching his arm. After a moment, the pilot looked up, and his face was illuminated by the light of the rising moon. Jas could see glints in his dark eyes as he looked intently at her. He turned his body toward her and held her arms.

As he leaned closer, Jas closed her eyes, waiting for his kiss.

But a screech broke through the air, and she heard the flapping of wings. Carl exclaimed, and Jas opened her eyes. Flux had landed on his head.

"G'day, Jas," the creature said. "Carl, you didn't say we were having visitors."

# EIGHT

"This is some place," Carl said as they drove up the long, wide driveway toward Sayen's home four days later. Magnolia trees in flower bordered the pavement, their huge, creamy goblet-shaped flowers cupped toward the sky. "Sayen told me her family was well off, but I didn't think she meant *this* well off."

Jas had spoken into an intercom at the gates before their autocab had been allowed through. From there, it had been a five-minute drive through immaculate grounds to the house, or rather, the mansion. The cab stopped and they got out.

Jas didn't normally ever think about the clothes she wore or how she looked, but it was impossible not to feel a little self-conscious in such an intimidating setting.

One of a pair of huge doors opened, and a maid in a traditional black and white uniform appeared. "Good afternoon, madam, sir. Would you please step this way?"

They followed the maid as she led them across a wood-paneled, wood-floored—*real* wood—hallway and through several sumptuous sitting rooms. Jas had a feeling that each room had a special name. That was the lounge, that was the parlor, she decided as they passed them. That room was for the gentlemen to withdraw and smoke after dinner, and that one was for the ladies' morning sewing circle. It was like a film set.

The maid took them into a conservatory at the back of the house. It filled with orchids of all shapes, sizes, and colors. Somewhere out of sight, a fountain played.

Sayen was lying in a chaise longue next to the glass outer wall, an animal on her lap, accompanied by a woman in a wicker chair. Jas guessed the woman had to be Sayen's mother, though she didn't look much older than her daughter. Enough money could buy very effective anti-aging therapies. At the sight of them, the woman got up.

"Ms. Harrington, we met at the hospital, I believe, while Sayen was recuperating? How wonderful to see you again," she said. "And you must be Mr. Lingiari. Please, come and sit down, both of you. What can Jessica get you to drink?"

Sayen looked stronger than she had when Jas had last seen her. She sat up and smiled. "Hi. It's great to see you. Thanks for coming."

After a few minutes' small talk, Sayen gently hinted to her mother that she should leave her alone with her friends, and the woman left, telling them to ask Jessica for anything they wanted. Anything at all.

As soon as the woman was out of earshot, Sayen said, "The maid's name is Florence, and she appreciates it if you call her that. Mama calls all our maids Jessica. She says it's because she can't remember their names. It's so embarrassing."

"You look amazing," said Carl. "It's hard to believe you were in such a bad way."

"Thanks, Carl. I feel pretty good. I'm nearly back to normal. I had to learn to do just about everything again. But I'm not complaining. I'm grateful to be here. And that reminds me..." She turned to Jas. "I never thanked you properly for what you did for me. Not long after I woke up in stasis, Carl told me that it was you who saved me. He said it was you who refused to give up when everyone else was saying I was a goner. If it weren't for you, I wouldn't be here. I'll never forget that, and, believe me, neither will my parents."

Jas struggled to think of what to say. "It wasn't anything—"

"Shut up, Harrington," said Carl. "You were a bloody hero."

Then she *really* didn't know what to say. The best option seemed to be to change the subject. "Thanks. I mean it. But we haven't only come here to see you, Sayen. We wanted to talk to you about something face to face."

Sayen sat up straighter. "Really? What is it? This sounds interesting. I've been so bored while I've been recuperating. Tell me what it is."

The eager anticipation on her face changed to sorrow and concern as Lingiari told her about his missing parents. He spoke for several minutes, and after he finished, no one spoke for a while.

"Carl, I'm so sorry," Sayen said quietly.

"I went over to his parents' place to help him," Jas said. "It's exactly like he says. It's totally weird. They've vanished into thin air, and no one's noticed anything suspicious. Not at the time they went missing nor since.

"You're the smartest person we know, Sayen. We were wondering if you could think of anything we or the police haven't done yet to find out what's happened to them. No creds have been taken out of their bank accounts since the last time they were seen. They lived in the same place all their lives, and everyone in the area knew them, but no one has any idea what could have happened."

"It *is* very strange," Sayen said. "Carl, I don't want to scare you, but do you think that it might have something to do with the Shadows?"

"I do," he replied. "We both do," he added, glancing at Jas. "Though it doesn't make a lot of sense. My parents haven't been replaced. They're just gone. And what would the Shadows want with them? They're just farmers."

Sayen's expression was troubled. "It might not be your parents they want. It could be their land. The Shadows need places for their traps, places not too far from human habitations, but not so close that they'd be easily discovered."

"Yeah, I had the same thought, to be honest. I flew all over the farm, but there's nothing there."

The word *yet* hung in the air, unspoken.

"When we arrived back on Earth," said Jas, "we were given the same tests that we went through on Dawn. *Dawn*, which was invaded by Shadows. I told them there might be a Shadow on the ship, but they said the tests were foolproof. How could they be foolproof if a Shadow got onto Dawn?"

"Yeah. And if they got onto Dawn, maybe they're here," said Lingiari.

"I've been thinking about what happened on K. 67092d and Dawn," Sayen said. "There's so much that doesn't add up. How long has the government known about Shadows? Long enough for them to set up at least two testing centers, on Dawn and here, for people exposed to them, but I haven't seen anything in the media about them. Have you? I've been searching for days. Why are they keeping the Shadows a secret? Do all the prospecting companies know about them? Is the government doing anything to stop them from spreading? Are the Transgalactic Council and Unity involved?"

"They made us sign a secrecy agreement on Dawn," Jas said. "It was really shady. And they wouldn't tell us what they did with any Shadows they caught."

Sayen frowned. "There has to be a way we can find out."

She rose from her seat and the animal on her lap jumped down. Lingiari gazed after it as it trotted away. "Is that a dog or a cat?"

"Neither, or both," said Sayen, "depending on how you look at it. Beau's a cag, or a dot. I don't know what the official word is."

"It's a hybrid cat and dog?"

"Yes, he is. He was a present to welcome me home. He's soft as a cat to cuddle, but loyal as a dog. He doesn't scratch up the furniture, and he takes himself for walks if you want. And you can teach him tricks. He's the ideal pet."

She opened the French doors, and Beau ran outside. They stepped into the garden—except her family garden was more like a park. A lush, vivid green grass carpet flowed down a slight incline at the back of the house and out as far as the eye could see. Ornamental trees dotted the verdant expanse, and in the distance was a bright, silvery lake with...Jas stopped. It couldn't be.

"Are those flamingoes?" she asked, pointing at the moving pink dots on the watery expanse.

"Yeah," Lee replied in a mildly abashed tone, as if she'd been asked the question many times before and found the admission a little shameful. "Do y'all want to come with me for my daily walk?"

"Hey, the temperature's cooled down a lot," Lingiari said. "It's..." He looked up at the cloudless sky, leaving his sentence hanging.

Lee sighed. "It's air-conditioned."

"It's what?" said Jas. "You mean...the whole place?"

"Yeah. I sometimes forget how it must seem to strangers."

"But, how?" asked Lingiari.

"There's a force field dome over the house and grounds. You drove through it, but you wouldn't have noticed. Underground machines cool the air, and the dome prevents the air inside from mixing with the air outside."

"Woah," Lingiari said. "Can you fly through it?"

"Yeah. I could explain how the force field works, but it's a little complicated."

"That's okay," Jas said. If Sayen found the explanation complicated, it would be beyond her and Lingiari's understanding. "Where do you want to walk?"

"I usually go to the lake and back. My mama and daddy get antsy if I go too far. I have to stay in sight of the house."

"I guess what happened to you was pretty tough on them," said Jas.

"You don't know the half of it. My mama always wanted to wrap me in cotton wool, but my daddy encouraged me to spread my wings. Now, they're both the same. It's like I'm five years old again."

Lingiari had drawn a little ahead of them. Jas wondered if he was going to trip over his feet because he wasn't looking where he was going. He was looking upward, as if trying to spot the force field holding the cool air in. The pilot stopped and turned. "Hey, I just remembered something. When you were breaking the comm links on the *Galathea's* defense units, you said you used to tamper with the android servants at home. Is Florence an android?"

"Yeah, she is. They all are. Me, mama, and daddy are the only humans in the house."

"You're kidding," exclaimed Jas. It was her turn to stop in her tracks. "Then, what was all that about her preferring to be called by her name? You're saying they have feelings?"

"Our androids aren't like your defense units, Jas. The ratio of human cells to synthetic components is much higher than usual. They aren't commercially available. To be honest, they sit the border of the legislation on android ethics. But they've always seemed happy to me. And it's better than using humans for menial work, don't you think?"

Lingiari asked the question that was also on Jas's lips. "Sayen, what the hell do your parents do? I mean, if it's okay to ask."

"You know, that's a good question, Carl. I wish I knew. When I was younger, I tried asking them a few times. My brother and I had a competition going to see who'd be the first to figure it out. But they always said it was better that I didn't know." She smiled a little wistfully. "It's something that brings in a lot of money, that's for sure. My grandparents aren't nearly so well off.

"And my parents know plenty of important people. We've had all kinds of visitors over the years—people on the news, celebrities, government ministers, heads of global corporations, and so on."

They were nearing the lake. The flamingoes looked almost unreal. Their feathers were the color of fairy floss, and they were standing on one stick-like leg each. Jas thought she'd heard that they were extinct in the wild.

She'd often heard the phrase, *how the other half live*, but Sayen's family didn't belong to the other half, they belonged a tiny fraction of the very richest of Earth's population. It was lucky for the navigator, and maybe, with her family connections, it would be lucky for them too in their quest to find out about the Shadows.

# NINE

Sayen studied her reflection in her dressing room mirror. She wanted to look smart and professional. Her silver-blue pant-suit achieved just the right effect, she concluded. The color looked good against her blonde hair, and the suit's lines were neat and fitted her figure perfectly. If she wanted her interviewer to take her seriously, she would have to look the part, even if she had no intention of staying in the job longer than it took her to snoop behind the scenes, and even if her mama and daddy had told her she didn't even need to interview.

They'd pleaded with her not to go back to work, but when they'd finally relented, they'd said any job that she wanted was hers, providing she had the skills and qualifications. She only had to ask and they would arrange it. But she couldn't risk the Global Government thinking she was there for any other reason than that she wanted to work. She didn't want to be observed beyond the normal level of interest in a new employee.

She made a final check of her appearance before going downstairs to say goodbye to her parents. They were each in their home offices. Her mother was reading something. As she looked up, it was clear she'd been crying.

"Sayen," her mother said as she went in, "for the last time, why?

Why can't you stay here and have fun doing whatever you want? You know that you only have to give the word, and we'll make it happen for you."

"Mama, I told you. What I want is a job. I'm dying stuck in here all day. Can't you at least try to understand that?"

"I'm trying, honey, I'm trying. But when I think of seeing you after your accident..."

"But I got better, didn't I? I'm better than ever. And I want to *do* something with my life. Not spend it hiding away from the tiniest little thing that might hurt me."

"Oh, sweetheart, I'm just worried about you. And when you have kids of your own you'll know how I feel."

"I'm sorry, Mama. Can you at least wish me well?"

"Of course I wish you well. I always wish you well, honey. Come and give your mama a hug."

Sayen's father didn't say anything to her when she went to see him. She was interrupting a vidcall. He asked the person he was speaking with to excuse him for a moment, and he came over to Sayen and wrapped his arms around her. After planting a kiss on her head, he turned back to the screen, giving her a half wave. He hadn't gone on and on trying to dissuade her like her mama had, but she could tell he was just as against the idea.

As she went downstairs and out to the chauffeur-driven heli that awaited her, she tried to ease her guilt at making her parents worry about her with the thought that, though it was true she really did want to get out of the house and start working again, she also had a more serious and less selfish reason for applying for the government job.

———

The downdraft from the heli messed up her hair as she got out on the roof of the GGSHQ, or Global Government Security Headquarters. It was a stroke of luck that the place was within an hour by heli from Sayen's family property. She didn't think her parents were ready yet to agree to her living away from home, if they would ever be.

A man in a suit was holding open a door, and she crossed the roof to go through it as the heli took off. The man smiled at her, and they went down in the elevator. Sayen thought he looked familiar. The more she glimpsed him from the corners of her eyes, the surer she was that she knew him, but she couldn't remember from where. She was sure that if she saw him in the right context, she would know him right away, but there, he seemed out of place. Or was her confusion an effect of the mind transfer treatment she'd undergone?

She faced the man. "Excuse me, do I know you?"

"I don't think so, ma'am," he replied.

They'd reached their floor, and the doors opened. The man told her the room number as Sayen stepped out, but he didn't accompany her. He remained in the elevator as the doors closed, and Sayen was left none the wiser. She shrugged. Maybe she would get a chance to talk to him later if she got the job. What was she thinking? Of course she'd get the job. She only had to go through the motions.

———

The Minister for Global Security was a large woman. In her expansive kaftan and long, straightened hair, she didn't really look like she was responsible for the security of every living human being on the planet, but her manner made up for her relaxed dress code. When Sayen was shown into her office, the woman didn't look up from her interface for several long moments.

Sayen wondered if she should cough or something. She hadn't expected this kind of reception.

"Sit down," said the woman without looking up.

Sayen sat opposite her and folded her hands in her lap, wondering if she was in for a long wait.

The woman swiped her interface, and the screen turned black. Only then did she lift her head. She looked into Sayen's eyes for an uncomfortably long time.

"Sayen Lee," she said.

"Yes, ma'am, I'm here for—"

"I know why you're here." She reactivated her interface and brought up a new screen. After scanning the information, she glanced at Sayen and then back at the screen.

"You served aboard the *Galathea,* a prospecting starship belonging to Polestar Corp, which visited the planets K. 67092d and Dawn, among others. You were critically injured." She looked at Sayen again. "It says here that you made a full recovery." Her gaze roved Sayen's face and the upper half of her body. Sayen shrank a little at this frank inspection, but she supposed the woman had to be sure she was fit to work.

"Yes, ma'am. I'm completely well again."

"Your personal record stands up to scrutiny, and your qualifications and transcripts are excellent. There doesn't seem any doubt in your ability to perform your duties after the relevant training. Very well. I accept your application. Your employment begins Monday. Your position is probationary for six months."

The interview seemed to be over. The Minister for Global Security hadn't asked her if she had any questions. Didn't they *always* ask if you had any questions? Sayen rose from her seat uncertainly.

As she went toward the door, the woman spoke. "Talk to my secretary. He'll tell you where your office is and anything else you need to know."

"Uh, thanks. Goodbye."

The woman didn't reply.

Sayen closed the door and went down the hallway. That had to be the quickest interview she'd ever had. She poked her head in at the first open door. An older man in an expensive navy blue suit sat at a desk inside the room. His hair and beard were snowy white and closely clipped.

"Hello," he said in a British accent. "You must be Ms. Lee." He stood and went to Sayen to shake her hand.

After her frosty experience in the Minister for Global Security's office, she was relieved by the man's kindly smile that crinkled the skin around his eyes. Though she only intended to stay in the job as long as she needed to, she hadn't relished the thought of spending even a short time working there if they were all like the kaftan-wearing woman. Then she scolded herself for the thought. Hadn't she decided she wanted to take risks and do more challenging things with her life?

"Yes, that's me," she said.

"Wonderful. I'm Mr. Lombard, but you can call me Bernie. Do come and sit down, and we'll go over everything so you're ready to hit the ground running on Monday."

Sayen took a seat next to the man, and he explained the ins and outs of her role. Cyber intelligence seemed as interesting and difficult as she'd imagined it would be.

After they'd been speaking for a while, Sayen felt comfortable enough to ask Bernie about their boss. "Is the Minister always so...formal?"

"Hmm...I understand why you ask. You see, things are quite tense around here at the moment. We're dealing with threats on several fronts, which you'll find out about as you begin your job. In fact, I and a few others would usually be the ones conducting the interviews for positions like yours, but the Minister has taken it upon herself to speak to each applicant individually, and double-check all the background searches we do on them. It's admirable, really. We can't take the slightest risk when it comes to global security."

"Oh, I understand."

"I'm sure you do. Shall we carry on? We have quite a bit to get through this morning."

"Yes, of course."

As she listened to Bernie telling her what information she was to look for and how she was to look for it, Sayen made a mental note every time she heard anything that might lead her to the Shadows.

# Ten

Carl had returned to Australia, but he was regretting his decision. There seemed to be nothing he could do there, and waiting for Sayen to investigate the possibility of there being Shadows on Earth was agonizing. Every moment that passed increased his chances of never seeing his parents again. Every moment might mean the difference between life and death. He wondered if he would be more useful on the other side of the world with Sayen and Harrington.

Unable to bear the quiet, empty farmhouse any longer, he'd rented a small flat in Sydney, close to the spaceport in case he needed to be somewhere in a hurry. Flux had stayed on at the farm in case anything new turned up. The little fella could get into places and see things that would be impossible for a human. If he had anything to report, he would tell Mrs. Jesson, who would then contact Carl.

At first, the messages that had arrived from Sayen had been discouraging. She hadn't been able to find out anything about the Shadows, even though in her role she had access to highly classified material. Along with Jas, they'd concluded that it was very strange, considering that they were a known threat. The Global Government had commissioned Dawn as a quarantine and testing area, and scientists on Earth were testing exposed arrivals from deep space. So

Shadows weren't that much of a secret. But no one was talking about them, and the government hadn't seemed to hold any information on them.

Then Sayen had discovered that there were hidden files—files that even she wasn't supposed to know about. They'd agreed they had to contain something worth knowing. But for days on end, Sayen hadn't been able to get into them. Each day that she failed, Carl had been more and more convinced that the files had to contain what they were looking for. If someone of Sayen's caliber couldn't crack them, they had to be something very special.

Carl was out walking the waterfront at The Rocks when the call came. He took out his interface. Jas was requesting a vidcall. Could this be it? Had Sayen uncovered the truth about the Shadows? He pressed the accept key, and Jas appeared on the screen.

"Sayen's gone missing," she exclaimed.

"What? She...how?" he asked.

"Carl, can you get over here? Her parents are going crazy. They want us to go and see them. They won't talk over any messaging service. They're insisting on speaking to us face to face."

"I'll be there as soon as I can. Meet me at the spaceport, and we'll go from there. I'm hanging up now to call a cab. Be careful, Jas. If anything's happened to Sayen because she was snooping, you and I could both be in danger."

———

Mrs. Lee looked very different from the last time Carl had seen her. When they arrived at the door, she let them in herself. Her face had lost its color except for her eyes, which were red-rimmed. She was a ghost of her former self, as if all life had been drained from her. Mr. Lee was waiting in the first room they came to. He was trying to put on a brave front, but it was clear that beneath the veneer, he was crumbling.

"Thank you for coming so quickly," said Mr. Lee. "Please, sit down."

"It's no problem," said Carl. "Has there been any word from Sayen?"

"Nothing," Mrs. Lee said. "Not a single sight or sound of her since yesterday evening."

Harrington said, "Is it possible she—"

"Ms. Harrington," said Mrs. Lee. "Let me show you something." She handed over an interface. On the screen was a message from Sayen to her mother, saying that she would be spending the weekend with a friend, and her mother was not to worry about her. "It's a lie."

"Something's happened to her," Mr. Lee said. "You two seem close with Sayen, and I've a feeling you might know something about it." He held up a hand to silence Harrington as she began to speak. "We don't have time for denials. We have to get our daughter back, and we need you to help us."

"I wasn't about to deny anything, Mr. Lee," Harrington said. "We'll do all we can to help."

"I'm certainly glad to hear it. Please begin by telling me what *you* think might be the reason for her disappearance."

Carl and Harrington explained about the Shadows.

"Yes." Mrs. Lee nodded. "Sayen did tell us what had happened on her last mission. And you really think they might have something to do with what's happened to my daughter?"

Carl went on to tell the couple about his missing parents and his and Harrington's suspicions that there might be some kind of cover-up going on about Shadows on Earth. He told them that Sayen had been trying to uncover information in the Global Government's databanks. By the time he'd finished, Sayen's parents' expressions were grave. Mrs. Lee put her face in her hands.

"I'd heard the rumors, Carleen," said Mr. Lee. "We both had. If only we'd known what she was trying to do. We could have stopped her. Why oh why did I help her get that job?"

"You mean you already knew about the Shadows?" Carl asked.

"No, we didn't," said Mrs. Lee, raising her head, "but we knew something was going on that we weren't being told about. Craven and I work for the Government. We've been in the job for over thirty years, and we know it inside out. A few months ago, we began to suspect that we were being deprived of information and excluded from certain meetings. Any subtle inquiries we made were met with silence and a closing of the ranks. There was obviously something big and highly sensitive going on. It must have been to do with these Shadows." She looked upward as if in supplication. "Dear Lord, if I'd known Sayen was getting herself mixed up in governmental intrigues, I would never have let her get involved."

"These people..." Mr. Lee looked gravely at Carl and Harrington. "You have no idea what they're capable of."

"My little girl," said Mrs. Lee softly. "Craven, what are we going to do?"

"Everything we can, Carleen. We're going to do everything we can to get her back. We still have friends. Don't forget that.

"Mr. Lingiari, Ms. Harrington, we need your help. Sayen has touched on something sensitive, and she's been taken. Whoever it was who took her, they have to be very high up. It has to be people who are confident that their actions will be beyond reproach. There aren't many who are above our circles of influence. Thank you for being frank with us. Now that we know what Sayen was doing, we can begin to turn the wheels that will bring these people's actions to light.

"Unfortunately, for the time being, we can't leave our home. Due to our connection to Sayen, the chances are that these individuals may try to take us too. We can't do a thing in person to go get to our baby girl. We would ask her brother to bring her back, but he's at the other end of the galaxy."

"Wait a minute, are you saying you know where she is?" Carl asked.

"We do," Mrs. Lee replied. "We know exactly where she is. She's on an air transport, and it's out over the Atlantic, heading toward Africa. We're keeping track of it." In response to Carl and Harrington's surprised expressions, she went on, "When Sayen was undergoing her cloning treatment, we had a tracer inserted into her body. Was it overstepping the mark? Yes. Was it invading her privacy? You betcha. Do I regret it? Not for a second." She gazed at them defiantly.

"Whatever the rights and wrongs of what we did," said Mr. Lee, "if we hadn't done it, I doubt we'd ever see our darlin' again."

"Where is she?" Carl asked. "We'll get her back."

"Come with me," Mrs. Lee said, rising. "I'll show you how to trace her and give you anything else you need. Whatever it might be, just ask."

# ELEVEN

Sayen sat in darkness. She was hot. Stripping down to her underwear had provided some relief, but not much. Though her enhanced skin provided some protection from the heat inside the box where the Shadows had put her, breathing in the hot air had raised her body temperature to uncomfortable levels.

She guessed the box wasn't much more than a meter in every direction. The ceiling was too low for her to stand up, and the walls were too close together for her to lie down outstretched. They were made of metal, and they were warm to the touch. There was no ventilation.

That morning, when she'd arrived for work, the Minister had been out of the office. Sayen had been glad because it meant she would be left to her regular work without being interrupted to research something in particular. She'd anticipated the opportunity to exploit the crack she'd found in the security surrounding the files on the Shadows. She'd thought she'd disabled any unauthorized access alerts. She'd been wrong.

After only minutes of reading, wide-eyed, the files on the Shadows, Bernie had entered her office without knocking. Gone were his twinkling eyes and cheery expression. It had all been a facade. Bernie had the expression of a corpse. As he'd grabbed her, two more men had come in, including the man who'd met her that first day whose face she couldn't place.

Sayen had fought, of course. She'd resisted with every ounce of her newly enhanced strength, but after she'd broken one of the men's arms, Bernie had knocked her out.

Blindfolded and with her wrists bound with wire, she'd come around aboard a heli, and they'd flown for seven or eight hours before touching down. She recalled stumbling through vegetation, the muzzle of a weapon of some kind pressed to her skull, before being pushed into the box.

Since then, she'd managed to work the blindfold off of her head, but as there was no light in the box, it made no difference to her. She still had little idea where she was, except that it was somewhere hot. From the length of the flight, she guessed she was somewhere in Africa.

The Shadows had her. She wondered how long she had before they would try to make a Shadow of her too. That would not happen. She wouldn't let it. The thought of a Shadow Sayen returning home to her parents turned her stomach. She would rather die than expose them to danger.

She was dizzy with the heat, and her skin was slick with sweat. She licked her arm to try to relieve her dry, swollen mouth. She stopped mid-lick. What had she been thinking? She was forgetting her physical enhancements. Maybe she could break out of her prison.

Sayen wasted no time. She'd located the door by feeling the walls, and she'd pushed it once before. This time she *really* pushed it. The metal bent under the pressure she applied, but the door didn't open. Sayen shifted back in the box. Bracing herself against the opposite wall, she put both her feet against the door and pushed with her legs. As she gasped with the effort, the door buckled. Bright light streamed through chinks on either side. She'd nearly gotten it open.

Bending her knees, Sayen drew up her legs. She spread her arms for balance and gave the door a massive kick. Whatever was holding it closed broke, and the door flew open, revealing lush vegetation. The rich, 'green' aroma of the jungle rushed in.

The daylight was incredibly bright after the hours she'd spent in pitch darkness, but Sayen's enhanced eyes reacted to the change immediately.

Outside, someone shouted.

Sayen scrambled out of the box. She was in a clearing of knee-high grass and plants, bordered in the distance by tall trees hung with moss and vines. Figures were running toward her across the clearing. The nearest escape route seemed to be the forest. She set off toward the trees at a sprint, heading for the safety of the darkness between the trunks.

She heard more shouts coming from behind her. Time seemed to slow down. Every step she took, she expected to feel the pain of a laser burn. Would she feel the beams hitting her, or would it all be over before she knew what had happened? She was running fast, faster than an unenhanced human could ever run. Another ten seconds and she would make it. She could hardly believe her luck had lasted so long. Why weren't the Shadows shooting?

Then it came. Something exploded against her back, and suddenly she couldn't feel her legs. The impetus of her running carried her forward, and she found herself sliding through the vegetation face down. A horrible slicing sensation across her face and the bare skin of her arms and legs were the last things she felt before she lost consciousness.

———

Something was tugging at her ankles, and her back hurt. Her back hurt a lot. Sayen opened her eyes to see a jungle canopy passing overhead, the blue sky visible in patches between the leaves and branches. She lifted her head to look forward. Two men were dragging her, holding one of her ankles each. She was being pulled down a track.

Her undershirt was pulled up, and the rough track was scraping the skin off her back. She felt like she was being shredded. She struggled violently and ripped her ankles out of the Shadows' grips. In a moment, she was up and running again.

But she didn't get far. That time, they were ready. Within moments, she felt another explosion against her back.

The next time she came around, she was lying on her front. The second thing she registered was pain from all over her body. She fought the urge to move. As soon as they knew she was awake, the Shadows would stun her again. She needed a better plan than running to get away.

Slowly, she opened her eyes. Blades of grass obscured her view. The blades were stained red, with her blood, she guessed. She wasn't inside a Shadow trap yet, at least.

Someone was approaching her. More than one person. Large, powerful hands grabbed her around the waist. She was lifted onto a man's shoulder. Sayen tried to remain limp so that the Shadow man would think she was still unconscious. She held her eyes only slightly open as she tried to take in as much of her surroundings as she could.

There was the structure she'd been expecting to see: the hexagonal blocks of a Shadow trap, deep within an African jungle, where it would be easy to hide. The trees were close together, no doubt helping to screen the trap from the overhead view of planes and helis.

If she could just get a few seconds' head start on the Shadows, if she could just make it far enough that they wouldn't have a clear shot at her with a stunning laser beam, she could get away. From the sounds around her, Sayen guessed the man was accompanied by three or four more Shadows.

They'd reached the trap. As soon as they entered the hexagonal doorway, the cool interior raised goosebumps on Sayen's skin. She would have to act now, before it was too late.

The Shadow carrying her stopped, and his shoulders shifted as he moved to lower Sayen down. As his hands fastened around her and raised her, the man's head came into view. Sayen drove her elbow into the side of it. His skull swung away sharply, and there was a loud report as his neck cracked. His body jerking, the Shadow hit the floor. Sayen fell with him, but she broke away and landed on her feet.

The other Shadows were immediately upon her. She grabbed the nearest one and drove its head into the stony wall. Its cranium shattered, and the Shadow woman slid to the ground, leaving a trail of blood, hair, and brains.

Another Shadow had hold of Sayen. His arms wrapped over hers in a bear hug. Sayen broke his grip and was about to turn and attack him, but another Shadow kicked her feet out from under her. She fell. Her chin jarred against the floor, sending a shockwave through her head. Her mouth filled with blood.

As she tried to rise, she felt a third explosion in her back. *No,* she screamed inside. They'd stunned her again. She'd failed. She was going to die. She was facing the doorway. Bright green vegetation framed by a dark, hexagonal hole faded from her sight.

———

She was alive, but she could see nothing but darkness. Sayen reached out and felt familiar, smooth metal. She was in a box like the one the Shadows had put her in before. But she'd bent and broken that one. They must have put her in a new box.

Wincing, she sat up. Every inch of her was sore. Her lips felt funny. She put a hand to her mouth and found that it was swollen. Dried blood encrusted her chin.

Something must have gone wrong. The last thing she remembered was being inside a Shadow trap. They'd stunned her for the third time. She'd thought that the Shadows would kill her, and a new Sayen would appear. That was what people thought happened. Or had they got it wrong? Were the Shadows' victims kept in prison while their replacements took over their lives?

Feeling around the inside of the box, Sayen found the edge that marked the door. She kicked it with all her might, but the thing didn't move. She gasped in pain at the shock that ran up her legs. The Shadows must have reinforced the door somehow.

She kicked it again, but the door didn't move a centimeter. Exhausted and in pain, she flopped to the floor. So much for her enhancements. She was trapped.

A scraping sound came from outside. Sayen was thrown to one side as the box tilted. It was being lifted up. She swayed as the box was moved. She was being taken somewhere.

# TWELVE

Carl looked out of the shuttle window as they sped back to London. Harrington was distracted, mailing someone on her interface. The last time they'd looked at the tracer dot that marked Sayen's location, it had shown she was in Gabon.

Far beneath, a dark seascape sped by. They were gaining on the sunrise, flying toward it over the ocean. He and Harrington had argued. He'd wanted to fly directly to Africa.

They didn't know how long they had before the Shadows killed and replicated Sayen, but Harrington had insisted that they needed to equip themselves properly before attempting a rescue. They would have only one chance, and they had to make it count.

Carl couldn't erase from his imagination the image of Sayen being taken into one of the Shadow traps. He hoped that the aliens would think twice before killing and replacing the daughter of one of Earth's most influential families. Whatever the creatures were, they weren't stupid.

In Carl's experience, they worked smartly, targeting the top individuals in a hierarchy and keeping their actions secret as long as possible. There was a small chance that replacing Sayen with a Shadow was a risk they didn't want to take at that stage.

He suspected that the Shadows' method was to replace as much of a population as they could before they were discovered, and then subdue and replace the rest. Why they did it and what their ultimate plan was, he couldn't guess.

He wondered what Sayen had found out before she was taken.

Beside him in the shuttle's passenger cabin, Harrington closed her interface's screen and sat back.

"Did you get what you wanted?" Carl asked.

"Not yet. Someone's working on it. If he can get the stuff, it'll be ready by the time we arrive."

"So what is this stuff that's so important?"

Harrington gave him a sidelong glance. "Just stuff." When Carl raised his eyebrows, she added, "It might make all the difference. You know I wouldn't delay rescuing Sayen otherwise."

Carl sighed and returned to staring out the window. "Yeah, I know."

He wished the shuttle would go faster. He wished he was flying it. He would have them in London and then on to rendezvous with the heli that was carrying Sayen in no time. As well as his concern for his friend, his impatience was driven by the urge to find out more about the Shadows. He was desperate to locate his parents.

As soon as they were out of the spaceport in London, Carl and Harrington ran to catch an autocab to take them to meet her contact.

Harrington had arranged to meet him at an underpass not far from a freeway. The place was rank with the odor of stale piss and the acrid smell of unwashed bodies and clothes. The contact was accompanied by his mates, and they reminded Carl of the dero who had touched him for some creds the first night he'd arrived back on Earth. The groups of under-educated, under-privileged naturals seemed to be growing day by day. Carl wondered how they survived.

As the autocab pulled up, all but one stepped back, leaving a small man with dirty, balding hair and several days' beard growth standing alone. He had an old bag slung over his shoulder.

The autocab stopped, and Carl and Harrington got out. The small crowd of naturals drew back farther as Harrington stood to her full height. Carl had got used to her size, and though he was tall himself, he'd forgotten how imposing she was. In their current situation, among the kind of people present, it certainly came in handy.

The man with the bag looked up at Harrington. "I got it all. Everything you said."

"Let me see," said the security officer.

"All right." He took the bag off his shoulder and opened it. He held it at waist level, so that Harrington had to stoop to see inside. As she did so, the deros who had stepped back moved forward. *Drongos.* They didn't have the imagination to understand what the security officer would do to them if they attacked.

Carl also stepped forward, unzipping his jacket as he moved. He reached inside it and pulled out a weapon. Just the handle of it, enough to show the deros what he carried. At the sight of the weapon, they lowered their heads and shuffled back to their former position.

Harrington was inspecting the contents of the bag. She straightened up. "Got a reader?" she asked the man.

He pulled one from a capacious pocket. Harrington took the bag from the man and zipped it up. She held her wrist to the man's reader and typed in a figure. Nothing else was said.

Carl and Harrington got back into the cab and left. When the vehicle had left the underpass and was out on the freeway, Harrington turned to Carl.

"Can I see it?"

"What?"

"You know," she said, gesturing toward him.

"Harrington," Carl exclaimed, pretending to be shocked, "this isn't the time."

The security officer rolled her eyes, reached over and unzipped his jacket. She pulled out the weapon from its holster under his arm. "Thanks for helping me out back there. I thought you had to be showing them something when they all backed off."

"I think I was helping *them* out more than you."

"True." She nodded. "So, how in hell did you manage to bring this with you on two trips across the Atlantic, and I'm guessing, your flight from Australia too?"

"I have my ways."

Harrington smiled wryly. She studied the weapon. "Not bad," she said, handing it back. She patted the bag on her lap comfortingly. "But these are better. Hey, could you use your magical method to get these through security checks? I was going to use my professional license exemption, but your way sounds better. I don't want to risk a nosey Customs officer having a quick look."

"Sure, if you want."

A moment later, Harrington's interface beeped. A message had arrived for her. "Krat, " she said when she saw who it was from.

"What's wrong?"

"I've been mentoring Makey. He got his refugee status and he's started studying to be a security officer. I forgot I had to meet him this afternoon." She pressed accept, and the kid's familiar face appeared on the screen. Harrington explained that she was going away for a while and she would help him out when she got back.

The kid frowned. "Where are you going? Is that Carl with you? Hi, Carl."

"Hi, Makey," Carl replied. "Look, we're just going off on a short trip. Shouldn't be too long."

The kid didn't answer for a moment. "Are you going to...to...can I talk about secret stuff over a vidcall? Is it safe?"

"No, it isn't," Harrington said. "Makey, what's wrong?"

"Those things...we both know about. I think they're here."

"At the refugee center?" Carl asked.

The kid glanced to one side before nodding. "Are you going to fight them? Because if you are, I want to come with you."

"Makey, if those things are there," Carl said, "it isn't safe for you to stay. But we can't help you right now. We're in a hurry. Can you get away? We can find you when we get back."

"I think I can. I don't think they realize that I know what they are yet, but, wherever you're going, I want to come with you. I want to fight them too."

"Makey," said Harrington, "you're too young. It's much too dangerous for you to come with us."

"Please give me a chance," replied the kid. "I keep thinking of what happened to my mam and sister. I can't think straight anymore. I can't sleep. It's eating me up. Please let me help you."

As Carl struggled to find a way to ease Makey's conscience, the kid added, "You need me. There's only two of you. And I know what they're like. I saw the ones that replaced Neeve and Mam."

"You're right, Makey," Harrington said, with a nod of agreement from Carl. "We do need a third person. Okay, you're coming with us. Bring a change of clothes."

They arranged a corner to pick Makey up, then Harrington ended the vidcall. She brought up the screen that was tracing Sayen's tracker.

"They're moving her," she said. "She's left Africa, and she's traveling south."

Carl took the interface from Harrington to study the direction Sayen was going. The flashing dot was moving slowly but steadily away from the coast of South Africa. "Unless they're heading to an island, it looks like they're taking her to Antarctica."

Harrington had an inscrutable expression on her face.

# THIRTEEN

Hours later, they were in the air again, flying south to Antarctica. Harrington had been subdued the whole way from London. Carl wasn't sure if it was because she was worried about Sayen or if there was another reason. They couldn't talk about what they were about to do in case they were overheard by other passengers in the shuttle, but the woman also hadn't said a word about anything else.

Makey made up for Harrington's silence. He was excited to be taking part in their rescue attempt. As they were descending over McMurdo Sound, he said, "I read about this place in the refugee center. I've been catching up on information about Earth. They didn't teach us much about it on Dawn. All we learned was that humans had destroyed the environment and polluted the air. They taught us that humans had disrespected Earth Mother, and that she punished them by not allowing plants to grow and by bringing earthquakes and hurricanes."

"Well, that isn't completely wrong, apart from the Earth Mother part," Carl said. "The climate's still being affected by three hundred years of industrialization. The geography's changed a lot as the average temperature has risen. Antarctica's been melting for decades, and it hasn't stopped. Not likely to any time soon, either. You can't reverse rising global temperatures easily.

"It snowed here in the past, and at one time the whole continent was covered in massive sheets of ice. Now, the ice is only a hundred or so meters thick, and it's decreasing every summer. No more snow's fallen in years and it isn't likely to. It never did snow a lot in the first place. Looks like we've seen the last of it in our lifetimes."

Makey frowned as he looked out of the shuttle window over the semi-frozen continent.

---

McMurdo Sound was like a big country town. Carl guessed that only a few tens of thousands of people lived there, judging by its size. It was mid-morning by the time they'd got out of the spaceport and into the city. The streets were quiet.

Not many shuttles flew to Antarctica. They'd had to wait precious hours for the next available flight from London. Thankfully, Sayen didn't seem to have moved in all that time, according to the dot on the interface that showed the location of her tracker. Carl guessed that the Shadows must have decided to keep her in one place for the time being. That was what he hoped anyway. He didn't want to think about the other possible reason for her lack of movement.

"You trained here, didn't you?" Carl asked Harrington as they left the spaceport.

"Yep," Harrington replied.

"So, you must know the terrain pretty well."

"Yeah."

"And the conditions."

"That's right."

Carl waited for her to continue, but she didn't. Harrington had never been much of a talker, but Carl wondered about this especially silent streak she seemed to be going through.

The security officer pointed. "We can get vehicles over there."

Antarctica was the coldest place Carl had ever been. He pulled out a second jacket from his bag and put it on over the first as they walked over to the vehicle rental place.

When they got there, Harrington picked out three snowmobiles. The vehicles came equipped with snow goggles, thick mittens, and snowshoes. An assistant loaded the snowmobiles into a pickup truck and drove them to the edge of town. After Carl and Makey practiced driving the machines, the three of them set off across the flat, icy landscape.

On the horizon all around, the dirty white of the land melted into the cloudy sky, so that it wasn't possible to tell where one began and the other ended.

When McMurdo Sound was no longer visible behind them, Harrington stopped. Carl and Makey parked their vehicles beside her.

Carl got out the interface that showed Sayen's location. Harrington looked over his shoulder.

"It's that way," she said, nodding at a part of the landscape that looked no different from the rest. "As I see it, the place she's in has to be crawling with Shadows. There's no way we can take them all on. The best we can do is go inside, grab Sayen, and get out as fast as we can."

"Right," said Carl. "How do we do that?"

Harrington opened the bag of illegal stuff she'd bought from the dero. "This might help." She got out a couple of large aerosol cans.

"We're gonna freshen them up until they disappear?" Carl asked.

"No," Harrington replied, straight-faced, "*we're* the ones who are going to disappear."

"That stuff will make us invisible?" Makey asked.

"Not exactly. It bends light. Anyone who's looking at something sprayed with this will see what's behind the object, unless they're at very close quarters. Whatever you spray it on isn't exactly invisible, but unless it moves, you probably won't notice it. In this landscape we have an advantage because it's harder to see things anyway. We lose that advantage when we go inside."

"So the Shadows won't see us unless we move?" asked Makey.

"That's right."

"I think we're gonna need to move to rescue your friend."

"Yes, we will, but you don't have to worry about that," Harrington said. "I want you to wait outside." She continued over his protests, "We need someone waiting to take Sayen back to the snowmobiles if Lingiari and I get caught. We don't want our effort to be wasted. We'll be relying on you, kid, in case something goes wrong."

"But I can help on the inside too," he said. "I want to help."

"Harrington's right," said Carl. "The more of us go in, the bigger the chance is of one of us being spotted. You've gotta think about the whole picture."

Makey nodded reluctantly.

"Good," said Harrington. "Now, let's spray ourselves before we get any closer to the place. We need to go on foot from here. We could spray the snowmobiles too, but they would hear them, so there's no point."

"So that stuff's illegal?" Carl asked. "Is it used by the military?"

"No, it isn't even available for restricted use," Harrington replied. "There are a few reasons, I think. One is because it contains a tiny amount of mythranil, which is banned of course. Another reason is because the substance failed safety tests. It causes psychological effects, probably due to the mythranil. Some test subjects developed psychoses.

"And I think the Government might also have banned it because of the havoc it would cause if it got into the general public's hands. Imagine the crimes people could commit if they could turn invisible."

"Hold on. So what you're saying is, this could make us insane?" Carl asked.

"It's a very slight possibility," Harrington said. "Are you ready?" She held up the can.

"Er...I suppose so."

"Lift up your arms and spread your legs. Hold your breath for as long as you can while it dries."

Carl did as she said. He heard a hissing sound, and tiny droplets of the invisibility spray landed on his skin, which tingled unpleasantly. He fought an urge to touch his face. Harrington's footsteps crunched on the ice as she walked around him. He heard the hissing sound again as she sprayed the back of his body.

"You ready, Makey?" she asked.

After a little while, when Carl's lungs were bursting, he exhaled. Harrington was finishing up spraying the kid. A very vague shape the same color as the landscape stood where Makey had been. If Carl hadn't been looking directly at him, he wouldn't have known he was there.

"My turn," said Harrington, holding out the can.

He began spraying her. Harrington's face and hair seemed to melt away into the pale gray ice behind her. Her shoulders and torso disappeared, and then her hips and legs. It was easy to spot any patches that he missed because they remained suspended in mid-air.

He turned to look for Makey.

"I'm here," Makey said.

The kid had moved. His voice came from somewhere to the right of where he'd been standing.

"Right," Harrington said. "If you want to show where you are, lift your snow goggles. We can't spray our eyes, so it's a good thing we're wearing them or we'd have to keep our eyes closed to slits to avoid being seen."

The woman's almond-shaped, deep reddish-brown eyes, eyebrows and a small portion of her face appeared briefly as she removed her goggles to demonstrate. They quickly disappeared into the landscape. When she moved, she was visible, but only vaguely, as if Carl were seeing her through a screen.

"Woah, what's that?" Makey asked. "What's happening?"

Carl felt it too. It was like he was floating in space. The landscape had become translucent and insubstantial. Then a moment later, he was in Antarctica again.

"It's the spray," Harrington said. "Try to ignore it. The effect wears off after a while. Let's go."

# FOURTEEN

In the void, the Shadows waited.

Generation was proceeding at an acceptable pace on the planet called Earth. An early infiltration had occurred when the humans were unaware and unprepared. The process was always risky and vulnerable to failure in the beginning. Most often, the subjects would realize that one or two of their number had been replaced, and they would kill the ones who had replaced them before they had an opportunity to introduce more subjects to the traps.

But the initial invasion of Earth had succeeded before the humans had known what was happening. By then, it was too late. The quarantine they'd put in place after they understood the risk from their experiences on other planets had been doomed. The test they'd developed was effective, but the testers were mere humans. Replacing them had been easy.

Light years from Earth across the physical realm, on a trap planet, the most recent generation had nearly failed. Only one of their number had succeeded in deceiving the humans and surviving when their starship had crashed. That one had arrived on Earth. Passing a test was simple when the tester was also one of them. That one from the trap planet had joined the generators.

They had replaced humans in many organizations that

controlled Earth affairs, and their plan to introduce more subjects to the secret traps was succeeding. The moment was approaching when they would no longer have to hide, and large-scale generation could begin. Already, they had acquired many tracts of land in areas close to human habitation. At an appropriate time, traps would be activated in these places, and the humans could be replicated on a large scale. There were so many of this species, it would matter little if they destroyed those who resisted.

In these early stages, killing subjects was not desirable. It caused disturbance and confusion in the target population and raised suspicions. That problem had occurred in the area called Australia when two subjects had resisted. The effects of destroying those subjects were only just dying down.

Another impediment to the scheme had occurred when a human had succeeded in accessing information they held on the generation process. Attempts to replicate the human to prevent it from revealing the information had failed. The subject was not entirely organic, and the mechanism had faltered, as it always did with synthesized substances.

A further complication was that this human had a familial relationship with two others in positions of high influence. Replication was not possible, and yet they could not allow the subject to escape. If it alerted the population at large, all their plans could fail.

They could not allow that to happen. They needed more time to infiltrate and conquer the physical realm.

The Shadows debated the problem of the existence of the part-synthetic human they had imprisoned. If replication was not possible, it seemed the only option was to destroy the subject. The effects would not be desirable, but perhaps they were unavoidable.

Replication. Generation. Domination. The plan had to succeed.

# FIFTEEN

The air inside Sayen's metal box was getting colder and colder. The Shadows had taken her on another long flight, and she guessed she must be traveling south. She'd never known such low temperatures. Wearing only her underwear, she would have been suffering from hypothermia without her enhanced skin.

The Shadows hadn't been careful with her box as they'd loaded her onto the heli, and they were the same when they unloaded her. She was thrown from side to side, and at one point the box was upended, and what had been the ceiling became the floor. Sayen was desperately thirsty and hungry. For most of the flight she'd drifted in and out of consciousness.

Lying curled into a ball, Sayen wondered what the hell she'd been thinking of when she'd decided she wanted to finally live her life and not be overly cautious anymore. She wished she'd listened to her mother when she'd begged her to stay home, safe and secure. After nearly dying aboard the *Galathea*, she'd been crazy to put herself in danger again. She should let people like Jas and Carl handle the Shadows. She wasn't cut out to be a hero.

As she lay unmoving, Sayen tried to figure out why she hadn't been replicated. She was sure that had been the Shadows' intention, but something must have gone wrong. She wondered if it was something to do with her enhanced body. Maybe Shadows couldn't replicate synthetic materials, and so the cloning process wouldn't work.

The box had been still for so long, she began to wonder if the Shadows were going to leave her there forever. It wouldn't be a good way to die, but she couldn't get out, no matter how hard she tried. She had bloody bruises on her arms and legs to prove it.

A scraping sound came from outside. Something was being dragged across the metal. Sayen heard the rattle of chains falling, and at last the box opened.

She didn't recognize the expressionless faces of the four Shadows that stared in. These were different from the ones at the last place. All of them were pointing weapons at her.

"If you try to run or fight us, we will kill you," one of the female ones said.

Sayen reflected that they were probably going to kill her anyway, but she decided to play along for now. Grimacing with pain, she crawled out of the box and unsteadily stood up. They were inside a windowless room. It looked like some kind of classroom. She was inside a building, not a Shadow trap. The room was square and empty.

"Come with us," said the Shadow who had spoken. The four of them formed a guard around her, two in front, two behind, and together they went through the door. As they moved along, more Shadows passed them. Sayen's guard didn't speak to the others or even look at them. They passed ten or twelve Shadows.

Sayen was dismayed. They'd been going about five minutes, and the building seemed quite big. If it was full of Shadows, that meant there were already many of them on Earth.

How had the aliens gotten there?

A door opened as they arrived outside it, as if whoever opened it was aware of Sayen and her escort without seeing them. They went through, and Sayen found herself in something resembling a medical center. She shivered. At the best of times, she hated these places with their invasive machines. Then she caught sight of something that made her blood run cold. Half-hidden behind a large scanner was a long metal table fitted with restraints. A trough ran around the edges, leading to a pipe that disappeared into the floor. It was an autopsy table.

"Lie down," commanded the female Shadow, indicating the narrow bed that protruded from the scanner.

"Why?" Sayen croaked. "What are you going to do to me?"

A moment's silence passed. Carl had said he thought the Shadows were telepathic, and now Sayen was sure of it. They never spoke to each other, yet they seemed to know what the others were going to do before they acted.

A male Shadow shrugged, as if he thought the decision they had come to was unimportant. "We are going to investigate your physical body. We want to know why we could not replicate you, and we want to better understand the human form. We have attempted to do this investigation on ourselves as replicants of humans, but the process is uncomfortable and causes injuries. Human bodies also heal too slowly. We have no use for you because your body will not replicate, so we will take this opportunity to increase our knowledge."

Sayen thought she was going to faint. Her first impulse was to run, but she knew she wouldn't get far without being stunned again and brought back. Her stomach turned at the thought of waking up while being operated on by one of these creatures.

She had to take them all out at once to have a chance of escaping, and she would have to attack quickly to prevent them from communicating telepathically with others in the building.

Could she do it? All her attempts so far to escape had failed. Having an enhanced body wasn't enough. You also needed the skills and knowledge of how to use it. Sayen had been smart all her life. Why couldn't she find a way out of her predicament?

She swallowed. First, she needed time to think. "What...what's this machine?" she asked, indicating the scanner. "What does it do?"

"This machine allows us to see your internal structures and gives us information on how they work in unison. Readings taken while you are alive are the most useful to us. We will perform the invasive procedures last."

Legs trembling, Sayen lay down on the bed. A scan wouldn't

harm her, and she still had no idea how she was going to get out of the situation. She wished she had Jas with her. Jas would know what to do. Jas would protect her.

The narrow bed was activated, and Sayen slid inside the machine. Whirrs and clicks started up, and her mind whirred too.

*Four of them have weapons. Four weapons is a lot, but I only need to get one and kill them all before they have a chance to shoot me.* She grimaced. *Yeah, that's all, Sayen. How're you going to do it?*

Too soon, the machine stopped and the bed she was lying on slid out of it. Three Shadows stood around her and two were looking at a screen. Of the ones standing near, only one had its weapon trained on her. The others had returned theirs to holsters around their waists. Sayen estimated it would take them at least a second—maybe longer—to draw and fire.

But the moment she reached for the weapon pointing at her, the Shadow holding it would shoot, and it would be all over for her. She was sure the Shadows wouldn't mind giving up on their scientific investigations and killing her if they thought she was a risk to them. Though she was shaking with fear, she would have to keep her cool and wait for the right moment.

"Sit up," said the man.

One of the Shadows at the screen came over to her, holding an ophthalmoscope. They must have noticed her enhanced eyes on the scan. The Shadow held up the instrument in its hand to Sayen's face and leaned toward it to read the display panel on the back.

Sayen blinked slowly, twice, to activate her enhancement. Her eyes zoomed in on the skin of the Shadow's face, and Sayen could see it in minute detail—the fine hairs sprouting from pores, the tiny sweat glands, the ridges and furrows, even a miniscule, blind mite. She shuddered. Shadows really were physically identical to the humans they replaced.

Who had this Shadow replaced? What had been her job? Had she been married? Had she had a family? To create the five Shadows in the room, five people had died. Sayen thought of Carl's missing parents, and wondered how many people the Shadows had killed. How many more would kill they if they weren't stopped?

She thought of her parents being replaced by these evil aliens. Her fear began to give way to rage. If she didn't make it home, it would break her parents' hearts. She wasn't going to let that happen.

She was furious at these *things* that had trapped her.

"Your eyes are partly synthetic," said the Shadow. "Their capabilities exceed the limits of natural human eyes. Do many humans have modifications like yours?"

"Yes," Sayen spat. "Lots of us have. That's why you couldn't replicate me, and why you won't be able to replicate them. And the enhancements I have are nothing compared to most of theirs. They'll *kill* you."

The Shadow moved its gaze from the display screen to look directly into Sayen's eyes. "I think you're lying. We have replicated many humans. You are the first that we couldn't replicate."

Sayen locked eyes with the creature for a moment, until it broke under her stare and turned away.

Another Shadow approached with an otoscope. They'd noticed her enhanced hearing during her scan, too. As the creature examined her ears, she watched the others in the room, noting their positions and their level of attention to her. They were paying her less mind than at first.

"We want you to run on this," one of them said, pointing to a treadmill. Sayen went over to the machine, and the Shadow attached a mask to her face to measure her respiration. It turned on the machine, and kept a weapon trained on her while it adjusted the controls.

Sayen walked on the treadmill, then jogged, then ran, as the machine sped up. All the while, the Shadow looked from her to the machine's display and back to her. In the rest of the room, Sayen could see three of the other Shadows, but she didn't know where the final one was.

She was lucky. The Shadow she couldn't see was the one that didn't have a weapon. She couldn't risk looking around to find where it was, or she might alert the Shadow watching her as to her intentions. She would just have to take a chance that she would locate the unseen Shadow before it could react.

The Shadow by the treadmill continued to watch. Its gaze flitted to her again. Then to the treadmill display. To her. She was sprinting now, faster than humanly possible. But with her enhanced body, she was barely panting. Her eyes were locked on the Shadow's.

To her. To the display. To her. To the—

Sayen pushed off with her right foot. She overtook the speed of the treadmill. Leaping over the front of it, she grabbed the Shadow's weapon and kicked it down. Its head cracked on the floor, but Sayen didn't see the impact. As it was falling, she was already turning and firing. One Shadow fell with a scream, a red, smoking hole in its chest. Another raised its hands in self-defense as the aim of Sayen's weapon traveled toward its face, but the beam sliced through its palms. A larger cavity opened where its mouth had been.

Sayen spun round. The third Shadow had made it to the door and was opening it. She got it in the back before it could take a step outside.

Where was the fourth? She had to stop it from broadcasting to the others. She scanned the room, but there was no sign of the creature. There was only one possible place it could hide.

She went to the corner of the room and looked under the autopsy bed. The Shadow's eyes met hers. She saw fear in them. Sayen hesitated for a split second. Then she remembered the woman whose life the Shadow had taken.

Her jaw firmed. She raised the weapon and fired.

# Sixteen

They must have walked two or three miles in their snowshoes, Carl estimated. His nose, fingers, and toes were numb from the cold, in spite of the exertion, and his face smarted from the steady, chill wind. His mind was also spinning from the effects of the invisibility spray. One moment he was on solid ground, the next it seemed like he was stepping into eternal nothingness.

Keeping track of the other two was also hard. Every few minutes they would all speak to indicate their location and move closer if they'd drifted too far apart.

Harrington had coated three weapons with the invisibility spray and handed one each to Carl and Makey, emphasizing that they had to take special care to know what they were shooting at to avoid shooting each other. She'd also pointed out that if they dropped their weapon, it was as good as lost.

Though she'd sprayed the bag of equipment she was carrying, she hadn't treated anything else inside it. Every so often, the interface that showed Sayen's location would appear mysteriously in mid-air and float around for a few moments before disappearing into nothingness again.

After one of these appearances, Carl heard Harrington mumble to herself.

"Shouldn't we be getting close?" he asked.

"Yes, we should," she replied. "According to the readings, Sayen's being held only two or three hundred meters from here."

The landscape in front of them remained bare and empty of life.

"Do you think the readings are wrong?" he asked.

"No, I don't think so."

"Then where is she?"

"I've been thinking about it. The Shadows are operating in secret for the moment. Any place where they congregate has to be hidden to avoid causing suspicion. I think Sayen's right where this thing says she is. Except she's underground."

"The Shadows have an underground base here?" asked Makey.

"I spent a few years living here," Harrington replied. "There are research facilities all over the place. It wouldn't surprise me if one of the old superpowers built a secret underground facility. If the Shadows occupied one, it would be the perfect hiding place for them."

"Krat," Carl said. "How are we going to get inside?"

"We'll figure out a way," Harrington replied. "Makey, this is where you wait. You remember what Sayen looks like from seeing her on the *Galathea*, right? She looks the same now, just conscious. If you see her, go to her and help her back to the snowmobiles."

"But—"

"Makey, that's an order. If you want to work in security, you'd better learn to follow them."

Carl heard an adolescent huff come from Makey's direction.

"Let's get going, Jas," he said. It had been many hours since they'd first learned of Sayen's disappearance. Every moment they delayed could mean the difference between success and failure.

"Just a second." A roll of thin rope appeared from the security officer's bag. She put it on the ground. "This is our rendezvous. It's not great, but it's better than nothing. Makey, stay here until you see Sayen, in case we need to find you."

Carl and Jas went the final distance together. They talked as quietly as the low whistle of the wind would allow.

"How are we going to get in?" Carl asked.

"The entrance has to be disguised to look the same as the surroundings, or we'd see it by now. But the Shadows have human bodies. In this environment, they need heat, and heat will escape through any gap."

A pair of binoculars appeared from thin air and floated over to Carl.

"What do you see?"

Carl held the binoculars up to his eyes, and the landscape was transformed to grey shapes beneath a glowing sky. Except in one place. Four bright lines formed a square only a few meters from where they stood.

"We're right on top of them," he said. He removed the binoculars and focused his gaze on the spot that had shown the heat signature. As he went nearer, the faint lines marking the edges of a hatch became visible. "Over here." Now that he looked closely at it, the ice over the hatch didn't glisten like the rest. It was artificial, but without looking directly at it, he would never have been able to tell.

He felt something swipe him. It was Harrington's hand. She grabbed his arm.

"Great," she said. "I can see it too. According to the tracer, Sayen's about twenty meters farther on in the same direction." She sighed. "I was hoping we wouldn't have to do it this way. If we could kill a guard and slip in, we'd have a little time before they realized what was happening. But we don't have an alternative. We'll have to surprise them and rely on chaos and confusion."

"What do you mean?"

"I'm going to blow the door in."

The bag rustled.

"This has a two-minute fuse," Harrington said as an explosive device appeared. "The second it blows, we go in. After that...krat. I don't know. I don't know what we'll find in there—how big the place is, or how many Shadows there are. We're going to lose each other the minute we're inside, and we won't be able to talk or we'll give ourselves away. I guess we just have to find her, get out, and get back to Makey. Whatever happens, don't wait for me. Go to the snowmobiles, I can find my own way back."

"The same for me," said Carl. There didn't seem much more for either to say.

They withdrew to a safe distance.

"Cover your ears," Harrington said, just before the explosive blew. As a gaping hole appeared in the ice, Carl was already running toward it. He leapt in and straight down into the Shadows' base. The door had ripped the hand bars from the wall before embedding into the floor. Carl landed on it and moved quickly away. As he expected, he heard a thunk as Harrington jumped down behind him.

Smoke from the explosion filled the air. Carl headed in the only direction that was clear. Shadows were already approaching the scene of the explosion. He slipped past them easily and went deeper into the base.

As he ran, he wondered what he was looking for. Where would the Shadows keep their prisoners? Sayen could be anywhere. Harrington had been right. The place did seem to be a research facility. He'd already passed several labs. A chill sweat broke out on him. Had the Shadows brought Sayen there because they wanted to experiment on her?

He was heading into an area of classrooms. He doubled back to return to the research laboratories, though he dreaded what he might find.

A Shadow ran out of a doorway, and Carl crashed into it. The creature landed heavily and stared around in confusion. Carl jumped over the Shadow and sped away, wondering at what he had seen. For a moment, Carl had experienced the drifting into nothingness that was an effect of the invisibility spray. At that moment, he'd looked at the Shadow, and seen a faint light around the man, like sunspots on his retinas on a sunny day. He ran on.

No shout or cry came from behind him, but if the Shadows were telepathic as he suspected, the information about invisible assailants was probably being broadcast.

He had to find Sayen fast.

The Shadow base was eerily silent. No alarms were ringing due to the explosion at the door. No one was shouting commands. But Carl could hear something else. It sounded like a fight was going on. He could hear grunts, gasps, and the sound of bodies hitting the floor.

As he turned a corner, he came upon a strange sight. Four Shadows were wrestling with an invisible opponent. Carl got a glimpse of a pair of beautiful, reddish-brown eyes. Harrington's snow goggles had come off and the Shadows had caught her. If he didn't do something soon, they would hold her still enough to get in a shot.

He aimed to fire, but he risked hitting Harrington. The disorientation effect of the invisibility spray hit him again. The Shadows before him glowed faintly. He blinked, and the glow was gone.

He had to concentrate. He would have to take them out close up. Before he could move, Sayen appeared, running toward them from the opposite direction. She was in her underwear, and she was a mess —covered in bruises, scratches, and dried blood. But she was alive. Now he just had to save Harrington and get Sayen out.

The woman's eyebrows rose at the sight of the struggling Shadows, and she slowed her pace.

"It's Harrington," Carl called. "They've got her. Get out of the way. I'm going to shoot."

Sayen looked in his direction, her face brightening in recognition of his voice. She slowed to a stop. The Shadows, on hearing him speak, loosened their grip on Harrington. They also noticed Sayen.

She had a weapon in her hand. She raised it and shot one of the Shadows in the stomach. As it fell to the floor, another was thrown head first into the wall by an unseen force. Carl shot a third, which was coming in his direction, trying to find the source of the words he'd spoken. The fourth aimed at Sayen, but the beam from her weapon cleaved its skull.

"Carl, Jas, where are you?" Sayen said.

Carl ran to her and grabbed her. "I'm here. Let's go. The exit's this way. Harrington, are you behind us?"

"Yes, I'm coming. Go."

Gripping Sayen's arm, Carl ran with her back to the blown-in door. When they reached it, they had a problem. With the hand bars ripped off, the hole was too high to reach. Then Carl had an idea.

"Climb on my shoulders, and I'll lift you up."

"Where are you?"

"Here." He put her hands on his shoulders and squatted down. When Sayen was aboard, he rose to his feet. Sayen was in reach of the edge of the hatchway. He felt her stand on his shoulders to scramble out. He'd done it. They'd saved her.

"Makey's due east, Sayen. He's waiting for you, and he'll take you to McMurdo Sound."

"Krat that, Carl, I'm not leaving without you." She was leaning over the hatch looking down at him.

"You'll have to. I can't make it up there."

"I might not be able to see you, but I can pull you up."

"You can't. I'm too heavy."

"You really think so? Try me." She gave two small grunts. "I've anchored my feet in the ice. Grab my hands."

Carl jumped and gripped the woman's small hands. He swung there for a moment, then, unbelievably, he found himself being lifted upward and out of the Shadow base.

The moment he could reach the edge of the hatchway with his knee, he levered himself the rest of the way. Sayen was grinning.

Now they just had to get Harrington. He looked into the hatch and quickly drew his head away as Shadows in the corridor fired at him. He caught a brief glimpse of return fire from Harrington below him. She was using the door as cover.

"Harrington," he shouted down.

"I've set a bomb," came her voice directly below him. "Run. Get Sayen away."

But the woman was scrabbling back to the hole. "Jas, take my hands." She thrust her arms into the hatch, and screamed. Her face was twisted in pain, but she heaved an invisible Harrington out of the hole.

They ran.

The ground shuddered, and Carl was thrown down as the Shadow base exploded behind him. Smoking debris began to rain from the sky. He scrambled to his feet, and went to continue, but the body of a Shadow fell in front of him. Carl halted in horror. The thing was still alive. It had a weapon in its hand. It was aiming at Carl. Rooted to the spot, there was nothing he could do.

Then the weapon sailed out of the Shadow's hand. Someone had kicked it away. Harrington?

The Shadow died.

# SEVENTEEN

"That's it, Makey," Harrington said through her teeth. "When we get back to London, you're on your own. No more mentoring. You're not fit to work in security or anywhere else where people put their lives in your hands."

The security officer was somewhere off to Carl's right. They were nearly back at the snowmobiles. He could see them a short distance away, black against the pale gray ice.

Harrington's words were the first she'd spoken since they'd left the remains of the Shadow base. Her pitch was low and calm, but it was clear she was in an absolute rage.

"What? Why?" came the kid's voice from his left.

"I gave you a direct order to stay by the rope. You disobeyed. You followed us to the Shadow base. If there's one thing you must never, ever do, it's disobey an order."

"Come on, Harrington," Carl said. "He saved my life when he kicked that Shadow's weapon away."

"That's how it looked to me, too," added Sayen. She was still wearing very little clothing, and she was walking barefoot across the ice, but she'd assured them that she was fine. She'd explained that the body enhancements that had enabled her to lift both Carl and

Harrington out of the Shadow base also protected her from extreme heat and cold.

Across her forearms, however, the skin was burned and blistered where the beam from a Shadow's weapon had scored it when she'd reached into the hole for a second time. Without her enhanced skin, her arms would have been severed.

"Don't interfere with things you don't understand, Carl," Jas said. "You were lucky, kid, that's all. You could have died, or you could have gotten the rest of us killed. You never disobey an order. If you don't get that, it's over. Forget it."

Carl said, "Jas, don't you—"

"This is none of your business," she exclaimed.

Anger rose in Carl in return. The woman's temper got on his nerves, and in this case it wasn't justified. Makey was just a kid, and he'd been a big help at a sticky moment. But before Carl could reply, Harrington continued, "When we get back to the snowmobiles, we need to change our clothes and wipe off the spray. Then we head straight to the spaceport. There are probably Shadows in McMurdo Sound, and I don't know how long we have before they're alerted about us."

The invisibility spray came off when scrubbed with handfuls of ice. By the time he was free of the sticky substance, Carl was freezing. His hands were red and raw from holding the ice, and he could barely feel them. He thrust them into his mittens, but that made little difference. It was odd seeing Makey and Jas slowly reappear as they cleaned off the spray. Sayen stood by, her arms wrapped around herself, watching them all in amusement.

"How are we going to get Sayen on a shuttle?" Makey asked. "She doesn't have any ID."

"Don't worry," Sayen said. "I don't think it'll be a problem. But I do need some clothes. I don't suppose you have any to spare?"

Makey was the closest in size of the three of them to the petite woman, but she still looked ridiculous in his pants, rolled up at the ankles, and his sweater, which hung almost to her knees.

They decided they couldn't risk taking the time to get her

anything more suitable. They had to get out of McMurdo Sound before the Shadows made a move against them.

Before they set off, Harrington mailed a one-word message to Sayen's parents: Success.

Jas was silent all the way to the spaceport, and Carl didn't say much either. He remained angry with her over her tirade at Makey. He was beginning to wonder what he'd ever seen in her. She could be moody and difficult, and her outbursts of temper were annoying.

Harrington's message seemed to have born fruit when they arrived at the check in for the next flight to the U.S. The clerk didn't ask to see any of their IDs, and neither did the shuttle staff when they boarded.

Carl, Sayen, and Makey sat three abreast, while Harrington sat across from them. From the look on her face, Carl would never have guessed that they had just saved their friend from grave danger and taken out twenty or thirty Shadows. He didn't know if he would ever figure her out, and he wasn't sure if he wanted to try. He turned to Sayen.

"So, what did you find out that made them come for you?" he asked in a low voice, taking care not to be overheard in the public passenger cabin.

"I'll explain later," she replied. "But one thing I can say is, they're good at mimicking us. I thought my manager was a sweet man, but it turned out he was one of them. We can't trust anyone."

Carl thought of his parents. Would he ever find them? And if he did, could he be sure it was really them?

Across the aisle, Harrington's interface beeped. She swiped the screen to read the message. Her sour expression turned sourer still. Wordlessly, she handed the screen across to Sayen. As she read it, the woman's face fell.

She angled the device so that Carl and Makey could also see it.

*Please do not bring our daughter home. We're so sorry. They know who you are. It's no longer safe to come here. You must disappear. Don't use anything that will allow you to be traced. A friend will meet you at the spaceport you're traveling to and give you a package. Good luck. S, we love you, darling.*

Sayen looked like she was about to cry. Carl put an arm over her shoulders.

"Don't worry. We defeated them back there, like we did aboard the *Galathea*. They're not invincible. We'll find out who they are, and we'll destroy them. Whether they're in government, or corporations, or the military, or even if they've made it to the Transgalactic Council itself. We'll get them all. They aren't going to win."

# UNDERWORLD

# ONE

Sayen was the first to notice that the shuttle they were in wasn't flying to its scheduled destination. She was sitting in a window seat and was in no mood for talking. After telling Carl what she'd found out at the Global Government Security Headquarters, their conversation had drifted to silence. She was worried about her parents. She wondered what their message meant in terms of their own safety. They'd written that it was no longer safe for her to go home, but had they meant that it was unsafe for her because the Shadows were looking for her, or that their house was under threat of attack? She had no way of finding out because they'd also told her not to do anything that would allow them to be traced, and that included contacting them.

Her thoughts had preoccupied her so much that she hadn't really been registering her view of the landscape below. When her ears popped, the sensation jolted her out of her distraction. The shuttle was descending. She scanned the ground for a familiar sight of her state's capital, and with growing alarm she realized she didn't recognize what she saw. Instead of a large metropolis, below them was a small town. On the horizon was a mountain range that she knew, but it lay in the wrong direction.

She clutched Carl's arm on the seat rest beside her.

"Something's up, isn't it?" he asked in an undertone.

"Yes," Sayen replied quietly. "We're landing in the wrong place. How did you know?"

"We started descending too soon." He leaned over her to peek out the window. "Do you know where we are?"

Sayen nodded. "At least three hours' drive from where we should be." She looked past him toward Jas and Makey across the aisle. The kid was asleep, his head lolling against the security officer's shoulder. The woman was staring at the back of the seat in front of her, her face set and expressionless.

"The pilot hasn't made an announcement," Carl said, "so he's in on it." He reached across the gap between his seat and Jas's and pulled on her sleeve.

She snapped out of her reverie. "What?" she asked him, frowning.

Sayen waved to get her attention. She pointed out the window and shook her head in an exaggerated gesture. Jas's eyebrows rose. She mouthed the word *krat* and pushed Makey upright so that he woke up. As he opened his eyes, she put her finger to her lips and leaned over to whisper in his ear.

Around them, a hum of conversation rose in the cabin as some of the passengers also began to notice the shuttle wasn't landing where it was supposed to.

A ping sounded from above as the overhead speaker came to life. "This is your pilot speaking. I'm sorry to report that bad weather has forced us to divert to Silversville. An autobus will ferry passengers on to your scheduled destination. We apologize for any inconvenience. We will be landing in fifteen minutes. Please stay seated with your seatbelt fastened."

Sayen looked at the clear blue sky outside. *Bad weather?* The rest of the passengers weren't buying the excuse either. Angry voices rose on both sides of the cabin and call buttons chirped as people demanded the attention of flight attendants. The attendants all seemed to have disappeared, however. A few men and women undid their safety belts and got up out of their seats, and the volume of protests and complaints inside the shuttle rose.

"Are y'all thinking what I'm thinking?" Sayen asked the others. They nodded. There was no need to spell it out. Shadows were in control of the plane. The only question was, was this a general kidnapping, or did the aliens know that Sayen and her rescuers were on board? There weren't many shuttle flights from Antarctica. It wouldn't have taken a genius to narrow down the possibilities as to where they were, and the news of her escape from the Shadows' base must have gotten out by now.

Jas was standing and taking down her bag from the overhead locker. After putting the bag on her seat, she said to Sayen and Carl. "We can't let them stay in control of the shuttle. If we go along with their plan, they're going to have a nice reception committee waiting for us when we land. Carl, can you fly this?"

"Probably," he replied.

"If you can get us on the ground without killing everyone, that'll be good enough. Sayen, how are your arms? Can you hold a weapon?"

Sayen's forearms were still painful from laser burns she'd received during her escape. "Yes, I can."

"Great. Short, sharp bursts, okay? If you melt a hole in the shuttle, we're all dead." Jas turned to Makey, who was craning his neck, trying to hear what she was saying. "You stay right where you are. You're just another passenger, okay?"

The kid scowled. Jas still hadn't forgiven him for not following orders when he'd taken part in Sayen's rescue. She grabbed her bag and surreptitiously pulled out a weapon for Sayen and Carl. "Let's go."

The three of them made their way to the front of the cabin, which was already blocked with angry passengers trying to find the flight attendants. The attendants all seemed to have retreated into the pilot's control room. Sayen hoped that none of them were human.

"Get back to your seats," Jas shouted. "Everyone, for your own safety, return to your seats and fasten your seat belts."

She got some attention, but not enough. Most of the passengers ignored her. "Who do you think you are?" asked a woman, shrilly.

"We want answers. My husband is waiting for me at the spaceport. This diversion is unacceptable."

Jas raised her weapon and pointed it above the crowd. The woman gasped and stepped back. "She's got a gun. Oh Lord, she's got a gun." That got everyone's attention. The angry passengers melted away like overnight frost under the morning sun, and in a few moments their path to the pilot's cabin door was clear. The place was filled with the sound of seatbelts being hastily fastened.

Sayen and Jas advanced, and Carl brought up the rear, covering them against Shadows that might be among the men and women watching.

Jas raised her weapon to fire it at the lock on the door, but Sayen grabbed her arm and shook her head. The Shadows could be expecting them to do just that, and they would shoot as Jas went through the door. Jas frowned at her, puzzled. As Sayen put her ear against the wall, the woman's brow cleared and she lowered her gun.

Sayen listened with her enhanced hearing. No voices could be heard inside, which wasn't surprising as the Shadows communicated with their minds, but she could detect the sounds of movement and —if she listened very hard—breathing. She held up four fingers to Jas. The pilot and three flight attendants were inside. She dropped two fingers and pointed with the others, indicating the positions of two Shadows. Jas nodded and aimed her weapon. A faint *Oh my Lord,* repeated, came from behind.

Sayen aimed at where she estimated the pilot's head to be and prayed that she hit it and not the window. With a mutual exhaled breath she and Jas fired, then altered their aims and immediately fired again. The shuttle lurched, and Sayen fell onto a seat occupied by an obese man. The cabin door swung open and a laser beam shot out, narrowly missing Sayen but hitting the obese man in the gut. He shrieked, and screams and yells from the other passengers echoed his cries.

Jas shot again, and the Shadow that had fired fell out of the doorway, half its head missing. She'd killed it, but at least one of their shots had pierced the shuttle. Air whistled out, and the door began to slam shut but was prevented by the body of the dead Shadow. An alarm sounded and oxygen masks fell from overhead. Jas and Sayen jumped over the fallen Shadow and ran through the door to the flight deck, quickly followed by Carl. Two Shadows lay dead on the floor, and the pilot was slumped dead in his seat, a smoking hole through his back.

Another hole had been melted in the window, and Sayen fought not to be dragged toward it. She grabbed a serving tray that one of the attendants had dropped and flung it over the hole. The air pressure inside the cabin held it in place, and the whistling stopped.

Carl had already dragged the pilot out of her seat and was strapping himself in. As he adjusted the controls, the shuttle's steep descent began to slow.

"Where are we going?" he asked.

"Anywhere that isn't where they were taking us," Jas replied.

"Okay, I'll find an unihabited area outside the city."

Sayen removed the headphones and mic from the pilot and listened with one ear. "Please report on your position," said a voice. "Please respond."

"Who is this?" Sayen asked. "Who am I speaking to?"

A gasp sounded, then the headphones went dead. Her eyes met Jas's. "The Shadows are at space flight control too," she said.

The aliens' spread seemed to grow wider each time she encountered them, but the exchange with space flight control had told her one thing useful: the aliens couldn't communicate telepathically over long distances. For that, they relied on electronic comms, the same as humans.

# Two

By the time Carl landed the shuttle a few miles from the capital, the passengers were subdued and quiet. Makey had joined Sayen, Carl, and Jas in the pilot's cabin. The obese man sprawled unmoving in his seat, a large pool of blood beneath him. None of the passengers had made a move to attack, so either there were no Shadows among them, or they were remaining anonymous.

Landing a space shuttle on an area of unprepared, natural landscape didn't hurt the shuttle, but it destroyed the surrounding area. When they opened the doors, the smell of burning plants and scorched earth drifted inside. As they were trying to figure out a way to traverse the ten-meter drop to the ground unharmed, one of the passengers spoke up.

"Hey, what's going on? What's going to happen to us?"

"It's too much to explain now," Sayen answered, "but those things we killed weren't people. They're aliens called Shadows. They look exactly like us, and they're trying to take over the planet."

That drew intakes of breath and exclamations from the passengers. The *Oh my Lord* woman started up again.

"We can't help you," Sayen continued. "They're after us, and we have to get away. Maybe you can call for help, but please be very careful. The Shadows might come and pretend to rescue you, only to make you another of their victims. It'll be better if you can make your own way home. After that, tell others what happened here, but watch who you speak to. If anyone you know has disappeared for no reason for a short time, they might be a Shadow."

The passengers murmured as they digested this information. A young man stood up, and Jas instantly aimed at him. The man blanched and raised his hands. "Woah there. I just wanted to say, use the emergency slide to get down. That's what it's for."

*Of course.* Sayen opened the casing beside the door and activated the mechanism. A bright yellow slide inflated all the way to the ground. "Thanks," Sayen said.

"No problem. Good luck to you," replied the man, sitting down.

Jas went to retrieve her bag from her seat. The curious heads of the passengers poking out into the aisle retreated as she passed them and popped out again as she returned to the front. Sayen hoped Jas had plenty of stuff in that bag of hers to help them survive.

"Thanks for saving us, honey," piped a voice. It was *Oh my Lord.*

"Ready?" Jas asked Sayen and the others.

They jumped onto the slide one by one, and scooted out of the way immediately when they hit the bottom. The ground was still smoking from the shuttle's engines. Sayen coughed, and her eyes watered. Fifty or so meters away were some low hills. She suggested they made their way over to them as they were in the direction of the capital. She was thankful for the enhanced skin on her bare feet. In their hurry to leave Antarctica, they hadn't even stopped to buy her some shoes.

As they went along, Sayen glanced over her shoulder. The shuttle passengers were beginning to leave, sliding down to the ground. She wished them well but also feared for them. The Shadows seemed to be everywhere, surely and steadily infiltrating every avenue of life, so that soon no one would know who was their family or friend or colleague, or who was a Shadow.

In a few minutes they reached the hills and started climbing the slopes. She estimated that twelve to fourteen kilometers lay between them and the city. It was late afternoon, and if they wanted to sleep in a bed that night, they had a long walk ahead of them.

Her stomach sank as she remembered what her parents had said: *don't use anything that will allow you to be traced.* The minute they used the credchips embedded in their wrists, they would be identifiable. If they couldn't pay for anything, how were they going to stay in a hotel, or buy food? How would she buy herself some shoes? And she needed a change of clothes. Walking around in Makey's oversized loans wasn't only uncomfortable, she looked so ridiculous, she would stick out like a sore thumb.

If they were to avoid detection by the Shadows, they had to disappear, her parents had said. How they were going to do that, she didn't have the faintest idea.

As she mulled over their problems, the four of them climbed higher into the hills, following narrow tracks created by hikers. Makey led them. He seemed to have a knack for finding the quickest path through the undergrowth and often found a new track when none seemed to exist. An hour passed, then two, and still they pushed on. The sun was getting lower, and the hills stretched out before them. They were heading in the right direction, Sayen was sure, but the city remained out of sight.

"Let's rest a while," Jas said as they were passing a piece of flat, grassy ground.

They sat on the grass. Carl pulled stalk to chew and lay down, spreading out his full length on the ground. Makey sat with his back to them. He was probably still mad at Jas, or maybe she was still mad at him.

"Hey, Sayen," Carl said, "your parents said someone would meet us at the spaceport with a package. Maybe we should go there and try to find them?"

"Our flight should have landed there hours ago," Sayen said. "Do you think they'd still be waiting?"

"No," Carl replied, his face twisting with disappointment, "you're right. They'd be long gone by now."

"It wouldn't be safe for them to wait around," Jas agreed. "The Shadows will have announced that the shuttle crashed, or another excuse. They might not believe it, but there wouldn't be anything they could do. And the spaceport's so far away, we'd never make it there. I don't know what to do. I'm out of ideas."

Something had been nagging at Sayen, and then seemed a good time to bring it up. "There's one thing I can't figure out—how did y'all know where to find me? Did you find out about the Shadow base and guess I must be there?"

Carl sat up and shared a look with Jas. Neither replied to her question.

"What's wrong? Why won't you tell me?" Sayen asked.

"Sayen, I'm sorry," said Jas. "I forgot you didn't know." She pulled an interface out of her bag, brought up a screen, and handed it to her.

Sayen studied the blinking blue spot and the map surrounding it for several moments before she began to understand what Jas was telling her. "Hold on, is this me?" Her mouth fell open as the penny dropped. "My parents had me fitted with a tracer? I'm carrying a *tracer*? You've got to be kidding me." She jumped up, and Jas quickly took the interface from her. Sayen clenched her fists and looked down at her body. "Do you know where it is? Did they tell you?" She probed the skin of her stomach, hoping to feel the hard edge of a chip.

"They didn't say," Carl said. "Sayen, they were worried about you after what happened on the *Galathea*."

"I'm a grown woman, and my parents are keeping tabs on me like I'm a little girl. *Worse* than if I were a little girl. Can they even do that? It's illegal, right? It's an invasion of...*krat*. My own parents." She sat down again.

"Well," said Carl, "looking on the bright side, if they hadn't, we would never have found you. You'd still be back in the Shadow base, being experimented on."

Sayen threw him a dark look. He was right, of course, but that didn't make her feel any better. All her life her parents had been overly protective, and it had made her fearful to try new things or do anything remotely risky. She'd finally overcome that fear, only to learn her parents weren't prepared to let her go and stand on her own two feet.

"We've got to find that tracer and get it out of you," Jas said.

"Yes, we have," Sayen replied, then, suspecting that Jas's reasoning was different from hers, she added, "Why?"

"You know all about the Shadows on Earth now, and they know you do. They're trying to keep their operations secret, so they'll want to stop you from spreading the word about them. If they find out that your parents fitted you with a tracer, they'll try to use it to find you." She looked at the interface in her hands. "Come to think of it..." she said as she got up. She went over to a rock and put the interface down on it. After searching for a moment, she found another rock and brought it down heavily on the interface, shattering the plastiglass screen. Jas continued to hammer the interface until it was nothing but small fragments. Finally satisfied that the device was completely destroyed, she said, "We can't be too careful. Let's get out of here."

# THREE

On the quarantine station in its low Earth orbit, Dr. Sparks was bored. He'd pondered the question at length, but he hadn't been able to understand exactly why Polestar insisted it had to be *him* who performed assessments on the Paths. It was true that he'd been the physician aboard the *Galathea* when it crash-landed on K.67092d, but he hadn't even seen the things before they'd been taken to quarantine.

But Polestar in its infinite wisdom had somehow connected the Paths with the only scientist on board who was well versed in the complexities of the human body, and it had ordered him to conduct tests on this new species. He could have refused, but then he would have been out of a job and without a good reference to show a new employer.

He regarded the Paths on the other side of the transparent barrier and yawned. The shapeless, fungi-like upturned bags were among the least interesting aliens he'd come across. They just sat there, not doing anything, apparently existing on nothing but ordinary air, as they didn't eat any of the variety of foods offered to them, and they didn't drink or absorb water or any other liquid.

All they seemed to do was emote. Anyone within a few meters of the creatures inevitably felt whatever the Paths themselves felt at the time. Or that was how it seemed. That was supposed to be one of the things he was investigating.

It occurred to him that maybe his boredom wasn't his, but theirs. He took several steps backward to test his suspicion. From previous tests he'd gathered that the vicinity within which the Paths had an effect on humans seemed to be limited. He left the room and went a short distance down the corridor. He was still bored.

"Sparks," said a lab tech, Rogers, approaching him, "how are you doing? Found out anything about your mushrooms yet?"

"No," intoned the doctor. "I don't suppose you have some free time? I need another human subject to test their emoting."

"Me, sit in a room with those things? You must be joking. My emotions are my own, and not to be tampered with."

"The feeling wears off almost as soon as you leave the immediate area," said Sparks. "It's completely harmless as far as I can tell."

"And it's that *as far as I can tell* that makes me repeat my response. No. Sorry." Rogers moved away. "Good luck."

He was right to be cautious, of course, Dr. Sparks mused. No one knew the long-term effects of exposure to the Paths. He hoped that wasn't something that Polestar would like him to find out. Their instructions had been annoyingly vague. He didn't think the company itself had any idea what it wanted to know, or what to do with the creatures.

Returning them to K.67092d was out of the question. Not only was the planet occupied by hostile aliens, but the Paths didn't appear to be natives of the place. No one knew where they'd come from. Sparks had scoured the Transgalactic Council databases on life forms existing and extinct, but he'd found nothing that remotely resembled them. None of the Council's experts had even been able to help with educated guesses.

Sparks wondered when Polestar would finally give up their investigations and put the strange aliens in a zoo.

He returned to his observation room. The Paths hadn't moved, but he hadn't expected them to. He sat down and brought up his latest unfinished report to Polestar on his screen. It was very short and thin on meaningful detail. He didn't think Polestar would be satisfied with it. If only he could get someone to agree to be a test subject, maybe he would find out something new. He wondered if the strength of the emotions conferred differed according to a variable within the subject.

Sparks rested his elbows on the frame around the window to the Paths' room. He steepled his fingers and gazed intently at the aliens. There had to be something else he could say. *Something.*

He blinked. For a brief fraction of a second, the Paths had seemed to change in some way, but the moment had been so short, he wasn't sure what the change had been or if his eyes had been deceiving him. He folded his arms and leaned on the window frame again. Maybe this was it. Something new that he could put in a report. He determined to not take his eyes off the aliens until the change happened again.

Sparks didn't have to wait long. After a couple of minutes, the Paths very briefly faded before returning to full visibility. He was right. They *were* doing something. He set a timer.

Two minutes and twenty-four seconds later, the creatures faded again. Sparks made a note and returned to his observation. Exactly two minutes and twenty-four seconds later, the same thing happened.

The fading seemed to be regular behavior. A fourth bout of fading supported Sparks's hypothesis. His head tilted to one side as he watched. The phenomenon was so subtle, he doubted that he would have noticed it if he hadn't been staring directly at the creatures for a sustained period of time. It occurred to him that the Paths could have been doing the same thing ever since they'd collected them on K.67092d, but no one had noticed.

He turned his attention to his screen and brought up a vid from the camera that had been filming the room that held the aliens. It took him longer than twenty minutes to detect the first fading, but once he'd seen it, the ones that followed at regular intervals were easy to spot.

Sparks smiled to himself as he brought up his report to Polestar. This new behavior he'd observed should fill it out nicely. He began to speak into his mic and his words appeared on the screen. He recorded what he'd seen directly and the corroborating evidence from the vid. He would include a copy of it with a note regarding the timing of the behavior.

As he scrolled down the report to the section on his conclusions, he paused as he wondered what to say. What did the behavior mean? Were the creatures capable of entirely disappearing? Transparent organisms weren't unusual, on Earth or elsewhere in the galaxy, but the Paths didn't seem to be turning see-through. Their entire body faded, as if they were very slightly and very momentarily *not there*. And it happened at a regular rate, almost like a heartbeat. Could it be possible that they weren't fading, but they were going somewhere? Were they able to move, but without a conventional means of locomotion, and to places not in their immediate vicinity?

Sparks gasped as another idea popped into his head. Was it possible that the Paths could move in time? Did they fade as they moved briefly into the future or the past? The most famous xenobiologists had long speculated that beings with such capabilities might exist somewhere in the galaxy, given the wealth of variety in species already discovered. Some species could do things no human had ever dreamed of.

But he must not get ahead of himself. There would be plenty of time to test his hypotheses later. He grinned. He hadn't felt this excited about practicing science since he'd been at medical school. His speculations made him feel young again.

He needed an independent verification of his observation. The fading was so difficult to spot that, even with the vid evidence, it was possible he was imagining it. He would ask a colleague to watch the Paths with him. Springing to his feet, Sparks suddenly checked himself. His elation felt odd. Was it real? Was he experiencing a genuine emotion, or was he being influenced by the Paths?

The shapeless aliens sat in their quarantine room innocently.

No, Sparks was sure their range didn't extend to the observation booth. He'd tested them on several subjects. No. He was only happy because he'd found out something interesting and was finally relieved of his terrible boredom.

He went to find Rogers.

# FOUR

It was the early hours of the morning when Sayen and the others made it to the outskirts of the city. They were still several miles' walk from downtown, where they hoped to find the kind of people who could help them in their new, cred-free lifestyle. Makey clearly couldn't go any farther that night, however. The kid was stumbling with tiredness, and Jas and Carl also looked pale and drawn.

They'd come across a stream as they descended the hills, and the water had seemed clean enough to drink. All four of them had been extremely thirsty by then and willing to take the risk. Sayen's stomach had ached with hunger for a few hours, but now she only felt a little weak for lack of food.

The suburban houses at the city's edge offered little hope of rest or sustenance. Knocking on a random door was out of the question. Whoever answered wouldn't waste much time in calling the police. Dusty and haggard from their walk, they looked like the kind of people who made suburbanites uneasy. Sayen was barefoot and wearing oversized clothes. She was also covered in scratches and bruises from her escape from the Shadows.

"We should stop and rest up as soon as we can," she said. "We can walk the rest of the way in the morning."

"Yeah, okay," Jas replied. "If we come across a park or recreational ground, we can rest there."

It wouldn't be too hard to find such a place, Sayen knew. The residential districts of her home city were planned for convenience and for bringing up the precious children of parents who'd invested a large proportion of their income in them even before they were born.

Sure enough, halfway down the next street was a small park. Daily watering had kept the grass green during the summer heat, and shade trees provided protection from the blazing sun. Drifts of the previous year's leaves had accumulated under the hedges that surrounded a playground, and the four of them made themselves as comfortable as was possible in the circumstances. Sayen was asleep within minutes.

Not long later, it seemed, the closing of a car door awakened her. Where she was sleeping, she had a view of the road, and her heart stopped when she saw what kind of car it was. Two uniformed police officers were walking toward them.

Carl was sleeping along from her under the same hedge. She edged toward him and pushed his shoulder with her foot. He shifted but didn't wake until she pushed him again, harder. He mumbled as he woke up. The police officers heard and altered their direction, heading right for them.

Sayen was already forcing her way through the leaves and stems to the other side of the hedge, and Carl followed seconds later as he realized what was happening. Jas and Makey were on the far side of the playground. Sayen and Carl ran across to them, keeping below the height of the hedge, but the officers spotted their movement.

"Hey, wait up," called one of them.

The cop's voice woke Jas. Sayen saw her eyes snap open, and she crawled quickly over to Makey and shook him, holding a finger to her lips as he stirred.

Sayen had spotted an exit to the playground in the opposite direction from the police. She pointed toward it wordlessly.

"Hey," called the officer again, more stridently.

Now they'd been seen, there was no point in trying to hide. All four sprinted toward the exit and through it before running down a road. Sayen suspected that the police were only trying to move them on, and it seemed she was right as no shots were fired and there were no more shouts.

Sayen kept her pace slow enough for the others to keep up. They raced the length of three streets before drawing to an exhausted stop.

When the others had caught their breath, she said, "I guess a neighbor saw us and made a call."

Jas nodded. "They don't want us down and outs in their area."

"Exactly," Sayen said.

They walked slowly on through the moonlit streets, assuming the same thing would happen wherever they stopped in that upmarket neighborhood. Solar-powered streetlights cast a soft orange glow. The others were beyond tired, but they had no choice but to march on. Gradually, the houses lining the streets became smaller, and they directly abutted the road with no security fences. The houses also became older and shabbier, and more cars and auto-cabs drove past.

When Makey staggered and fell, they had no choice but to stop. They had wandered into an area of apartment blocks and small convenience stores. Sayen and Jas helped the kid into a large block's recessed entrance, and he lay down under the security panel. Jas sat with her knees drawn up and her head resting on her folded arms, and Carl curled in an uncomfortable-looking ball on the hard pavement. Sayen sat in a corner with her back against the apartment block door and leaned her head against the wall.

It seemed only moments later when she found herself falling backward. She managed to jerk awake just in time to prevent herself from hitting the back of her head hard on the floor. It was dawn, and the door she'd been leaning against had opened. A pair of legs in pants and heels were stepping over her, their owner cursing *good-for-nothing panhandlers*. The woman who had opened the door let go of it, so that it would have hit Sayen if she hadn't put out her hand to catch it.

She held onto the door as the woman left, not giving them a backward glance. Jas and Carl were blinking awake. Makey snored gently, his mouth hanging open.

"Hey, look," Sayen said, nodding toward the building's interior.

"We can get inside?" asked Carl. "What good's that gonna do us? Are you saying we should break into an apartment?"

"I thought about it," Sayen replied. "We could find an empty one by buzzing them all and seeing which ones don't answer, but I don't know how to get past the door security. There might be other stuff inside the building, though."

"Yeah, that's right," said Jas. "It might have a gym."

Carl looked at her like she was mad.

"Showers," she explained. "Clean water."

They woke Makey up and went inside the building. The elevator was operated by retinal scan or voice recognition, but the fire door to the basement opened with a push, and they went down two flights of stairs. They found a gym. The equipment was sparse and old and so were the showers, but the water was hot and it was free. They had no soap or towels, but right then that didn't matter to Sayen. They all went into shower stalls.

Sayen stripped off her clothes and turned on the shower, sighing with pleasure as the warm water cascaded over her body. Her enhanced skin was already almost healed. The scratches she'd sustained in the jungle were now only slight grazes, and her bruises were light yellow. Bending over, she lifted her feet one by one and checked the undersides. They were holding up well considering the many miles she'd walked without shoes. If it hadn't been for the enhancements her parents had paid for, she could never have survived the last couple of days.

Her conscience twinged as she remembered her anger over the tracer they'd put inside her. She still thought it was wrong, but she didn't doubt their love for her.

"Sayen," came Jas's voice from beyond the shower curtain, "are you nearly done? We have to go. Someone's bound to turn up in a minute, and we can't risk another run in with the police."

"Okay," she replied as she reluctantly turned off the water. Leaning forward, she ran her hands across her head, trying to wipe away as much water as she could. She reached up to the basket that held her clothes. Wrinkling her nose, she put on the dirty underwear and clothes, tugging them over her wet skin.

They went up onto the first floor and outside. Air and her body's warmth quickly dried Sayen off as they went deeper into the city. The place was waking up, and they began to attract attention from passersby. The area they were in was still too affluent for them to pass unnoticed, but this was Sayen's home city, and she knew where they had to go. When they reached the oldest, dirtiest, most dangerous area, they wouldn't get any more stares. In their unkempt, hungry, desperate state, they would fit right in.

# FIVE

With no possibility of using their embedded credchips, Sayen and the others had to make a hard choice. They'd finally reached the area where the people the vidnews called 'underworlders' lived, and they stopped to discuss their next move.

Sayen knew she was less streetwise than the others, so she was content to go along with what they decided. It was clear that they would either have to steal to survive—running the risk of arrest with nothing but an implausible story to tell in their defense—or sell the only assets they had: the contents of the bag Jas had carried all the way from the shuttle.

The decision didn't take long to make. They decided to keep Jas's two weapons and Carl's that he'd brought from Australia. They would sell everything else. The invisibility spray could have been very useful to them, but it was also very illegal in the way that personal weapons were not, and their risk of chance encounters with the police was high now that they were homeless. The spray, the explosives, and the rest of the bag's contents would have to be sold, but with the proceeds they could buy food and maybe somewhere to sleep while they figured out what to do about the Shadows.

They decided they would try to find a buyer as quickly as possible.

Considering that it was around midday, the street they'd stopped on was quiet. Few cars seemed to drive through the underworld zone, and the ones they saw were customized, self-driving models that didn't seem to be going anywhere in particular, but only cruised up and down the streets.

It was fortunate that the street wasn't busy with traffic, as children roamed it. Even toddlers who could barely walk had been allowed out by their parents, and they tottered around, sometimes in the care of slightly older siblings, and sometimes ignored by all. Older youths also loitered a short distance away from Sayen and the others. They were unashamedly staring at them.

The adolescents seemed to be the kind of people who might know buyers for Jas's equipment. They walked over and approached one of the group, who seemed to be the ringleader. A sycophantic female follower clung to his elbow. She bore a tattoo on her right cheek of a symbol that Sayen didn't recognize. The young man bore the same tattoo on his neck.

"You want something?" he asked.

"Yes," replied Jas, "we have some stuff to sell." When the young man's face hardened and his hand went to side, Jas continued, "Not the same stuff you sell. Do you know anyone who might be interested in buying some military supplies?"

His hand left his side, and his expression relaxed. "No, I don't," he said, but his gaze fell to the bag Jas carried.

"You sure, mate?" Carl asked. "If you do know someone, they might be disappointed not to see what we've got. What if we were to go over to the next neighborhood and do our business there? Whoever's in charge round here won't like it if the opposition get hold of what's in that bag."

The girl clinging to the ringleader hooded her eyes as she looked up into the face of her idol. She was about fourteen years old, Sayen guessed, though her face was heavily made up. The artificial coloring looked like crayon on her youthful skin. Sayen mused that she'd been learning to speak French and play badminton when she was fourteen.

The ringleader made up his mind. He shrugged and turned away. Picking up the girl under her arms, he lifted her to his lips. She squealed in excitement as he kissed her, and the rest of the gang laughed.

When it became clear that he was intent on ignoring them, Jas and the others turned and left, but they hadn't gone far before Jas spun around, her weapon out. The teenagers had followed and were right behind them. The gang rushed forward.

Beams shot out from Jas's gun, and she hit all of them but the ringleader. He was also holding a weapon, but he didn't get a chance to fire a single shot. The color drained from his face as he stared at Jas.

"I only stunned your friends," Jas said. "I don't like hurting people. But I can make an exception for you."

After a moment of internal struggle, the teenager's stare wavered, and he lowered his weapon. "I'll take you to Erielle."

He led them along the street and down a narrow alley. It was windowless, and the blank brick walls rose five or six stories high on either side. Only a few old doors broke the monotonous facade. To Sayen, it looked like something out of an antique black-and-white movie. She glanced over her shoulder to the alley entrance. The figures of the street gang were silhouettes. She hoped Jas knew what she was doing.

They arrived at a plain door covered with peeling, cracked paint. The young man knocked in a specific pattern, and the door opened. After a brief exchange with two men, they stepped out and one moved toward Jas with his hands raised, ready to pat her down.

"No," Jas said. "We're not giving up our weapons, and we're not coming inside. Your friend Erielle can come out here if she wants to do business."

"Forget it," said the man, waving dismissively. "Run away and play."

"Wait," Jas said. "I think I have something to interest you." With her free hand she reached into the bag and pulled out a device the size of her fist. "I estimate that this would take the whole building down, with your precious Erielle inside. But I'm not sure. Do you think I should find out?" She flipped open the casing with a thumb.

"Whoa, geez, lady," exclaimed the man, throwing up his hands. "We'll be back in a minute." He and the other guard went inside. The teenager who had brought them quickly left.

They waited for several minutes, until Sayen was beginning to worry that Jas really would blow the place up. But then the door opened and a woman stepped out. She was about early forties and lean, but well-defined muscles lined her arms and neck. A scar scored her cheek and ran down to her chest, and Sayen couldn't help but gasp a little at the sight of it. She rarely saw any form of physical abnormality.

She couldn't understand why the woman didn't get the scar fixed. Cosmetic surgery didn't cost a lot, and you could get it for free if you let students use you for practice.

Her sharp intake of breath had attracted Erielle's attention. Sayen fought to smooth away the expression of disgust on her face, but she wasn't fast enough. The woman had caught sight of it, and in response, she looked from Sayen's toes to her head, finishing with a gaze of pure loathing directly into her eyes.

Then the silent encounter was over, and Erielle turned her attention to Jas and the device in her hand. Her anger seemed to dissipate into mild surprise, as if she hadn't quite believed that someone was really in her alley threatening to blow the place up if she didn't come out. But Erielle was more bemused than frightened. She leaned against the alley wall, her arms folded over her chest. She was wearing baggy, dark pants and a loose tank top over bare breasts.

Still saying nothing, Erielle scrutinised each of them each in turn except for Sayen, who now merited barely a second glance. The woman had clearly made up her mind about her character. As Erielle looked at the others, Sayen could almost see the cogs of her mind turning.

"Are you interested in what we have to sell or not?" Jas asked. "We don't have all day, and we won't have trouble finding another buyer."

"You're a Martian, right?" Erielle asked. "The height and the coloring."

Jas replied, "We aren't here for small—"

"And you—you're Australian," said Erielle to Carl. "But you," she said, turning to Makey, "you, I can't place, unless—"

"Let's go," Jas said to Sayen and the others.

"Okay, okay," Erielle said. "Calm down. Come inside, and we'll talk." When Jas hesitated, she added, "You can keep your weapons."

# Six

Erielle lived in what Sayen could only describe as a 'natural' house. From the human doorkeepers to the rooms at the top of the building, it seemed to have no modern appliances. No elevator—they had to climb five floors—no interfaces on the walls, no aircon, no control panels; in fact, Sayen wasn't even sure if the place had an electricity supply until they reached their destination and she saw the lighting.

Erielle led them into a large room on the top floor. Unlike the rest of the place, the room looked relatively comfortable. A rug covered the bare boards, and worn, thick, soft floor cushions were piled here and there next to low tables. The walls looked like they'd been painted by hand, each a different bright color. Simple wooden cupboards had been decorated with intricate, multi-colored designs.

"Sit down," Erielle said, nodding toward a corner. "You look hungry. I'll get you something to eat."

They did as she invited, and she went to the door and bellowed, "Sark, food," before closing it and joining them. She sat cross-legged opposite the group across one of the tables.

Jas was looking annoyed. "We're only here to do business. I want to know how much you'll give us for what we have. Let me show you."

"She doesn't beat around the bush, does she?" Erielle said to Carl and Makey, though for all the attention she paid Sayen, she didn't exist. When the men didn't answer her, she turned to Jas. "All right, show me."

Jas took out the contents of her bag piece by piece and placed them carefully on the table. Erielle's eyebrows rose when Jas produced the invisibility spray. The woman's carefully constructed mask of indulgent tolerance fell for a moment, and a look of excitement leaked through.

When Jas had emptied the bag, Erielle sat back. "I can't deny it. That's quite an impressive haul."

The door opened and a woman entered, pushing the door with her back as her arms were occupied with holding a large tray stacked with dishes.

Jas began returning the equipment to her bag, and in the space she cleared on the table, the woman placed the tray. Sayen felt like her stomach was going to climb up out of her throat to get something to eat.

"We aren't here to eat," Jas said. Sayen's stomach squirmed in disappointment. "Tell me how much you'll give us for our stuff."

"You don't trust me? You think I poisoned the food?" asked Erielle. "I'm hurt. Truly." She picked up a handful of rice and beans and pushed it in her mouth.

Sayen thought she heard Makey whimper with hunger.

"I bet the kid could eat something," Erielle said, her mouth full. "Couldn't you, hun?" She swallowed and took a bite from a piece of bread.

Makey's eyes reminded Sayen of her catdog—a genetically designed begging machine.

Jas sighed. "Oh, okay. Eat, everyone."

No one needed telling twice. Sayen leaned over to the table and helped herself. She'd eaten the rarest foods prepared by the world's top chefs in the fanciest restaurants, but nothing compared to the pleasure of eating at the underworlder's hangout that afternoon after two days of nothing but water.

While she and the others ate, Jas and Erielle negotiated the sale of the military items. Jas sneaked the odd piece of bread dipped in stew, and one or two leaf-wrapped parcels of spiced rice as they talked. The discussion took some time. Erielle had guessed that they were new to the underworld. As her talk with Jas spread to wider things, she filled them in on useful information about her society, such as the major forms of currency underworlders used to trade with when they had no creds to buy goods in shops.

A mild narcotic called kratom was most often used where a straight barter of goods wouldn't work, Erielle told them. She explained that the amount of food they were eating cost about twenty-five grams of kratom. An hour with someone whose main asset was their body cost about the same. Erielle paid her guards fifty grams of kratom a day, she said, but their bed and board were free.

Clothes and consumer products were mostly stolen, she told them without a shred of shame. Some underworld societies existed out of town, where a few crops were grown—mostly kratom. Electricity was 'diverted' from the main supply. Sayen strongly suspected that Erielle had a hand in many of the activities that kept her society running.

If you were an underworlder, Erielle explained, living there was mostly safe, though life was tough and children grew up fast. If you weren't an underworlder and you wandered into the territory, you were fair game. Most of the 'digifreaks', as Erielle called non-underworlders, came there to buy drugs or sex, but they took their chances on being robbed or worse.

When Sayen had taken the edge off her hunger, she began to wonder why Erielle was taking the time to explain all this to them. Why didn't she get what she wanted and show them the door?

"Thanks for telling us this," she said.

The woman's eyes flashed at her. One of them was slightly pulled out of shape by her scar. She ignored Sayen's interruption and returned to her conversation. Jas seemed to be getting tired of it, however, or maybe she was suspicious of Erielle's motives.

"Yeah, thanks for the information," she said, "and the food. But we really need to get going. So, what's your offer?"

"What's the hurry?" Erielle asked.

A muscle in Jas's jaw twitched.

"I'm going to buy everything you have," the underworlder continued, "and for a good price, but I want you to indulge me just a little longer." She got up and went to the door before bellowing down the stairs, "Sark, plates."

They waited in silence for the woman to come and clear the dishes. Makey had collapsed onto the cushions and was fast asleep. Guarded looks were passing between Jas and Carl, and Jas turned her gaze to Sayen, too, more than once. Her eyes warned her to be on guard.

When Sark had retreated, Erielle leaned her elbows on the table. "A Martian, an Australian, an offworlder—I think—and the cream of our genetically engineered society. Sounds like the start of a joke. But it's no joke to you, is it? I wasn't lying when I said I'd buy your stuff, and you're lucky you ran into me. I'm no angel, but I'm the best of my kind you'll find around here."

She reached over and took Jas's hand. Jas watched warily, but allowed the underworlder to turn it palm upward on the table. Erielle traced a slightly raised, almost imperceptible square bump on Jas's wrist with her finger. Jas's embedded credchip. "Do you know what people around here do for these?" Erielle asked. She reached higher and with the same finger she drew a line across Jas's throat. "You wouldn't have lasted the night if you hadn't happened to stumble in here. Weapons or not. Us underworlders are very good at what we do, and we'd be prepared to risk a lot to get access to all your bank accounts, especially little ol' perfection over there. I bet you've got millions just sitting in an instant-access, haven't you, hun?"

Sayen shivered as the woman's eyes rested on her again.

"And don't imagine we'd do anything so refined as to force you to deposit everything you had in a reader. Oh no. We don't need your number to get past bank security. All we want is your chip, and certain people will get it whichever way is fastest. Lift your skin with a razor, cut off your hand, whatever. They'd kill you before or after. Doesn't matter to them, as long as you're not alive to tell anyone what happened."

Sayen was thankful that Makey wasn't listening to this. Even Jas looked taken aback.

"It's a bit of a shock to find out these things happen, isn't it? You don't hear about it on the vidnews. Stick around here a while, and you'll find out there's a lot of things you don't hear about on the vidnews."

The underworlder paused to take a small container out of her pocket. She opened it and took out a pill, which she swallowed without water. Jas frowned and drew back her hand. She glanced at Sayen and Carl.

"Where's the kid from?" Erielle asked.

"Dawn," Carl replied. "We picked him up from there when the planet was being attacked by Shadows."

Sayen wondered at the advisability of telling the underworlder about the Shadows. Though it was unlikely she'd had any dealings with them, there was nothing to be gained by being careless. But Erielle didn't pick up on the reference.

"Dawn?" she echoed, looking shocked. "I guessed he was from a colony, but I had no idea..." A flicker of sorrow crossed her face before she went on. "You said the planet was being attacked? What happened to the rest of the colonists?"

"Still there, the last we heard," Carl answered. "But the Government sent troops to defend them."

"What's Dawn got to do with you?" Jas asked.

The underworlder shook her head. "Just an old friend of mine went there." She smiled wryly. "I guess you think we're pretty strange living like this, don't you? Out of the system, no modding, no creds, no interfaces to glue our noses to day in, day out."

"I thought you didn't have a choice," said Jas.

"Everyone has a choice. Life's full of them. That's what you digifreaks don't realize. Sure, before you're born, your lives are laid out for you. Your parents program you with whatever looks, talents, intelligence they want, if they can afford it. You grow up indoctrinated into the system, scrambling for creds, watching the vids, believing the propaganda that passes for news. But even then, you have a choice—only you don't realize it. I had all that, but I turned my back on it. I chose this."

Tiredness was closing Sayen's eyelids. She yawned and wondered why anyone would choose to live as the underworlders did. Through half-open eyes, she glimpsed Jas throwing her a sharp glance.

"Still, it's easy to get taken in, I admit," continued Erielle. "A lot of people I used to know believed the Government's lies about Dawn being somewhere they could live freely and naturally. I lost a very special buddy because of that. Someone I loved. I didn't go with her. I didn't see why we couldn't or shouldn't live outside the system right here. It's a free planet, right?" She laughed.

Carl was also yawning.

"Sayen," Jas said, "wake up Makey. We're leaving."

"Hey, what's your problem?" asked Erielle. "We haven't decided a price yet."

Jas grabbed her bag and tried to stand, but stumbled. "You misborn," she muttered as she sank to her knees.

Carl toppled over, and Jas also hit the floor. Out of her control, Sayen's head fell forward. The last thing she heard before she lost consciousness was the underworlder's laughter.

# Seven

It had been Sparks's idea, but he'd wanted Rogers to do the actual experiment. He thought he should find out if the Paths' flesh faded even when separated from the main body. But the truth was, his years at medical school had taught him that his strengths didn't lie in science. He was more comfortable in dealing with the face-to-face, human side of practicing medicine, not the nitty gritty of diagnosis, interpreting test results, and prescribing treatments. Emotions, he could do. Science, not so much.

After much persuasion, Rogers had agreed. He was in the Paths' quarantine chamber, wearing a biohazard suit. His air supply was provided by a long tube that stretched from the back of his suit to a unit on the wall. Not that any protection would save him from the onslaught of emotions the Paths would project when he approached them.

Sparks hadn't yet discovered how the telepathy worked. That was no surprise. Though telepathy was rare among intelligent species in the galaxy, it did exist, but no one had found out the substance or mechanism that transmitted brain waves from one mind to another. Not even the aliens who had telepathy had found the secret. It was one of the galaxy's great unsolved mysteries.

So Sparks hadn't expected to find out how the Paths transmitted.

All he'd done was measure the effects. His results allowed him to predict just how Rogers was feeling right then.

"A lot of fear," came the man's voice over the intercom. Sparks checked that the interface was recording. "Getting stronger," Rogers said as he went closer to the Paths, holding aloft a scalpel. "Urgh, I don't know how you talked me into doing this, Sparks," he said. "I feel awful."

"Just a small sample, and you're done," Sparks replied into the mic. "I appreciate it, Rogers."

The man muttered to himself as he went closer. Sparks watched the Paths carefully. They were due to have one of their fading spells. Right on time, the creatures became slightly transparent. No change there. As usual, they didn't move, despite their obvious fear of the human getting closer to them, holding something metal and sharp.

Sparks felt a tiny bit sorry for the aliens. If he'd known how to administer an anesthetic, he would have. But it couldn't be helped. The sooner he found some useful information about the Paths to convey to Polestar, the better. He hoped that then he would be relieved of the assignment. It was well past time for the project to be handed over to real scientists.

"About to take a sample," said Rogers. His voice shook slightly. "I can tell you, it's certainly making me question my choice of profession, if this is how all my subjects feel."

"It'll be over in a moment," Sparks said in what he hoped was a reassuring tone.

The scalpel sliced into the flesh of a Path, and at the same moment, Rogers yelled. His arm began to shake as if he were fighting for control of it. He grunted as he lifted his hand and forced it down again to take a section of flesh.

His arms wobbling dangerously, Rogers transferred the tiny section to a glass microscope slide in his left hand. He tried to turn, but his legs also began to wobble. In a moment, he'd lost control of them, and he fell, dropping the slide and scalpel as he went down.

Sparks thumped an alarm on his interface and raced to the man's aid. He grabbed a hazard suit from the wall, hastily donned it, and sealed the flaps. He pulled open the door to the Paths' chamber and ran over to the prone Rogers. The man had fallen on the scalpel. It had pierced his suit and cut his thigh. Blood dripped from the wound, but it didn't look serious.

Rogers was in danger of contamination from exposure to the air of the room, which could contain anything the Paths might excrete as a defense mechanism. Sparks grabbed the man under his arms and began pulling him to the door. A couple of colleagues had turned up in response to the alarm. One of them lifted Rogers' legs, and they carried him out of the room between them.

Without waiting to remove Rogers' or their own hazard suits, they carried the affected man toward the station's medical center. Medics met them halfway with a gurney. They were also suited up.

Sparks and his colleague lifted Rogers onto the gurney, and one of the medics also leapt aboard and began cutting open the hazard suit. The other grabbed the bar and pushed the gurney, running with it down the corridor. Sparks also ran to keep up, watching as Rogers was cut free of his suit.

He couldn't understand what was wrong with him. The cut from the scalpel hadn't looked too bad, and any emotional effects from contact with the Paths should have worn off by then. Yet Rogers was staring unblinking and apparently unseeing at the ceiling as he was rushed along. His mouth worked wordlessly, though Sparks could hear a faint droning hum or moan escaping his lips.

# EIGHT

Jas reached up to her head as she woke. It hurt so much she was almost surprised to find it wasn't locked in a vise. She squinted against sunlight as she opened her eyes and registered that she was lying somewhere hard, cold, and bare. She tried to sit up. At the second attempt, she managed it and also closed her mouth, which had been open. Her gums and lips were painfully dry.

*Krat. Krat. Krat.* That misborn Erielle had drugged their food and taken the antidote herself before the drug had taken effect. She gasped as pain from her wrist registered. She looked down. It was covered in dried blood. Where her credchip had once been was now a raw gash. The impact of this discovery was beyond cursing to express. She could only stare at the wound for several moments as her heart and stomach plummeted to her feet.

She was sitting on a sidewalk, she realized. She turned to find her friends. All three were behind her in various states of consciousness. Makey was sitting up like her and staring in disbelief at his bloody wrist. Sayen was still out, and Carl was just opening his eyes.

Erielle and her crew had dumped them in an anonymous, empty street. Jas's bag was gone. Aside from the wounds in their wrists, the loss of their credchips didn't matter a lot. They couldn't use them without giving away their location, and it was only creds that they'd lost, not something more serious. But to have the chip physically removed was violating to a degree Jas had never experienced.

"What's happened?" Makey asked. "Did they cut that thing out of me?"

"Yeah, and me too," Jas replied. "All of us. The food was drugged."

"Krat," Carl mumbled.

Sayen awoke and gasped at the sight of her wrist.

"I only had mine put in a few days ago," Makey said. "Does that mean all our money's gone?"

"Bloody deros," said Carl as he sat up and checked out his wrist. "Yeah, they've got the lot."

"And everything we had to sell," Jas added.

"I guess we're lucky they didn't cut off our hands or kill us, like Erielle was saying," said Sayen.

"Guess so," said Jas, wondering why the woman hadn't done just that. She looked up at the sky between the roofs of the surrounding apartment blocks. "I reckon we've been out a couple of hours. Plenty of time for them to empty all our bank accounts. They won't have to worry about us reporting the crime now."

She couldn't believe what an idiot she'd been. Why had she gone into that woman's place? Why had she let the others eat the food and eaten it herself? How could she have been so stupid?

"What are we going to do now?" asked Makey.

Jas rubbed her face with her hands. The movement broke open her wrist injury, and a line of fresh blood snaked down her arm. She stood and pulled her shirt sleeve down over her wrist wound. "At least they left us our clothes."

"Erielle was right," said Sayen. "I do—or did—have millions of creds in my account. They could've given me some shoes at least."

This brought a subdued chuckle from the others. Carl held out his uninjured hand for Jas to help him to his feet. Jas gripped it tightly and pulled. Makey and Sayen also stood up.

"Well, my plans haven't come to much," said Jas. "What do you guys think we should do? I'm kratted if I know."

"We'll have to deal with the Shadows soon," Carl said. "We can't survive like this for long."

"Yeah, we haven't yet discussed just what we're going to do about them," said Sayen.

"It's hard to know *what* to do," said Jas. "Sayen, I never asked you what you found out about them when you were at the Security Headquarters."

"I told Carl while we were on the shuttle. The Government knows about them, but they've put a media ban on any mention of them. To avoid mass panic was the reason they gave, but I found a memorandum saying it was important to show the Transgalactic Council that they had the situation under control. The Council have been banning traffic to and from planets where the Shadows are known to be established. If I recall correctly, the Government didn't want to jeopardize Earth's trade agreements with other galactic nations."

"Misborns," Jas said.

"Oh, and those tests on Earth and Dawn that you two took?" Sayen said to Jas and Carl. "Fake. Or mostly fake. There's only one test that actually works. It's a scanner, and it detects a glow around Shadows that no other species has. All the other tests are only to confuse the Shadows about what we're using to identify them."

"Really?" Carl said. "You didn't tell me that. I saw the same thing in the Shadow base. They were surrounded by a glow. Did you see it, Jas?"

"No. I didn't get a chance to notice much before one of them ran into me and got my goggles off as we struggled. What did you see?"

"It was just like Sayen says. A kind of aura. I wondered if it was an effect of the invisibility spray."

"Well, that might be useful information," said Sayen. "We can detect them if we have the right scanner. Then they can't hide by disguising themselves as our friends and relations."

"I wish I'd hidden that invisibility spray," said Jas, "instead of trying to sell it. I wonder if it was because you were looking through the spray on your goggles, Carl, or if the stuff altered your brain chemistry."

"No point in speculating right now," Sayen said. "What are we going to do about the Shadows? We can't find and destroy them all by ourselves, and I don't know who to tell about them. Who can we trust? It was a Shadow at the Global Government Security HQ who had me abducted, and I swear the Security Minister is a Shadow too. She was really creepy."

"If Earth's government is compromised," Jas said, "it seems to me we need to go one step higher."

"That's the Transgalactic Council, right?" Makey asked.

"Yeah," said Carl, "but how the hell we contact them, I don't know."

A hand clutched Jas's arm. It was Sayen. Her eyes were wide and her mouth was open. Jas followed her gaze and looked down the street. A group of underworlders had appeared at the end of it, and they were heading in their direction. Had Erielle decided that leaving them alive had been a mistake? Had she sent her cronies to finish them off?

"Shouldn't we run?" asked Makey.

"Not unless you want to be shot," Carl replied.

The underworlders were aiming weapons at them. They wouldn't stand a chance if they tried to escape, and they had nothing to defend themselves with. The only good news was that if Erielle had wanted them dead right away, the underworlders would have fired at them by then.

"You're coming with us," said one of them as soon as he was within speaking distance. They had no choice but to do as he said.

# NINE

Erielle was a lot less friendly than she'd been earlier, in Makey's opinion. Instead of inviting them up to her room with the comfortable cushions, she had them shown into a basement. He didn't like the place. It was cold and damp and had no windows. His three friends also looked worried about what had happened, which didn't make him feel any better.

There wasn't even anywhere to sit down. All four of them stood waiting in silence, but they didn't have to wait long before the underworld leader appeared.

Her shaved head and narrow eyes were even more intimidating the second time round. Makey wondered why she'd called them back after drugging them and stealing those things called credchips. The amount given to him as his refugees' allowance had been so pitifully small, he wished she'd just asked him for it. It would have been a lot less painful than having the thing cut out of his wrist.

Erielle was standing with her arms folded across her chest. She pointed at him. "You," she said, "here." She lowered her hand to point at the ground next to her.

"No," cried the other three.

"You wanna argue about it?" asked Erielle. "I've got ten people with guns out there." She jerked a thumb toward the door. "You gonna fight me for him?"

"It's okay," Makey said. "I'll go."

He crossed the space and felt the pull of his friends' gaze as they looked at him across the divide. Erielle folded her arms again. "The people who I sent to download your creds have disappeared. I want to know where they've gone, and what you're going to do to help me get them back."

"We don't know where your friends are," said Jas, "but we can make a good guess at who's taken them."

"Who would that be?" asked Erielle. "And let me make it clear: if I find out you're lying, the kid here gets it."

"Geez, woman," Carl said, "why would we lie to you? The things that took your people would've taken us if we'd tried to use those chips."

"Things? What things?" Erielle asked.

"Shadows," Jas said, and she proceeded to tell the underworlder what had happened aboard the starship *Galathea* and on Dawn. Carl and Sayen offered more information as she spoke. When they told Erielle about the Shadows on Dawn, Makey noticed her glance at him.

After half an hour or longer of explaining, Jas finished with their intention to try to contact the Transgalactic Council in the hope that they could help.

Jas stopped speaking, and Erielle seemed at a loss for words for a while. "Is this true, kid?" she asked Makey. When he nodded, she said, "But you would agree with them, wouldn't you?" She deliberated a little while longer before sighing and saying, "It's so bizarre, I don't think anyone could make it up. I guess I believe you."

"So will you help us?" asked Jas.

"What do you mean?"

"We have to do something to stop the Shadows. You can help us get a message to the Transgalactic Council. We can't do it by ourselves. You saw what happened as soon as someone tried to use the credchips that identified them as us. We can't go to the Government because we don't know who we can trust."

Erielle snorted with laughter. "Me? Help you digifreaks? Your kind have been making our lives a misery for centuries. All we ever wanted to do was live the way we wanted—naturally. And what did you do? You ruined our Earth for us. You made us the lowest of the low. We have no respect, no voice, and no power. Naturals are shunned and ridiculed wherever they go.

"*Help* you? Forget it. You can all go to hell. These Shadows you're so worried about won't be interested in us underworlders. According to what you say, they prey on people in authority or who have something they want. We don't have anything to offer them. Who knows? Maybe they'll turn out to be better masters than our current ones." She winked sardonically. "No, I think you've told me enough. I'll do what I can to get my people back from these Shadows, though it sounds like there isn't much hope. I should have known to steer clear of digifreaks. They only ever bring trouble."

She turned to Makey. "You can stay with me. I made a mistake in letting you go with them. You belong here with us. You understand our beliefs, and as a son of a Dawner, I owe it to your parents to look after you."

"I don't want to stay here," Makey said. "I want to go with my friends."

"That's a bad idea," said Erielle. "If you go with them, you'll die. No one survives outside digifreak society without help."

"I don't care. They're still my friends, and they saved my life more than once. I trust them. I don't trust you. Look what you did to me," he exclaimed, lifting his arm and pulling down his sleeve. The wound was thick with dried blood.

Erielle looked down. "I'm sorry. I wasn't thinking. I was forgetting that you were one of us."

"I'm not one of you," exclaimed Makey. "This isn't what the people of Dawn were about. I don't know what you underworlders think, but this life doesn't have anything to do with living naturally and caring for Earth Mother. I don't believe in that stuff, but even I know that."

"He's got a point," said Carl.

Erielle scowled at him. She turned to Makey. "After you've lived with us for a while, you'll understand."

"How many times do I have to tell you? I'm *not* living with you. And I'm not going to be lied to anymore. I've had enough of that. What are you going to do to make me stay? Are you planning on keeping me a prisoner here? Is *that* what being an underworlder's about? Keeping kids locked up?"

Erielle bit her lip. "No, I won't keep you prisoner. You're right. That isn't the underworlder way, unless—"

"Unless you aren't underworlders, like my friends. It's one rule for you and another for everyone else," Makey interjected contemptuously. He was amazed to see the older woman redden slightly. He hadn't been trying to embarrass her. He was only angry at the idea of being separated from his friends, and he'd said what he really thought.

"You're wrong if you think the Shadows won't come after you," Jas said. "When we first encountered them, they went after the highest in command, it's true. But we had every reason to believe they would have gone for the entire crew eventually, and then they would have returned to Earth aboard our ship to help infest the planet. I can't think why they wouldn't work their way through the whole of Earth's population eventually and replace even underworlders with their kind. Look at what happened to the people who tried to use our credchips. It's already started.

"Erielle, I get what you're saying about what your people suffer. I really do, and these last few hours have opened my eyes to things I was never aware of, but believe me when I say this isn't an 'us and them' thing. We have to put away our differences and work together if we're going to defeat these aliens. It's going to take everything we've got."

Holding up a hand to Jas, Erielle said, "Okay, okay, enough. I need to think. You can all stay here tonight. I'll get some food sent in." Reacting to the looks on their faces, she added, "Drug-free food. You have my word."

She left them. Carl went over to Makey and ruffled his hair. "Nice one, kid."

Makey grinned. Finally, he'd done something useful.

# TEN

Sparks stood nervously outside Rogers' room. The nurse had told him that the lab tech had shown signs of coming around, and he peered at the man lying in the isolation room. He was worried about what Polestar would make of the incident. He might be held responsible.

Inside his room, Rogers smacked his lips lazily, and his eyes half opened. Sparks felt a surge of relief. He pressed the intercom button. "Rogers, can you hear me? Are you awake?"

"Hmmm...who's that?"

"It's me, Sparks. How are you feeling?"

Rogers tried to rise, but slumped back down onto his bed. "Where am I? What's happened? Oh, wait, I remember. The Paths."

"Yes, that's right. You're still on the station, in the medical center. How are you feeling? You had some kind of fit."

"I did, did I?" Rogers, with some effort, managed to rise to his elbows. He scanned the room until he spotted the observation window Sparks was looking through. "There you are. How long have I been out?"

"Four and a quarter hours. Do you remember what happened? You'd just taken a sample when you passed out."

"Hmmm...yes, I do remember." The lab tech reclined on his

pillows. "I was in a state of terrible fear, brought on by the Paths. Urgh...it was awful feeling their terror. I think they thought I was going to kill them. I'm never doing that again. So don't even think of asking me." His eyes swiveled to the right to meet Sparks's.

"No, of course I won't," Sparks said.

"Good. So...I cut once, and then again to take the sample, and I thought that was it. Their ordeal would be over, and I would be able to get out of range of those odd creatures, and then...then, well...I was suddenly in the most wonderful place I've ever been."

"Really?" asked Sparks. "What do you mean? You didn't go anywhere—except straight here to the medical center as fast as we could take you. You must have been hallucinating."

"I suppose I must have, but that isn't how it felt. It felt very real. I was floating in infinite space. And...now, let me see...I seem to remember that I was sure *I* could become infinite too, and fill the space. Or I could choose to become infnitesimally small. But that wasn't the best part, oh no. I was serenely, blissfully happy. The happiest I've ever been in my entire life. No cares or worries bothered me. Nothing mattered at all, except *being*, you know?" His face seemed to shine as he relived the memory. "Ahhh...it was quite wonderful. I wouldn't mind going there again, in fact, if it were possible."

"Extraordinary," Sparks mused. The Paths had accessed the technician's emotions, but not as he would have expected when they were under threat. He would have expected them to continue to project their negative emotions in order to make whatever was threatening them go away. They'd projected their fear of the approaching lab tech with his scalpel, as he'd expected, but when the lab tech actually assaulted them, they'd overwhelmed him with bliss.

Their strategy had been effective. The result was that Rogers collapsed and didn't cut them again. But as a long-term behavior, it didn't make much sense. The creatures were providing a reward in response to attacks. Wouldn't a hostile species that experienced the reward be tempted to attack again?

"Sparks," Rogers said. "Are you listening? I said, do you know how long they plan to keep me here?"

"Sorry, I was miles away. I don't know how long you'll be here, I'm afraid. Until they're sure you haven't been infected by an agent from the Paths, maybe? When you collapsed, your scalpel cut through your hazard suit. You've been exposed."

"Bugger," Rogers said. "Oh well. I suppose it means I get out of work for a while."

"Yes, enjoy it while you can," said Sparks. "I'll let the nurse know you're awake. I'll be back later to check how you're doing. Is there anything you need?"

"I don't think so. I'll call the nurse if I do."

"Okay. Rogers, one more thing before I go. I'm curious about this state you were in. Do you think you could write me a report about it?"

"Doesn't look like I'm going to have much else to do for a while."

"Great. Thanks."

"You know," Rogers said, "I was a little peeved at having to go near the Paths again. Those creatures give me the willies. I like my emotions to stay my own. But now, I'm kind of glad you asked me to help out. Whatever it was they did to me, I'm glad I had the experience. I doubt I'll ever forget it."

It was the quiet shift, and after Sparks left Rogers, his words helped Sparks sleep more easily. The man was positive about his experience, and Sparks hoped he wouldn't have too much explaining to do. He also had something especially interesting to put in his next report to Polestar. With a little luck, the company would hand the project on to the big league xenobiologists now that he'd discovered something unusual.

The following morning, on his way to the canteen to eat breakfast, he passed the Paths' quarantine chamber and found the whole place, including his observation office, had been sealed off with security tape. The master of the quarantine station was there, and when he spotted Sparks he approached him and slapped him on the shoulder. "Just the man I wanted to see. I comm'd you three times. Is your button turned off?"

Sparks looked down at the comm button on his shirt. He had

indeed accidentally thumbed it off as he was attaching the device. He turned it on. "Yes, sorry. What's going on? Why's the area been cordoned off? Has something happened to the Paths?" He wondered if Rogers had harmed them somehow when he'd taken his sample. Maybe they'd bled out over night. He hadn't gone back to check on them because he'd been too preoccupied with the lab tech.

"I thought you hadn't heard. One of the researchers broke into the Path chamber during the quiet shift."

"What?" exclaimed Sparks. "Why would anyone do that?"

"As far as we can tell, it was because she'd heard about Rogers' experience yesterday. He told the nurse, and she passed the story on. She didn't see any reason not to, she says, and I guess she's right. It was just a little bit of gossip to her. The poor woman; she's distraught now. She's saying it was all her fault."

"What was her fault?" asked Sparks, standing on his tiptoes and craning to look into the chamber.

"The researcher got it into her head that what happened to Rogers sounded pretty nice, and she thought she'd like to try it herself."

Sparks's eyes grew round. "No."

"Yes. She took a knife with her. I don't know what she intended. Thankfully, she didn't have the opportunity to do much damage."

"I'm glad to hear it," said Sparks. "I take it they weren't too badly cut?"

"They were hardly cut at all."

"And the woman? Did she have a fit like Rogers? I take it you've placed her in confinement?" He leaned closer and lowered his voice. "Is she a natural by any chance? I've always thought there should be some kind of vetting for professional positions."

"No. The reason she didn't cut the Paths very much was because she didn't have the opportunity. She died."

"She's dead? They killed her?" Sparks almost squeaked.

"She's lying in there right now. She was cold by the time someone noticed the chamber door was open. She'd used her security clearance to disable the alarm."

"Dead?" Sparks repeated. He needed to sit down.

He pushed past the master and stepped over the tape that covered the door to his observation room. Collapsing into his chair, he caught sight of the deceased administrator in the Paths' quarantine chamber. She was right next to them. They hadn't moved or changed position, but the woman was on her back, her arms and legs spread out. The most beautiful smile Sparks had ever seen was emblazoned across her features.

# ELEVEN

"What are you planning to tell the Transgalactic Council, if you ever manage to contact them?" Erielle asked. The day following their capture, Sayen and the others had been allowed to climb the stairs to her private room once more. Though, from the way Erielle continued to ignore her, Sayen doubted she would have received the same respect if she'd been alone.

"We'll tell them what's been happening here on Earth," Jas said. "We'll tell them the Shadows have infiltrated the Global Government, and that whoever hasn't been killed and replaced believes that the problem was dealt with, and the Shadows are no longer a threat."

"That's a long message." Erielle smiled sardonically. "And why would the Council believe you?"

Jas had been resting her elbows on the low table that separated the two women. She leaned back. "Why would they believe us? Why wouldn't they? It isn't the sort of thing someone would make up."

"You don't think so? There's plenty of crazies around. Sometimes modding goes wrong, you know. Some people aren't right in the head, and they often end up here. Plenty of conspiracy theorists. The Council wouldn't take much persuading from someone high up in government to convince them that you're insane. Hell, I bet they receive a thousand messages a day from crackpots in one corner of the galaxy or another. Why do you think they'd treat yours any differently?"

Jas frowned and looked down.

"What do *you* think we should do?" Carl asked.

"I'm not sure. Tell me more about these aliens."

They told her all they knew, and when they arrived at Sayen's investigations at the Global Government Security HQ, she took over the story and related what she'd read in the hidden files. She also explained how her manager, Bernie, had turned out to be a Shadow and had arranged for her to be abducted and nearly replaced by a Shadow herself. Erielle didn't look at her as she spoke, but she listened.

"So you can identify Shadows, no matter how closely they resemble their victim, with one of these special scanners?" she asked.

"That's what I read," Sayen replied.

"And that's what I saw, too, when we rescued Sayen," said Carl. "We were covered in that invisibility spray you stole from us."

"Ha, consider it payment for your bed and board," Erielle replied. "Well, we can't use that. That's long gone down the pipeline. Much too hot to keep. But if you had a scanner, you could identify a Shadow and capture it. A Shadow found in Earth territory would be good evidence to show the Council."

"We don't need to identify a Shadow," Sayen said. "I know one. The man I was working under at the Security HQ. If he's still there, we could try to kidnap him."

"That British guy you were telling us about?" Carl asked.

"Well, that's who the victim was, yes," Sayen replied. "Now, a Shadow's doing a great impersonation of him. Unless that thing's gone somewhere else, he'll be at the HQ."

"Yeah," said Jas, "we could kidnap a Shadow to prove we aren't crazy. But what then? How would we get it to the Transgalactic Council?"

"One thing at a time," Erielle said.

"It's some kind of a plan," Carl said. "Sayen, the HQ's in this city, right? How far from here?"

"Not far. About half an hour by autocab."

"I can't think of a better alternative," Jas said. "Let's do it. Tonight. The longer we wait, the more people will fall victim, and the Shadows will move closer to catching us. Sayen, think of everything you can remember about this creature. What time it leaves the office. How it goes home—if that's where it goes. We'll ambush it in a quiet spot if we can. Erielle, how many of your people can you lend us?"

"People? You can't have any of my people. You're on your own."

"What?" Makey exclaimed. "I thought you were going to help us."

"I *am* helping you. By letting you and your friends go. That's what you wanted, wasn't it? I've had your wrists treated. I've even listened to your cockeyed plans and pointed out how stupid they are. What more do you want from me?"

"I expected you to help us defeat the Shadows," said Makey. "Don't you want them forced to leave Earth? My friends told you what happened on Dawn. You said there was someone you loved there. Don't you care about what happened to them?"

Erielle's brief expression of sadness was quickly followed by a stony look. "My lover made her choice. She could have stayed here and continued to fight the Government, but she didn't. She left with the rest of the Earth Mother cultists. I learned my lesson then. Look after yourself. No one else matters. The Transgalactic Council doesn't give a krat about us underworlders. If these Shadows come to us, we'll fight them. But we'll fight on our terms and in our own way, not because some digifreaks want us to."

Jas sighed and shook her head. "Will you give us our weapons back at least? Explosives? You know we'll need everything we can get."

Erielle said, "Okay." She looked at Makey. "Are you sure you won't stay here with me? I was hoping we could talk about Dawn. Maybe you knew my friend. I'd have liked to hear news of her. "

"I haven't changed my mind. I know who my friends are, and I know the right thing to do, even if you don't."

The corner of Erielle's lip lifted. "You sound just like my friend. Maybe you did know her."

"I think you should stay here, Makey," Jas said. "In fact, I insist. I'm not allowing you to come along."

"What?"

"Like I told you in Antarctica when you ignored my order, you're a danger to yourself and others. I can't trust you, so you aren't coming with us."

"Oh, come on, Jas," said Carl.

"And like I told *you*, this is none of your business."

Carl let out a snort of frustration and folded his arms.

Sayen said tentatively, "Jas—"

"No. This isn't up for discussion. The kid isn't coming with us. He's too young, and he's too unreliable. I'm not going to risk both your lives or mine so he can feel good about himself."

"It isn't about feeling good about myself," Makey exclaimed, rising to his feet and clenching his fists. "Those misborns killed my mam and my sister. I want to fight them just as much as you do."

"Hey," shouted Erielle, "simmer down." When their gazes turned to her, she continued, "I changed my mind. The kid goes with you, or you don't get any of your stuff back. I'm not having digifreaks telling us underworlders what we can and can't do. The kid goes with you, or you leave here now with nothing but the clothes on your backs."

Jas glared at the woman.

"Take it or leave it," Erielle said.

Carl said, "We'll take it, right, Sayen?"

"Yes, we'll take Makey with us," she replied. "Give us our things, and we'll get along." Time was passing. The Shadow Bernie would be leaving work soon, and they didn't yet have a plan for his capture. Sayen also felt Jas was being unreasonable. Most of the time, she was nice, but sometimes she could be pig-headed. She didn't know what her problem was.

Erielle called for the weapons and explosives she'd taken from them and handed them over to Jas. The woman took them without a word. She looked furious.

Sayen had another problem that needed addressing urgently. "Erielle, do you think I could get some shoes?" she asked, pointing at her bare, dirty feet. The sight of them made her squirm. What wouldn't she give for a hot bath and clean clothes as well?

Rolling her eyes, Erielle made the request by her usual method of shouting downstairs. Almost miraculously, a worn pair of running shoes arrived that were only about a size too big. Sayen slipped them on and tied the laces, trying hard not to think about the residue from someone else's feet that was touching her skin.

# Twelve

Erielle not only returned everything she'd taken from them besides the invisibility spray, but she also loaned them one of the strange self-driving cars the underworlders used and gave them a map to a safe, unoccupied house on the edge of her territory. She said they could use it as long as they wanted.

Carl was pleased at the loan of the car. He loved driving cars. He'd learned how when he was in his early teens, when self-drivers had already been mostly replaced by auto-drive cars. A couple of old relics lived among the farm machinery in the barn. Charging their batteries took forever because they were so old, but it was worth the wait to be in control of a vehicle instead of being carried around like a baby.

Jas and Carl sat in front. Sayen and Makey were in the back with the bag of equipment between them. The light was beginning to fail.

"You sure you can handle this?" asked Erielle, leaning down to look through the car window.

"Yeah, no problem," Carl said as he searched for the headlight switch. He tried one, and the windscreen wipers started up. He tried another, and the windows closed. Erielle stepped back to avoid being decapitated. The third switch he tried turned on the headlights, though their beams were weak.

Carl lowered the windows. "Got it. Are you sure we won't be stopped by the police? Are these cars still legal?"

"They're still legal, but, yeah, you might be stopped. I don't know what you can do about that. I guess you'll just have to take the chance. You could always walk there, but it'd take hours, and I don't know how you'll kidnap a Shadow without a vehicle. You can't hire an autocab without ID. This is the best y'all can do, I reckon."

"I think you're right," Carl said. "We'll get going."

"Good luck," Erielle said. "Take care, kid," she said to Makey. "Remember, there's always a place for you here. I'd like to hear about Dawn sometime."

"I'll come back and tell you all about it."

"You look after him," Erielle said to the others.

"Thanks for the shoes," Sayen said.

Erielle didn't reply. She stepped back. Jas also said nothing. She sat with her arms folded, staring ahead.

Carl didn't know what was the matter with her, and he wasn't sure that he even cared. She had a mood on, and like always, she wouldn't open up about whatever was bothering her. He'd thought they might have had something going after they'd nearly kissed back at the farm in Australia, but ever since they'd rescued Sayen, the coldness of Antarctica seemed to have crept into her bones and heart.

"Got your seat belts on?" he asked the group generally as he searched for the button to start the engine.

"All buckled up," came Sayen's response from behind him.

"Hey, Sayen," Carl said, "you know where we're going, right? Why don't you come sit up front here and direct me?"

"Sure," Sayen replied, and she and Jas swapped seats.

Jas's knees pushed into Carl's back as she squeezed into the smaller space. He preferred that slight discomfort to her taciturn presence beside him. He started the engine, and the former navigator gave her first set of directions.

As they gradually drove farther and farther from the underworlders' domain, the traffic became heavier and pedestrians grew sparse. It wasn't long before they were driving through the business district, attracting many second glances in their out-of-date, self-drive vehicle. Carl grew nervous. Surely it wouldn't be long before they were stopped. As soon as they were asked for their IDs, the game would be over.

"Second left," Sayen said. "We're a few minutes' walk from the Security HQ, but I don't recall any parking nearby. Not public parking anyway. And we would never pass the security check to get into the underground car park. But if I'm right, there's an alley down this street," she said as Carl turned the vehicle. "We can wait there until it's time for Shadow Bernie to leave work."

Dusk was falling, and the street lights were turning on.

On their way over, Sayen had explained that their target usually left the office around seven o'clock every evening and departed in his personal government car. Because Sayen left by heli, she'd never seen the car, so she wasn't totally sure that what he'd told her was true.

"It's over there," she said to Carl, pointing to a narrow, dark opening on the left-hand side of the street.

He indicated and pulled in. The alley was only as wide as the car. Tall office blocks rose on either side. There was no exit except for the busy street at the other end of the alley. Carl didn't drive far in. With nowhere to turn around, he would have to reverse the car out.

"What's the time?" asked Jas, leaning between the front seats.

The car clock read six thirty.

"We don't have long," she continued. "The Shadow might leave work early, and we can't risk a practice run. It won't be long before someone reports us for suspicious behavior. We have to get the Shadow tonight. Do you have any idea what direction it might go?" she asked Sayen.

"I don't."

"Then we'll have to watch the car park exit and follow its car when it leaves," said Jas.

"It's not going to be easy," Carl said. He looked at the falling darkness in the alley. "What if the car windows are tinted?"

"We just have to do our best," said Sayen. "We don't have to wait very near the exit. My eyes can zoom in, though I can't see through darkened windows."

"Okay," Jas said. "When we spot the Shadow, we follow it until we're in a quieter part of the city. Then I'll shoot out the car wheels. As soon as the car stops, we've got to move fast. We won't have long until the police get there. But be careful. We don't know what weapons it might be carrying, and there might be more than one of them in the car."

"Right," Carl said. "Sounds like we're all set. Sayen, where do we go from here?"

After she gave him the final directions, he reversed out of the alley. They had to wait a while for a pause in the traffic before he could enter the street and pull away. Following Sayen's instructions, he drove them to a spot about fifty meters from the Security HQ car park exit. It was at the back of the building, and the street only served the car park so there was no other traffic. They waited.

The exit was automated. No visible human guard threatened to become curious about their presence, but Carl was sure that cameras would be covering the street. It was the Global Government Security Headquarters, after all. They wouldn't have long before they were challenged. He hoped their target wasn't working overtime that night.

A light flashed, signaling that a car was about to leave. A limousine appeared, its windows tinted black. There was an audible sigh of frustration from everyone. Would they ever be able to recognize the Shadow? Automation had done away with the need for transparent windows in cars. What if the entire Government fleet was the same?

The limousine left at the opposite end of the street from them. The light at the exit flashed again, and another car appeared. It was an unmarked van. Carl's stomach tightened as the van turned in their direction. Was this a security van coming to check them out? The van passed, though two women sitting in the front seats gave them curious looks. Once it had passed them, Carl's stomach relaxed.

A third car appeared. This car's windows were transparent, and Carl could make out one person sitting in the front seat.

"Is that him?" Jas asked Sayen.

"No, it's just another of the Government personnel."

The car turned toward them. As it drew closer and the occupant's face became more distinct to Carl, his heart skipped a beat. He knew this person. Where did he know him from? As the answer came, he felt the blood drain from his face.

"That's not your Shadow??" he asked Sayen.

"No, I'm sure. Shadow Bernie's much older. But I recognize him. I saw him on my first day."

"Look away," Carl barked as the car drew closer. He turned to face the back of the car, looking into Jas's puzzled eyes. She bent her head down as the car passed.

Carl's heartbeat quickened as he watched the car driving away in the reflection of his rear view mirror. He noted which way it turned as it left the street. He put the car into drive, turned the steering wheel, and followed.

"What are you doing?" cried Jas. "Sayen said that's not him."

"It might not be Sayen's Shadow, but it's a Shadow all right," Carl said. "It's Alef from the *Galathea*."

# Thirteen

"Who the krat's Alef?" Jas asked as Carl sped down the street. The acceleration pushed her back into her seat.

"Alef from geo-phys," Carl replied.

"I knew I'd seen him before," exclaimed Sayen, "but I couldn't remember from where. I didn't recognize him out of uniform, and I was only with him for a couple of minutes."

"Geo-phys like Margret?" Jas asked. "I was right. There was another Shadow aboard the ship. So he went into the trap with her and got replaced at the same time?"

"Yep, he must have," answered Carl. "You remember when we were trying to get onto the bridge? It was Alef who helped me tackle Loba, before the misborn got away from me. I left Alef behind when I chased after him."

"But why would he help you take down Loba if he was a Shadow himself?" asked Jas.

"I dunno. Maybe he had a problem with him, or he saw that things were going south and decided to play the long game. Whatever his plan was, it worked. He made it all the way here with us, and now he's joined his mates in the Global Government."

Carl pulled out into the rush hour traffic. His head was fixed firmly ahead as he kept his eyes on the Shadow's car. Jas stopped talking to him to let him concentrate on following their target. She opened the bag next to her and took out a weapon. Tapping Sayen on her shoulder, she passed the weapon forward to her. She took another for herself and peered around Carl's head. He was drawing closer to the Shadow's car, though four or five vehicles separated them.

"What about me?" asked Makey.

Jas frowned and took the third and final gun out of the bag. "Self-defense only," she said as she handed it to the kid.

They were leaving the inner city district, and the roads were becoming quieter. Jas wondered where the Shadow was going. Did the Shadows continue their pretense of being human and return to their victims' homes each night? Or did they have a secret meeting place where they all congregated?

Houses and apartment blocks of a residential district surrounded them. Carl had moved their car closer, and they were only two cars away from the Shadow's vehicle. Jas hoped the strangers' cars that lay between them and the Shadow's would leave that road soon. They'd been following it for a while; she worried that it might have noticed them.

"Can you get around these cars, Carl?" she asked.

"I can, but overtaking on a street like this would be too noticeable. It's better that I stay back a little while longer."

Jas rubbed the edge of her weapon nervously. She had those prickles she always got when something bad was going to happen. But she couldn't do anything about it. They had to go ahead with the plan. They wouldn't get a second chance.

"Be careful, everyone," she said. "And Makey, let us handle this. Stay in the car."

The kid tutted.

"Here we go," Carl said as one of the intervening cars turned down a side road. At the next exit, the second car did the same. There was nothing between them and the car in front carrying the Shadow Alef.

Jas checked over her shoulder. A few vehicles were behind them, but it couldn't be helped. She hoped they would get out of danger fast when the shooting started. She and the others would only have a couple of minutes to snatch the Shadow before the police arrived.

"I think he's seen us," Carl said. "He keeps turning to look back."

"Right, let's go," Jas said. "Drive up his ass, Carl."

She lowered her window, and Sayen lowered hers. Jas undid her seatbelt so that she could lean out and take aim. She fired. Her shot went wide, but Sayen's hit true, taking out the back wheel of the Shadow's vehicle. The car began to veer across the road. Jas fired again and hit the front wheel on the same side as the car turned its longer side toward them. The Shadow ducked down and disappeared from view.

An explosion sounded from behind Jas, and their car rocked. "Krat," shouted Carl. The car began to swerve. "We're being shot at. We've got Shadows behind us."

Jas's stomach fell as she turned. The van that had passed them outside the Security HQ car park was right behind them. While they'd been following the Shadow Alef's car, they'd been followed themselves. She reversed her aim and shot at the window of the Shadow van. The beam melted a hole in the plastiglass and hit one of the Shadows in the chest. It fell to one side, but the van continued on.

Their own rear window was hit by a shot from the remaining Shadow's weapon, and the car filled with smoke and the acrid stench of burning plastic.

They crashed. Jas was thrown forward into the back of Carl's seat. As she sat up, she saw that they'd hit the Shadow Alef's vehicle, which straddled the road. Carl revved the engine and backed up so fast that Jas was thrown forward again. Her weapon was knocked from her grasp and fell onto the floor.

She bent down to pick it up. Sayen was firing and the tires of their car screeched as Carl did a u-turn and pulled away. Jas was rocked backward, but managed to grasp the fallen weapon. As she regained her seat, she noticed that the handle was sticky with something.

They were heading toward the Shadows' van. It was heading

toward them. Carl sped up, seemingly intent on meeting the other vehicle head on. Jas leaned out of her window and fired at the Shadow in the front of the van. She didn't hit it, but it had to lean over to avoid her blast, and its own shot went wide.

The van filled her vision. They were going to hit it. But at the last split second, it pulled to one side. As they flew past, they clipped its wing. They sped into the night.

They'd escaped.

They'd failed to catch a Shadow, but at least they'd gotten away alive. The wind from their open windows blew away the smoke in the car. Wondering what the sticky stuff was, Jas turned her weapon around in her hand. In the dark street it looked black, but as they drove under a streetlight she saw that it was red. Blood. Her weapon was covered in blood.

Had she been hit? She quickly checked herself. She didn't think so. Her heart stopped as she realized Makey hadn't said anything for a while. Hardly daring to look, she turned her gaze to the kid. His eyes were closed and his head lolled to the side. His front was soaked in the blood running from his neck.

# Fourteen

They screeched to a halt outside Erielle's place. Sayen leapt from the car and bolted down the alley that led to Erielle's door. She hammered on it and screamed. Carl was on her heels, carrying Makey in his arms. Jas had her hands pressed to Makey's neck, but the blood wouldn't stop steadily leaking out. His face was white. By the time Carl reached the door, it had been opened by one of Erielle's guards. The man's puzzled face changed to one of alarm when he saw the wounded kid.

"What is it?" Erielle asked, appearing at the bottom of the stairs. She gave a look of horror as she spotted Makey. "In here," she said, opening a door. Carl carried him over and Jas followed, her hands still clasped to the kid's neck.

Erielle spat, "I told you to take care of him."

"And I didn't want him to come," Jas retorted, shouldering Erielle aside as she went into the room.

It was a makeshift medical treatment room, containing a couple of outdated hospital beds, a glass cabinet of bottled drugs, drawers labeled with the names of medical equipment, and some basic medical devices and instruments.

Carl laid Makey down on one of the beds. Jas had the heel of one hand on his neck, and the other heel pressed on the first, but blood dripped onto the sheet.

"He got hit by a shot from Shadows behind us," Jas said. "He didn't say a thing. Maybe he passed out immediately. He's lost a lot of blood."

"I can see that," snapped Erielle. "He's in shock. He needs a transfusion."

"Can you do that here?" Sayen asked.

"We could if we had any blood, but we've had a few accidents to treat. We used the last of it just yesterday. Krat."

"We can give him ours," said Sayen.

"Do you know what blood type he is?" Erielle asked.

"No," Sayen replied. "I don't think he has any medical records either. He only arrived on Earth a few weeks ago."

"He needs universal donor blood," Jas said.

"I know," said Erielle. She bit her lip. "We usually steal it, but it's a complicated operation. He can't wait. We'll have to do a smash and grab. It won't be easy, but we have to try. I'll go now. Keep the pressure on his neck. If his heart stops, there's a defibrillator in that cupboard." She turned to leave.

"I'll come with you," Sayen said. "I can help."

"No. Stay here. You'll only get in the way."

"No, she won't," said Jas. "Take her. You can use her. Believe me."

Erielle looked doubtful, but she didn't offer any more objections. As she left, Sayen followed close behind.

They took the car Carl had driven. Two more underworlders came with them. Sayen sat in the back and fastened her belt. Erielle sat in the front with the driver. As the car pulled away, they closed the doors. They were soon speeding through the streets.

"There's a clinic a few minutes away," said Erielle. "They have artificial universal donor blood. I know because we have someone on the inside who supplies us. But the clinic's closed for the evening. We'll have to break in."

"I might be able to disable the security," Sayen said.

"I'll give you a minute to try," Erielle replied. "If you can't do it..." She pulled out a weapon with a huge muzzle, "...we blast our way in."

The underworlder sitting next to Sayen said, "There's a police station right around the corner. We won't have time to get away before they catch us."

"We have to try, or that kid's gonna die," Erielle said.

The underworlder muttered to himself.

They arrived. The clinic was a small place, only serving the immediate neighborhood, it seemed to Sayen. It stood on the street corner. A high, metal-paneled fence ran down the side. The frontage was solid brick except for a glass door. As they passed, Sayen could see a receptionist's desk and a few chairs in the waiting room.

They pulled up a few doors down and walked back to the clinic's entrance. It was securely locked. Inside, the light of the alarm panel winked. There was no way to access the security control from the outside.

"Better blast it," said one of the underworlders.

"I bet that door's laser-proofed," Sayen said, "if they're storing drugs in a neighborhood like this."

The underworlder looked offended, but Erielle said, "She's probably right."

"What about around the back?" asked Sayen.

"The fence is four meters high. We'll never get over it," said the underworlder.

"Speak for yourself," said Sayen. "Give me the blaster," she said to Erielle. The woman hesitated before handing it over.

Sayen trotted around the side of the building. The underworlder's estimation of the height of the fence was about right. She crossed to the other side of the street and sized it up. When Erielle and the underworlders appeared, she called, "Bring the car around," and ran toward the fence.

A few steps before she reached it, she jumped, springing from her right foot. She sailed up and caught the top of the fence with her fingertips. Quickly pulling herself up, she climbed over before landing in the yard behind the medical center. The fence cast the place in deep shadow. Sayen blinked her eyes to night vision, and the scene swam into a green-hued view.

The yard was bare save for garbage bins bearing signs for different kinds of medical waste. The back door was locked tight, and like in the front, there were no windows.

She had no choice but to try to blast the door. Laser-proofing was expensive. Maybe they wouldn't have taken the extra precaution with the back door. It would trigger the alarm, but she couldn't help that. She pulled the blaster from the waistband of her pants and fired it, concentrating its beam on the door lock. The metal glowed red, then white. That had to have triggered the alarm. Sayen wondered how long she had before the police responded. Probably less than a minute.

She threw her shoulder against the door, bursting it open. Not slowing her pace, she sped through and into the center. As she went, she realized that she should have asked Erielle where they kept the blood. Too late for that. But the clinic was small. The blood shouldn't be too hard to find.

She was in some kind of consulting room. Various scanners and other medical equipment stood against all the walls. Where did they keep the medical supplies? She threw open another door. She was in the doctor's office, with a simple bed, the physician's desk and interface, and chairs. Sayen ran through, upending a chair as she tripped over it in her hurry.

Flinging open another door, she found herself in the waiting room she'd seen from the front. Bright lights oscillated over the walls, shining in from outside. The police had arrived. A car door slammed. They were coming over to the clinic. Did they have a key to the place?

*Where were the supplies?* Sayen spotted another door. She sped through it. At last, she was in the supply room. It was full of cabinets and refrigerator units. All were locked, but they bore signs. Her eyes roved feverishly. She must have only seconds. She saw it.

Sayen grasped the handle of the unit containing the blood bank and forced it down. The lock snapped off, and the door opened. She grabbed handfuls of bags of artificial blood, expecting every moment to feel a police officer's hand on her shoulder.

She raced out. Passing through the waiting room, she caught sight of an officer standing outside the front door, looking in. At the same moment, the officer saw her. He raised his hand to his belt and shouted. Sayen ran out of the waiting room door in a heartbeat, through the office and treatment room, and outside into the yard.

"Hey, catch these," she yelled and flung the bags of blood over the fence, praying that the others were still there and waiting; praying that they were good at catching.

From behind her came the sound of movement. The police were in the building. She had to jump the fence immediately, but the yard was small. She had hardly any room for a running start. She backed to the clinic, ran, and leapt. She didn't make it to the top of the fence. Her fingers tried to grasp the smooth panels before she slipped down and landed heavily.

"Stop where you are. You're under arrest," shouted a police officer.

She had less than a couple of seconds before it was all over. Sayen took another run at the fence. This time, she jumped onto one of the garbage bins and launched herself upward. Her hands gripped the top of the fence. She'd made it. She pulled herself up. Below her, a bright laser beam shone out and sizzled against the fence.

She dropped down into the street, but it was empty. Where were Erielle and the underworlders? Where was the car?

Then she saw two vehicle reverse lights heading her way. The car was traveling backward to reach her. Sayen raced up to the opening rear door and threw herself in headfirst. The car sped away, Sayen's feet in their oversized shoes hanging out the open door.

# FIFTEEN

Makey's life hung in the balance over the next few hours. Erielle had transfused the artificial blood and carefully sutured closed the wound in his neck, but he didn't seem to get any better for a while. His pulse was weak, and he remained clammy and unconscious. Sayen, Jas, Carl, and Erielle took turns sitting by his bed so that someone would be there when—if—he woke up, or in case he got worse.

Sayen was asleep in the early hours of the morning when the news finally came. Carl shook her shoulder to wake her. "Makey?" she mumbled as she came to.

"Yeah. He's woken up. I think he's going to be okay. Do you want to come and see him?"

She sat up and pulled on her shirt and pants. She was in a sleeping bag in a communal bedroom. Underworlders lay around her in various states of sleep and wakefulness. She tiptoed out of the door that Carl had left open and went down one floor to the medical center.

The kid didn't look good. He was still as white as a ghost, and dark circles lay under his eyes. The wound on his neck was covered in a dressing, but angry red skin was visible at the edges, and fresh blood reddened the white gauze. Nevertheless, he managed to smile at Sayen as she went in. Erielle, Jas, and Carl were already there.

Makey's arms and hands lay listlessly on top of his bed coverings. He raised a finger. "Hi, Sayen. I guess I must look how you did when I first saw you aboard the *Galathea*, except you looked worse."

Realizing that he was reacting to her facial expression and was trying to calm her concern for him, she smiled in return—reassuringly, she hoped. "Yeah, well, you only have a scratch on your neck. I was nearly brain dead."

Her attempt at humor lightened the mood in the room a little. Jas and Carl chatted about what had happened in their failed attempt to capture a Shadow. Makey couldn't remember being shot, nor anything much after the shooting had started. No one was talking about what their next plan of action might be. It was enough for the moment that Makey hadn't died. Jas and Erielle seemed to have made their peace with each other.

The kid's eyes began to close, and Erielle suggested that they leave him alone to sleep and regain his strength. Carl volunteered to stay with him. As Sayen and the rest left, Erielle told Makey that he could drink some soup in the morning if he felt up to it.

She invited Sayen and Jas up to her room for a late supper or early breakfast, but Jas said that it had been a long night, and she would rather sleep. She left them on the second floor, and Erielle and Sayen continued up to the top of the building in a slightly awkward silence.

They went into Erielle's room, which was empty. Some dishes of food awaited them, along with a jug of some kind of home brew and beakers.

Erielle gestured for Sayen to sit down. She chose a cushion near the underworlder, across the table corner that separated them. Erielle's eyes were downcast as she ate.

After a while she said, "I didn't get a chance to thank you for what you did earlier. I was in too much of a hurry to get the blood into Makey."

"You don't have anything to thank me for," Sayen replied. "He's my friend. I was only doing what I could to help."

"If you hadn't been there, I don't think he would be alive now, and I would probably be in a holding cell."

"Like I said, I was just doing what I could."

Erielle lifted her dark brown eyes to Sayen's hazel ones. "I've gotta say, that's some modding you have. I've never seen anything like it."

"It isn't modding. My body's enhanced. We told you about the Shadows on our last prospecting mission, but we left out the fact that I nearly died. Jas saved my life, and she made them keep me in stasis until we got back to Earth. They couldn't revive me, so the doctors cloned my body and uploaded my mind into my new brain. Before they recreated my body, they offered me the option of choosing a few enhancements."

"Really?" Erielle's gaze lingered on Sayen's arms and chest. "Can you do anything else as well as you can run and jump?"

"I have super-sensitive vision and hearing, and my skin's extremely tough."

The underworlder reached out a hand, then hesitated, hovering over Sayen's bare forearm. "Can I?"

"Sure."

Erielle's fingers lightly stroked from her wrist to her elbow. A shiver ran up Sayen's spine.

"Strange," Erielle said. "It feels normal." Their eyes met for a moment. "But you're modded too, right?" Erielle asked. "You got the works at conception, didn't you?"

"You can tell?"

"Well, it's pretty obvious. You're flawless. Your face and body are completely symmetrical. The chances of being born looking so perfect naturally must be millions to one. And your intelligence is dialed right up too, isn't it? What's your speciality?"

"Math, I guess. I was a navigator. I *am* a navigator, I mean. When this mess is sorted out, I plan on returning to my job. Only this time I want to take advantage of my opportunities and not hide away from them. That's what I used to do, till I came close to dying. My parents were a little protective as I was growing up and—" She gasped.

"What's wrong?" Erielle asked.

"I forgot. My parents had me fitted with a tracker. I need to get it out in case the Shadows find out about it and use it to locate me."

"Your parents had a tracker put inside you? Wow. That's more than a little protective, I'd say, hun." Erielle frowned. "I might be able to get it out, but I'd have to operate on you in the medical center, and I don't want to move Makey. Things are still touch and go with him. If he's looking better tomorrow, I'll see what I can do then."

"Are you sure you can do it?"

"I used to be a doctor," Erielle said.

"You did?"

Smiling wryly so that her scar pulled her eye a little out of shape, Erielle said, "Is that really so hard to believe? I guess I don't look very professional anymore."

Sayen's gaze dropped to the underworlder's lean, bare arms before returning to her face and its disfigurement. "What happened?"

"Did you think I was a natural? I guessed you did. After all, why would anyone choose to live like this? It's true, most of us underworlders are naturals, but not all. I was modded at conception like you. I was given my smarts with a stroke of a geneticist's gene splicer too. I don't think my parents' payment was in the same league as yours, but I did okay from it. Got into a good university, then medical school." She paused and laughed. "I don't know why I'm telling you this."

"Go on, I want to hear," said Sayen. Her privileged upbringing was rare, she knew. She'd always been curious about what regular lives were like, but it had always seemed crass and insensitive to ask.

Erielle sighed. "I went into cosmetic surgery." As Sayen raised her eyebrows, she touched her scar. "I know. Ironic, huh? Anyway, you wouldn't think there would be much call for facelifts and so on these days, but you'd be surprised. Modding produces beautiful children, but after they grow up they get older, just the same as people always have. Sure, there's plenty of aging treatments these days, but nothing as effective as the surgeon's scalpel."

Erielle's tone was quiet and intense. Sayen waited patiently to hear what she had to say next. As the underworlder spoke, she was breaking a piece of bread into tiny pieces.

"One day, I got asked to do some pro bono work. I agreed. My job paid well, and I had time on my hands to do a little good in the world. It wasn't until I saw my patient that I realized how much in need of good the world was." She took a deep breath and released it. "It was a little girl. She was badly disfigured. I thought she must have been in an accident. But my contact—I never met the girl's parents—my contact told me that she'd been born like that."

"How come?" Sayen asked. "Was she a natural?" She had heard about the many genetic abnormalities that modding had just about eradicated.

"No, she wasn't a natural. That was the point. It was all done very secretly. My contact brought the little girl in the evening and asked me not to put anything in the system about the operation. The nurse who assisted agreed to never tell anyone. I had to record the anesthetic and other resources as wastage to account for them. The poor girl looked terrible. I wanted to do all that I could to help her lead as normal a life as possible."

"Hold on," interjected Sayen. "You're sure she wasn't a natural? I mean...I don't get it."

"Sayen, my contact swore to me that the child's deformities were the result of modding gone wrong. He said that there were more like her, but the parents were bribed or threatened to silence. Their fee for the genetic modification was refunded, and they were offered a second treatment free of charge. And the babies with the abnormalities..." She swallowed. Her eyes were wet. "The babies were whisked away somewhere. I don't know where. The parents of the girl who was brought to me had insisted that they wanted to keep her. But they had to keep her hidden away. Our world barely tolerates people conceived naturally these days—people who look normal, let alone anyone who's different."

Lowering her fork to her plate, Sayen tried to take in what Erielle was telling her. "You're saying that sometimes the process goes wrong, but they can't tell until the baby's born?" A thought chilled her: what if she'd come out not quite right, after all the modding that her parents had paid for? Would they have abandoned her?

"It's one of the many sickening secrets of our world," said Erielle. "Just one of them. After that, I tried to continue working as normal, but I found I couldn't. I would look at my wealthy clients, who wanted a little fat removing here, a slight wrinkle smoothing out there, and I'd wonder if they'd given up a baby who'd failed to meet their expectations; if they'd returned a child who wasn't up to spec."

Sayen was suddenly not hungry. She pushed away her plate.

Silent tears rolled from Erielle's eyes.

"I'm sorry," Sayen said. She lifted a hand and slowly wiped away one of Erielle's tears with her thumb, brushing her scar. Erielle met her gaze. "How did you get this?" Sayen asked.

"Car accident. When you don't use autodrivers, they happen." She shrugged. "I could have fixed it up a little, but it seemed kinda hypocritical. I'd left my job by then. I just couldn't stomach it anymore. I couldn't stomach living in the sick, fake world we've created. I came here and joined the underworlders. They're my people now."

"And I guess I represent everything you underworlders hate?" Sayen asked.

Erielle smiled and wiped her eyes. "Yeah, you do. I'm sorry for being a misborn to you before. Try not to take it personally. After what you did for Makey, I know you're not like some digifreaks I've met."

"What am I like?"

For a long moment, Erielle didn't answer, and the silence stretched between the two women. Their eyes didn't leave each other's faces.

It was Erielle who made the first move. She leaned over the table. Sayen met Erielle's lips with her own.

# Sixteen

Carl woke up. He was sitting in a chair, and his head and arms were on a bed. Disoriented for a moment, he sat bolt upright and looked around. As he realized where he was and remembered what had happened the previous day, he immediately swung around to Makey. The kid was motionless, and his skin was like alabaster. Carl leapt up and grabbed his shoulder.

"What?" exclaimed Makey, his eyes snapping open.

"Geez, I thought you were dead," said Carl.

"Ahhh," Makey said, wincing as he eased his shoulder from Carl's grasp, which made him move his neck. "No, I'm still around, thanks."

"Sorry. How are you feeling? Are you hungry? Or thirsty? Would you like me to get you something to drink?"

"Yeah, something to drink would be great."

Carl left him and ran up the stairs two at a time to Erielle's room to tell her the kid was awake again and needed her attention. He burst into the room without knocking. The underworlder was there and so was Sayen. Erielle was looking out of the window and Sayen was lying on some cushions beneath a cover. The two had been talking when Carl interrupted them, though he hadn't caught the gist of the conversation. They both looked at him.

For a brief moment, Carl wondered what Sayen was doing there. Everyone else slept in one of the several communal rooms on the second floor. As the realization dawned, he said, "Oh, krat. Sorry," and he began to back out of the room.

"It's okay. What is it?" Erielle asked. "How's Makey?"

"He's woken up, and he's thirsty. I thought you'd want to know."

"I do. Thanks. Could you get him some water from the kitchen? I'll be down in a minute."

Carl ducked out and went to get the kid a drink. By the time he returned to the convalescent's room, Jas was there. She was talking to Makey.

"It's out of the question," she was saying. "Even if you were well enough, which you aren't, it'd be far too dangerous."

Makey said, "But—"

"Look, I overreacted in Antarctica," said Jas, "and I apologize for it. But the basic facts hold true. It was totally idiotic of me to allow you to come along on that trip yesterday. I should have made you get out of the car and picked you up later, no matter what Erielle had said." As Makey tried to voice further protests, she continued, "No. You aren't ready. But listen. I will train you, I promise. If we have the opportunity, I'll start as soon as I can. But we've got to make our next move, which is to capture a Shadow. For now, I'm *ordering* you to rest and get better. Are you going to follow my order or not?"

Makey glowered. "I'm going to follow your order," he said eventually, with an air of disappointment.

"Are we continuing with the plan?" Carl asked Jas as he handed Makey a beaker.

"I don't know what else we can do," she replied. "Erielle's right. Without proof, the Transgalactic Council have no reason to believe us. If these scanners that detect Shadows exist, we can show them that we've caught one, and they won't be able to deny that they're here on Earth. Under the Transgalactic Treaty, they'll have to help us."

"It's a shame that bugger Alef got away last night," Carl said.

"Yeah, it is. Shadow Alef, you mean."

"Yeah, Shadow Alef. You know they aren't the same as their victims, but that doesn't stop you from feeling like they are."

"Tell me about it."

Carl remembered the Shadow of the army officer Jas had killed on Dawn. He cringed. He seemed to be constantly putting his foot in it that morning.

The door opened, and Erielle and Sayen came in.

"How are you doing, kid?" Erielle asked.

"I'm feeling better by the minute," Makey replied. Some color had returned to his cheeks, and his eyes were brighter.

"Great." Erielle went to the door and bellowed, "Sark, soup," before shutting it. "If you're feeling up to it, I'd like to move you out for about an hour while I perform a small operation."

"An operation?" Jas asked. "Was someone injured in the raid last night?"

"No, we all got away unharmed, thanks to this woman," Erielle said, putting her arm around Sayen and giving her shoulder a squeeze. "But I want to do this operation as soon as I can."

"It's my tracer," Sayen explained. "She's going to take it out so we can destroy it."

"Of course. I'd forgotten," Jas said. "Are you sure you can do it safely?" she asked Erielle.

"Yes. I've extracted various pieces of shrapnel in this room over the years. I have everything I need." She turned to Sayen again. "I'll use a local anesthetic, okay?"

As Sayen nodded, Erielle's words reminded Carl of something that had long been bothering him about the underworlders. "So, you're happy to use modern technology?" he asked. "You said some of your people went to Dawn. I got to know those people and they wouldn't have anything to do with modern medicine or anything else that they thought was unnatural."

Erielle rolled her eyes. "Yeah, that's what they were like. We aren't all like that. They're confused, in my opinion. It isn't modern technology that we reject; it's what comes with it. The Government uses technology to watch and control you digifreaks. The only way to avoid it is to refuse to take part in normal society. You think we'd choose to live like this if we could have all the benefits you enjoy with none of the downsides? Of course not. That would be stupid. But if we have to give them up to be free, we will. Now, I don't suppose you know where that tracer is, Sayen?"

"I don't. I don't even have a scar. They must have had it added as my body was being grown."

Erielle grimaced. "That might make it harder to get out. Let me think. They would have put it in the safest place possible. It's probably somewhere without many nerves, and not very deep or near any organs. Ah, I have an idea. Turn around."

Sayen turned her back to Erielle, and the latter lifted her shirt and pushed her hands down the base of her back, under the waistband of her pants. Erielle frowned as she palpated the flesh at the top of Sayen's buttocks. Her face brightened. "I think I found it. Just here. Give me your hand." She took her hand and placed it on a certain spot. "What do you think? Can you feel it? I've got a scanner that should confirm it's there. I'll get it out."

"Great," Sayen said, "and then, can I finally get some clean clothes?"

Erielle laughed and nodded. Sayen prodded the spot on her buttocks. She noticed Carl and Jas watching. "Don't you two have something else to do?"

Sark came in with some soup for Makey, and Carl and Jas went to leave through the open door.

"Wait a minute," Erielle said. "Before you go, have you had any more thoughts on how to catch your Shadow?"

"I haven't," Jas replied. "Have you, Carl?" He shook his head.

"I heard that there's a security meeting tonight at the HQ," Erielle said. "A few Government officials are flying in from overseas. Would your Shadow usually attend those, Sayen?"

"Yes, he would," Sayen exclaimed.

"Tonight?" Jas said excitedly, but her face fell. "That place will be locked down after our attack last night."

"Maybe," said Erielle, "Or maybe they think you wouldn't dare attack them again so soon, especially when all you've got is a beat-up old car and a few weapons."

"Maybe they're right," Carl said.

"But if I were to help..."

"You're going to help us?" asked Jas.

"I'd like to lend a hand. And I've got quite a lot of equipment that should make things more interesting."

"That's great," said Jas. "What made you change your mind?"

Erielle shrugged. "I guess I finally understood this isn't a 'them and us' thing."

# SEVENTEEN

"I can't believe you lied to me about the invisibility spray," Jas said to Erielle.

"You think I'm going to tell a digifreak the truth?" the underworlder retorted as she retrieved the can from a cupboard in her munitions room. "This stuff's so precious, I could sell it and buy enough blackmarket food to keep the whole neighborhood fed for a year."

"I understand, I guess," Jas said. "Still, if we'd had it when we tried to catch the Shadow, maybe no one would have been hurt."

"I know. No need to remind me. That's one reason I'm coming with you tonight. If anyone's going to get hurt fighting these Shadows now, it should be me. I wasn't thinking straight, and Makey suffered for it. I should have sided with you when you didn't want to let him come with you, or I should have lent you the best equipment I had. I messed up, and the kid nearly died. I hope I'm going to put that right tonight."

"Don't blame yourself," said Jas. "If I hadn't been so hard on him in Antarctica, he mightn't have been so insistent. But neither of us knew what would happen, and he's going to be okay." Jas took the blaster that Erielle handed her and passed it to Carl, who inserted it in the holster inside his jacket. "How's Sayen doing?"

"She's got a sore butt, but she should be up and around tomorrow."

"Did it take you long to find the tracer?" Carl asked.

"No, but it had worked its way in a little, and I had to dig it out. I melted it in a burner. Sayen's got a few stitches. She wanted to come with us, the idiot. I told her to get some sleep, and in the morning I'd have a shadowy gift for her."

Jas was a little puzzled by Erielle's attitude toward Sayen. At first, she'd seemed to hate the ground the woman walked on. Then that morning she'd been overly familiar and intimate when she'd examined her, and Sayen hadn't seemed to mind. Now she was talking about giving her a gift. She wondered what was going on.

Tucking the blaster that Erielle handed her into the belt of her pants, she said, "How are we going to get there?" If they had to use the car that the underworlder had lent them the previous day, it wouldn't take the Shadows longer than a split second to recognize it. Or a split second longer to blow it to pieces.

"I've got a vehicle that'll help us blend in," Erielle said. "You'll see."

———

They were leaving the alley that led to Erielle's place. The underworlder had covered herself in invisibility spray, including goggles to cover her eyes, saying that she would explain on the way. Jas worried about what she might have in mind. The spray brought its own set of problems, though it gave them plenty of advantages.

Another large, black advantage was parked out in the street. A long, low Global Government limousine sat in the road, its doors open. An underworlder was giving it a final polish.

"Whoa," Jas said. "How the hell did you get it?"

"Now that would be telling." Erielle's voice came from Jas's right.

"What a beauty," breathed Carl. "Can I drive it, or is it autodrive?"

"They're either or," Erielle replied. "but I was hoping you would want to drive it. The autodrive safety control will stop us from getting too close to other vehicles, and that won't work for what I have in mind."

"And what do you have in mind?" Jas asked.

"I said I'll explain on the way."

Jas hated the last-minute planning, but Erielle had wanted to have someone survey the Security HQ and report back. They got into the car and headed out. Erielle sat in the rear and outlined how they were going to kidnap Sayen's Shadow.

Sayen had given them a detailed description of their target, but many personnel would be leaving the headquarters that evening in Government cars, and they had to be sure that they had the right one. Erielle's plan was that she would slip inside and down into the car park, hopefully undetected as she would be invisible. Her contact had scoped out the place, and she said she knew where to go for a close-up view of people entering the car park after the meeting. Carl and Jas would circle the block until Erielle notified them via short range radio that the Shadow was leaving, after which they would follow the car as it left the car park and make a second attempt at a kidnapping.

"I don't like the idea of you going in there," Jas said. "The place could be crawling with Shadows. Being invisible doesn't make you as undetectable as you might think. I found that out when we rescued Sayen. If it weren't for her and Carl, a Shadow Jas would be walking around right now."

"I'll be careful," Erielle said.

"How are you gonna get back?" Carl asked. "Even if we had time to pick you up, we can't see you."

"I can radio to tell you where to stop for me, and I'll do that if for some reason things don't work out. But you'll be busy catching your Shadow. I can make my own way home."

"I still don't like it," said Jas.

"Do you have a better plan?"

Jas was silent.

They dropped Erielle off a hundred meters or so from the Security HQ. It was weird seeing the car door open and close but no one apparently get out. They checked their radios were working, and set off to begin driving around the block while waiting for Erielle's heads up.

"I really don't like this," said Jas.

"You keep saying that," Carl said.

"I keep feeling it."

The radio crackled and fell silent. It seemed weird to be using such an old technology, but Erielle had assured them that it was *because* radios were such an old technology that they were the most secure comms the underworlders had.

Tension between Jas and Carl chilled the atmosphere inside the car. There was so much she wanted to say to him, but she never knew how to start, and the timing was never right. Something had nearly happened between them in Australia, but now they seemed more distant than ever. Thinking back over the last few days and wondering why things were never easy between them, she realized that she hadn't been good company recently.

"Carl," she began before immediately drying up.

"Yeah?" His eyes left the road and flicked toward her for a moment.

"I...I'm sorry if I've been hard to get along with lately. It was going to Antarctica...it put me in a bad frame of mind. I've got some unhappy memories of my time there. I never thought I'd ever go back."

"No worries, Jas. Anything you wanna tell me about?"

"Not now. One day." Feeling a little better, she continued, "Hey, Sayen and Erielle have been acting a little weird toward each other. Is something going on between them, do you think?" she asked Carl.

"Yeah, of course. Can't you tell?"

"Oh yeah. Yeah, I thought so." In fact, Jas didn't find those kinds of things easy to notice. The added information drove her concern about what Erielle was doing a notch higher. If anything happened to the underworlder, Sayen would take it hard, and with her fears about her parents' safety, she had enough on her plate as it was.

A burst of static came from the radio. "I'm inside," said Erielle quietly. "Watching. Over." The radio was silent again.

Carl indicated and turned a corner. It was late evening, and the traffic was thin, which meant that they wouldn't be held up, but Jas worried that it also made their car noticeable and suspicious.

They'd passed the road leading to the car park once already. When they passed it again, a line of four limousines were queueing to get out. The meeting was over and the officials were leaving. Jas's heart pumped faster. It wouldn't be long now.

The radio gave a burst of static, then was silent. They drove the quiet streets for another turn. The suspense was agonizing. When would the kratting Shadow appear? Jas hated waiting. She itched to act.

"I think I can see him," came Erielle's soft voice over the radio. "He fits the description exactly."

Jas wished the underworlder wouldn't speak except when completely necessary. Though Erielle couldn't be seen, she could be heard.

"He's coming closer," continued Erielle. "I can see him better. Yes, I'm sure it's him."

Jas wanted to tell her to shut the krat up, but the sound of her own voice on the radio could also give the underworlder away.

"He's leaving now. Get—"

Erielle's words were drowned out by an explosion of noise. Jas and Carl jumped in their seats and looked at each other. The radio went dead.

"What was that?" Carl asked.

"I don't know. I thought I recognized the noise, but—"

"Do you think she's okay?"

"I don't know. But we have to move. She said he's leaving."

"I know. We're nearly at the junction with the car park road. I'm slowing down. We should see his limo soon...Krat."

There it was: a limo waiting to join the main road. And right behind it was another one. Both had heavily tinted windows. Which one contained the Shadow?

———

Jas's mind was whirring as she tried to concentrate on the limousine in front of them. What had happened to Erielle? They'd received no further comms from her since that burst of loud noise over the radio. She thought of Sayen waiting for the underworlder back at the house. And she worried that they were following the wrong car.

She gripped her blaster. What if a human was inside the vehicle? They'd wanted to capture the Shadow alive, but if it died in the firefight, she wouldn't lose sleep over it. Killing an innocent person was another matter.

Carl seemed to be thinking the same thing. "Hey, look, we're coming up to a ditch on the side of the road there. What if I just force the car into it instead of you shooting the wheels out?"

"Good idea," Jas replied. She turned to scan behind them. The road was empty. No Shadows had noticed them this time, as far as she could tell.

Carl sped up. The limousine in front edged away. Jas wondered what the occupant was thinking. Had they noticed, or were they too occupied with an interface inside? Carl sped up some more, and moved out toward the center of the road, but the bright headlights of a truck appeared around a bend in front of them, and he had to move back into their lane.

*Come on*, thought Jas. The ditch was coming to an end. If they didn't manage to force the limousine into it soon, the opportunity would be lost, and she wasn't sure how they would stop the car without violence.

Carl hit the accelerator, and Jas's head whipped back. He zoomed out, but another truck appeared ahead. He slammed on the brakes and zipped back behind the limousine. The ditch on their left ended, and was replaced by forest. They were now way outside the city. They had to stop this car, and soon, before it reached its destination, where they might have to contend with other Shadows.

"Krat. I'm an idiot," exclaimed Carl. "It's so long since I've been driving cars, I forgot."

"What?" Jas asked.

Carl flipped a switch and pressed the accelerator. The pitch of the engine's whine rose, and the car sped up, but it also *flew* up. In a few moments they were above the car they were following. Carl flipped another switch, and the engine cut out. They fell, landing directly on the front of the limousine, which rolled to a halt, its auto-drive safety system kicking in. Inertia carried their car forward, and they slid down onto the road.

Jas was out before the car stopped. She ran back to the limousine, her blaster in hand. The car's roof was dented, and she wondered if the damage was preventing the doors from opening, because the Shadow hadn't emerged and tried to escape. Carl was on the other side, holding his weapon. Their eyes met, and at a silently agreed moment, they pulled open the doors.

The occupant was sitting on Jas's side, looking more than a little surprised. It wasn't Sayen's Shadow. It was a woman with long, straight hair, wearing a kaftan.

# EIGHTEEN

They were nearly back at Erielle's place. A muffled thumping came from the trunk.

"Gee, I hope you're right," Jas said to Carl.

"I'm sure," Carl replied. "Well, pretty sure anyway."

Jas rolled her eyes.

"It has to be the Minister for Global Government Security," Carl said. "There can't be many women who wear kaftans to work at government headquarters."

"But is she a Shadow?"

"Sayen definitely seemed to think so."

Jas shook her head. If they were wrong, they were in deep, deep trouble. She wondered what the sentence was for kidnapping a Global Government minister. The courts would add assault to the charge, as they'd had to manhandle the woman to gag her and tie her up and lift her into the trunk. At least it was roomy and had plenty of air, and it was nighttime so the woman wouldn't get too hot. Still. They'd kidnapped a minister. She shook her head again.

When they arrived, an underworlder came out to meet the car. Carl popped the trunk, and they went around the back to get the minister out. The woman's hair was all over the place, and her eyes were nearly popping from her head. A torrent of angry protests were muffled by the tape over her mouth.

"Better get her inside quick," Jas said to Carl.

She fought and struggled as he picked her up and hoisted her over his shoulder before carrying her down the alley. They thought it was safest to deposit the minister in the basement room where Erielle had put them before. They gave her a chair to sit on, but left her gagged and bound. The door had a secure lock.

Sayen was lying on her front in Erielle's treatment room. Makey was there, too. It was the early hours of the morning, and both were sound asleep. Jas gently woke Sayen and explained in whispers that they needed her to identify someone.

Wincing, Sayen eased herself off the bed and hobbled to the door. Jas and Carl went with her as she made her slow way down the stairs to the basement. Their victim had gotten out of her chair and wriggled over to the door, and they hit her on the head accidentally as they opened it. A muted cry of pain escaped her gag.

She didn't look any less furious than she had when they'd gotten her out of the trunk of the car. Her face was red and sweaty beneath her tangle of hair.

"Why did you take her?" Sayen asked. "Why didn't you kidnap Shadow Bernie?"

"Long story," Carl said. "But, is that the Minister for Global Government Security?"

"Yeah, that's her all right," Sayen said.

Jas exhaled in relief. "And you're sure she's a Shadow?"

"Well, I wouldn't go so far as to say I'm *sure*."

Jas groaned.

"She wasn't with Bernie when I was captured and taken away," said Sayen. "But she acted like a Shadow when she interviewed me, and it sure seems like there are a lot of them in that place."

The woman jerked and writhed on the floor, and tried to shout.

"Let's leave her to calm down a little," Jas said.

There didn't seem much point in replacing the woman in her chair, so they left her where she was after telling her they would be back in a little while. As they were climbing the stairs, Jas's hand froze on the rail as a realization popped into her mind.

"That noise," she said. "I know what it was."

"What noise?" asked Sayen.

"Erielle radioed us from the headquarters' car park, but there was a noise, and she was cut off."

"*What?*"

"What was it, Jas?" asked Carl.

"It sounded just like the burst of a fire extinguisher, which is strange...oh, krat."

"What, Jas?" Sayen asked urgently. "What is it?"

She hesitated a moment. She didn't want to put the thought in Sayen's mind, but now she couldn't refuse to explain. "Erielle was covered in invisibility spray, but she had to speak to tell us when your Shadow was leaving. If someone had overheard her, and wanted to find her..."

"They could spray the area with a fire extinguisher, and the foam would show where she was," finished Sayen.

"I might be totally wrong," Jas said. "I'm sorry."

They continued to climb the stairs. Sayen's head was bowed as she slowly took each step. When they reached the top, she turned a stricken face toward them. "Do you know when she's supposed to be back?"

"She'll be here by morning at the latest, I think," Carl replied. "She said she'd come back by herself."

It was going to be a long wait. Jas hoped with all her heart that the underworlder had made it out and was now on her way through the streets, invisible, returning to the home she'd created for herself and her people. If she didn't show up, they would have to find a way to rescue her.

Erielle had helped them. Without her, they would never have been able to capture the—probable—Shadow in the basement. She'd shown that underworlders and the rest of human society could and should work together to defeat their common enemy.

# BURNED

# ONE

Jas was having a staring competition with the Minister for Global Security. She had locked eyes with the long-haired, kaftan-wearing government official, who was tied to a rickety wooden chair. Above them both, a single bare light strip illuminated the windowless basement room. Jas wasn't up to speed on the politics and politicians of Earth's Global Government—her brief visits to Earth between deep space missions didn't allow for it—but she'd been told the woman's name was Bathsheba Dubois, and that she'd been in office for three and a half years.

Three and a half years was plenty long enough for her to have been killed and replaced by a Shadow—a perfect copy of the victim, only inhabited by a hostile alien. What Jas had to find out was simple: was it the real Bathsheba sitting before her, or was it Shadow Bathsheba? If she was the actual Minister, Jas and her friends were guilty of the crime of kidnapping. But if it was a Shadow, Jas was one step closer to alerting the Transgalactic Council that Earth was gradually being infected and taken over by an alien menace.

Bathsheba was the first to crack. She broke her stare, and her eyes shifted to the side. Jas gave a slight nod of satisfaction. The minister seemed to be weakening a little, and now she might respond to questioning. As part of her training as a security officer Jas had learned how to interrogate effectively, but she didn't want to employ the harsher methods she knew. She had a distaste for them, and there was a chance the woman sitting before her was a human being.

"How did you know it was me in the car?" Bathsheba asked.

Jas straightened up in surprise. After removing her gag, she'd endured longer than an hour of furious threats and demands from the minister. Her question was the first real attempt at communication she'd made.

The truth was, Jas hadn't known she was kidnapping a Global Government minister when she'd attacked her limousine. She'd been trying to kidnap another, known, Shadow. Unsure of the wisdom of giving away that information, Jas replied, "It wasn't easy. You all travel in identical unmarked limousines. Maybe you should think about updating your security policy in that area."

Bathsheba shrugged. "A motorcade only draws attention to important officials. And these days, when a targeted airstrike from kilometers away is technically easy to arrange, anonymity is the best defense. It's worked pretty well."

"Until now."

Another shrug. "Security must be constantly revised and updated as threats develop and evolve."

She was stating one of the first principles Jas had ever learned. Bathsheba Dubois was no lightweight. She knew her stuff. But her statement wasn't evidence that she was the real Bathsheba. The longer Shadows spent living as replicants of their victims, the more they unlocked their memories and knowledge, and the more like them they became. Jas had heard that some Shadows even became confused about who they were, eventually.

What information could she get from the woman that would clearly identify her? Shadow Bathsheba could probably answer any question the original Bathsheba could. A certain emptiness behind the eyes or a vagueness in the gaze were some signs of a recently created Shadow replacement, but the woman showed neither of those symptoms.

"So," said Bathsheba, "what's your organization? What are you demanding for my return? You realize that the police are homing in on this location as we speak? You know, if you give yourselves up now, before it's too late, you might be spared the death penalty."

"Are you trying to tell me you've been fitted with a tracker?" asked Jas. "That's a lie. They would have been here a long time ago if that were the case. Don't worry. I know all about trackers. No. No one knows where you are. No one's ever going to find you."

Bathsheba's gaze wavered. Her anger had given way to fear, Jas detected, though the woman was trying to hide it. *Good.* Maybe she would reveal something that would give away her true identity. "Tell me what you know about Shadows," she said, watching the minister's expression closely.

Surprise flickered over her face but was quickly suppressed. "What a ridiculous question. Shadows are shade cast by objects standing in light."

Jas's lips thinned. "Don't waste my time and yours. You know what I mean. You know what Shadows are. The Government's been covering them up long enough. You've been pretending to the Transgalactic Council that you have the situation under control, and you've suppressed all reports about them in the media. But they're here, and they're taking over. You've let the situation get out of hand. Or maybe your victim did."

"Wait. You think I'm a Shadow?" Bathsheba sat upright. "Is that what this is about? That's why you kidnapped me? But that doesn't make any sense. You could have informed the vidnews channels if you really thought that. You could have—"

"Told the media you've silenced?"

Bathsheba paused. Her shoulders sagged. It seemed the natural reaction of someone in her position, but it could also be the mimicry of a Shadow.

"I'm not a Shadow," said Bathsheba. "I don't know how to prove it to you, but I'm not. Listen. If you know about them and you're fighting them, we're on the same side. Protecting Earth from Shadows is the Global Government's number one task. The longer you keep me here, the closer we come to losing that fight. You have to let me go so I can do my job."

Jas snorted. "From what I've seen, we stand a better chance without you in power."

Her face reddening, the minister replied, "You have no idea what you're talking about. You have no idea the lengths I've gone to in order to fight this menace."

Jas stepped closer and bent down so that her face was inches from Bathsheba's. "The tests you use aren't working. Shadows are flooding onto the planet. The parents of a very good friend of mine have gone missing, probably taken by Shadows. There are Shadows in the refugee institutions. There are Shadows in your own offices. Whatever lengths you've gone to, they *aren't enough*."

Behind her, the door opened. It was Sayen, looking tired and in pain. Less than a day ago, she'd had an operation to remove a tracking device her parents had placed in her. The wound had to be sore.

"You," gasped Bathsheba, her eyes widening. "Then you aren't a Shadow. I thought not when I interviewed you, but when you disappeared..."

"No, I'm not," Sayen replied. "Can I talk to you?" she asked Jas, who followed her outside.

"Erielle still isn't back," she said, after Jas closed the door. "It's nearly dusk. She should have been here hours ago. Something must have gone wrong. She's been captured, or hurt. Maybe she's stuck at the Security HQ, Jas, and she can't get out. Maybe she's unconscious, and she needs our help. She's covered in invisibility spray. How are we ever going to find her?" Sayen's voice had been rising as she spoke, and her lower lip trembled.

"Let's go upstairs." Jas locked the door and helped Sayen mount the steps to the first floor. The missing underworlder leader hadn't escaped her mind, but she wasn't sure what they could do. The last they'd heard, it had sounded like she was in great danger. Since then, the radio contact they had with her had been silent, even when they'd risked hailing her. But they couldn't storm the Global Government Security Headquarters. They didn't have the firepower. And even if they managed to get inside, what then? They had no clue where she might be.

But Sayen and Erielle were lovers, and Jas didn't want to crush her hopes that the underworlder might still turn up alive and well. "We'll talk to her people and see what they suggest. They must be just as worried as we are. How's Makey doing?"

"He sleeps most of the time, but he seems to be getting better. I dressed his wound. It's healing up."

"That's great. Why don't you go back to your room, and I'll talk to the underworlders about Erielle. Do you know where Carl is?"

"He said he was going to get some sleep, but that was a while ago."

"Okay, thanks. You try to sleep, too, and try not to worry. We'll do our best to find Erielle. I promise."

Leaving Sayen in the underworlders' medical treatment room, Jas went to find Carl. The pilot was alone in the communal bedroom. He was lying on his back, but he was awake. His hands behind his head, he was staring out the window into the twilight. He looked sad and wistful. Jas wondered if he was thinking about his missing parents.

"Carl?" she said, breaking him from his reverie.

He sat up. "Did you find out if that woman's a Shadow?"

Jas shook her head.

"Krat."

"I don't know how we're going to know for sure. But that isn't what's on my mind at the moment. Would you come with me to talk to the underworlders about Erielle?"

"She still not back?"

"No, and none of them seem to be doing anything about it."

"That's not good."

The building was strangely empty and quiet. They didn't find Erielle's followers until they'd climbed right to the top, where her private rooms were. When they went in, they found all the underworlders gathered there. A meeting was going on, but silence fell abruptly the moment Jas and Carl showed their faces.

"Something we can do for you?" asked a large man, who appeared to have been addressing the rest. His tone was sarcastic. Jas recognized him as one of the men who had accompanied Erielle and Sayen when they had stolen the blood that saved Makey's life.

"I think you all agree Erielle has to be in trouble," Jas said. "If you have a plan for some way to find her, we'd like to help."

"What a generous offer," said the man. "But, sorry, whatever we decide to do, your *help* won't be needed."

# Two

Jas rattled the padlock on the cabinet. It was a simple mechanical device, typical of the underworlders' dislike and distrust of technology. Luckily for Jas, that meant it would also be simple to break. She lifted up the blaster she was holding, preparing to hit the lock with its handle.

"I'm not sure this is a good idea," said Carl, grabbing her arm before she could bring it down.

"Carl, if the underworlders turn against us, we won't stand a chance unless they're unarmed." But her friend's worries made her pause. They both looked at Erielle's weapon cabinet while they decided what to do.

"When they find out we stole their guns," Carl said, "they're definitely gonna turn against us." He let go of her arm.

"You saw that guy at their meeting. He was talking them into throwing us out, or worse. And what are we going to do then? Sayen can barely walk, and Makey's too sick to move. Who knows what they'll do with the minister we kidnapped." She sighed. "I agree it might turn out not to be the best move, but in our current situation, I don't think we have a choice. Offense is the best defense."

After the underworlder's rejection of their offer to help them find their leader, the rest of them had stared at Jas and Carl in silence until they left. Whatever they thought of the large man's comments, it was clear that the underworlders still thought of them as outsiders. Their presence at Erielle's place was on very shaky ground. Jas knew she would feel a whole lot more comfortable with their weaponry under her control.

Carl seemed to have run out of arguments. "I suppose you're right. Go ahead."

Jas raised her blaster again and brought the hard edge of the handle down on the lock. The metal rings on the door that held the lock bent, but they didn't break. Jas tried again, but the welding held firm. The lock was turning out to be a lot tougher than antique vids implied. She would have to blast it.

She turned the weapon in her hand and aimed it before delivering a short beam. It sizzled the metal, and the lock clanked as it hit the floor. Erielle's cabinet of wonders opened before them. She had a variety of weapons in there. Jas was familiar with most of them, though some were so old she'd only ever seen pictures of them.

They hastily filled a bag with the cabinet's contents. They didn't know how long the underworlders' meeting would go on. Jas was worried about Makey and Sayen lying unprotected in the medical center.

Soon, the cabinet shelves were empty, and their bag was bulky and heavy. Its weight didn't reassure Jas, however. With their criminal connections, the underworlders would have few problems replenishing their supply. Stealing Erielle's stock was, at most, only buying them a little time.

"That it?" Carl asked, leaning over Jas's shoulder to peer into the dark recesses of the cupboard.

"Yeah, we've got everything."

"Krat."

"What's wrong?"

"Where's the invisibility spray?"

Jas's heart sank. "You're right. It isn't here. I swear Erielle put it back before we left for the security HQ. Someone's taken it already."

"Yeah. Someone's thinking ahead. Probably that fella who was running the meeting."

"Nothing we can do about it now. We've got everything else. Looks like I was right to be cautious. Let's get downstairs to the medical center."

Both Sayen and Makey were in bed but awake when Jas and Carl appeared with their cache of weaponry. Carl explained what had been said at the underworlders' meeting, and neither of them was slow to understand the danger they were in.

"Jas, did you get anywhere questioning the minister?" Sayen asked.

"Well, once she stopped cussing me out and started talking...I don't know. Either she's doing a good job of acting like the real Bathsheba Dubois, or she isn't a Shadow."

Sayen grimaced. "I really thought she was. She was so cold toward me. And the fact that she was interviewing all the job applicants, it seemed like she was trying to assess me to see if I was worth turning into a Shadow."

"I think she might have been interviewing candidates herself because she was worried about Shadows infiltrating the department," said Jas. "She was trying to check for them."

Sayen shook her head. "Things must have gotten really bad. We've got to do something."

"Of course, and we're trying," Jas said. "But it looks like our plan of catching a Shadow has failed again. We still don't have anything to convince the Transgalactic Council that Earth's politicians have been lying."

The door flew open and banged against the wall. The underworlder who had been addressing the meeting stood in the doorway, and the space behind him was crowded.

"We've come to a decision," said the man. "You can stay one more night, then you're all to leave first thing in the morning. Erielle's not coming back from the look of it. You guys were only ever here because she wanted it. No one else did. We've lost friends because of you. You're bad luck, and you're trying to drag us into a fight that's none of our business. If it were up to me, you'd be out of the door right now, but some people feel sorry for the kid. So we've agreed, you've got one more night. In the morning, you can pack up your stuff and get out."

"We can't leave in the morning," exclaimed Sayen. "Makey isn't nearly well enough yet. He almost died. He can't just get up and leave."

"Look..." said the man, approaching Sayen until he was within a few inches of her.

Jas slowly reached inside the bag of weapons, which the man seemed to have mistaken as containing their belongings.

"I could've died or gotten arrested stealing blood for that kid," he continued. "And why? He isn't one of us. He's a complete stranger. I only did it because Erielle asked me to. But now she's gone, and we're going to see a few changes around here."

Jas wondered if those changes included him taking over in Erielle's place. He was standing only a short distance from the petite navigator. With her enhancements, she could take care of herself, but Jas didn't want him thinking he could bully them into doing whatever he wanted.

"You're crowding my friend," she said. "Leave us alone. We've heard what you have to say, and we'll talk about it. If it suits us to leave in the morning, we'll go."

The underworlder lifted a corner of his mouth. "You're going whether you agree to it or not," he said. But he moved back. "I'll be back at dawn." Pushing against them with his broad frame, he broke through the other underworlders who were peering in through the door, following the proceedings with great interest.

Carl closed the door on their curious faces and leaned his back against it. A tense pause followed. "Hey, Jas, give me a hand with this," he said, indicating a tall metal cupboard full of medical equipment. Together, they positioned the cupboard in front of the door. It wasn't much of a barricade, but the door didn't have a lock and it was the best they could do.

"I'm sure I'll be well enough to move in the morning," Makey said. The kid's appearance belied his words. He was pale, and the bones of his face were clearly outlined beneath his skin.

"Even if you were," Jas said, "which you're not, we aren't going anywhere. We've kidnapped a government minister. The minute anyone in the street sees her, the game's over for us. And where would we go? We don't have any creds to pay for a place to stay."

"That's not strictly true," Sayen said. "Do you remember the first time we tried to kidnap a Shadow, Erielle gave us a map showing us a safe, empty house. She said we could stay there a while. I've still got the map."

"You do?" said Jas. "That's great, but I don't think we should move until you're both well enough, and maybe not until we decide what to do with the minister."

"What *are* we going to do with her?" Sayen asked.

"Krat knows."

A shout came from upstairs, followed by the rumble of many feet running down toward them.

"Looks like they found out about their weapons," said Carl.

"What weapons?" Sayen asked.

Jas opened the bag she was carrying. Sayen's eyebrows rose, and her mouth fell open as she looked inside.

# THREE

Jas and Carl had their backs to the cupboard they'd put in front of the door, and their legs were braced against the floor. Incoherent shouting was coming from outside, and the cupboard rattled as the underworlders tried to break through. Jas pushed back as hard as she could, but her feet began to slide across the floor as the door was slowly forced open.

"Kratting digifreaks. Give us our weapons back," shouted a deep voice. "Thieves," called another. "Erielle should never have let you in. You've been nothing but trouble since you first showed your faces." "Open up," demanded a third. "Give us what's ours now, or you're gonna regret it." The voices of the angry underworlders resounded through the crack they were forcing wider.

As Jas gasped with the effort of trying to hold back the furious men and women, Sayen got out of bed. She winced as she hobbled over.

"No," Jas and Carl said at once. But they were no match for the underworlders forcing their way in. Sooner or later, they would be pushed aside.

Favoring her good leg, Sayen stood between them and leant the strength of her enhanced body to their efforts. The cupboard slowly moved back and the door closed, shutting out the yells and shouts.

As the door shut, Jas reached down into the bag of weapons she'd dropped when she'd rushed to stop the underworlders from getting in. She pulled out a blaster and went to stand grimly at the edge of the cupboard next to the wall.

*Just let them try.*

She didn't have to wait long. The underworlders must have gotten something they could use as a battering ram. A heavy weight struck the door, and the cupboard, Carl, and Sayen were thrown forward. A gap appeared, filled with triumphant underworlders. Their expressions quickly changed when Jas shoved a blaster in their faces.

"If you don't leave us alone," she said, "I'm going to barbecue the first head I see."

The gap was suddenly empty. She nodded at Carl, who pushed against the cupboard and closed the door.

"How long's it gonna take them to get some more guns?" he asked.

"Not long, I don't think," Jas said. "Not with their connections. But we've got a little more time. I wish I knew who took that invisibility spray."

"My bet's on our grumpy friend," Carl said.

"I think you're probably right. It looks like he was one of Erielle's right-hand men. I doubt she told many people about that spray."

"He's probably been maneuvering for a takeover for a while," Sayen said. "I'd love it if Erielle came back and put him in his place."

"We'd all love it if Erielle came back," Jas said. "And let's hope she does. But for now, we've only got ourselves and a little time until the underworlders gather enough firepower to force us out. We should take turns keeping watch tonight. I'll go first. You all try to get some sleep. We might have to leave tomorrow, whether we're ready or not."

"No, Jas," Carl said. "You sleep, and I'll take first watch. You didn't sleep all last night, and you've been up all day. I managed a nap this afternoon. Get some rest, and I'll watch the door."

He was right. She was exhausted, and that made her a liability in a fight. She spread some blankets on the floor and lay down. Carl took her place by the doorway, a blaster in his hand. Jas's eyes were only closed for a moment, however, before they snapped open and she sat bolt upright.

"What's wrong?" asked Sayen, who had made her way over to her bed.

"We've been forgetting something," Jas replied. "The most important thing. The minister."

"Krat. You're right," said Carl. "How long has she been in the basement by herself?"

"Sayen," Jas said. "It's awfully quiet out there. Can you hear anything?"

Sayen returned, limping, to the doorway. She put her ear against the wall. "They're right outside," she said quietly. Her eyes widened. "I can hear footsteps going downstairs. There's only one room down there. They're going to get the minister."

"Krat. Krat. Krat," exclaimed Jas. "We can't let them take her. Carl, open the door." Dipping her hand into the bag, she pulled out the first gun she touched. It was a small beamer, but anything would do. Carl was pushing their barricade out of the way. "Sayen, get something to protect yourself with. Carl, come with me, and bring that blaster."

"I'll come too," said Makey.

"Don't be stupid," Jas replied. "Stay here."

By the time Jas and Carl left the medical treatment room, the underworlders had all disappeared downstairs. Jas tiptoed after them, and Carl did the same. From the top of the stairs, Jas could see that the door to the basement room was open. She raced down, taking multiple steps at a time. She didn't know what they might do to the minister. They could have decided that keeping her was too much of a risk and were going to kill her.

She burst into the room, seemingly just in time. The large underworlder who wanted them to leave had a knife to the terrified woman's throat. At the sight of Jas he tensed and grabbed the minister, as if intending to block his body with hers. Jas fired before he could take another step. He slumped to the floor. The rest of the underworlders backed away.

"I've only stunned him," Jas said. "But that can soon change. Against the wall. All of you." The underworlders shuffled back, their eyes on her blaster. "Carl, cut her free. We'll take her upstairs with us."

Picking up the knife the fallen underworlder had dropped, Carl quickly sliced through the minister's bonds. The woman tried to rise to her feet, but either long sitting or simple fear had made her legs weak, and she staggered. Carl pulled her upright and put her arm over his shoulders. As he helped her to the door, Jas walked backward, keeping her aim fixed on the underworlders. Their would-be leader was already coming around. Jas was sorely tempted to put an end to his threat once and for all, but she couldn't bring herself to kill the man in cold blood. As well as the immorality of shooting him while he was defenseless, she also knew that her act would unite the underworlders against them. She hoped that people loyal to Erielle still existed among them, and though they might not be future friends, they might be allies.

No underworlders appeared in the doorway to the basement room as Jas, Carl, and their captive made their way up the stairs. They ran into the medical room, Carl still supporting the minister. The second they were safely inside, they replaced the barricade.

Her hair disheveled and her face a mask of shock, Bathsheba Dubois collapsed onto a chair and put her face in her hands.

"What happened?" Makey asked.

"I think our friend was going to kill her," Jas said grimly.

The minister's head lifted. "He said...he said if I didn't tell them everything I knew about what happened to confiscated mythranil, he would...he said he would cut my throat."

"Myth?" Jas asked. The underworlder's actions were beginning to make sense to her. Myth was an outrageously expensive drug. The man had to be an addict. If he were to take over as underworlder leader in the neighborhood, he would have the connections and resources to fund his habit. That was why he was in such a hurry to take Erielle's place.

# Four

It was a long night. Jas had insisted that Sayen rest and not keep watch. She slept head to toe with Makey in his bed. The minister took the other bed, but slept fitfully. When she did sleep, she snored and kept everyone awake.

Carl made Jas sleep again while he took the first watch. She curled up on the blankets on the floor. The underworlders' house was quiet. They seemed to have given up on dealing with them for the moment. He wondered if they were waiting on something—a new supply of weapons to arrive, for instance—or if they were arguing among themselves about what to do next. There had only been a few supporters down in the basement with the wannabe leader. He didn't seem a very likable bloke. He doubted that all of the others were behind him. There were probably quite a few who were holding out hope that Erielle would return. Though her leadership style was rough and ready, she'd seemed fair. She'd appeared to care about the people she led. He had a strong feeling the new guy only wanted to exploit them.

He watched Jas as she slept. The faint lines that time and a stressful job had worn into her face faded away, and she looked younger and more carefree, though he wasn't sure that she'd ever really been carefree. From the little she'd told him about her childhood, she'd led a lonely life. When they'd been watching for their Shadow target to leave the security headquarters, she'd told him something had happened to her years before in Antarctica that had made her never want to go back.

Sometimes, with the way she acted, Jas was a hard person to warm to. But Carl had found that, whatever she did that pushed him away, he couldn't help but be drawn back again each time. There was something different about her. Something he couldn't define in words, which connected with him deep inside. The longer he spent with her, the stronger the feeling grew.

He hoped that they would both make it out of whatever was coming, but if they didn't, he would be glad for the moments he'd spent with her.

After a few more hours, he yawned and rubbed his eyes. A pale, pre-dawn light was coming through the window. Carl had watched and listened for the underworlders all night, allowing Jas and the others to rest. He stood and stretched. His movement caused Jas to wake.

She sat up and saw that dawn wasn't far away. "What's the time?" she asked quietly. "Why didn't you wake me?"

"I was enjoying watching you sleep," he said.

"Right...That's a little bit creepy, Carl."

"You pull faces like my granny used to make when she was trying not to fart."

Jas opened her mouth in outrage. "No, I don't." She frowned. "Do I?"

Carl raised his eyebrows at her but didn't answer, as if he were trying to be kind.

"Oh, shut up. Of course I don't." She got out of bed. "Here, give me that blaster. You try to get some sleep. The underworlders might leave us alone for another hour or two." She came over to him and took his gun. "I don't really pull faces, right?"

He patted her on the shoulder. "Don't worry, Jas. It's kinda cute."

She narrowed her eyes at him as he went, smirking, to the blankets she'd just vacated. He lay down and turned on his side before allowing sleep to overwhelm him. Before he could sink into its depths, however, a massive thump against the door threw the cupboard to the floor. Medical devices, instruments, and other equipment spilled out. Jas stunned the first underworlder that burst into the room. He was unconscious before he fell onto his face, apparently breaking his nose, as blood flooded from beneath him.

Carl was already up and leaping to join her.

"The next one, I shoot to kill," shouted Jas. The underworlders took no notice. More were pouring into the room. Jas yelled as she was hit. Carl smelled her burnt flesh. The underworlders weren't pulling their punches. A man screamed as Jas's shot caught him square in the stomach. He stared in disbelief at the burning, gaping hole before his eyes rolled back and he toppled like a felled tree.

This made the rest pause, but only for a moment. Someone behind urged them on. The would-be leader, Carl guessed. Then he noticed the attacking underworlders' wild eyes and glistening skin. They were running on something. Their instigator had given them a drug to erode their judgment and get them to take part in this suicide mission.

As these thoughts sped through his mind, Carl was firing at the encroaching underworlders. He severed a man's leg at the knee. The sight of this caused another to turn and flee, despite the workings of the drug in his system. His action caused a body jam in the narrow doorway. The sound of screaming came from behind Carl. It sounded like the minister.

Jas's face was twisted with pain from the wound on her shoulder, but she fired off another shot, hitting a barrel-chested man who was managing to force his way through the struggling bodies. She got him in the neck and must have hit an artery because blood spurted out, pulsing with the man's heartbeats. He didn't seem to even notice. He continued to shove and shoulder the others aside until finally he was free, and he took an exultant step into the room. He lifted a weapon—new supplies had obviously arrived—and aimed at Carl.

In response, Carl squeezed his trigger, but he needn't have bothered. Before he could fire a shot, Jas scored a hit and the man fell upon the other she'd stunned. That one was now beginning to rise, but the weight of the falling, dying man smashed him to the floor and pinned him down.

Outside, a shout cut through the yells and cries of the attacking underworlders. They paused, and the noise quieted.

"I said, what the krat's going on?"

It was a man's voice: deep, confident, and commanding. Though it was unfamiliar to Carl, the underworlders clearly recognized who it belonged to. The effect was immediate. Those who had been trying to force their way in through the ones trying to get out ceased their efforts. The jam in the doorway disappeared as the attacking under-worlders seemed almost to melt into thin air. Carl peered out into the hallway. There was no sign of the would-be leader, but the owner of the powerful voice stepped into view.

He was tall. Well over two meters. But he wasn't lanky like Carl. His height was matched in proportion by his girth, though he didn't seem to have an ounce of fat on him. The man's appearance was striking, and Carl took note of his coloring. His skin was a deep olive, and his thick, wavy hair was reddish-brown—a color that matched his eyes. The man was a Martian, like Jas.

In two strides of his well-muscled legs, he was in the room. His gaze roved over Makey and Sayen, who were sitting up in bed, then to the minister, who had drawn her covers up to her nose, and finally to Jas, Carl, and the one trapped and two dead underworlders. With the toe of his boot, he lifted the corpse off the underworlder pinned beneath it, and the bloody-faced man scrambled to his feet and was gone in the blink of an eye.

The newcomer put his hands on his hips. "Who the krat are you?"

# FIVE

Everyone in the room froze for a moment as they took in this new turn of events. Carl was first to break the ice. He stepped forward and held out his hand. "Carl Lingiari." The man took his hand and enveloped it in his own large, powerful grip. "Ozment. Just Ozment." He turned to Jas. The pain from her shoulder wound was etched on her face.

"You need something for that. Erielle can treat you. But where is she? What's going on here?"

"Erielle's missing," said Jas.

Ozment's eyes widened, and his hands fell from his hips. "What? No. For how long?"

"About thirty hours," Carl replied.

Raising a hand and running it through his hair, Ozment said, "Krat. Where did she go?"

"Don't you wanna ask your mates?" Carl asked. "You're one of her crew, right?"

"No. Not exactly. And from the way they took off when I arrived, like mice caught eating the cheese...if Erielle's not here...I'm guessing Durfy's behind this."

"Is he a big bloke?" asked Carl, and he went on to describe the underworlder.

"Yeah. I warned Erielle about him, but she obviously didn't listen to me. Too trusting." He turned to Jas, who was lifting the neck of her shirt, trying to peak underneath to her shoulder. "Let's get you seen to, then you can explain what's going on here."

Jas turned her attention to Ozment. "Yes, and you can explain who you are and what you're doing here."

A slight smile curved his lips. "Fair enough."

"Let me do it, Jas," Sayen said, easing herself out of bed. "I've been in enough doctors' offices and had enough treatments to be able to figure some of this out. I'll try to find a painkiller." She began pulling out drawers and riffling through their contents.

Ozment took a package from his back pocket and opened it. Inside the folded leather were some dried leaves. He picked out a few and handed them to Jas. "While you're waiting, chew on these. They'll take the edge off the pain." As Jas hesitated, he added, "It's kratom. It won't hurt you. People have been using it for thousands of years."

Jas took the leaves and put them in her mouth. As she began to chew, her nose wrinkled.

"Yeah, it's bitter. I'll make some kratom tea in a little while and sweeten it with honey to take away the taste."

Sayen made Jas sit down. She'd found a pair of scissors, and she used them to cut away the burned fabric, exposing red and blistered skin with a blackened patch at the edge of Jas's shoulder. Sayen winced and sucked air through her teeth. "Looks like the beam only grazed you. You were lucky. You could have lost your arm. I'll inject a local anesthetic that'll numb the wound for a while. Then I'll clean it up and put a sterile dressing on."

"Thanks," said Jas. "It's great that you can help now that Erielle isn't here. We can't risk any hospital visits with so many Shadows around."

"Shadows?" asked Ozment. "Looks like a lot's happened since my last delivery."

"I'll explain," Carl said.

But Jas interrupted, "No, don't." She turned to Ozment. "I'm sorry. I think you might have saved all our skins back there, but we don't know who you are. We can't trust everyone who walks in the door. We don't have that luxury."

Ozment shrugged. "That isn't unreasonable, I guess. How about I tell you who I am? Then you can have your turn."

"It doesn't matter who you are," said Jas. "This isn't a situation where we can trade secrets. I'm sorry. Thanks for your help."

Jas's words were followed by an awkward pause. Ozment shrugged again and went to Bathsheba's bed. She still had the covers drawn halfway up to her face as she stared at the man. "Do you mind if I sit here?" he asked her. Silently, she shook her head. Carl wondered why the woman didn't tell him who she was. He supposed she didn't want to give away her identity, especially since she'd had her life threatened twice in the last couple of days.

Bathsheba's bed creaked as Ozment sat down, flattening the edge of her mattress. Looks passed between Sayen, Jas, Makey, and Carl. It didn't look like the newcomer was going away for a while.

"This is what Erielle injected me with when she removed my tracker," Sayen said to Jas, holding up a bottle of clear liquid. "Are you okay with me using it on you?"

Her jaw muscles clenched, Jas nodded.

"How come the underworlders took off when you arrived?" Carl asked Ozment.

The Martian opened his pack of kratom and pinched a few leaves. He put them in his mouth and began to chew before he answered. "I guess they're a little scared of me. Either that or they don't want to lose their main supplier." He lifted a haunch as he returned the package to his back pocket. "I bring their kratom. Every month or so. Not so regular that the authorities get a handle on my delivery schedule."

"Erielle told us about it," Sayen said, holding a hypodermic syringe full of anesthetic poised over Jas's shoulder. "She said it's the main currency around here."

"Kratted stuff," Jas said between her teeth as Sayen slid the needle just beneath her skin. "I was constantly confiscating it and having it destroyed aboard ship. I don't know how the misborns used to smuggle it aboard."

"It's no more harmful than alcohol," said Ozment. "In a lot of ways it's less so."

"Yeah," Jas said. "I used to confiscate alcohol too."

Ozment smiled and moved his kratom cud from one side of his mouth to the other. "So you worked on starships?"

Jas frowned. "Krat."

The Martian laughed. "Don't worry. You don't have anything to fear from me, I swear. I just told you I'm a drug dealer. You could call the police right now, but I'm guessing you won't."

A pregnant silence stretched out. Carl felt an instinctive trust for the man, but he also knew that Jas was right. They shouldn't give away their identities and intentions to just anyone who walked in the door.

Ozment leaned back and stretched out his arms behind his back to support himself. "My story's pretty simple. I'm a farmer and kratom grower, down in the Everglades. Erielle's been my contact for a long time. I trade kratom in the city for items you can't get in the swamp."

"But you didn't always live in the Everglades, did you?" Carl asked. "You're a Martian."

"There's no denying it, as this woman will testify." He winked at Jas. "The original gene therapy that protects against radiation leaves an indelible mark on all that planet's inhabitants. But that was a long time ago. I've lived on Earth more than twenty years. I'd like to go back to Mars some day. Visit my folks. My old home. But I'll have to wait until the Government allows felons to space travel."

Intent as they all were on Ozment's life story, no one noticed the approaching footsteps. The underworld leader wannabe, the man Ozment called Durfy, appeared at the door. Ozment straightened up and fixed the man with a glare from under his brows. "I was wondering when you'd show your face. Been causing trouble again, I see."

"There's no trouble here," Durfy said. "Or if there is, I'm not the one causing it. I don't know what these folks have told you, but they roped Erielle into some risky business, and now it looks like she isn't coming back. I was just trying to make it clear to them that they've outstayed their welcome."

"You sure made it clear enough," Ozment replied. "But, whatever's happened to Erielle, if these people are here under her say so, that stands until we know for sure she's gone. She's no fool. You know that. If she trusted them, so should you. And you've got no authority to be evicting her guests anyway. You know the rules. Everyone gets to vote on a new leader. You can't just step up and take over, however much you might like the idea."

Durfy bristled a little at this accusation. "Who said I was trying to take over? I was concerned for the others' safety with these strangers hanging around. Four people have gone missing due to them."

Carl gave a snort of derision and rubbed the scar on his wrist where the underworlders had cut out his credchip. "Listen, mate. The only one up to no good around here is you. You gave your friends something and riled them up to attack us. Until Erielle's back or we find her, we're sticking around, whether you like it or not. You got it?"

Durfy gave Carl a dirty look, but he left.

The tension in the room eased. Ozment's arrival had averted a crisis, but Carl didn't know how long they had before Durfy managed to rally enough support to evict them and assume Erielle's position.

# SIX

A kind of normality returned to Erielle's household. Sark offered to cook them breakfast, and Ozment left to arrange the unloading of his kratom delivery. Despite the night's sleep Carl had kindly allowed her, Jas felt bone weary. The local anesthetic Sayen had injected was wearing off, and her wound ached with a pain that reached out from her shoulder, all the way down her arm, and to the back and front of her torso. She would have liked nothing more than to lie down again and sleep the rest of the day away, if she could ignore the pain. She'd been hit before, but this time seemed worse than the others. She hoped the wound wouldn't become infected.

Makey was still far from recovered, and Sayen was hobbling around with her sore butt. Carl was the only one left whole and healthy out of the four of them. Jas didn't have the luxury of slowing down or taking it easy. They seemed no farther forward with their plan of capturing a Shadow to take to the Transgalactic Council.

Bathsheba Dubois had finally relaxed enough to let go of her covers. She was resting her arms on them. As she caught Jas looking at her, she said, "What are you going to do with me? Are you going to let me go now? If you take me into the city and drop me somewhere, I'll walk away. I won't tell anyone about you, or about this place. I promise."

Jas shook her head. "You know we can't trust you. And, anyway, kidnapping you is the least of our worries. We're trying to do something more important than you, or me. We're trying to save the Earth from invasion."

"Yes, yes, I know. The Shadows. But the Government nearly has the situation under control. There's no need for you to do anything. In another few months, we'll have rooted out the last of them, and—"

"No, you won't," exclaimed Jas. "You don't have any idea how bad the situation is. We have to do something. Now. I don't care about quarantine and trade embargos. That's all about money. I'm talking about lives. Human beings who are right now being murdered and replaced by aliens. If you ministers won't put a stop to it, we will."

"All right, all right," Bathsheba said, raising her hands. "I hear what you're saying, and you've convinced me. If you set me free, I promise I'll take your message back to the Global Government. I'll insist they hold an inquiry about the true state of affairs regarding the Shadow invasion of Earth."

For a moment, Jas almost couldn't believe her ears. *An inquiry?* She couldn't believe that someone who was responsible for the safety of every human being on the planet could be so out of touch and so blind to the reality of what was happening. Jas did the only thing she could in response to the minister's ridiculous words. She laughed. Loudly, uproariously, she laughed until her stomach ached.

When she could laugh no more, she wiped her eyes. Bathsheba was looking at her and the others—who had heard the conversation and had the same reaction as Jas—as if they were mad. Then she began to sob. Her face in her hands, between muffled sniffs, she said, "Please, please let me go. I don't know what's so funny about what I said, but you have to let me go. That man...that man was going to kill me, and it's only a matter of time before he returns to finish me off."

Jas felt a twinge of guilt. It was true. Bathsheba had come perilously close to losing her life only a few hours ago. Prior to that she'd been chased, captured, gagged, tied, put in the trunk of a car, driven to an unknown destination, and finally been held captive against her will among a group of strangers who seemed intent on doing her harm.

But though she felt a little sorry for Bathsheba, she definitely didn't want to let her go just yet. There was still a remote chance that she was a Shadow. After all, Sayen had been convinced that the Shadow who'd had her kidnapped had been a nice, older man.

"What if I tell you how you can test whether I'm a Shadow?" Bathsheba asked. "Would you let me go then, if I can prove to you that I'm not?"

This caught everyone's attention.

"How would you do that?" asked Sayen.

"A year or so ago," Bathsheba said, "we received a shipment of scanners from the Transgalactic Council. Shadows had appeared and begun to spread across the galaxy, and they wanted us to protect Earth by scanning everyone who arrived from other planets. We had to invent a whole load of other tests to put Shadows off the scent of the new technology, but it's only the scanner that works."

"We know that," said Sayen. "I found out about it just before the Shadow working in your office arranged my capture."

"You're proposing that we scan you?" Carl asked the minister.

"Yes, exactly."

"And how are we going to do that?" asked Jas.

"The scanners have a finite life. We have to replace them every three months. A new shipment is due from the Council next week."

"And...?" Jas asked.

"Well, I never thought I'd be saying this, but I can give you the information to help you steal one. If you manage it, however, you have to test me. When you know for sure that I'm not a Shadow, you have to let me go. Is it a deal?"

A Shadow scanner? It was exactly what they needed. Otherwise, they were operating by guesswork. They would have only one chance to show the Transgalactic Council that there were Shadows on Earth. They had to get it right and be sure they had a real Shadow to prove what they were saying.

"What do you think, guys?" she asked Carl, Sayen, and Makey.

"How well-protected is the shipment?" Sayen asked.

"That's the advantage of my suggestion," Bathsheba replied. "It isn't that well-protected. Research has shown that the more attention you draw to something with a heavy deployment of security, the greater the chances are of an attack. The scanners are arriving in a shipment of regular imports from deep space. Only I and one other trusted person know the carrier, and the day, time, and place of the arrival."

"When is it?" asked Jas.

"In six days."

"I don't know," Jas said. "We aren't in much of a state to be breaking into a spaceport."

"I'll be fine in a couple of days," Makey said.

"I'm up for it," said Carl.

Sayen said, "I'll be better soon too. My skin's completely healed. It's just the muscles underneath that are still a little sore. But I don't know that I agree with this idea. It'd feel like we're abandoning Erielle. After all she did for us, we should try to find her. I keep thinking that she's out there somewhere, hurt but unable to get any help. We should at least return to the Security HQ and scout around a little. Something bad has happened to her, or she'd be back by now for sure. As long as there's a chance she's alive, we shouldn't give up on her."

"You're right," Jas said. "We owe her, and if it weren't for the problems with these kratted underworlders, I would have gone out looking for her before now. Maybe we can do both. If this shipment of Shadow scanners isn't due until next week, we have plenty of time to look for Erielle."

"And," Carl said, "we don't have to decide right away if we're going after the scanners. Maybe something else'll turn up."

Ozment appeared, and the discussion immediately dried up. The Martian rubbed his hands together and said with a smirk, "My entrance hasn't had that effect since I had too much kratom and walked naked into a local government planning meeting."

# Seven

As soon as he heard about their plan to try to find Erielle, Ozment wanted in on it. At first, Jas wouldn't accept his help, but Sayen had pointed out that Jas's and Carl's faces were already known to the Shadows at Security HQ from their first kidnapping attempt. It wouldn't be long before they were noticed and apprehended. Now that the invisibility spray had gone missing, they couldn't get too close to the building, but Ozment was someone Erielle would recognize as a friend, and he certainly stood out, making him easy for her to see.

Finally, Jas relented. "You're still not one hundred percent, so I don't think you should come," she said to Sayen, "but I'm not comfortable with leaving you, Makey, and the minister here unprotected. Durfy and his lackies might have backed off for the moment, but who's to say they won't change their minds, especially if Ozment's out of the picture for the day?"

"I can deal with them," Sayen said. "Durfy knows what I'm capable of. He was there when I broke into the medical center to steal the blood for Makey, and he's no fool."

"No, he isn't," Jas replied. "Which is why he drugged up a bunch of his followers and used them as cannon fodder before he showed his face in here. Two underworlders died. That's two too many. I don't want any more deaths. I hope you don't mind me saying, Sayen, but you don't exactly look intimidating. It wouldn't take much for Durfy to persuade the underworlders to risk an attack against a sick kid, a soft politician, and a little woman."

Sayen bit her lip. "I guess you're right. I don't want to hurt anyone."

"Then I'll go by myself," Ozment said. "Just give me directions."

"No," said Makey. "At least two of you have to go. You'll be safer in pairs."

"True," Jas said. "I'm glad to see you're getting a little better understanding of security, Makey. Okay. Ozment and I will go. As a pair of Martians wandering around, we'll be noticed, but people will think we're tourists. Just a couple out doing a little sight-seeing. Carl, you can stay here as an extra deterrent to the underworlders."

"But how're you going to get there without me?" Carl asked. "You can't park that limo anywhere. It'll stick out like a sore thumb. And that old car we used for the first kidnapping is a self-driver. Can you drive, Jas?"

"I can drive," Ozment said. "We have plenty of self-drivers down in the Everglades."

Carl looked as though he still didn't agree, but he said nothing.

———

Life at Erielle's place had become seriously disorganized in her absence. No one seemed to know who they should talk to about borrowing the car they needed to get to the Security HQ. Some underworlders seemed to believe that Durfy was in charge, and that they were no longer welcome there; others appeared frightened to speak to them. A few were simply apathetic, lying semi-conscious in the communal bedrooms, heavily drugged up.

Ozment's expression became graver as he and Jas continued their inquiries. "The sooner we find Erielle and bring her back here, the better," he said after they had interrupted two men paying what had seemed to be too much unwanted attention to a young woman. "Back home, there's plenty to do on the farm. It keeps people focused. Living in the city seems to bring out the worst in people. They need someone strong, with a clear purpose. Someone who leads by example. Erielle's is one of the best underworld neighborhoods. I hate to think what's going to happen if she's gone."

Finally, they happened upon Sark in the kitchen. Of all the house's inhabitants, she appeared to be the only one who had continued as normal, faithfully cooking three meals a day for the entire household. They found her instructing three small boys on how to peel potatoes. She was leaning over them as they gazed in dismay at the large pile at their feet. When Jas and Ozment appeared, she straightened up, and her usually sharp face broke into a smile.

"Good to see you again, Ozment. Thanks for bringing our supplies. I've been a little busy with my apprentices, or I would have come and found you."

"It's good to see you too, Sark. I hope you haven't been too disturbed by the commotion going on around here."

She waved dismissively. "Oh, I don't ever get caught up in all that nonsense. People come, people go. Sometimes they fight a little. No one bothers Sark if they want their supper."

"I'm glad to hear it," Ozment said. "And a delicious supper it is too, every time."

Sark smiled in a way that said she knew he was buttering her up, but she didn't mind. "So, what can I do for you?"

"We were wondering if you knew how we could borrow a vehicle to use on an errand we'd like to run."

"I sure do." Her expression clouded. "Are you going to look for Erielle? I heard she still isn't back."

"That's right. We are."

"Then wait here a minute, and I'll go and arrange it right away. I was hoping someone would do something. I couldn't bear it if anything's happened to that sweet woman."

While Sark was gone, a couple of the small boys tried to sneak away, but Ozment clapped his large hands on their boney shoulders and turned them around. They slunk back onto their stools and picked up their potato peelers and a potato each. They looked in puzzlement from the peelers to the potatoes, as if trying to figure out how the two fit together. The third boy was busy stabbing his potato with the pointed end of his peeler.

Sark returned and told them a car with a full battery would be out in the street for them in a moment. They thanked her. As they went outside, Jas said, "Those poor boys. That looked like a dirty, boring chore Sark had set up for them."

"You're thinking, wouldn't it be easier to put the potatoes in an electric peeler? Or better yet, buy them ready-prepared? Or even better, just buy the whole meal and heat it up?"

"I guess so," Jas said as she got into the car on the passenger side.

Ozment sat in the driver's seat. "Well, you know, we do the same thing down in the Everglades. We teach the kids how to prepare and cook food. We also teach them how to clean, do simple first aid, how to build shelters, hunt, and grow their own vegetables, fruit, grains, and beans. It might seem like a waste of time to you digifreaks, but you never know, one day humans might need all the old skills again just to survive."

He started the car, and they set off. He continued, "But it's more than that. We teach our kids these things not only so they know how to look after themselves without help from technology, but also so that they learn patience, attention to detail, concentration, how to work with others...lots of things. It isn't all about survival skills. I know we must seem like backward savages, but it's a good life we lead. It's an honest and happy one."

Jas hesitated to reply, but she couldn't square Ozment's statements with what she'd seen of the underworlders so far. "I don't know. Do you really think the underworlders hereabouts are happy? They don't seem to be leading very honest lives. "

"It's harder in the city. There's a lot of crime and a lot of prejudice against naturals. Sometimes they have to do unsavory things to survive. They would be better off in the country. I've often tried to persuade Erielle to come down and live with us, but her followers are used to city life. They won't leave, and she won't leave them."

They were exiting the underworld neighborhood and heading downtown to the business and government district.

Jas tried to imagine where Erielle might have gone if she were injured. She regretted not arranging a place where they could meet in such an eventuality. They'd only spoken in terms of the success or failure of the plan.

Ozment broke into her musings. "Where are you from on Mars?"

"Valles Marineris Five."

"Oh, krat. I'm sorry." He glanced at her. "But, you're...?"

"I was a baby when it happened."

"I see. I didn't think there were any survivors."

"I was the only one. My parents got me into a survival capsule just in time, but it was too late for them. The colony records were destroyed, so I don't know who they were. When I was twelve, the authorities shipped me to Earth to finish my education." She preferred to deal with the inevitable questions all at once. It got the subject out of the way.

Ozment considered a moment, then asked, "Did you know...you might be one of us?"

Jas turned to him. "What do you mean?"

"There were Green Earthers at Valles Marineris Five."

Jas slumped back. *Green Earthers, like the people on Dawn?* "How come? Surely Green Earthers wouldn't have wanted to undergo the anti-radiation gene therapy?"

"For the sake of forging a new life on a new, unspoilt planet, some of them were prepared to bend their morals a little. And, after all, it's just the once. As you know, the effect gets passed on, even to children naturally conceived, so there's no need for any further modding or unnatural alterations. All of us get to be this beautiful color." He gave her a wink.

The idea that Jas's parents might have been Green Earthers had never occurred to her. She'd always thought of them as ordinary colonists—adventurers, maybe, excited at the idea of life on a colony planet, or trying to escape poverty, or running away from some kind of trouble. She'd never thought that her mother and father might have been underworlders.

# EIGHT

Jas directed Ozment to park in the alley where she and the others had stopped before their first attempt to kidnap Shadow Bernie.

"Where should we start looking?" he asked.

"The HQ is a couple of streets away, but I can't go near that place. The Shadows there know me. Out here should be safe enough for a little while. How about you go and check out all around the building? If she's there, she'll see you, and maybe she can attract your attention."

"But you said she went inside? If she's hurt, wouldn't she be there?"

"The only reason she got in there was because she was covered in invisibility spray. If you try to go in without ID, they'll arrest you. We have to hope that she managed to make it outside." The pit of Jas's stomach ached. "It's been two nights. I can't believe her supposedly loyal followers haven't tried to do something to find her."

"I think Durfy's behind that. There aren't many who'll go against him. But we're trying to do something now at least. Tell me where to go."

Jas explained how to get to the Security HQ. When Ozment left, she got out of the car and walked up and down the alley. She'd had a crazy hope that Erielle might have made her way there and was waiting for someone to come, but of course Erielle hadn't known they'd stopped in that spot.

She went to the end of the alley and looked out into the bustling street. Cabs and private cars buzzed by. Occasionally, a single-seater, low-slung autobike flashed through the traffic, most likely speeding, but few paid attention to speed limits. Computer-controlled cars meant that serious accidents were a thing of the past. Jas mused that Carl would probably love to ride an autobike.

There were few pedestrians. In the business districts, people went from their cars into the offices and back again. There was little reason to wander the streets. If Erielle was somewhere nearby, that fact would work in her favor. Few pedestrians meant few people likely to stumble across an invisible, injured woman.

Of course, the most likely reason for Erielle's absence was that she'd been killed or captured by Shadows. Jas hoped that if that was the case, that it was the former rather than the latter. She didn't want to face the problem of a Shadow Erielle turning up.

Standing in the street without any obvious purpose, Jas was attracting stares, so she returned to the car. After another twenty-five minutes, Ozment also came back. He'd found no sign of the missing underworld leader.

"That place is crawling with security agents, on foot and driving," he said. "People in suits and uniformed guards are patrolling the area. I had a look around, but there was no sign of any blood or anything that might lead us to Erielle. I hung about as long as I could. If Erielle was conscious, she would have seen me. I listened out in case she called me, but I didn't hear anything."

"Krat. I guess it was too much to hope for. Let's walk the route she would have taken if she were trying to get home. Maybe we'll find her on the way."

They set off. Jas put her arm through Ozment's but grimaced and went to his other side. Her shoulder wound was still painful. She linked arms with him again, so that they looked like a couple out for a stroll. The man's arm was firmly muscled. Jas imagined he must have a lot a physical labor in his work growing kratom. As they walked, they stopped at any likely spot where Erielle might be—in alleys, behind dumpsters, in disused doorways. They softly called her name, and surreptitiously ran their feet along the ground, hoping to meet an invisible obstruction.

"You know," Ozment said, "we could always break into the head-quarters. If they caught her, they might still be holding her there."

"I'd like to think so," Jas replied, "but I doubt it. When they captured Sayen, they took her away to a trap immediately."

"A trap?"

Jas had forgotten Ozment still didn't know about the Shadows or the reason why Erielle had gone with them to capture someone from the Security HQ. She sighed. "Okay. I'll explain. But, please, you can't tell anyone. The reason why will become clear."

"If it might help Erielle, I can keep a secret."

"I'm sorry, but, honestly, I think Erielle's beyond our help. Do you still promise to keep this to yourself?"

"I do."

Jas looked into the man's reddish-brown eyes. As had lately become her habit, she searched for signs that he might be a Shadow. She saw none, and she had no bad feelings about him, but that didn't stop her from worrying that she might be mistaken. She wondered if she would ever lose that feeling about every new person she met.

She sighed again. "Let's go back to the car and drive through the area we've covered. Then we can park again and explore farther from there. When we've checked everywhere Erielle might be, I'll explain. I don't want to delay our search for her. We've delayed long enough."

They looked for the missing woman for the next few hours, but Erielle was nowhere to be found.

After they'd covered all the ground they could, they parked. Jas explained to Ozment about the Shadows and briefly went over what had happened since they'd first encountered them at K. 67092d.

"So, there's really no way to tell these Shadows apart from their victims?" Ozment asked when she'd finished.

"It depends. If you see one soon after they've made the switch, there's something odd about them. They look kind of empty, like there's nothing behind their eyes. And they lose concentration easily.

We think they communicate telepathically and that sometimes they're having a conversation in their heads. But after a while, when they're used to their new bodies, no, you can't really tell. Not until one of them attacks you, of course.

"And the funny thing is, the closer you are, or the more friendly you feel toward one of them, the harder it is to notice they aren't who you think they are." She swallowed. "I was affectionate with a man on Dawn, and I didn't realize he'd been swapped with a Shadow. I just thought he was upset at me about something. He nearly got me into one of their traps. I ended up having to kill him."

"His Shadow, you mean."

"Yes, his Shadow. Of course."

Ozment was quiet for a moment. He looked out the car window. They'd stopped at the edge of the underworlder territory, and they were surrounded by dilapidated, abandoned, derelict buildings.

"If those misborns have captured Erielle," he said quietly, "we have to get her back."

"I want to too. But she probably isn't at the headquarters anymore. Anyway, I wouldn't even know how to get inside. I know you said we could break in, but that's the Global Government Security building for krat's sake. It isn't like you can pop a lock on a window and sneak inside."

"No. When I said break in," Ozment said, "I didn't mean like a burglar. I meant *break* in." He started the car. "I'll show you what I mean."

He drove the short distance back to Erielle's place, but he passed by the final turn and instead entered the next road, which was wider. A huge truck was parked at the other end of Erielle's alley.

"That's yours?" Jas asked.

"How else do you think I make my deliveries?"

"That's a monster."

He smiled. "Wait till you see inside."

They got out of their vehicle and went to the truck's cab. Ozment unlocked it, and Jas climbed in. The interior had a sweet, slightly rotten odor, which she assumed was the smell of kratom. The wide seats were covered in cracked, very soft material that also exuded an unusual smell. It took her a moment to realize what the material was.

"This is leather, isn't it?" she asked.

"Yeah. The truck's pretty old, but she's a good one, and we've made some modifications." Ozment looked up the street and checked the surround-view screens on the dashboard. The road was empty. He turned and opened an almost invisible, square door behind the seats. Jas saw a sloping tunnel with indentations for hands and feet, leading up into darkness.

"We created a false roof. Up there's a toy to keep the Shadows busy while we try to find Erielle."

"I admit I'm impressed, but why would you need heavy weaponry? That seems a little excessive, even for a kratom grower."

"When you live on the fringes of modern society, Jas, you need all the protection you can get."

"Okay, Ozment, but I don't see how a mortar or whatever it is that's up there will get us inside the HQ. It'll take a lot to get through their defenses."

"Okay, check this out." He thumbed a button, and the cab juddered as a metal wall rose to cover the windscreen. As darkness fell inside, the dashboard lit up with an electronic display that included a screen showing images from cameras on the outside. "That's reinforced, laser-proof steel. With that in front, and the power of this truck's engines, we could punch right through a solid wall."

# NINE

When Jas and Ozment returned to Erielle's place, all hell had broken loose. Durfy had persuaded the other underworlders to launch another attack. This time, Jas got to see him at work from another perspective. He was standing on the stairs, watching as the drugged-up men and women tried to force their way into the medical center.

They'd arrived not a moment too soon, for the resistance inside the room had clearly collapsed, and the underworlders were streaming in. Ozment shouted at them as he had before, but he had less of an effect, maybe because his delivery was unloaded and safely in their possession. A shriek came from inside the room.

There was only one way to stop them, Jas realized. Instead of targeting the underworlders, she ran straight to Durfy. His gloating expression vanished when he saw her. He fumbled for something inside his jacket, but Jas had a weapon pressed against his temple before he could reach it.

"Call them off," she barked. "Now, or so help me, I'll—"

"Okay, okay," Durfy muttered.

Jas stuck a hand into his jacket and pulled out a blaster, which she tossed to Ozment. She forced Durfy down the stairs and into the medical center. The room was in chaos. Several bodies lay on the floor. Three underworlders were grappling with Sayen, and another was in a fistfight with Carl, who was trying to protect Makey. The remaining underworlders were dragging the minister from her bed. She was clinging to the headboard with her fingertips, but as Jas went in, they ripped her away and lifted her onto their shoulders.

The minister shrieked for a second time. Ozment followed them in and set upon the underworlders who were fighting with Sayen.

"Stop them, now," Jas shouted at Durfy.

"Okay, everyone, that's enough," the man said half-heartedly.

Jas ground the point of her weapon into his skull.

"That's enough," he repeated, louder. When the underworlders still didn't respond, he said, "A new run for everyone who stops now."

That message got through, and the antagonists stopped fighting. The ones holding the minister dropped her onto the bed. Sayen took a moment too long to understand what was happening, and she thrust her elbow into the side of a man's head, sending him spinning to the floor. As she did so, she became aware that the fight was over. "Ooops, sorry."

"What about her?" asked an underworlder, indicating the minister. "You said she could get us some myth."

"Looks like I was wrong," Durfy replied.

"You're only saying that 'cos she'll kill you if you don't," said the underworlder, looking at Jas, who was maintaining her position with her gun pressed against Durfy's head.

"Come on, guys," said Ozment, his hands on his hips. "Take a look at yourselves. What are you doing? These people are Erielle's guests. What kind of hospitality is this? Is this what underworlders stand for? Fighting women half your size?" He eyed Sayen, who was surrounded by three unconscious men. "Dragging old ladies from their beds?" The minister's eyes flashed, but she said nothing. "Is this what Erielle taught you? Is this how she'd like you to behave?"

"They're digifreaks. They don't deserve our respect," said an underworlder.

Ozment sighed and shook his head. "This is what comes of living out of touch with nature. *All* living things deserve your respect, especially other human beings. Sometimes we have to lie, and steal, and cheat. Sometimes we even have to kill. But we don't do it unless we have to. And we certainly don't do it for the sake of a run. What's wrong with you people? What nonsense has this man been whispering in your ears?"

"Oh, quit with the lecture," said another underworlder. "You come up from the country, thinking you can tell us what to do and how to live our lives. You don't live on the street. You don't know anything."

"Hey," Jas said. "I'm sick and tired of living here anyway. You don't want us here, so we'll leave. Just let us go in peace, okay? We'll be out of your way by this evening."

"You sure, Jas?" Carl asked.

"Yes. Are you well enough to move, Makey?"

"Yes, I am. I've been up and walking around today."

"Great."

"You're right," Sayen said. "It's time for us to go. But, in case you were wondering, she comes with us." She pointed at Bathsheba.

"No," Durfy said. "I'm not agreeing to that. She stays."

"Yeah, she can tell us where the myth is," said an underworlder.

"No, I can't," Bathsheba said shrilly. "I have no idea where it's kept. I can't help you with that. But when the police catch you, I do have the authority to uphold the death penalty if I feel you have threatened global security, which you can be assured I do."

"*If* the police catch us," said the underworlder. "Not seen a cop around here in the last five years. Anyone else?"

Another underworlder puffed air between relaxed lips. "I don't know. Probably not worth the risk. I heard that myth isn't all it's hyped up to be anyway."

"Look," said Ozment, "you let them walk out of here free—all of them—and I promise I won't hold a grudge. Delivery as normal next month. You don't want to lose your kratom, do you? Or the food I bring you? Come on, guys, see sense."

"Okay, let them go," said the second underworlder who had spoken. The first began to protest, but the others drowned him out with calls of agreement.

Durfy was scowling. "You've got an hour," he said between his teeth before stalking out of the room. The rest of the underworlders left with him, except the ones who were unconscious or dead.

"We're going to Erielle's safe house?" Sayen asked Jas.

"It seems for the best, don't you think? Do you still have the map?"

"I do. I take it you didn't find Erielle?"

"No, we didn't. I'm sorry."

Sayen looked down. "I guess it's better than finding her body."

Jas put a hand on her shoulder. "There's still hope. Ozment here has an idea for storming the security HQ and rescuing her, if she's there."

"Storming that building?" Sayen snorted and shook her head. "No chance."

"You haven't seen his truck."

———

It took them less than an hour to pack up what little stuff they had. A lot of Erielle's medical supplies and equipment had been trashed in the fight, but Sayen picked through them and gathered up what she could that she thought might be useful. Makey still required regular dressing changes and antiseptic sprays, she explained. Sayen seemed to be taking along a lot more than that, Jas thought, but she didn't object. With Erielle gone, the remaining underworlders seemed to be descending into a state where medical treatment would be low on their agenda.

They asked Sark if she wanted to come with them, but the woman said no. There were many young and innocent mouths to feed, and she wouldn't ever begrudge a meal to the worst of them. They were all human beings, after all. Ozment told her she was a person after his own heart, and that he hoped things were better when he returned in about a month.

They drove to the safe house in his truck. The cab was large enough for them all to squeeze in. Carl was so impressed with the vehicle he could barely speak. It wasn't far to their new place, but it was difficult to get there through the streets of the old neighbor-hood. Ozment had to drive out onto wider roads, then approach the house from a different direction.

Eventually, he stopped outside. It was a small building, dwarfed by newer, but still very old apartment blocks on either side. The yard was overgrown, and it looked like no one had set foot on it in ages. The gate was ajar, and the windows were blank and dark. It was late dusk, and no lights shone from inside, which Jas was glad of. Everything indicated the house was unoccupied. She hoped none of Durfy's followers would find them there and try to force them out, for a few days at least.

She pushed at the gate, but it was stuck and wouldn't open any wider. She tried again. The hinge gave a moan. It was no use; the gate would only open wide enough for her to squeeze through. They would have to lift their belongings over.

As she stepped through, her foot caught on something, and she fell. Astonished, she looked back at whatever had tripped her. There was nothing there. It had been something large, soft—and invisible.

# TEN

"What's wrong, Jas?" asked Sayen as she saw the woman's expression. They were on their way into the safe house, and she was holding a bundle of clothes they'd brought with them from Erielle's place. She gazed in wonder as she saw Jas drop down and begin manhandling something Sayen couldn't see. *Something she couldn't see.*

The clothes fell from her grasp, and for a moment she was frozen. Then she was at Jas's side, and she too could feel the warm, soft, invisible body beneath her hands. "Erielle," she gasped.

Jas had a handful of grass, and she was rubbing it on the prone figure. Bits and pieces of Erielle began to appear as she scrubbed off the invisibility spray. Her clothes, a part of an arm.

"Wait," said Sayen. She had figured out how the underworld leader was lying. She pushed her onto her back and pressed an ear between her breasts. "Be quiet," she hissed, as exclamations of realization came from Makey and Carl. The street had no traffic, but it still took several long seconds before Sayen heard a heartbeat. It was slow and faint, but it was there.

"Get the door open, Jas," said Ozment.

Sayen found Erielle being pulled from her grasp as the large man scooped her up in his arms. She followed him into the dark house and the first room they saw. Inside was a dusty, old sofa. He laid Erielle down on it. Someone found the light switch. Someone else was asking for soap and water. All Sayen could do was hold Erielle's invisible wrist and feel for the thready pulse. Then she heard the underworlder murmur.

"Wait, she's saying something," Sayen said to Jas, who was cleaning the spray from Erielle's face. She leaned close. Only Erielle's right cheekbone, ear, and eye were visible. Her skin was translucent and drawn tightly over her cheekbones. Her eye was sunken in its socket. Sayen bent down to her mouth.

Erielle was speaking so softly, she could barely make out what the woman was saying. "Oh-seven-three...four-seven...two..."

"Can you understand?" Jas asked.

Sayen nodded. "Wait a minute." She listened some more, and Erielle repeated herself twice. "Okay, Erielle, I've got it now," she said, but the woman didn't seem to hear her because she continued to repeat the numbers.

"What's she saying?" asked Ozment.

"I don't know. It's a set of ten numbers. Could it be a key lock? Or a code? Do underworlders use encryption codes?"

"Not that I've ever heard of," said Ozment. "Ten numbers? What if it's just a phone number?"

"A phone number? Of course. It might be just that. Could you call it for us?"

"I've got an interface in the cab of the truck. It's untraceable. Come with me."

Sayen followed the Martian to his vehicle and climbed inside. She spoke the number into the interface, and a call went through, but it was a long time before the callee picked up. A middle-aged man's face wearing a suspicious expression appeared on the screen.

"Hello? Who is this?"

"Hi," Sayen said, "you don't know me, but please don't hang up."

"Why can't I see your face? If you're selling—"

"I'm not selling anything. I got your number from someone

who's in need of help. She's saying this number over and over again. I think she wants me to call you."

The man's expression changed from suspicion to annoyance. "I'm sorry, I think maybe you have a wrong number. Anyone I know who's in need of help would go to the..." He paused, and a look of recognition began to dawn on his face. "Who is this person?"

"Her name's Erielle, and she's very, very badly hurt."

"Erielle," breathed the man. "After all this time. Where are you calling from? I'll be right there."

Ozment gave the man the address. He frowned as he took it and seemed to momentarily reconsider his decision, but before he hung up, he said he would be there in twenty minutes.

When they got back inside, Jas had cleaned all the invisibility spray from Erielle, and at the sight of her, Sayen nearly collapsed. A deep laser wound ran across both her thighs, halfway to her knees. The muscle was visible, and Sayen thought she could even see bone. Her arms were also a mess. Unable to walk, Erielle must have dragged herself on her arms all the way from the Security HQ. She bore dark red scabs from her elbows to her wrists.

Jas was dripping water into her mouth, but some was running out unswallowed, as Erielle continued to mouth the phone number over and over again.

"She made it all this way," said Sayen. "Why didn't she come back to us?"

"I guess she couldn't make it any farther," Jas said. "Not even a few more streets. She must have seen the safe house, dragged herself inside, and collapsed."

"How long has she been lying there?" Sayen asked. "Oh why didn't we come here earlier? If only we'd left last night."

"We're here now. We've found her, and she's safe. Did someone answer your call?"

"Yes. I think it was an old friend from when she was a doctor. He said he's coming over."

"She used to be a doctor?" Jas asked. "I never knew, but it makes sense."

Sayen knelt by the sofa and looked more closely at Erielle's thighs. They were a mess, and at close range, Sayen detected a putrid, rotting odor. The wounds were going bad. Sayen prayed that she was right in guessing that the man she'd called was a surgeon, and that—somehow—he could save Erielle's legs.

Then it hit her. "What are we doing?" she said. "This is crazy. Erielle could die. Nothing's worth that. I'm going to call an ambulance." She went to return to Ozment's truck, but she found her way barred by the man's large frame.

"No," he said. "Erielle wouldn't want it."

"You don't know that," said Sayen. "I'm pretty sure she'd want to live." She tried to sidestep Ozment, but he moved to block her again.

"I do know that," he said gently. "I've known her a long time. She *would* rather die than be a part of a system that's caused so much pain and suffering in our world."

"You mean the medical system? That's saved so many lives and cured so many people?" Sayen asked shrilly. "Erielle told me what she found out, but this is different. This is life or death."

"This isn't the time for a debate. I can see how deeply you care about her. We have to respect her wishes."

Sayen clenched her fists and tried to hold back the hot tears that sprang unwanted to her eyes. Deep down, she knew Ozment was right. In the short time she'd known Erielle, she'd made her disgust for modern health services and their obsession with human perfection very clear. But Sayen felt so helpless. She couldn't bear to stand by and watch Erielle pass away.

There was a quiet knock at the front door. Ozment moved aside, and Sayen ran to open it. The man she'd called was waiting, a black case in his hand. He glanced from side to side before entering.

The sight of Erielle made him pause a moment, as if he didn't recognize her at first. He shook his head and went to her side. "My dear friend, whatever's happened to you?" he asked. Opening his case, he said without looking around, "I need one person to assist me. The rest of you, out."

"I'll help," blurted Sayen, and she sprang to the man's side.

# Eleven

Three days had passed, and they had three days still to go before the shipment of Shadow scanners from the Transgalactic Council arrived. They'd found dried food stored in the safe house to keep them going. Jas was in the back yard. Once, a lawn must have grown there, but now the area was a mess of weeds and trash that had blown in from the street. The sun was hot and the air was humid. She sat alone on an old swing seat on the porch, leaning against the decayed wooden slats, which were coated in ancient, flaking paint.

The mysterious man Sayen had called had just delivered the news that, after several dicey moments, it looked like Erielle would live. The man never gave his name, and whenever he turned up, he spent most his time with his patient. They had turned the living room into a bedroom as the man had advised, saying that he didn't want to risk even moving Erielle to another room.

The underworld leader's wounds were free of infection at last and on the mend, and she was able to eat and drink normally. He'd said she needed surgery to walk again, but so far she'd refused all mention of such treatment.

Try as she might, Jas couldn't understand why anyone in their right mind would rather be paraplegic than undergo restorative surgery. But that was Erielle's choice, she decided, and ceased worrying about it. She had to plan their next course of action, but the gentle rocking of the seat and the heat of the day were sending her into a doze.

They no longer had to concern themselves with finding Erielle, which meant they no longer had to go through with Ozment's plan of storming the security HQ. They could focus instead on stealing one of the Shadow scanners. But the spaceport where the scanners were arriving was a state away, and they had to make their attempt when it was dark. They would have to spend a night on the road on their way there, Jas calculated. She needed time to scope out the site in daylight and plan the best method for breaking in and getting out alive.

In her bedroom were all the weapons that she and Carl had taken from Erielle's stash, and Ozment had some serious artillery in his truck, so firepower wouldn't be too much of a problem. It was really that there were so few of them that made the project risky. She didn't want anyone to get hurt. If only she had ten or fifteen deep space defense units, she would feel much more confident.

The back door opened with a squeak of rusty hinges, and Makey came out. He no longer wore a dressing over the wound on his neck. It was healing nicely, and a shiny, pink scar was forming. Jas got the impression that the kid was rather proud of it.

"Hey, Jas," he said. "Did you hear the news? Erielle's going to be okay."

"Yeah, I heard. It's great news."

Makey sat down next to her, pushing the swing backward. "So what are we going to do now? Are we going to break into a spaceport and steal some scanners?"

"Hmmm...so you overheard the minister? Well, I was just thinking about that, but I'm not sure what you mean by *we*."

"Awww, come on. You have to let me come too."

"I *have* to? Do I?"

Makey groaned. He jumped to his feet, performed a mock salute and said, "Permission to come too, ma'am."

Jas laughed. "Sit down. I don't know. I haven't decided yet, to be honest. Someone has to stay with Erielle, and I'm guessing I won't be able to separate Sayen from her, which is a shame because with her enhancements, she's very useful."

"But that means only you, Carl, and Ozment will be there. That isn't enough. You need me."

The kid was right. Though she hated the thought of taking someone so young into such a dangerous situation, they would need everyone they could get. And Makey seemed to have learned his lesson since Antarctica. She didn't think he would disobey another order so lightly again.

"Well..." she said, and Makey's expression brightened. "We'll see." His expression fell. "How about I give you some training, and if you do well enough, you can come."

"That sounds great," he exclaimed. "Can we start right now?"

"Not yet," Jas replied. "We'll wait until the sun swings round into the yard. It'll make the laser beams less easy to see from a distance. You showed you were a good shot when you and Carl saved my life on Dawn, but some target practice never hurts. For now, go to your room and do the exercises I showed you to build up your core strength. I'll call you when it's time."

Makey didn't need telling twice. He was gone in a moment. Carl caught the door as it swung to behind the kid and closed it. He took Makey's place next to Jas and spread his arms along the back of the seat. Neither said anything, but the silence between them felt comfortable.

After a little while, Carl said, "I was talking to Ozment about his farm."

"Oh yeah?"

"Yeah. Sounds like a great place. They grow all kinds of crops down there. Keep goats and pigs too. Got a good set up."

Carl seemed to be leading up to something, and Jas wondered what it was. Was he planning on going there when this business with the Shadows was over?

"Seems like a nice guy," Carl went on.

He was on edge about something. Jas could tell from the way his accent had gotten stronger. She liked the sound of his Australian drawl. It gave her a warm feeling.

"Ozment?" she said. "I was suspicious of him at first, but I think you're right. He's okay."

"I suppose you and he get along pretty well. With him being another Martian, I mean."

They had both been looking out into the view from the back yard, which was of a derelict building site that had been abandoned, leaving only the foundation. At Carl's sentence, however, Jas turned to look at him. He continued to gaze steadily out and wouldn't meet her eyes.

"Oh Carl, don't be an idiot."

He finally looked at her. "What do you mean?"

"I like Ozment, but not like that." She sighed. "The last time I got close to someone, I ended up bashing in his Shadow's head with a rock. Even if I did want something more with Ozment—which I don't—this isn't the right time. A lot of people are going to lose the ones they love before this is all over. It doesn't make a lot of sense to open ourselves up to more hurt."

"Yeah, I suppose you're right."

Jas returned her gaze to the distance, and another silence fell. The sun's beams crept slowly into the yard, lighting up the weeds and the insects that flew and danced among them. After a little while, Jas leaned her head against Carl's shoulder, and he wrapped his arm around her. They stayed in that position, neither saying a word, until Makey burst out of the house, asking breathlessly if it was time for target practice yet.

# TWELVE

The next day, as Jas was teaching Makey some hand-to-hand fighting techniques, murmuring voices came from Erielle's room, growing louder. Soon, shouting could be heard. Erielle was arguing with her doctor friend.

"For krat's sake, see sense, woman," shouted the man. "You were always stubborn, but this is ridiculous."

Erielle retorted, "Just forget it, okay? You'd never understand."

"And what's *that* supposed to mean?"

"I said, forget it."

"Forget it? After I've brought you back from the brink of death? After I've ventured into this gangland for you? Do you know the cabs won't even come down this street? They stop at the end, and I have to walk the rest of the way, risking life and limb at the hands of your underworld thugs."

"Hey," exclaimed Erielle, "don't talk about my friends that way."

"Did your friends save your life? Are your friends offering to operate on you and give you back the ability to walk? When I heard you were in trouble, I hadn't seen you for twenty years. I didn't know if you were alive or dead. But I came. I came because I was told you needed me. But apparently not. Apparently, I'm not one of your *friends*. That's it, Erielle. It's over. I suggest you forget my number, because the next time I receive an anonymous call, I won't be answering it."

Loud footsteps rang from the hallway, and the house resounded as the front door was slammed shut.

Makey was lying on the floor, where Jas had thrown him. He raised himself up on his elbows. "I don't think he'll be back."

"No, I don't think so either," Jas agreed. "But Erielle sounds a lot better. I'll go in to see her later. Come on, get up. Now, you work the same move on me."

Makey stood and waited for Jas to run at him. When she did, he grappled her and hooked his foot behind her ankle. She landed on her back. "Well done," she told him from the floor. "That should work on someone taller than you who has some momentum going. You can use that to unbalance them and—"

Sayen flung open the door and marched in. She threw herself into a chair and crossed her arms. "Oh, sorry," she said when she noticed Jas and Makey. "You carry on. I just had to get away from Erielle. She's driving me insane. I've tried everything I can think of to get her to change her mind, but she's adamant. She'd rather spend the rest of her life scooting around on a board with wheels than get her legs fixed. Can you believe it?"

"I don't understand it either," Jas said, "but if she doesn't want the surgery, what can you do?"

"But you should see her legs. They're healing up all right, but they look awful. There's hardly any tissue left where the laser hit her. It isn't only a matter of her never walking again. If she doesn't have treatment, she's going to be in pain for the rest of her life. She doesn't say anything, but she's in constant, severe pain all the time already. You can see it on her face. I think she hardly sleeps at night because of it. Ozment's been doping her up with kratom, but I don't think it's enough. Who would choose to live like that?"

"Most of the Dawntowners would," said Makey. "The older ones, anyway. The first generation colonists, they were almost all like that. I never really understood it either, but Erielle's way of thinking isn't that unusual to me."

Sayen shook her head sadly. "I just don't get it."

"Me either," Jas said. "But don't forget she grew up in a different time from us. That seems to have something to do with it. Today's generation of underworlders don't seem to hold the same strong opinions about global control through technology. They seem to be mostly naturals who can't get jobs, or addicts. I think the old Green Earthers developed their ideas when the world was changing rapidly, and people had to decide whether or not to continue with technological development. People like Erielle only see the bad that technology brought with it."

Sayen sighed. "She's told me what happened that opened her eyes to the things she hates about the world today, and it was terrible. But I still don't understand. If she allows her friend to operate, it doesn't make her a participant in the way our society's run. It doesn't mean she's doing those things herself."

"For some people," Makey said, "it's the same thing. My da thinks he's tainted if he touches anything 'unnatural' as he puts it. He has to go and wash himself afterward. It's strange, but it's the way he thinks."

Ozment came into the room. "Erielle's asking for you, Sayen."

She got up to leave.

"Wait a minute," Jas said. "We're setting off tomorrow. Are you coming, or do you want to stay here? We can't take the minister with us. We need someone to guard her for another few days. And Erielle..."

Her expression sad, Sayen said, "I can't leave her. Not yet." She went out.

"We need to talk," Jas said to Ozment. "Are you still on board with helping us steal a Shadow scanner?"

"Yes, I am." He rubbed his hands together. "It's been a while since I did anything downright criminal."

"You don't count growing kratom as criminal?" Jas asked, her eyebrows raised.

"I'm nothing but a simple farmer," Ozment replied. "I can't help it if my crops have special properties." He winked at Makey.

"Hey, no corrupting the kid."

"Wouldn't dream of it."

Jas narrowed her eyes at him. "So, let's figure out our route, and what we need to take."

"I've got the route figured out already. We can stop overnight at a national park. I can park the truck behind some RVs where it won't attract too much attention. We'll blend in with the tourists. It's busy there this time of year."

"Sounds good. We'll have to leave some weapons here for Sayen. She'll be by herself with an invalid and a hostage to protect. I wouldn't put it past Durfy and his clan to figure out where we are. I don't like leaving her."

"We can give her plenty of guns," said Ozment. "Once we're inside the cargo warehouse, there shouldn't be much need for fighting. The guards will be on the perimeter. My truck will get us through that. Smash, grab, and run." He grinned. "Like the old days."

# THIRTEEN

They came from across the abandoned building site in the early hours of the morning. Jas was asleep. She'd tied Bathsheba to the other bed in the room. She hadn't liked doing it. Over the days that the minister had been living with them, Jas had grown accustomed to her. She didn't think she was a bad person, just misguided and out of touch, and perhaps too sure of herself. Jas believed she genuinely hadn't known that the Shadows had infiltrated Earth to the extent they had. As she fell asleep, Jas had been looking forward to the day they could let the older woman go.

The first Jas heard of the underworlders' attack was the tinkle of glass breaking. As her eyes flicked open, she reached for the blaster next to her bed. Her waking brain tried to compute where the sound had come from. It seemed to have been from the kitchen, which was below Jas's room. Carl and Makey shared the bedroom next door, Ozment had his own room at the front of the house, and Sayen and Erielle were in the living room.

Jas was already up and moving toward the door. The sound of someone breaking a window hadn't woken the minister. She lay on her back on top of her covers, wearing the same kaftan she'd worn when she'd been kidnapped. Jas contemplated untying her for her own safety, but decided against it. She was safer exactly as she was. If she ran off into the underworld territory at that hour of the night, she wouldn't last five minutes.

It had to be Durfy's gang. But were they there for Bathsheba, or had someone discovered that Erielle was there? Had Durfy come to assassinate the underworld leader so that he could take her place? Jas's stomach tightened. Erielle was entirely unable to defend herself, and Sayen was unarmed.

As she left the room, the door on her right opened. Carl emerged. Makey followed. They'd been woken by the noise too.

"Wake Ozment," Jas told Makey in an undertone. On bare feet, she went downstairs, her gun at the ready, Carl behind her.

All was dark. No streetlights were working, and the night was cloudy. Jas paused at the bottom stair, peering into the velvet blackness. She held her breath. Was someone in the hallway already? Watching her?

A slow creak came from the kitchen door. Jas was thankful for the rusty hinges. She lifted her weapon to fire, but she hesitated. What if it wasn't an underworlder, but Sayen, who had gone into the kitchen for a drink of water in the night? What if the sound she'd heard had been Sayen dropping a glass?

But the door to the living room began to open, and Jas knew where Sayen was. She fired at the dark figure emerging from the kitchen. There was a scream followed by shouting. The form that Jas had shot thumped to the floor. Scuffling and the sound of furniture being overturned was loud in the house.

The living room door had closed at the first shot. Jas kept her gun trained on the kitchen, but no one else emerged. She glanced up at Carl, who was on the steps above her, also waiting for the next move from the underworlders.

Jas was blinded by something on her left. A laser beam had shot right through the front door, narrowly missing her head. Her retinas burned, and she could see nothing but a red glow. "I'm blinded," she gasped to Carl. The hiss of his weapon told her he'd fired back through the door. He pushed her to one side.

"Get upstairs," he said. "Check on the minister. Ozment's here."

Groping on her hands and knees, Jas climbed the steps and felt her way along the hallway, trying to blink away the scarlet glare. Finding the doorknob by touch, she went into her bedroom. The minister was awake and asking her what was happening.

"The underworlders have found us," Jas replied. She searched for the bonds that tied the woman to the bed and began to untie the knots.

"They've come for me again?" Bathsheba asked nervously. "What if I tell them what they want to know? They'd let me go then, wouldn't they?"

"No, I don't think so," Jas said. She'd noticed the deep hatred the underworlders bore toward the woman, even if the minister hadn't. It wasn't only their hope that she could lead them to hard drugs that drove their desire to capture her. She didn't want to frighten her, but she didn't imagine Bathsheba would last long in Durfy's hands.

No more sounds of fighting were coming from downstairs. It looked like the underworlders had given up their attack for the moment. Jas's sight was also returning. Dark gray shapes were appearing from the fading red. Bathsheba's anxious face shone palely in the scant light. Jas was wondering what to do next—should they go on the offensive and drive the underworlders away, or should they wait until dawn—when someone ran up the stairs and along the hallway. Carl burst into the room.

"The kitchen's on fire," he exclaimed. "It's out of control. We've gotta get out."

"Krat. They're forcing us to leave. They're going to pick us off one by one the minute we go outside." Jas was untying the final knot at the minister's wrist.

The woman ripped her hand free and clutched at Jas. "Help me. I don't want to die."

"Then do as I say," Jas replied. "Is Ozment helping Erielle?" she asked Carl.

"Yes."

"Stick with Makey, then, Carl. Don't let him out of your sight. Tell everyone to wait in the hallway. We're coming. "

"Stay safe, Jas," Carl said, and he was gone.

She grabbed the bag of weapons. Everything else, she left. "Put on your shoes," she told Bathsheba. "Come with me and don't leave my side, no matter what happens."

The woman took Jas's last instruction literally. She clutched her arm in an almost painful grip. Jas swung the bag of weapons over her shoulder with her other hand and together they left the bedroom. Smoke from the kitchen made the dark house utterly impenetrable to sight. Jas reached for the banister rail. From below came the sound of coughing. They had only seconds to get out before smoke inhalation rendered everyone unconscious.

Bathsheba was gibbering frightened nonsense at her side as they felt their way quickly downstairs. "Calm down," Jas hissed. She was worried the woman would do something stupid in her terror and get them all killed.

"Ozment," she said into the choking smoke. "You've got to get your truck open. You'll have to go first. I'll cover you."

"I have to carry Erielle," he replied.

"No," came Sayen's voice, "I can do it. I can. Trust me."

"Okay," Ozment said.

Jas was at the front door. She slid her hand across it, found the handle and turned it. As she raised her weapon to fire through the gap, she was thrown roughly aside. It was Bathsheba. She ran out, shouting, "Don't shoot. Don't shoot. I'll—"

The buzz of laser fire was followed by a terrible shriek. The minister collapsed. Jas gasped, but she'd seen from where the underworlders were firing. She returned fire, shouting at Ozment, "Go. Now."

The large man sped over the short distance to his truck and was inside in a heartbeat. The laser proof steel shields rose up and slid into place around the cab. "Sayen, Erielle," shouted Jas, firing again into the darkness.

Sayen ran low across the front yard, carrying the crippled woman over her shoulder in a fireman's lift.

"Carl, fire at that alleyway. I'll take this side. Let's go."

Jas, Makey, and Carl raced to Ozment's truck. On the way, Jas glimpsed Bathsheba. She was on her back, her stomach and chest open, burned, and bleeding, her eyes flickering closed. Then the image was gone. Arms were pulling Jas into Ozment's cab. The engine was already running. The door was slammed shut, and they were driving into the night.

# Fourteen

Carl leaned an arm on the open window of the truck and watched the countryside speed past. Though the cab was large, it wasn't meant to hold six people, and he was hot, cramped, and uncomfortable. Erielle was lying in the narrow space at the back, but everyone else was crammed across the long bucket seat at the front. It didn't help that the air-conditioning seemed to have given out under the strain of trying to cool six bodies. Only the breeze pouring in the window gave some relief.

"How long now?" Carl asked Ozment and immediately regretted it. He sounded like a whiny kid. The fact was, as well as the confined conditions bothering him, he hated it when someone else was driving.

"Couple more hours," came the reply.

Carl couldn't wait to arrive at the national park that was to be their halfway stop on the way to the spaceport. He was sure the others felt the same. The general mood was very low. Jas was deeply cut up about the death of the minister, Carl could tell. He didn't think she should blame herself so much. If the woman hadn't been trying to brush the problem of the Shadows under the carpet, she and a lot more people would still be alive.

Sayen had a line between her eyes that never seemed to go away.

She was worrying about Erielle, no doubt. The underworlder wasn't really well enough to be moved. Ozment was concentrating on the road. Makey was the only one who seemed relatively cheerful.

They'd been driving through flat farmland for hours, but the mountains that had been far distant were drawing close, and the fields had given way to sparse woods. The air outside grew cooler as dusk drew on, and they drove into the shadow of the trees. Slowly, the road began to slope upward.

"Can we stop for some water?" Sayen asked Ozment.

"Sure. There's a camping store along here somewhere, if I remember right. We can have a rest stop and stock up. We'll need sleeping bags. Gets cold up in the mountains at night."

"We can't pay for anything," said Jas. "Erielle's crew stole our credchips, but we couldn't use them anyway. The Shadows know that we know about them. They're looking for us."

"Don't worry. I'll pay. You can pay me back with labor on my farm." He turned and winked to show that he was joking, but his words caused an ache of homesickness in Carl. He would have given a lot to be back on his parents' farm, dusting crops with Flux beside him in the cockpit. He hoped the little fella was doing okay in his absence. He wished he could call him.

"What do you grow, apart from kratom, I mean?" Jas asked Ozment.

"Bananas, avocado, watermelon, guava, eggplants, mangoes, papayas, oranges, peaches, peanuts, sweetcorn, tomatoes, squash, beans, passionfruit, lychees, lettuce—"

"Whoa, you grow a lot of stuff."

"Yeah, I don't only deal in narcotics, you know. I run a mean sideline in fruit and vegetables too."

His joke broke the tension somewhat, and the cooler temperatures and prospect of an imminent escape from the close confines of the truck's cab also sparked a shift in mood.

"Do you drive this route when you go to the city?" Jas asked.

"No. It's pretty, but the freeway is faster. I've been here for a break a few times, though. The road's wide enough for the truck."

"Is it busy this time of year?"

"It didn't use to be, but lately it's become popular with alien tourists. It's within a few hours of the spaceport, and they can spend a day or so here in a typical Earth landscape before heading off on a tour of the major sites."

Makey sat up. "Aliens? I've only ever seen the haidiren. What are they like?"

"You see all kinds of weird and wonderful creatures up there. Should be interesting for you."

Ozment's comment also piqued Carl's interest. Though he'd visited more planets than he could easily count, shuttle pilots on prospecting missions were generally required to remain with their spacecraft in case of an emergency evacuation. And his parents' farm was far from the tourist areas where visiting aliens were commonly seen.

"Won't we stand out?" asked Jas. "We hardly look like tourists. The last thing we want to do is attract attention."

"Maybe a little," Ozment replied. "But I don't see how that can be helped. We'd stick out more at a regular truck stop, that's for sure. There aren't many truckers who try to squeeze six people, including an invalid, into their cabs. Besides, the only authorities up there are the rangers. They see all kinds of folks and don't pay them any mind as long as they follow the rules. We should be okay."

Carl settled back in his seat and let the refreshing air from the window cool the sweat on his neck and chest. In another few minutes a single story cabin appeared on the side of the road. The camping store had parking space for RVs around the back. Carl, Jas, and Ozment went into the store while Sayen and Makey stretched their legs.

A warm, musty, pleasant scent of wood greeted them inside the camping store. It was filled floor to ceiling with equipment for basic through luxury camping. A red-cheeked young woman sat behind the counter watching an interface on the wall. Jas and Ozment went to look at the sleeping bags, and Carl went over to see the screen, which was showing the latest vidnews. He'd been attracted by a flash of a building that looked familiar. As he watched, he found his suspicion was correct. The screen displayed an aerial view of the Global Government Security Headquarters.

"Can I help you, sir?" asked the woman as she noticed Carl standing there.

"No, thanks. I'm waiting for my friends."

An image of Bathsheba Dubois appeared, looking very different from when Carl had last seen her. She was in a Government meeting with other ministers, looking commanding and dignified. He remembered her fury at being kidnapped, and her descent into terror of Durfy's crew.

Another image appeared. It was an older man with white hair and a beard, closely clipped. He was well-dressed in a tailored navy suit. The unseen anchor announced that since her disappearance, the security minister's secretary had been representing her at meetings, but as the police were no further with their investigation to find the missing official, a stand-in would be chosen as a temporary replacement.

The older man fitted the description of the Shadow Bernie that Sayen given them. So a Shadow had been taking part in Government meetings. Carl wondered if whoever was in line to be Bathsheba's replacement was also a Shadow. They had to contact the Transgalactic Council urgently before the aliens got any further in their takeover of Earth.

"Isn't it terrible?" the assistant asked Carl. "That poor woman. I wonder what they did to her? I guess there's no hope she's still alive after all this time."

"What did who do to her?"

"Didn't you hear? It's been all over the news."

"No, I've, er, been out in the woods for a couple of weeks."

"The police suspect she was kidnapped by that old Green Earthers cult that was supposed to have died out decades ago. It was before my time, but I heard they were pretty crazy. They say the cult's been revived, and they've turned to terrorism to try to get their way."

"Green Earthers, huh? They were a little before my time too. Did they publish their demands?"

"Not that I've heard, but the authorities seem pretty sure it was them."

Ozment and Jas appeared, their arms full of sleeping bags, bottles of water, and packets of snack food. After Ozment paid, they left.

"You've got a credchip embedded then?" Jas asked him as they went back to the truck.

"The farm's legit," he said, "even if not everything we grow on it is. There's only so much you can trade vegetables for."

"Traitor," said Jas with a wry smile.

# FIFTEEN

ayen fixed two sleeping bags together and slept next to Erielle
that night to share her body warmth with the injured
woman. She couldn't stop worrying about her. Though her
old doctor friend had saved her life, she was still far from better and
not in any fit state to be traveling for hours in a truck.

Erielle never mentioned it, but the underworlder was clearly in a
lot of pain. Ozment had supplied her with kratom pellets that kept
her in a sedated haze most of the time, but she was often pale and
sweaty before it was safe for her to take another dose. Erielle had
feeling in her legs but it was impossible for her to move them. When
they were accidentally moved or even touched by others, she would
cry out. Apart from requests for water and help with other basic
needs, she said very little. Sayen wondered how long it would be
before they could go somewhere safe, where Erielle could rest and get
better.

She tried to make herself comfortable on the floor at the back of
the truck, where she and the others had lain down after pulling into
the campsite after dark. Ozment had left the truck door ajar to let in
a little air. After hours of agitated fidgeting, Erielle was finally
breathing in the slow, steady manner that indicated she was asleep.

Sayen needed some exercise, however, before sleep would come to her.

After unfastening the sleeping bag as quietly as she could, she got up and padded across to the door, where she slipped on her shoes. She dropped onto the asphalt of the car park and headed for a trail that led up into the trees. It was a clear night, and the moon's beams and starlight made it easy to see without the help of her night vision.

Sayen hiked up the sloping trail for a kilometer or so, enjoying the freedom and the short respite from the harrowing events of the previous few days. Now that she had the leisure to go over everything in her mind, she could hardly believe all that had happened since she'd been captured by the Shadows at her workplace. It had been only a couple of weeks since she'd left home by heli.

Thinking of her home made her wonder what was happening to her parents. Carl and Jas had said they were afraid to leave their estate. She hoped they were safe from the Shadows there. They had to be worrying about her, too. A sudden realization made her gasp. When Erielle had destroyed her tracker, the signal from it must have disappeared. Did her parents think she was dead?

Her eyes filled with tears. She'd never wanted to upset them or make them worry about her. She wished there was a way she could get a message to them to let them know she was okay, but she couldn't think of a method that wouldn't put either her or them in danger.

Sayen was so preoccupied with her thoughts, she didn't notice the aliens approaching her on the trail ahead until they were almost on top of her. They seemed to suddenly loom up out of nowhere. More than two meters tall and wide, four insectoid aliens bore down on her, black silhouettes against the starry night sky.

She gave a small scream, and the aliens stopped, seeming to only just notice her.

"I do apologize," one of them said. "We did not detect your scent among the many strange and wonderful odors of this environment." As it spoke, a second set of sharp mandibles protruded from the outer pair and dripped with mucus.

"Oh my word," gasped Sayen, stumbling backward.

"Please do not be alarmed. We are entirely harmless. Our species is noted for its natural pacifism, in fact. But we understand that our appearance is alarming to humans. That is why we are exploring this landscape at night, while most humans are sleeping. Please forgive us for frightening you."

Sayen swallowed and took a deep breath. Her heart was racing. "It's okay. You didn't scare me a lot." She was lying, but the creature seemed genuinely mortified that they had given her a shock. "Do...do you like it here? Have you been on Earth long?"

"From what we've seen of it so far," said the alien, "we like it very much. This area is particularly attractive. You must be very proud of your planet."

"Thanks. You're very kind," Sayen replied, slipping into the formal small talk she'd learned to use when speaking to important friends and associates of her parents. The whole situation felt slightly bizarre. "I, er, I hope you enjoy the rest of your vacation."

"Thank you. I am sure we will. It has been very pleasant to make your acquaintance."

"Likewise," Sayen said. "Well, I guess I'll be going."

"We hope you enjoy your walk," said the alien.

"Thank you. I'm sure I shall." She stepped to one side and suppressed a shudder as the aliens passed by, the claws on the ends of their ten pairs of legs faintly scratching against the wood chip path. She remained where she was until the creatures disappeared around a bend in the trail. Exhaling deeply, she went on.

At a high point on the track, the trees thinned out enough to allow a view of the surrounding countryside. Clusters of tiny artificial lights marked the nearby towns on the plain below, and the roads that joined them were traced with the minuscule moving headlights of cars and trucks. Sayen squatted down for a while, her arms wrapped around her knees, as she wondered which of the houses and vehicles contained not humans, but Shadow clones.

After a while, it occurred to her that Erielle might have woken and be in need of another dose of kratom. She returned down the trail to the car park and crept into the truck. The underworlder was sleeping as soundly as she'd been when Sayen left her. She climbed inside the warm sleeping bag and settled down, finally able to drift off to sleep.

———

She was woken the following day by the sounds of movement and quiet voices. Erielle was already awake. She'd managed to sit up and pull herself backward on her arms so that she could lean against the truck wall. She gave a wan half-smile as she looked into Sayen's sleep-filled eyes.

Sayen yawned. "How are you feeling?"

"A little better. You should get up soon if you want to get some breakfast."

Sayen pushed back the sleeping bag and sat up. Jas, Ozment, and Carl were sitting cross-legged next to the truck door, which was wide open. Brilliant sunlight streamed in, and the sound of birdsong was loud.

"Where's Makey?" she asked Erielle. "Has he gone to take a shower?" She hoped there were showers at this place.

"No, I sent him on an errand."

"What kind of errand?"

"You'll see."

"Time to get up," Ozment said as he noticed she was awake. "We're leaving soon. We've got to get to the spaceport while it's still daylight so that we can get a good look at the place."

"Okay, okay," Sayen replied. "Have you eaten?" she asked Erielle.

"Yes. There's some left, but like Ozment said, be quick."

"I'll take you to the bathroom first."

"I don't think there'll be any need for that."

Makey climbed inside, carrying two long, straight branches. "This wood's great," he said. "I heard about trees, but I never imagined how useful they could be. Life on Dawn would have been so much easier if trees had grown there." He handed a knife to Ozment, who slipped it into a sheath at his side.

"Will these do, do you think?" he asked Erielle, holding up the branches for her inspection. He'd cut them to the same length, which was somewhat longer than a meter. At the top of each the branch split into a fork.

"Oh, you got him to make you crutches," Sayen exclaimed. "Wait, let me find something we can wrap around the ends for padding."

When she'd made the crutches as comfortable as she could, she carried Erielle to the door, where Makey held them upright for her. Slowly, she lowered the woman until her armpits rested on the branch forks. Her right leg was less damaged than her left, and Erielle gingerly put her weight on it while trying to take most of the strain on her arms.

She let out a gasp of pain and fell forward. Makey caught her and held onto her while she tried again. Once more, she couldn't take the pain, and she collapsed.

"That's enough for now," Sayen said. "Have a rest, and we can try again later."

"No, I want to do this."

Unable to hold it back, Erielle cried out as she hopped forward one step. She fell down. Neither Sayen nor Makey were quick enough to catch her.

"Erielle, this is stupid," Sayen said. "There's no need for this. Let me carry you."

Erielle glared at her from the ground. "Makey, help me up, please." She slipped the crutches under her arms, and the young man pulled her to her feet.

The next time she tried to walk, she managed two steps before crashing to the ground again.

"Erielle—" A hand gripped Sayen's shoulder. She turned to see Jas.

"She's doing pretty well, don't you think?" Jas asked.

"No, she's going to hurt herself. We can get her some proper crutches or a wheelchair. And it's much too soon—"

"Sayen, why not let her do it her way? I thought you hated your parents being overprotective of you."

"This is different. My parents are totally over the top. I just don't want her to hurt herself. I care about her."

"I know. Look, it's nearly time to go. Eat something and get ready. We've got five or six hours' driving ahead of us."

# Sixteen

A heat shimmer hung over the spaceport landing pad. Jas squinted in the glaring sunlight at the cargo bay. They'd parked the truck a little way down the road.

Jas wished she had some binoculars to see more detail. Then she remembered the weapons they'd brought from Erielle's place. She dug into the bag and pulled out an old-fashioned rifle with a sight. Peering through the crosshairs, she could see close up the perimeter fence around the spaceport, the massive shuttle hangars, the passenger buildings, and the warehouse that stored the cargo waiting to be loaded onto flights or ready for pickup.

If Bathsheba Dubois had been telling the truth, the shuttle flight carrying the Shadow scanners would be arriving at 7 pm. At 8:15—to allow time for offloading and transfer to the storage area—anonymous governmental trucks would pick up the scanners for distribution to the various spaceports around the world that handled deep space arrivals. They would have a window of about half an hour to break in and steal a scanner.

"What can you see?" asked Makey, who was crouched beside her on the rise that overlooked the spaceport.

"I can't see guards anywhere, for one thing," she replied. Turning to Carl, she asked, "You've spent a lot of time hanging around restricted areas in spaceports. Is it normal to have no guards?"

"It's not a military installation. They aren't expecting to be attacked. There are probably a few guards on site, but not many, and they wouldn't spend all day patrolling."

"That's good for us," Jas said, "but what about protection from theft? There have to be some valuable shipments that pass through."

Carl nodded. "The storage areas are sealed up pretty tight. Only cleared personnel can get access after retinal and voice checks. What we have to worry about are motion sensors. While the spaceport's in operation, they're turned off because the workers are constantly moving cargo in and out of storage. But overnight, the motion sensors are activated. They're trigger alarms, and they shoot whatever moving object they detect."

"Krat," Jas said.

"But if we break in while the place is open, these sensors won't be activated, will they?" Makey asked.

"Not right away," said Carl, "but the minute they realize what's happening, you can be sure as hell that system will be the first thing they reach for. Which means we've got to be fast. As soon as we're sure the scanners are inside the warehouse, we should break in, take one, and get out of there."

"Do we know where in the warehouse they'll put the scanners?" Makey asked.

Jas gazed through the crosshairs again at the huge spaceport. "Nope."

———

It was 7:45. The shuttle carrying the scanners had arrived and Jas had observed its cargo being unloaded and moved toward the warehouse. They'd returned to the truck. Erielle and Sayen had moved to the back and taken weapons with them. They were going to prevent guards from entering the rear of the truck. Ozment was driving, and Jas, Makey, and Carl were all armed with blasters.

Jas's greatest fear was that they wouldn't be able to find the scanners before the motion sensors were turned on, or that the sensors would automatically activate the minute they broke into the warehouse. If that happened, they wouldn't stand a chance. They would be trapped inside the truck, unless...

"Are you sure this is tough enough to break through the warehouse wall?" Carl asked Ozment.

"Should be," he replied. "But I can't say as I've ever tried. Buckle up, everyone." He was driving at the speed of the traffic on the approach to the spaceport, but soon he would have to veer off the road and across the open land surrounding it.

"Hey, listen up, take one of these," Jas said, pulling more guns from her cache and handing them to Carl, Makey, and Ozment.

"Aren't these a little outdated?" Ozment asked as he took a weapon from her.

She'd given them each a pistol that fired rounds and not the laser beams of modern weapons. "Yes, they're old, but they might be just what we need. The motion sensors are probably laser-proofed, but they might not be bulletproof. Here." She gave them each a magazine of bullets. "There aren't many. They probably don't even make these anymore. So every shot is going to count."

They were nearly at the spaceport. "Okay, this is it," Jas said. "Remember, we find a scanner, get it in the back of the truck, then get the hell out of there."

The truck swerved and began to judder as Ozment left the road, went down a bank, and across rough dirt and rocks. They were about a minute from the spaceport. Jas wondered if anyone had noticed them yet. They were thirty seconds away. The perimeter fence and the corrugated metal wall of the warehouse were rushing up toward them.

Ozment pressed a switch, and steel walls flew up around the cab and slotted into place, leaving only a narrow slit in front of the driver. The juddering was violent as Ozment increased speed. "Get ready," he shouted.

As they struck the fence and then the warehouse, Jas was thrown forward. A great rending and tearing of metal could be heard all around. When it stopped, she opened her eyes. "Are we in?"

Ozment peered through the slit. "We're in. Go."

Jas threw her door open and leapt out. She landed awkwardly on broken boxes of goods strewn around the cab. "Be careful," she called to the others. At the far end of the warehouse, workers were running away. Automated forklift trucks in the warehouse aisles continued to operate, lifting and carrying stored items.

Only the cab of the truck had made it through the wall. If they were going to load up a scanner, they needed access to the rear doors. "Ozment," Jas called. "You've got to pull the whole truck in."

Carl and Makey were setting off on the search for the scanner. As Jas joined them, the truck engine revved, and the warehouse was filled with deafening noise as Ozment destroyed more of its wall and knocked down a massive shelf of goods to bring the rear of the truck inside.

Where were the scanners? They probably had only seconds before someone thought to activate the motion sensors. "Let's check up near the entrance," Jas said. "The scanners were only supposed to be here a little while before they were picked up."

They moved down an aisle. In front of them was a forklift, trundling in their direction, a pallet of boxes balanced on its forks. Suddenly, a laser beam flashed out, and the truck burst apart. The boxes fell and smashed, spilling their contents.

"Krat," Jas said. She froze. Makey and Carl also stopped.

"What do we do now?" Makey asked.

"Wait."

Jas's eyes were on the forklifts in their aisle. Another beam flashed out and hit a moving truck, and this time she saw the motion sensor that was responsible. It was on the ceiling, moving to fire again as it detected the final surviving forklift in their aisle. As the third beam shone, Jas lifted her weapon, aimed, and shot. A massive bang echoed around the warehouse, and the sensor exploded. Plastic and metal debris rained down. "Makey, you spot and take out the motion sensors. We don't have long before they run out of targets except for us. Carl, let's find this kratting scanner."

They set off. Shots rang out as the kid traced the beams flashing from the ceiling. Jas and Carl ran low and kept to the sides of the aisles. Jas hoped that the forklifts would attract more attention than them from the motion sensors.

At the end of the warehouse, near the open doors, a couple dozen boxes shaped like large coffins were stacked.

"You reckon that's them?" asked Carl, who had spotted the boxes too.

"Got to be, don't you think? We'll just have to take a chance. It isn't like they would have labeled them."

Another laser beam flashed out, this time low down from the warehouse entrance. Guards had arrived and spotted them.

"Krat," Jas said. "I hate to do this, but..." She pulled a grenade from her jacket pocket, set it and tossed it through the doors. As it exploded, she and Carl ran toward the boxes. She grabbed the end of one, and Carl grabbed the other end. They slid it off the pile, but it was so heavy, they couldn't hold onto it. The box fell to the floor. "We'll have to push it," Jas said. "Quick."

They both pushed and dragged the box back toward the aisle. Right next to Jas's hand, a laser beam burnt the container. She spun around to see a guard ducking back behind the door. She fired her old-fashioned propulsion weapon. The round pierced the laser-proofed door, and a cry sounded.

They reached the relative safety of the aisle, but the box was so heavy, they were only inching it along. Makey fired. The guards had entered the warehouse. If they didn't find a faster way of getting the box to the truck, the place would be swarming with them. As Jas grunted and strained, she glanced up and caught sight of a figure that gave her hope. Sayen was racing toward them. She'd left the truck and come to help.

But a motion sensor detected her. Its beam caught her side, and she staggered and fell. Jas shot the sensor. Sayen got up and continued toward them more slowly. When she reached them, Jas saw her left arm and back had been burned. Her face was twisted in pain.

"Let's move this thing," she gasped, and she placed her right hand next to Jas's. With her help, the box slid easily along. As they made their way back to the truck, Makey fired at the guards that were trying to pursue them.

Ozment also approached to lend a hand. "The truck's rear doors are open. We've just gotta get this inside."

They were nearly there. Behind the truck was a gaping hole where Ozment had driven the truck through the wall. Jas saw movement. "Krat. The guards have come around this side." A beam flashed from inside the truck, and a guard fell. Erielle was firing at them. Another guard appeared and was caught on the shoulder by a beam from Erielle's gun.

"Makey, cover us," Jas ordered.

He fired shot after shot through the hole while the other four hoisted the box into the truck. In another moment, the doors were closed and they were back in the cab. Ozment reversed the truck out of the warehouse, buckling and breaking more of the wall. The guards outside fired, but their laser beams sizzled uselessly.

They rocked and swayed as Ozment forced the truck around in a tight curve to get back to the road. Then they were out in the traffic, heading away from the spaceport.

# SEVENTEEN

Whoops and hollers filled the cab as they sped from the spaceport. As soon as they were a safe distance away, they stopped the truck and opened the box. Inside they found exactly what they'd hoped for. They'd done it. They'd stolen a scanner. Sayen and Ozment helped Erielle into the cab and they set off once more. Jas leaned back in her seat, and for the first time in days, she relaxed.

They still had to capture a Shadow, and that wouldn't be easy, but they were much further along with their plan than they had been only a day previously.

Ozment was driving with a huge grin on his face.

"You seem pretty pleased with yourself," she said to him.

"It always feels good when you stick it to the man," he replied.

"Where are we going now?" Makey asked.

Jas realized that they hadn't even considered their next step. There could be no going back to Erielle's safe house, even if anything remained of it after the fire. Durfy and his associates wouldn't be pleased by their return.

"You're coming with me to my farm," said Ozment. "I thought that was obvious."

"Great," said Makey.

"Yeah, thanks, mate," Carl said. "Great idea. We can rest up for a while, and Erielle can get better."

Sayen nodded in satisfaction.

A shadow flickered over the cab, as if something had passed by overhead. Over the sound of the truck's engine, Jas thought she heard a high-pitched whine.

"What was that?" Makey asked.

"Sounded like a heli," Sayen said.

The truck shuddered as something hit its roof.

"Krat. We're being fired at," exclaimed Ozment. On the dashboard, in the screens showing the rear- and side-views, the dark shapes of two helis could be seen, hovering over the truck like mosquitoes in search of blood.

"Carl, take over," Ozment said. "I'll deal with them."

Jas remembered the false roof of the truck that Ozment had told her about, and the 'toy' he had up there.

Ozment and Carl awkwardly swapped seats, and Ozment crawled into the back of the cab and opened the hatch. He disappeared up the dark tunnel leading to the roof. The truck shuddered again, and Carl fought to keep it on the road.

The dark countryside was speeding past. Jas gripped a handle over the window to keep her balance. She pressed a button, and the plexiglass retracted into its slot. Leaning out, she saw the two helis overhead. They were flying erratically, as if the pilots were unused to the controls. *As if they were being flown by newly formed Shadows.*

An arc of fire spat from the truck roof, and the rotor blade of one of the helis flew off, spinning crazily down before it hit the road. Sparks erupted from it as it skittered along, and cars swerved to avoid it. A dull rumble and flash of flame signaled the damaged heli crashing into a field at their rear.

"He got one," Jas exclaimed. She was aiming at the remaining heli, but its haphazard movement made it difficult to follow. The shot she fired went wide. Something erupted from the heli's base, and a third shudder ran through the truck, followed by a loud bang. The heli had scored a direct hit, but it was firing at the largest target —the truck's roof, probably aiming for the weapon Ozment was firing. *Better that than the wheels*, Jas thought. If the Shadows took them out, it would be game over, but her stomach clenched at the thought of the man in the false roof.

Another line of fire flew up from the truck. A hole appeared in the center of the second heli a moment before it was consumed in a ball of flames. The fiery ball hit the road behind them and rolled away, leaving a trail of burning debris.

"Second heli down," exclaimed Jas. "Ozment did it."

The cab was filled with cheers and laughs of relief. The stomach-churning zigzagging of the truck ceased as Carl was able to keep it straight. He accelerated, quickly increasing the distance between them and the scene of carnage behind.

Jas scanned the dashboard screens and took a look out of the window at the night sky and the traffic that was beginning to fill the road around them again. It seemed there was no further pursuit. She hoped it would be a straight run now to the safety of Ozment's farm, and their next plan.

Suddenly she realized the Martian still hadn't climbed down.

Sayen had had the same thought. "Ozment's taking his time." She leaned over the seats and called his name through the open hatch.

The missing man made no reply. Jas's heart sank. "Krat," she muttered, adding, "I'll check on him." She undid her seatbelt and climbed over Sayen to reach the hatch. Slotting her fingers and toes into the depressions in the tunnel, she climbed up.

The first thing she saw was the back of a low swivel chair and Ozment's arms and legs splayed out either side of it. Fighting the dread that rose up and threatened to overwhelm her, Jas climbed out into the narrow, low space. Ozment was seated behind a missile launcher. The roof above him had been retracted, and his position was open to the sky. An easy target from above, it was a suicidal spot.

The Martian was still alive, though from the state of his chest, he seemed to be holding on by willpower alone.

"Hey, Jas," he whispered.

She took his hand. "Hey, Ozment. You did a brave thing. You saved us."

"It was worth it." He smiled. "It was good to know you guys. Especially you, Jas. Good to see another Martian." He coughed. Blood ran from his mouth.

"I'm glad I met you, too." She couldn't say any more.

"Fight the fight, Jas. You know what I mean."

She gripped his hand tighter. Ozment looked up at the stars, and then he was gone.

Jas stayed for a while, wishing she'd had more time with him. They hadn't talked about Mars, or his life since coming to Earth, or his farm. There was so much she didn't know about this man who had given his life so nobly.

It was Sayen calling to her that broke her from her trance.

"I'm coming," she replied. She went down the tunnel feet first and climbed out into the cab. The others seemed to tell from her face what had happened.

Only Makey needed confirmation. Very quietly, he asked, "He's gone?"

Jas nodded as she resumed her position by the window. No one spoke. From behind the seats came the sound of Erielle weeping.

Her face set, Jas looked out, unseeing, into the night.

# Eighteen

They buried Ozment in the corner of a field next to a deserted farm track about a kilometer off the freeway.

Erielle managed to hobble from the truck to the burial spot on her crutches. She sank down to the ground next to the freshly filled grave and bent her head as if in silent prayer.

Jas wondered if she was commending Ozment's spirit to Earth Mother. She didn't really understand the beliefs of the under-worlders. They seemed to be a very personal thing and something that had changed from the older to the younger generation.

"Jas, do you want to say anything?" Sayen asked.

She shook her head. "I'm no good at that stuff."

"I can recite the funeral rights they say on Dawn," said Makey. "I remember them."

"Okay," said Erielle. "I think he might have liked that."

Makey began, "Earth Mother, accept this man who is returning to you. Take his body as nourishment for living things. Return his soul to the natural spirits from where it came. Spread it wide, and let him delight in life once more, part of the whole which is you..."

Jas gazed down at the mound of crumbly soil, moister and darker than the surrounding ground. Ozment's grave was under a tree. She thought he would have liked it. She made a mental note of the place so that if anyone who knew him wanted to visit, she could tell them the spot. She bit her lip. He'd been so full of life, it hardly seemed possible that he was gone. And so young. He'd had so much more living to do.

As she mulled over these thoughts, a rage rose in her. The Shadows had taken yet another life. They had to be stopped. She would halt them in their tracks, and she would make them pay for every human being they'd killed.

She became aware of silence. Makey had finished speaking. She heaved a sigh. "I guess we should get back to the truck and decide what we're going to do next."

Sayen helped Erielle to her crutches, and the two left the graveside, followed by Carl and Makey. Jas was the last to leave. Before she went, she whispered, "Goodbye, friend."

———

Carl sat behind the steering wheel of the parked truck with Makey next to him. Erielle was now well enough to join them on the seat. Sayen scooted over as Jas approached, making room for her next to the window.

"Where are we going?" Makey asked.

"I don't know yet," Jas replied. "I'm not sure that it's such a good idea to go to Ozment's farm. It's a safe hiding place, yes, but I don't think that hiding is what we should be doing right now. We have to contact the Transgalactic Council. We can't stop the Shadows without their help. We have to show them what's happening here."

"What is there on Ozment's farm, Erielle?" Sayen asked. "I'm guessing there isn't any kind of deep-space linkup?"

"I haven't been there for years," Erielle replied, "but, no, I don't think there's anything like that."

"All those places where you can send a deep-space comm are off limits to us," Carl said. "We don't have a krat's chance of breaking into any of those places. We don't have a Shadow as proof yet either."

"Hmmm...I'm not sure about that," Sayen said.

"You mean we do have a Shadow?" Jas asked.

"No, I meant about not having access to a deep space comm device."

"Really?"

"I'm pretty sure my parents send deep-space comms all the time."

"Then why haven't they told the Transgalactic Council about the Shadows?" Jas asked.

"They probably have, but for some reason they aren't being taken seriously."

"They did tell me and Carl about being shut out of meetings and having information withheld," Jas said. "You think we should go to your parents' place? They told us we couldn't go back there. That it wasn't safe."

"It doesn't seem very safe not to go there, though, does it?" said Sayen. "Think about it. We've got no creds and no place to go except Ozment's farm, which doesn't help us over the long term. How will we survive with only this truck? Heck, we don't even have the creds to pay for a battery recharge."

They had discussed removing Ozment's credchip, but they didn't have the equipment for inserting it into someone's wrist even if they'd been prepared to despoil his body, which they were not.

"My parents' house is damned near impregnable," Sayen continued. "If we can just get inside with a Shadow and contact the Council...I reckon it's our best option."

Jas wondered how much of Sayen's reasoning was influenced by her concerns for her mother and father, but she was making some good points.

"It's no good," Carl said. "If your parents are being watched by Shadows...if Shadows are surrounding the place, the minute we go near it they'll capture us. We'll never get in."

Sayen sighed. "Yeah, I guess you're right. I guess it was just wishful thinking."

"What about if your parents knew we were coming?" Erielle asked. "If they were ready for us? Could they fix things so that we could blast through the Shadows and drive right in?"

"Maybe, but we can't contact them," said Jas. "Sayen's parents warned us not to use anything that will allow us to be traced. The Shadows will instantly follow every comm her parents receive to its source. They'll swoop down on us and catch us."

"But if it were an anonymous message from a moving source?" Erielle asked.

"An anonymous..." Sayen's eyes widened. She touched the interface on the dashboard. "Ozment said this interface was untraceable. I used it to call your old doctor friend, and he couldn't see any caller ID."

"I doubt it's strictly untraceable," Erielle said. "Even our best isn't up to that. But the Shadows won't know who's calling, and they won't be able to see or hear the message. If you make the call while we're on the move, we'll be ten kilometers away before they figure out where it came from."

"It could work," Jas said to Sayen. "Your parents could tell us if they can get us inside their home. If they can, we don't even have to find a Shadow before we get there."

"Huh?" Carl said. "What good's it going to do to turn up at Sayen's parents' place without a Shadow?"

"I didn't say that," Jas replied. "If they're surrounding the place, they won't be hard to find. We can grab one on the way in."

Carl started up the truck. "I don't know if it'll work, but it's worth a try."

"I think so, too," Sayen said, smiling for the first time in days.

As they drove away from Ozment's grave, Jas watched it retreat into the distance. In her heart, she promised him that she wouldn't give up until she had defeated the Shadows and avenged his death.

'Fight the fight,' he'd said. She wondered what he'd meant. Something more than fighting the Shadows? He'd dedicated his life to struggling against the Global Government. Jas had never thought about them as a force for evil, but it was true that they were neglecting their duty to protect Earth's citizens. Had Ozment meant that they should fight them too? Had he meant that she should take up the underworlders' cause, perhaps following in the footsteps of her parents?

She turned to face forward. They were entering the freeway, and the open road stretched out before them. What the future held, Jas couldn't guess, but she wondered if it might somehow also lead back into her past.

# TRAPPED

# ONE

Things were getting desperate. They'd eaten the last of the food two days previously, and the water had run out the day before. Jas sat in the cab of the truck and wondered how much longer they would last if they didn't succeed in breaking through the Shadows' siege of Sayen's home.

Carl had parked the truck a kilometer or so away. Its battery was almost dead. Jas hoped they were far enough from the house to avoid detection. Sayen's call to her parents from the untraceable interface had gone through, and after they'd gotten over their joy at hearing her voice, they'd diverted the call to an encrypted line.

Neither of Sayen's parents had left home for weeks. They hadn't even ordered food deliveries in fear that the Shadows would take the opportunity to invade. The aliens were watching them, they'd said, and though they might have been able to leave, they didn't know where to go or who they could trust. Her parents had activated a force field around the home, but they would momentarily drop their defenses at an agreed time to allow the truck in.

Jas was sure that the minute the Shadows saw the truck, they would recognize it as the one that had been used to steal a Shadow scanner from the spaceport. Maybe they even knew exactly who was inside. Their reach had stretched far—deep into the recesses of the Global Government.

The Shadows were certainly in no doubt about who Sayen Lee was. Their attempt to kill her after she'd breached the Global Government's secure files on them had failed. Jas and Carl had defeated the Shadows in their attempt to take control of the starship *Galathea*. Young Makey, the sole escapee from the Shadow invasion of the colony planet, Dawn, had gone missing from his refugee institution. Perhaps only Erielle, the wounded underworlder who had helped Jas and the others, was as yet unknown to the aliens.

They were the ones who the Shadows knew had discovered their secret invasion of Earth. They were the ones who were a danger. If they could reach the Transgalactic Council before the Shadows had taken Earth, and bring the might of the Unity military forces down upon the fledgling offensive, the aliens might yet be defeated.

But the group would have one chance and one chance only to reach the safety of Sayen's parents' estate and transmit a deep space comm to the Council.

"What's the time?" Makey asked, though it could be clearly seen on the dashboard. The kid was understandably nervous.

"We've got ten minutes," Carl replied. His arms were resting on the truck's steering wheel as he watched the cars passing.

Jas's tongue and mouth were thick with thirst. Her stomach had given up complaining about its emptiness the day before. Even if they had their credchips, they couldn't buy anything without the Shadows immediately identifying and capturing them. Jas wasn't too concerned about their lack of provisions. If they didn't get inside the Lees' house, they probably wouldn't survive anyway. However, she was worried about Erielle. The woman was still recovering from severe laser burns to both legs. Until the day before last, she'd seemed to be recovering, but the lack of water and food had weakened her far more than the others. She was drifting in and out of consciousness as she lay on the cab floor behind the seats.

"So, where are we going to find our Shadow to scan?" Sayen asked. "If we can't prove to the Council what's happening, there's not a lot of point in my parents sending a deep space packet to them."

"They shouldn't be too hard to find," replied Jas. "I'm guessing it'll be whoever's shooting at us. We just have to capture one without killing it."

"That all?"

"That's all."

"You realize I've gotta raise the shield around the cab before we get close?" Carl asked. "As soon as they see us, they're gonna start firing."

"Krat," Jas said. The laser proof steel wall had protected them on more than one occasion, and they would need it now, but it would deprive everyone but Carl of a view outside. She hadn't figured that into her plan. If it had been just her, she would have taken her chances with no shield, but she didn't want to expose the others to the risk.

"What if I have a look around for someone to target before we go in?" Sayen asked. "Don't forget my enhanced eyes allow me to see a lot of detail at a distance."

"We can't risk being spotted while you do that," Jas replied, "and besides, whoever you see is going to change position before we get close enough to grab them. Krat. I don't know how we're going to manage it." She turned the problem over in her mind.

"Six minutes," Carl said. "I'm going to start her up in four. We've only got a thirty-second window. Jas, we don't have time to be hanging around chasing Shadows. If we delay, they'll figure out what's happening, and they'll get inside Sayen's place themselves."

"No," Sayen said. "We can't let that happen. Jas, how about we give up on catching a Shadow on our way in? We can try to do that once we're inside. There isn't a shortage of them in the area according to what my parents told me."

"I don't like it," said Jas. "They'll know we're there, and they'll be on the defensive. They might guess what we want to do because they know we kidnapped the minister. Your parents haven't attacked them, but they know *we* could. If we don't grab one when we have the opportunity, we'll lose the advantage of surprise."

"If we go in there with the shield down," Carl said, "they'll have clear shots at all of us."

Jas bit her lip. She couldn't decide what to do. For once, she wished someone else would take the lead. Her decisions didn't ever seem to be the right ones lately. The death of the minister they'd kidnapped weighed heavily on her. The woman had been incompetent at her job, it was true, but she hadn't deserved to die. Erielle had lost the use of her legs by trying to help them, and their friend, Ozment, whose truck they were in, had lost his life.

"Two minutes," Carl said.

"Krat it," said Jas. "Carl, tell me what you can see as we're driving in. If you can see a Shadow we might be able to capture, let me know, and I'll go after it. I guess it's the best we can do."

He started the engine. "Righto."

Jas took out her weapon and set it to stun as they pulled away from the curb.

Sayen's parents lived out of town on a huge estate. As well as a tall electrified fence surrounding the place, an invisible barrier formed a dome over the estate. When Jas and Carl had visited, Sayen had told them the barrier was to trap artificially cooled air, Jas guessed it had now been transformed into a force field to make the grounds impenetrable.

Their destination was easy to spot as an oasis of green in the surrounding dry, barren landscape. Jas had heard that the whole state had once been green and lush, but that rising global temperatures had changed the climate and dried up the rain.

Something had changed since her last visit. On the borders of the estate, opposite the front gates, construction of a large building was underway. This was how the Shadows were staking out Sayen's parents. They were building nearby, no doubt under the guise of a construction company. The shell of the first three floors were up already.

The truck was barreling down the road, only a minute from their destination. From a distance, the hard-hatted figures working inside the building were tiny and difficult to spot, but they didn't need to wait long before Shadows left the construction site and appeared on the road.

"Raising the shield," Carl said.

It slid smoothly into place, and the cab turned dark. A light blinked on. Jas was pushed back into her seat as Carl floored the gas. From all around came the sound of sizzling as the Shadows' lasers scored the shield.

"Nearly there," called Carl over the sound of the laser hits. The truck began to slow. If they entered Sayen's parent's estate at full speed, they would crash into the trees that lined the long, winding driveway.

"I see a Shadow you can get, Jas," exclaimed Carl. "On your side. Open your door and grab her."

They were all thrown forward as Carl braked hard. Jas flung open her door and put one foot down on the step, squinting in the glaring sunlight, trying to see the Shadow Carl had identified. The truck was still moving, and all she could see was a little girl, about eleven years old, holding a skipping rope.

"Get her," shouted Carl.

But Jas turned to him for confirmation that this was who he meant. *A child?* Laser fire hit the inside of the shield near her head, and she was nearly thrown from the truck as Carl pulled away violently. She retreated inside and slammed shut her door.

In another thirty seconds, the truck stopped. "We made it," Carl said. "We're inside."

They were safely behind the defenses of Sayen's home, but they had no Shadow.

# Two

The door that Jas had only recently slammed shut was wrenched open, and she was crushed beneath Sayen's mother as the woman leapt into the cab and climbed right over her. She grabbed her daughter, saying, "My baby. You're home. You're okay. I can't believe it. You're finally home."

"Mama, please," protested Sayen. "Calm down and get out of here. You're squashing Jas."

"I'm sorry, honey," she said. "I'm just so happy to see you again." She awkwardly clambered backward. Jas caught the woman's elbow as it was on its way into her face. She helped her as she climbed down from the cab onto the gravel of the driveway.

Jas also climbed down and moved out of the way so that the others had room to get out. Sayen's father embraced his daughter lovingly. The Lees' mansion was as Jas remembered it: massive and imposing.

Looking back in the direction they'd come, she saw figures peering through the estate's gates, keeping a respectful distance from the electrified metal. Smallest of the figures was the girl Carl had told her to capture.

He came over. "Why didn't you take her?"

"Do you really think she's a Shadow?"

"'Course she is. She's gotta be. Why else would a child be all the way out here in the middle of nowhere on a building site? Why would Shadows allow a human kid to hang out with them?"

"I don't know. I guess you're right. It just freaked me out for a moment. Krat. I missed our chance."

The Shadows were gazing at them and not even trying to pretend they were anything other than what they were. Even at a distance, she could see that their faces were expressionless. Up until then, she'd only seen rare glimpses of the natural state of the aliens. Most of the time they tried to mimic the humanity of the person they'd replaced. She supposed that they saw no need for pretenses now. A shiver ran down her spine. Not for the first time, she wondered who these mysterious aliens were, and what form they had before they copied human bodies to inhabit.

Behind her, Sayen's parents were urging them all to go inside, and she was happy to oblige. She'd had enough of Shadows for that day. For a lifetime, in fact.

"Wait, Mama, there's someone else," Sayen said. "Another friend. But she can't get out by herself. She's hurt. I have to help her." Sayen returned to the cab, where Erielle still lay, half hidden and unconscious.

"No, wait, honey," said her father. "Let Florence and Tyler do it." He motioned to the maid and butler who were standing in the doorway. The two android servants came down the steps, and at Sayen's instructions, they gently lifted Erielle out of the truck and carried her into the house.

With a final look at the watching figures of the Shadows, Jas followed the others inside.

At the sound of the door closing behind her, she relaxed for what felt like the first time in weeks. Whatever defenses Sayen's parents had against the Shadows, they seemed to be effective for the moment. There, they were as safe as they could be, even with the mysterious aliens sitting on the doorstep. It was odd, however, that this couple had military-style protection of their home. There hadn't been a war anywhere in the world in years, and the extent of their security went far beyond that needed to prevent burglaries or other home invasions. She wondered what it was that warranted the need.

"Oh, Sayen," exclaimed her mother, hugging her child again. "We thought you were dead. We thought the Shadows had caught you and murdered you."

"I know Mama. You told me so when I contacted you. Don't you remember? Now, where should Florence and Tyler put Erielle?"

"I think the red guest room would be best. That's nearest yours. I'll see what we can do for your friend. She looks very weak and dehydrated."

"Thank you, Mama. We all need food and something to drink. We haven't been able to buy anything for two days."

"That sounds awful," said Sayen's father. "Don't you worry. We'll see to it all. Florence will look after Erielle. Please, everyone, come through here and eat something. You must all be famished. And you two…" He turned to Jas and Carl. "Thank you for bringing my daughter home. I don't know how I'll ever repay you."

"You don't have anything to thank us for, Mr. Lee," said Carl. "Sayen saved our lives more than once."

"And mine," said Makey.

Sayen introduced the kid to her parents, and they went further into the house. Nothing was said for a while as the four ate and drank. No one could eat much after fasting for two days, but the water tasted like nectar to Jas.

"Where's Beau?" Sayen asked her parents.

Jas remembered the strange cat-dog hybrid that was Sayen's pet.

"I'm sorry," Sayen's mother replied. "We gave him away when we thought you weren't coming back. I couldn't bear to see him anymore. He reminded me of you."

Sayen sighed. "Okay. I'm going to check on Erielle." She put down her glass.

"She'll be fine," said Sayen's father. "You know Florence will give her the best care, just like the other maids used to give you when you were a little girl."

"I know, Daddy. I just can't rest until I see that she's okay." She got up and put down her napkin before leaving.

As Sayen closed the door behind her, Sayen's mother raised her eyebrows at her husband.

"If you don't mind my asking," said Mr. Lee. "Who is that woman, Erielle? Sayen didn't mention her when she called. She seems to have been seriously injured."

"She was," Jas replied. "She helped us kidnap the security minister—"

"That was you, was it?" said Mrs. Lee. "We saw the reports on the vidnews. She's been missing for days. Why would you do a thing like that? What's happened to the woman?"

"She's dead, I'm sorry to say. She got shot when we were attacked," said Jas ruefully. "I guess I should bring you up to speed. A lot's happened since we left you to go and rescue Sayen."

She and Carl narrated the events of their retrieving Sayen from the Shadow facility in Antarctica, their first encounter with Erielle in the underworld neighborhood, and everything that had happened since. It took a while, and long before they'd finished, Sayen returned from checking on Erielle. She and Makey also contributed to their parts of the story. Sayen took over to explain how they'd stolen a Shadow scanner and how their friend, Ozment, had died.

As Sayen spoke, Jas went to the window, which looked out over the lawn of the estate. The green sward led down to a lake with flamingoes. The fence that marked the rear boundary far away was obscured by trees. She couldn't see it clearly. She wondered if Shadows were patrolling behind the estate as well as in front. As she watched, a dark shape appeared in the sky, flying closer. A heli. Not one of the small, domestic four-seaters, but a military vehicle. Her hand went to her mouth.

There was only one explanation for the heli being in the vicinity: the Shadows' reach had now extended into the Global Government Air Force. She was silently grateful that the aircraft hadn't turned up a couple of hours ago, or they would never have made it into the house. As always, they seemed to be only one step ahead of the encroaching Shadows.

"Krat," breathed Carl, who had joined her at the window while Sayen was finishing off their story.

"I know," said Jas.

The heli drew close. A beam of blinding light flashed out from it. About thirty meters above the ground, the beam encountered a barrier. The light split and zigzagged outward and down, outlining the shape of the force field that protected the estate.

"What the hell was that?" exclaimed Mr. Lee, leaping up to look out the window. "A heli? Carleen, they've sent in the military. They certainly want y'all," he said to the others.

"It's the first time this has happened?" asked Jas. The heli had disappeared overhead, but it returned and swept a wide arc before approaching the house once more.

"Yes," Mr. Lee replied. "The Shadows have only been watching us up until now. They've never attempted an all-out attack." Another flash of intense light blazed from the aircraft and dissipated across the barrier.

"Will your force field withstand the charges?" Carl asked.

Mr. Lee rubbed his chin. "Yes—for a while."

Sayen's parents, Jas, and the others stood at the window watching the heli firing at the force field for a while, like it was a bizarre fireworks show. Eventually, the Shadows seemed to accept their efforts were pointless, and the heli flew off.

"Mama, Daddy," Sayen said as they returned to their seats. "Now it's your turn. What's been happening here? And how come you have all these defenses? You two have always been so secretive. I think it's high time you finally told me what it is you've been hiding from me and Phelan all these years."

"Oh, honey, I'm sorry. I know we haven't been open with you," said Mrs. Lee. "We were only trying to keep you and your brother safe."

"And I guess that's your reason for having a tracker put in my butt cheek," Sayen retorted, folding her arms.

"Well, as a matter of fact, it is," replied her mother. "We nearly lost you once. I wasn't going to risk losing you again."

"Mama," exclaimed Sayen, "how could you? That was an invasion of my privacy."

"I never checked up on you, I swear. I never once tried to find out where you were. You're a grown woman, I know that. I didn't do it to snoop on you. It was only in case of an emergency. Aren't you grateful now that I did it?"

Sayen glared at her mother.

"Now, now," said her father. "What we did, we did, for better or worse. As it turned out, it was for the greater good in this case. But we can't fix it now. Sayen, sweetheart, you're right. I guess it is time that you know the truth about us." He sighed. "When you know, I hope you'll understand why we could never give you or Phelan the slightest hint about what we do. It was for your own safety as well as ours."

There was an uncomfortable pause as Sayen looked expectantly at her parents. Neither seemed to know how to begin. "Well? Are you going to tell me or not?"

"Perhaps it's better that I show you," said Mr. Lee. "All of you. If you would step this way."

He led them out of the room and up the wide, winding staircase of his palatial home. At the top of the stairs, sumptuous hallways opened on both sides, lined with deep plush carpet and lit by old-fashioned, ornate lamps. Jas wondered what Sayen's childhood had been like with this vast house as her play space. It was the kind of place you could get lost in but not really mind for a while.

Halfway down a corridor, they stopped at a closed door. A device of a kind Jas had never seen before protruded at head height from the wall—a security console of some kind. Mr. Lee put a hand to a panel and his face to a hole. He breathed into a tube while a scanner read his eyes. A small click signaled as the door opened. "I'll add y'all to the security database so that you can have a free run of the house while you're here," he said as they went inside.

The room looked like an ordinary office. Chairs and a desk, several interfaces, and knick-knacks were all Jas could see. Mr. Lee ignored all these and walked directly across the room to an area of blank wall. After pressing a raised panel, he stepped back as a section of the wall slid away to reveal an elevator. He spread his arm wide to invite them in.

Sayen gasped. "Daddy? Mama? What is this?"

"Step in here, sweetheart," said Mr. Lee, "and I'll show you. Come on, everyone. I think we can all fit."

"I'm going to check on your friend, honey," said Mrs. Lee. "Your daddy can explain everything."

They crowded into the small space. Mr. Lee gave a voice command, and they descended. The elevator stopped, and the doors opened. Spreading out in front of them, covering an area as wide and deep as the entire base of the Lees' home, was a workroom and laboratory rolled into one.

"Wow," said Makey.

# THREE

Jas put an arm around Sayen, as the woman appeared to be about to faint.

"Daddy?" she asked weakly.

"I'm sorry, Sayen. I realize this must come as a terrible shock. I guess I'd best get this over with as quickly as I can. Please, everyone, come in and sit down." He led them into the massive room and pulled up a couple of laboratory stools next to a bench that was scattered with metal parts and tiny tools. As he left to find some more stools, Jas helped Sayen onto one of them. The normally chatty woman seemed unable to speak. She only gaped.

Uniform wooden benches occupied most of the vast space, but there were also fume cabinets and a wide range of machining tools, as well as many things Jas couldn't even recognize. On most of the benches were interfaces, and materials and instruments were spread about, as if work on something or things had been temporarily halted.

Mr. Lee brought over three more tall stools, and he and the others sat down. He laid a hand on Sayen's arm. "Sayen, this is what I could never let you or your brother know. I am breaking solemn oaths that I swore to uphold by telling you and your friends this. However, it looks like our government has been compromised, and to help save humankind, I must break my promises. My dear, your mother and I work for the Global Government in an absolutely top secret capacity."

"You...what do you mean? What is it you do?" Sayen asked, her voice almost childlike.

"I should probably have made up something to tell you both to stop you from wondering all this time, but I couldn't make up a believable alternative. Besides, neither your mother nor I could bring ourselves to lie to you. I know you and Phelan had a little game going on where you were trying to guess."

Jas wished the man would get to the point. They were under attack by hostile aliens. It was hardly the time for shilly shallying. But she supposed he'd been thinking about this for the last two or three decades.

"I guess you would call us inventors," he went on. "We design and create the prototypes of devices used for the purpose of espionage."

"You're spies?" exclaimed Sayen, her eyes wide.

"No, no, no," Mr. Lee replied. "We *make* the things used for spying. All kinds of things. The Government approaches us with a problem it needs to solve, such as how to gain access to some sensitive information, and we invent the appropriate device." He turned to Carl and Jas. "You remember I told you we were being shut out of governmental meetings? You probably thought we were involved in politics. We aren't, but we are privy to confidential government business. We have to be. If we don't know what's happening, we have no way of suggesting how we can help.

"About six months ago, we found we were not being invited to certain meetings that previously we had attended as a matter of course. We also received many invitations to leave our estate. The reasons we were given for our requested departure were weak. This was highly unusual. Our colleagues and acquaintances are aware of our general reclusiveness, which is partly natural and partly precautionary. It would be a serious blow to the Government if it were to lose our services. Its enemies would love to have the information we hold. Why would it invite us to expose ourselves to danger?"

He turned to his daughter. "Sayen, you and Phelan were also at risk. If anyone had taken you from us, we would have done anything to get you back, and enemies of the Government knew that. We have been excessively protective of you both, I admit. I hope you understand why now."

Sayen got up and threw her arms around her father. "Daddy, I'm so sorry. I'm sorry I got mad at you and Mama."

Jas glanced at Carl. He had his head down. She guessed he was probably thinking of his missing parents. She leaned over and gave his arm a squeeze. He looked up and smiled at her sadly.

"This place is sneck," said Makey. "Can I have a look around?"

"No, I'm afraid not," replied Mr. Lee. "Perhaps one day I'll show you some things, but not now. Let's head back up to my office, where we can look at the problem at hand."

They filed once more into the elevator, and he returned them to the room with the interfaces.

He pressed a hand on a wall screen, and it blinked on, displaying a chart. After several swipes of lines and figures, Mr. Lee nodded. "As I thought. They've cut us off entirely now. First, we lost our direct comm to governmental colleagues. A temporary fault, we were told. Then we lost contact with all out-of-state connections. We could send and receive local comms only. Now, everything's gone."

"Does it matter, though?" Jas asked. "We're surrounded by Shadows. All we have to do is capture one, scan it to check that it is what we think it is, then contact the Transgalactic Council. That's why we're here."

"Contact the Council?" asked Mr. Lee, his eyebrows raised. "You think we didn't think of that? It was the first thing we tried after you and Carl set off to retrieve Sayen. Just before you arrived, we'd sent a packet to our son's starship to tell him his sister was missing. Then after you left, we tried to contact the Transgalactic Council to inform them of, well, everything you'd told us—about the Shadows and so on, but our deep space comm link was gone. It's been gone all this time."

"What?" exclaimed Jas. "We're kratted then. If we can't contact the Council, Earth doesn't have a hope. We need their help. The

Shadows are moving fast. We already don't have the numbers to stop them on our own."

"Wait a moment before you give up," said Mr. Lee. "Listen. I despaired too when I realized what the Shadows had done, but I've been working on the problem since then. You saw that building when you came in? That's where they're housing the suppressor that's preventing deep space comms in and out of here. I've been trying to figure out a way to get inside the building and destroy the machine, but I'm seventy years old and hardly cut out for climbing around in the dark. Then I saw your truck…"

Carl looked up. His face had lost its gloomy look. "Now that's an idea. You mean we could just drive right in there and smash this suppressor down?"

"Something along those lines."

"I'll do it," said Carl.

"Hold on," Jas said. "Aren't you forgetting something? We need a Shadow to show them as proof first before you go smashing anything."

"Oh, yeah," said Carl. "Well, that shouldn't be too hard. It isn't like they're difficult to spot around here."

"It isn't going to be that easy," Jas replied. "They know we're here now, and we don't exactly have a history of friendliness toward them. They're going to be expecting us to do something. They'll be watching. The minute anyone steps out, they'll be on us."

"Shame you didn't get that Shadow girl while you could," Makey said.

"Hey, it wasn't easy," Jas protested.

"You mean a young girl with a skipping rope?" Mr. Lee asked.

"Yeah," Carl replied. "She looks about ten or eleven."

"I know her. She's out there all the time. I think they're trying to tempt us to go and talk to her. They seem to understand that humans are predisposed to be friendly toward children."

"Have you ever spoken to her?" Jas asked.

"Goodness no," replied Mr. Lee.

"Good call, Daddy," Sayen said. "I saw her too. She gives me the creeps. She'd probably shoot you the minute you got in range."

"She can't shoot us through the force field," replied her father, "but I don't want to hear whatever it is that thing has to say. Which reminds me, I must check on how the force field's holding up against that heli attack." He swiped and pressed the screen, bringing up an image of the estate grounds. Two helis were there now, and the sky was alive with their onslaught. Overlaid on the image were a set of fluctuating graphs.

"We're good for the moment," said Mr. Lee, "but I hope they don't have much more to throw at us. The generators can only provide a finite amount of energy."

"The sooner we catch a Shadow and take out that suppressor, the better," said Jas.

"Yes, but what then?" Sayen asked. "I've been thinking, if we do get a packet through to the Council, and they take notice, it isn't like they'll be able to come here and rescue us right away. We're going to be at the Shadows' mercy until help arrives."

There was a pause. Jas, like almost everyone else it seemed, hadn't considered what would happen after they achieved their goal. The Shadows knew they were there. They knew that the humans they had trapped were trying to wreck their plans. The aliens weren't going to give up until they were all dead and had their own Shadow clones as replacements.

Mrs. Lee stuck her head around the door. "Sayen, your friend's awake, and she's asking for you."

# FOUR

Sayen had always liked the red guest room the best, and if her mother hadn't suggested putting Erielle in there, she would have asked for it. The room was named for its deep red velvet curtains and rug, which contrasted beautifully with deep cream walls and furniture. There was also an amazing view over the gardens at the rear of the house and the distant hills, where the sun rose in the mornings. As a little girl, Sayen had taken her dolls in there to play and had spent many happy hours pretending that it was a royal court, and that the king and queen were receiving visitors.

It was a surprise to her to see the sour look on Erielle's face. The older woman was sitting up in the sumptuous double bed, looking much better than she had when they'd arrived. She was clean and wearing the sleepwear that Sayen's parents kept for guests. Her hair, which she normally kept close-cropped or even shaved, had begun to grow out in salt-and-pepper shades, and her gaunt face and frame showed the evidence of her many ordeals. But her inner strength and passion hadn't faded. Without her needing to say a word, Sayen could tell the woman's feelings were on fire.

She sat on the edge of the bed and took Erielle's hand. "Is something wrong?" she asked, almost timidly.

"So this is your parents' place?" her lover replied. "From the modding and enhancement you've received, I knew they had money. That was obvious. Maybe I was naive, but I never imagined quite *how much*."

Erielle's tone was harsh. Sayen felt like the woman expected her to apologize for her parents' wealth, as if it were wrong or somehow her fault. She looked down into her lap. "I thought you'd like it here. I thought it would be somewhere that you could rest and get better. And maybe with time, you might change your mind about your legs. My parents would—"

"Don't you dare," spat Erielle, raising a finger in warning. "Don't you dare say it. I am certainly *not* taking your parents' money to get my legs fixed. If I ever get them fixed."

Sayen let go of her hand. She wondered what had happened to that dynamic, ardent, loving woman she'd gotten to know only a couple of weeks before. Now, Erielle seemed full of nothing more than pain, anger, and hate. After all the arguments they'd had about getting her the treatment she needed to take away her pain and allow her to walk again, which the woman stubbornly refused to consider, Sayen could hardly bear being around her anymore.

She got up and went to the window. She looked out over the green lawns. The helis had disappeared for the moment. On the other side of the house, the sun was going down, and a deep shadow spread across the grass.

Sayen turned to face her lover. "Is it really so bad, Erielle? My parents have worked hard for everything they have. It isn't like they inherited their money. Every penny they have, they earned. I just found out that due to what they do, they were—are—also in a lot of danger. My brother and I too. I get that other people aren't so well off, but it isn't like that's my parents' fault. My mama and daddy aren't undeserving. They help keep the world safe, and they donate a lot of money to charity. They fund plenty of projects in poorer countries."

"You think it's generous of them to give away a portion of their billions?" asked Erielle. "Tell me, Sayen, what did you or anyone in your family go without so that they could donate that money? Did you suffer at all? Did you miss out? I'm guessing that, no, you did not. So what makes your parents' generosity so noble? Do you have any idea how many people your parents could help if they gave everything they have? Do you know how much good they could do? But they don't, do they? When you give what you can easily afford, it means nothing. Those charity projects are just an afterthought to your folks. No, instead of helping someone who desperately needs it, they'd rather have kratting *flamingoes* in their lake."

Sayen's face burned. No one had ever spoken to her like that about her parents and their money. Whenever she'd let it slip that her family was very wealthy, most people were mildly jealous, or they would ask her about what it was like growing up in luxury. No one had ever made her feel ashamed of something she had no control over, or embarrassed about the two people she loved the most in the world, and who had never shown her anything but their utter devotion.

She balled her fists. "And what if Mama and Daddy gave everything away, as if they *should*? What a joke that would be. You and your underworlder friends would only spend it on kratom, or booze, or myth. My parents worked hard. They used their brains. They made a *difference*. What the krat have you ever done except run away from your job and your responsibilities? You were a trained surgeon, and you gave it all up to lead a bunch of losers and misfits in their stupid, pointless, posturing, pathetic waste of time they have the arrogance to call their lives.

"Do you know what happened after you went missing, Erielle? I never told you. You were out of it most of the time, and I didn't want to upset you. But it took less than a day of your absence before everything you'd built up for so many years started to fall apart. All those people you'd led and cared for and nurtured? They didn't give a krat about you. *We* were the ones who wanted to go out and find you. It was Jas and Ozment who scoured the streets hoping to stumble across you. All the rest of your misborn underworlder friends didn't give a krat. All they cared about was where their next run was coming from. So I'm not going to apologize because my parents are rich. They have what they deserve, and so do you underworlders."

She stormed across the room, barely taking in Erielle's look of shock. She flung open the door and nearly walked directly into Jas, who was outside. With a snort of frustration, she side-stepped the Martian and stalked away.

Jas caught up to her in a few strides. "Er...things not going so well between you and Erielle?"

"Hmpf. I've had it with her, Jas. I don't know what I ever saw in her. I don't think I ever met anyone so pigheaded, arrogant, or holier-than-thou. I mean, who does she think she is, criticizing the only place where she's safe and can recover? You'd think she'd be just a little grateful—just the tiniest bit thankful that we had this place to escape to. But no. It isn't *humble* enough for her. Erielle's too good for my parents' home, where they've welcomed her as a guest. She needs a hovel to languish and die in just so she can feel *comfortable*. So her fine feelings of *equality* aren't offended."

Jas sighed and put an arm around her. "I don't get what you mean," she said with a small smile. "Stop beating around the bush and tell me how you really feel."

Sayen gave a snort of laughter. A little of her anger dissipated. "Thanks, Jas. I needed that. I guess I'm overreacting a little. Erielle said some ugly things about my parents and my home, but she's still not fully recovered, and she's in a lot of pain. I shouldn't forget that."

"Yeah," Jas said, "with Erielle's beliefs, it would be hard for her to wrap her head around a place like this. I had a little trouble myself when I first saw it, and I don't ever think about things like money or who has what. It's a little hard to take in."

"Maybe I'll go and see her again later," said Sayen. "When I've had a chance to cool down. I might apologize for some of the things I said. I don't want to be her enemy. I like her and I want to be her friend. But, you know, Jas, I don't think we'll ever be more than that again. We're just too incompatible." She looked up at her friend and smiled wistfully. "Sorry, my love life isn't your concern. What are you doing here? Did you want to see me about something?"

"I don't mind hearing about your problems, Sayen, but I'm probably not a good person to talk to. I'm not great at that kind of thing myself. Anyway, I came to tell you what we decided. You and I are going to capture one of the Shadows. Carl and Makey are going to figure out a way to take down the suppressor that's preventing the deep space comms. But we need to do our job before the guys can do theirs. We'll use the scanner to make sure we really have a Shadow. Then your parents will contact the Transgalactic Council and show them the evidence."

"And then what happens?"

Jas sighed. "I have no idea. But we'll do our part. We'll have tried at least. After that, it'll be up to more important people than us to figure out how to defeat the Shadows."

"The people more important than us haven't done such a great job so far."

"You're not wrong, but there's still hope. It sounds like your parents are respected and have a lot of important connections. The Council will listen to them. They'll have to help Earth if they want to stop the Shadows from spreading across the galaxy. I just hope there are enough people left to defeat the invasion here."

"Me too. So what are we doing? How are we going to capture a Shadow?"

"Now that we have your mom and dad's workshop at our disposal, I don't think it's going to be too difficult. What we want to do is find a Shadow when it's on its own, stun it, and bring it in here. We want to avoid a gunfight with the others if we can. We don't want to take more risks than we have to. We've been burned enough."

"I'm all for that. My skin recovers quickly from a laser burn, but it sure as hell hurts when it happens. So how are we going to know when a Shadow is on its own?"

"Your dad says he has something that will help."

# FIVE

The fennec fox looked like it was asleep, except for the fact that it wasn't breathing. Makey reached out and stroked its fur, which was about the finest, softest thing he'd ever felt. The animal was cold to the touch. This wasn't surprising because it wasn't real, though he was having a hard time believing it.

"It's so lifelike," he said to Mr. Lee, who was adjusting controls on an interface screen.

"Hmmm," replied the man, his head down as he concentrated on what he was doing. "That's the idea. If it's spotted, it should pass for the real thing, at a cursory glance anyway."

Makey, Sayen, and Jas were in the basement laboratory with Sayen's father, gathered around the animal he'd built as a surveillance device.

"Wouldn't it be better to use a mosquito or something a similar size?" asked Sayen. "The fox is small, but it wouldn't be that hard to spot and destroy if someone suspected what it was."

"It isn't that easy to spot in this landscape. It's very well camouflaged. Fennec foxes are notoriously difficult for predators other than man to catch. They're virtually invisible against a desert background, and they're fast and nimble. It was the first animal that sprung to mind when I first thought of creating something to spy on the

Shadows around us. I've used it successfully three times now. That was how I first located the suppressor within that building they're constructing."

"But wouldn't a mosquito be more maneuverable?" Sayen persisted. "I mean, at the first sign of trouble, it could fly away."

"You're right, sweetheart, but a mosquito's too small. Let me tell you how this thing works, and then you'll understand. A mosquito is fine and dandy for standard surveillance. In fact, I have a number of them just over there that I designed and made myself. But even with the latest in storage capacity, it isn't large enough. Now an animal like this is about the right size. Only a small part of this fox is given over to its locomotion, sensory, and transmitting equipment—of course, there's no need to include the other parts of the natural animal, such as its digestive system—the rest of it is given over to housing the operator's consciousness."

"What?" exclaimed Jas. "The person operating it...you mean it holds their mind? They embody this thing?"

"That's right. A direct mind connection with a surveillance device is far more effective than operating one at a distance. Anyone can do it, providing I link them up to its system. The capacity remaining aside from the space required for the other necessary components is roughly the size of a human brain. It would be an abomination to put a real brain in there, of course, but the material we use mimics the complexity of neurons and other cells that make up the human brain. Not perfectly. We haven't managed to achieve that yet. But perfection isn't necessary. It isn't like anyone's going to live in there."

Makey could hardly believe his ears. Since arriving on Earth, he'd been turned speechless more than once at the amazing things he'd encountered—things that he'd never even imagined while growing up on Dawn. But if he understood Mr. Lee correctly, this latest object was almost beyond belief. The man seemed to be saying that someone could transfer their mind to the animal and operate it from the inside, as if that person were the animal itself.

"What happens to the person's body while their mind is in the animal?" he asked.

"Nothing at all. All human functions necessary to life continue as before—heartbeat, lung function, metabolism, none of these requires the mind to work. Sadly, we used to see that in previous generations when people would suffer brain death but their bodies would continue to live on as if nothing had happened. Thankfully, no one has to suffer that indignity any longer."

"I meant what happens in the operator's mind? Can you be in the animal and aware of your body at the same time?" Makey asked.

"No, that would be too disorienting I think. I've set up the system so that isn't possible. Once you're in the fox, you're only aware of everything from its perspective. You see through its eyes, listen through its considerable ears, and feel through its fur and mouth. Of course, whatever the fox sees and hears, etcetera, is also displayed on this screen and recorded."

"And how do you get out of it again?" asked Makey.

Mr. Lee smiled. "I believe we have a budding scientist in our midst. When we have more time, I will explain to you exactly how to operate the device and how it works, though you'd probably have to study several degree-level courses to understand. It was Sayen's mother who programmed the consciousness transference. I have to admit I don't understand it too well myself. Suffice to say, the operator learns a mental sequence that triggers the return to their body. With luck, that should only happen when the device has returned. I wouldn't like to lose it in the field. It would take me days to make another."

Makey had a horrible feeling that, from what Mr. Lee was saying, *he* wasn't going to be the one operating the fox. His heart sank. He didn't think he'd ever wanted anything so much in his whole life, except maybe that his sister and mam could return from the dead.

Mr. Lee read his expression. "When this is all over, Makey, not only will I explain how to operate this fox, I will allow you to do so."

"Sneck," Makey exclaimed. "Thanks."

"But for now," Jas said, "I believe that Carl will want to talk to you about destroying that suppressor."

"Awww," Makey whined, "but that isn't until after you and

Sayen have caught a Shadow. That isn't for ages. I'd rather stay here and watch someone transfer their mind to that fox."

"Makey," said Jas in that voice that meant she didn't want to have to say anything else.

"Oh, okay. I'm going." He left them and went up in the elevator. He found Carl outside the front of the house, where he was inspecting the truck.

Though it was a tough vehicle, it had taken plenty of damage when Ozment had driven it through the perimeter fence and ware-house wall at the spaceport. The grill was buckled, and the top of the cab was crumpled. Black streaks ran down the sides from the heli attack.

"She's a beauty, eh?" Carl asked. "Don't you think?"

"Er," was all Makey could think to reply.

It didn't matter. The Australian was lost in his admiration of the vehicle. "Never had a chance to really look at her till now. I can remember trucks like this from when I was a kid. Big, ten-wheeled monsters with tires bigger than me. I used to dream of driving one across the Nullabor. Nothing around me but the desert and the sea. Nothing above but the sky. For hundreds and hundreds of kilometers. That'd be an experience. Not, mind you," he said, waggling a finger at Makey, "that it would beat flying. Nothing beats that. Still, it'd be great, wouldn't it?"

"I suppose so. Um, Jas sent me up here to talk to you about destroying the suppressor."

Carl's eyes and mind were still on the truck. He had his hands on his hips, and he was nodding thoughtfully at some scenario playing in his head. After a moment of silence, Makey's words seemed to register. "Did you say something, mate? Oh, yeah, destroying the suppressor. Yeah. That's our job. Right." He pulled open the driver's side door. "Hop in."

"Huh?" said Makey. "That's your side."

"Oh no. You'll be driving. I've got to get up on top."

"What?" Makey exclaimed. "You mean you're going to sit where Ozment died?"

"Someone has to. The Shadows have got two helis. The minute

we start this thing up, they'll be onto us. We won't have long before they figure out what we're going to do and try to take us out. Before they figure out what we're doing, maybe. If we've got no defense, we'll be sitting ducks."

"Then I'll do it. I'll go up there," said Makey. "I'm an ace shot. Jas said so."

"No. No way. You're too young. Jas won't hear of it, and I agree with her."

Makey clenched his jaw. He wished they would all stop treating him like a kid. "I'm not too young. I'm not allowed to do anything. It's like you all don't want me to grow up."

"It isn't that. Kid, we don't let you do stuff *because* we want you to grow up. We want you to have the chance."

Makey sighed. The man only wanted to look out for him. "Okay. Are you going to teach me how to drive?"

"That's right. Come on." They climbed up into the cab, and Carl began showing him the different controls and telling him what they did.

"You know," Carl said, "I used to imagine teaching my kid to drive one day. Keep the old skills going, you know. I never thought I'd be teaching a seventeen-year-old colony pup. Still, you'll do. Now, usually it'd be hard to find a place for you to practice driving a vehicle this size, but we're lucky. We've got acres of parkland to drive around in. We'll take her round the back of the house."

"Do you think Sayen's parents are going to mind us ruining their lawn?"

"Right now," Carl said as a heli rose up from beyond the half-finished building at the end of the driveway, "I think that's the least of their worries."

# SIX

Jas was inside the fennec fox. Wrong. She *was* the fox. The figures of Sayen and Mr. Lee were impossibly high above her, almost unrecognizable from her new perspective. To her left, she could see her own legs, as her body, which she'd temporarily left, sprawled unconscious in a reclining chair.

"How do you feel, Jas?" asked Mr. Lee, peering down at her. His voice was almost painful in her super-sensitive ears. "As I explained, you aren't able to speak, so nod if you're okay."

Jas tried to nod, and the fox's head obeyed her thoughts. The world moved up and down in response. She staggered, feeling extremely disoriented. If she'd had a stomach, she would have been sick.

"It'll take you a few minutes to accustom yourself to the experience," Mr. Lee said. "Take your time. Walk around a little."

"I still think *I* should be the one doing this," said Sayen.

"And I still think that we need your enhanced powers right here in case of an attack," replied her father.

Jas took a tentative step on her right front paw. Which leg came next? One of her back legs, probably, but which one? She tried to move her right rear leg and wobbled dangerously. That wasn't right. She quickly brought her left front leg forward to compensate. But then her right rear leg was in the wrong place. She returned all four legs to their starting points. This needed some figuring out.

Meanwhile, her mind was becoming aware of a rich range of sensations. The most noticeable were the signals coming from her nose. She smelled odors she could never have believed possible before. And so many of them. She smelled the sour, metallic aroma of the dust on the floor. The scents of Sayen and her father were heavy in the air. They smelled different from each other, but there were similarities that told Jas the two were related.

Her hearing was also turned up to a much higher capacity. She could hear the three humans in the room breathing and the sounds of their intestines moving, squeezing food and gas along. Somewhere, a fly was trapped in a web, and a spider was picking its way toward its victim.

Vibrations from the floor through her paws told her that Ozment's truck had started up outside. She could even detect the movement of air currents against the highly sensitive hairs inside her ears.

She tried to move her legs again. After putting her right front paw forward, she followed the movement with her left rear paw, then repeated the action with the legs on the opposite sides. That worked much better.

"Well done, Jas," Sayen said. "You're getting it."

Soon, she was running around the laboratory. Embodying a surveillance device in the shape of a small animal was fun, she decided. She wished she had more time to explore this new experience, but they couldn't waste a moment in capturing a Shadow. She nudged Mr. Lee's leg with her nose.

"You're ready?" he asked. "Good. Follow me."

He took her up in the elevator to the first floor and out into the conservatory full of orchids Jas'sd seen on her first visit. Mrs. Lee was there. She was with the maid, Florence. The android's chest was open, and Sayen's mother had both hands inside. She looked over her shoulder as her husband and daughter and a small, pale brown fox appeared.

"Jas, you seem to be doing fine," the woman said. "Good luck.

Don't forget the sequence for returning to your own body when you get back. Or if things get too hairy out there, activate the sequence and just leave the fox behind. We can always make another one. We can't make another Jas."

Jas wished she could thank her.

Mr. Lee opened the doors that led outside to the huge green lawn. Dusk was falling. "I'm going to show you a tiny place in the force field where you can slip through," he said. "It's too small for any human, even that creepy little Shadow girl. But you can fit it. You must come back the same way, and preferably unseen, though I can seal the spot if Shadows follow you and try to break through."

Jas, Mr. Lee, and Sayen walked across the lawn toward the woods that bordered the furthest reaches of the Lees' estate. The Shadow-controlled helis had stopped attacking for the moment. Jas wondered if they had only been testing the strength of the force field and were preparing themselves for a serious assault. She estimated they had a day or maybe two at most to carry out their plans. The Shadows were moving fast. It would be only a short time before they gathered the firepower to breach the Lees' defenses. Either that or they would have replaced enough of the population with Shadows to do away with the need for subterfuge.

Her paws crunched on the dry leaf mold beneath the trees as they entered the woods. The trees stretched only fifty meters wide. They arrived at the thick-wired fence that stood between the verdant private gardens and the surrounding desert landscape. Jas searched for watching Shadows, but there were none. It was a good sign. The aliens didn't seem to have the numbers to surround the place—yet. Mr. Lee led them along the fence to an area that didn't appear to be any different from the rest. Jas wondered how she would find it again when she returned from spying on the Shadows.

Mr. Lee took a pair of glasses out of his pocket. After putting them on, he scanned the fence where it met the ground.

"We have a hidden gate in this fence back near the house, but I'd have to turn off the electricity for you to open it. At this spot, you can return whenever you're ready. We don't have to prearrange a time."

"Couldn't the Shadows just dig under the fence, Daddy?" Sayen asked.

"They could try," he replied, "but it goes ten meters deep and it's electrified all the way down, though the underground part is insulated in plastic. Ah, here it is." He took a bottle from his jacket pocket, opened it, and shook a few drops of a clear liquid on the ground next to the fence wires. "Can you smell that, Jas?"

She trotted over and sniffed the ground. The stench was so powerful it made her reel backward. She gave a huge sneeze and shook her head.

Mr. Lee laughed. "I'm sorry. I made the pheromone a little strong, but it works. Humans can't register the scent, and I'm guessing that Shadow humans can't either. Only you will be able to find it, Jas. When you return, sniff along the border until you smell it, then pass through where the odor is strongest."

"But she can't," Sayen said. "Even a small animal can't fit through the gaps in the wires."

"There is no fence just there. Use these." He passed Sayen his glasses. "It's an optical illusion."

"Oh yes," she exclaimed. "I can see it. A small gap."

"Ordinarily," Mr. Lee said, "we would have only the electrified fence protecting the grounds and the air barrier to seal in the cool air. I've turned the air barrier into a force field that extends all the way to the ground, but left this tiny entrance open. However, Jas, take care not to touch the fence. It's still electrified."

*Easy for you to say,* thought Jas. *You can see the hole.* To her, the fence looked complete. She had only the pheromone that Mr. Lee had sprinkled and his word to rely on. Unfortunately, she couldn't tell him that.

Looking down at her from his great height, the man seemed to guess her concerns. "There's plenty of room for you. You won't be in any danger of electrocution providing you follow your nose, so to speak."

Jas approached the stink again and got ready to walk through the apparently solid wires. She took a final look at Sayen and Mr. Lee.

Sayen's hand hesitated, as if she were resisting an urge to give her a pat.

"Good luck, Jas," she said.

"Yes, good luck," said Mr. Lee. "We'll return to the lab and check your progress on the screen. Don't forget, you can activate the sequence to return to your body at any time. It's preferable that you return in the device, of course. It would take me longer than we have to make another one."

He was right. Time was of the essence. Night was falling. She had to go and find a Shadow for them to capture.

She set her nose toward the fence where the ground smelled strongest and went forward. As she was about to touch the wires, they seemed to suddenly melt away. In a moment, she was through and outside, standing on desert dirt instead of leaf litter. The ground was still hot from the day's sun, though the fur on her paws was doing a great job of protecting her from the worst of it.

Sniffing the air, she detected little but dry vegetation in the vicinity, and she could hear nothing but the warm wind passing over the dusty ground. She would have to walk around the estate to the front to find the Shadows.

# SEVEN

Makey turned the truck's steering wheel and followed the driveway as it led around the Lees' mansion to the gardens at the back. Driving the vehicle was a lot easier than he'd thought it would be. Not for the first time, he wondered why his Da and the Dawntowners thought that mechanical things were so evil. This truck didn't give off the bad gases he'd heard them talk about, which had polluted the air and made the global temperatures rise. It ran on electricity. The Lees had charged up the nearly dead battery soon after he and the others arrived.

Though he didn't like the truck as much as Carl did, he couldn't see anything bad about it. It was certainly going to be useful for taking out that suppressor Mr. Lee had told them about.

He pressed the brake. They'd run out of paved roadway. If they went any farther, they would be driving on grass.

"What's up?" Carl asked from the passenger seat. "You're doing great."

"Are you sure it's okay for us to do this?"

"Makey, if we don't drive this truck into that suppressor and destroy it, we're all gonna die. Do you think Sayen's parents would prefer a nice lawn over not dying? Geez, mate. Look, here's Mr. Lee. You can ask him for yourself."

Mr. Lee and Sayen were crossing the grass on their way back to the house. Carl lowered his window and called out to them, "Hey, Mr. Lee, is it all right if Makey gets some driving practice in on your lawn?"

"Go ahead," said Mr. Lee, "but first, let me show you something."

Makey turned off the engine, and they got out of the truck. They went inside and upstairs with Mr. Lee to his office, where he brought up an image on the large interface on his office wall. It was a mass of wave patterns, all flowing across the screen.

"Our sensors are picking these up. They're what's preventing us from sending a deep space packet to our contact at the Transgalactic Council. I'll show you what I've found." He swiped the screen, and it turned black. With a finger, he drew a sketch of an aerial view of the Shadows' building. "The suppressor is here." He drew an X at the bottom left corner. "That's the side facing away from us."

"Not next to the road, the other side?" Carl asked.

"That's right. If you crash the truck into this corner, you should destroy the machine."

"Won't that destroy the truck, too?" Makey asked. They were talking about driving into solid brick, not the corrugated metal wall they'd encountered at the spaceport.

"Yeah, I'd say so," Carl replied. "She's a tough old thing, but I don't think she'll survive that. More's the shame."

"And then what happens?" Makey asked.

"We fight our way out," said Carl, "or something. Don't worry, we'll figure it out. The most important thing is to take out that suppressor."

Makey swallowed. Suddenly, learning to drive the truck seemed like a piece of cake. He'd thought they'd reached some kind of safety at Sayen's parents' home, but of course that had been stupid. No one was safe anymore. It didn't matter, he decided. He would stop the Shadows, whatever it took, in memory of Mam and Neeve.

"You all right, mate?" Carl asked.

"Yeah, I'm fine. You were saying we have to drive the truck through here?" Makey pointed to the sketch on the screen. "Then I reckon we should come off the road where it bends. What do you think, Carl?"

"I think you're right." Carl put a hand on his shoulder. "Yeah, you're right. That gives us the best angle. Well done."

Makey smiled and felt a warm glow at the older man's words. Finally, someone was treating him like an adult. If only he had a dad a bit more like Carl or Mr. Lee.

"Do you really think you can do it?" Mr. Lee said. "You realize you'll be under aerial attack?"

"I thought about that," Carl replied. "Our friend, Ozment, built some kind of missile launcher into the roof of the truck. You can't see it from the ground. Poor fella died up there."

Mr. Lee's eyebrows rose. "You must show me. Maybe I can improve it for you."

They returned downstairs, and Mr. Lee took them into the conservatory, where his wife was still working on the android. "Carleen, would you come with us? I think you could lend us a hand with something."

They all passed through the conservatory doors and into the garden, where the massive, battle-scarred truck now blocked the view of the lawn, lake, and trees. Night lay over the estate, and the stars were coming out. Carl took them into the truck cabin and pointed out the homemade tunnel that led to the roof.

While Mr. Lee returned to the house for flashlights. Carl went up the tunnel, followed by Mrs. Lee. Carl called down to Makey, telling him not to join them because there wasn't room for more than two people, so he sat in the cab, feeling a little left out again and wondering what the others were doing.

Bobbing lights coming from the house attracted his attention. Mr. Lee had returned with an android servant. Both were carrying flashlights and ladders.

"Would you like to have a look too, son?" he asked as he placed a ladder against the side of the truck. Makey didn't need to be asked twice. He was out of the cab and up the ladder in a flash, while the android held it steady.

At the top, he found he was looking down into a pit sunk into the truck's roof. The top edge was level with the rest of the roof, so unless you were looking at it from a higher point, you wouldn't know the pit existed. Carl and Mrs. Lee were in there examining a large weapon. Makey had no idea what it was, but it looked powerful. Mr. Lee joined him at the top of a second ladder and shone a flashlight into the pit. The beams lit up the operator's chair that was next to the weapon. The seat was stained darkly with what Makey realized had to be Ozment's blood. And now Carl was going to be in the exact same position.

"Craven," Mrs. Lee said, "do you think you could make some kind of shield to fit over this thing? It won't withstand a single direct hit as it is."

"I sure can," he replied. "I can do it overnight. I'm thinking that tungsten/graphene alloy. I have a few sheets left. And I can reinforce the truck walls. What do you think?"

"Sounds fine. And I'll work on upgrading this for maximum firepower and automatic targeting. Don't you worry, sugar," she said to Carl. "Any of those helis comes within spitting distance of this truck, you'll be taking them out of the sky quicker than you can blink at them."

"Thanks, Mr. and Mrs. Lee," Carl said. "I appreciate it."

"No need to thank us," said Mr. Lee. "We're all in this together. Isn't that right, son?" He addressed his question to Makey.

"Yes, sir, that's right."

The blackness of the night was split by a dazzling burst of light. The air was filled with a sizzling, crackling noise. Makey was momentarily blinded. The beam that had struck was far more powerful than the ones the Shadow helis had fired earlier.

"What the hell was that?" Carl asked.

"Looks like the Shadows are back, and they've upgraded," said Mr. Lee.

"What was it, Craven?" Mrs. Lee asked. "Do you know?"

"Some kind of pulse cannon, I guess."

"How long can the force field take it?" she asked.

"We should make it through the night. I wonder if they've

guessed our energy is from solar power, and that's why they waited until nighttime to attack?"

"Lord knows," Mrs. Lee said. "I hope you're right and that we make it until dawn. There's nothing much we can do anyway. Might as well keep busy getting this ready. Can you lend us a hand, son?" she asked Makey. "We're going to need all the help we can get if we're going to finish by morning."

"Of course I can," he replied.

# EIGHT

The cool night air chilled Jas's nose and the tips of her ears, but the failing light didn't affect her vision. If anything, things seemed to become clearer and sharper. The desert was alive with sound as the nocturnal creatures were waking up and leaving the places they hid from the hot sun during the day.

She ran alongside the security fence, keeping a good distance from its electrified wires. It wasn't long before she reached the road. The pavement was deserted. She kept low as she scooted across, a fleeting shadow herself in the deep twilight. Silently, she made her way down the bank and across the distance that separated her from the Shadow's construction site.

All she had to do was to find a likely Shadow to snatch. One of the aliens alone in a place it probably wouldn't leave for a while, such as asleep in bed. Then she could return to the Lees' home and her own body, and she and Sayen could slip out, take the Shadow, and bring it back as quickly and quietly as possible.

When they had the Shadow scanner readout, everything would be ready to send to the Council.

The dark-windowed building was drawing nearer as she trotted along, wondering what she would find inside. She wondered if the

Shadows continued regular human lives when they lived in their replicated bodies, or if they behaved according to their alien minds.

Not panting with exertion after the long run felt weird. The side of the building loomed up. Jas slipped around the back, hoping to find a rear entrance. There was none, and though the windows were only frames without any glass, they were much too high for her to reach. She would have to enter at the front.

A few Shadows were hanging around outside as if waiting for something. None of them noticed her scurry behind them and into the cooler interior of the building.

On the first floor at least, the Shadows had constructed rooms with ceilings. They were bare and dusty. Where did they eat and sleep, she wondered. Surely their bodies had the same requirements as those of the humans they'd copied?

Jas ran silently down a corridor. She turned one corner, and then another. Still, she met no Shadows. What lay around the third corner made her stop in her tracks. A terrifyingly familiar, dark gray shape seemed to rear up. It was a hexagonal block, and in its center was a hexagonal hole. A Shadow trap. They'd built a trap within the building.

She froze in the center of the corridor, her shock making her momentarily unwary of the danger of being seen. Why had the Shadows constructed one of their traps out in the middle of nowhere? The Lees lived kilometers from their nearest neighbors. Had the aliens gone to all that trouble just to replicate Sayen's parents, and maybe herself and her friends? It seemed like overkill.

Her super-sensitive ears swiveled backward as a faint noise came from behind her. It was the sound of voices, as well as car doors slamming. Had more Shadows arrived, or...? Her heart sank as she viewed the trap's gaping hole. Was it some human victims? Were the Shadows supplementing their numbers at the site by bringing in people to replicate?

Her ears twitched. The voices were drawing nearer, and the floor vibrated faintly with many footsteps. She glanced left and right. The corridor was bare, with nowhere to hide. Doors had been fitted in the doorways, but they were all closed and impossible for her to open.

The voices were only a corridor away. If she didn't get out of sight soon, the approaching Shadows would see her. Maybe they would only be surprised at the sight of her, and they wouldn't try to catch her, but she couldn't take that risk. Desperately, she scanned the corridor again.

Her gaze fell upon a small gap between the edge of the Shadow trap and the corridor wall. It looked barely wide enough, but she could probably squeeze inside. She went in backward as there was no space for her to turn around.

No sooner had she hunkered down and peeked out than a group of people turned the corner and came into view. There were ten or twelve men and women in ordinary office clothes, and they were chatting about everyday stuff. At first, it was impossible to tell who was human and who was a Shadow, but within seconds, the difference was evident.

The humans in the group—about half of them—were puzzled and shocked at the sight of the Shadow trap.

"What the krat's that thing?" one of them asked.

"Is this some kind of joke?" another asked. "I thought we were going to discuss the building progress, not get taken on a theme park ride."

"Ha," a third said, "that's right. It looks like the entrance to a ghost walk."

"It's just a little diversion before the meeting," one of the Shadows said. "It'll be fun. Come inside."

"Oh, I don't think so," said the person who spoke last. "That place looks scary. I hated those kinds of things when I was a child. I'm going to skip it. I'll wait outside for you folks to finish your fun."

"Me too. I'm not going near it. Look, we appreciate it and all, but I think it might be better if we have the meeting and get it over with. We all have our families to go home to tonight, right?"

The group had reached the trap's entrance. "We insist," said a Shadow. "Come on. It'll only take a minute or two. There's nothing to worry about."

"Really, let's just have the meeting," said a man.

"No," a Shadow replied and pulled out a gun. The other Shadows did the same. The people were in the center, and the aliens surrounded them.

The humans gasped. One of the men tried to grab a weapon. The Shadow holding it shot him at point blank range, destroying his chest. There were screams as his lifeless body crumpled to the floor.

"Inside," commanded a Shadow, all pretense gone. It gestured toward the trap, its face expressionless.

After some hesitation, the humans shuffled in. Some were silently weeping. The Shadows brought up the rear, threatening with their weapons.

A sense of powerlessness and frustration overwhelmed Jas as the group passed inside the trap. The people were going to die and there wasn't anything she could do about it. If she'd been in her own body, she might have been able to save them, but as a tiny animal, she was powerless. She didn't know what to do.

*Go after them, Jas. See what happens.*

She jumped a little in surprise. She'd forgotten she was hooked up to the surveillance equipment back at the Lees' home, and that it was recording everything she saw and heard.

It had been Sayen's voice speaking through the linkup in her mind. *You think I should?* she asked mentally. *Maybe I should just find a Shadow we can snatch and get back to you guys.*

*No,* Sayen replied. *This might be the first and the last chance anyone has of seeing what happens inside a Shadow trap. Haggardy said he couldn't tell what was going on when he was forced inside one with the other officers of the* Galathea, *do you remember? But you have night vision. You'll be able to see clearly. The better we understand the Shadows, the easier it'll be to defeat them. We're recording all of this, and we can include it in the packet we send to the Transgalactic Council. If we can capture evidence of what the Shadows do to people, we won't need one of our own to show them.*

*Okay, I'll see what I can do,* Jas replied.

The corridor was empty. She left her hiding place and went through the hexagonal entrance, into the Shadow trap.

She'd first entered a similar structure on K.67092d weeks ago. As she went deeper in, following the sound of people and Shadows ahead, a dull chill settled over her. The feeling was partly due to the frigid atmosphere, and partly due to her memories of taking her fifteen defense units on one Locate, Investigate, Vacate procedure after another of the Shadow traps and failing to find anything wrong. She wished that somehow she could have been more thorough. If only she'd been able to find something to convince the *Galathea's* master, Loba, of the threat, so many lives could have been saved.

But it was too late for what-might-have-beens. At least now, she finally had her chance to find out what the Shadows did inside their traps.

# Nine

Replication. Generation. Domination. The plan had to succeed.

Time moved on within the physical realm. The invasion of the planet called Earth was reaching a crisis point.

Most of the schemes had been successful. Their kind now occupied important positions in the controlling and supervising organizations of the planet. They had destroyed and replaced humans in most tiers of the planetary hierarchy. In many cases, replication had taken place without attracting suspicion. In others, humans who had noticed the changes had themselves been quickly targeted and replicated. Soon, replication and generation could occur on a mass scale. The remaining human population would be eradicated.

Until then, it was vital that the galactic powers remain unaware of what was taking place on Earth. A severe threat remained: the six trapped humans.

They had the humans confined within a defended domain. Two were older than the others, and a familial relationship existed between them and one of the younger humans. The group included one adolescent. The two older ones were closely connected with influential agents on Earth and in the galaxy's governing body, named the Transgalactic Council. The other four had been identified upon their arrival. The one who was related to the older ones had infiltrated the digital records that held information on the secret invasion. Despite their best efforts, that human had not been copied and destroyed.

The other three humans were also known. Two had served aboard the starship that had crashed on a trap planet. The sixth human—the adolescent—had escaped from a planet under invasion and come to Earth aboard the same starship. The adolescent had absconded from the center it had been sent to.

Much information was known about these humans. They had inflicted substantial damage and successfully evaded capture many times. The risk their existence posed was extreme, yet all efforts to destroy them had failed. Rather, their menace grew greater. Other humans had been easy to trap and replicate. What made these different?

The threat they posed was growing greater. Already, four of them had broken into a spaceport and stolen a critical item. It was only after investigation had established *what* was stolen that its significance was realized. The air attack to destroy the humans and the purloined machine had failed. Now, they would be able to use the device to identify a human replicant.

The event increased the risk of defeat. Replication and generation depended on the replicants' ability to blend into the local population. If the humans used the machine to root out replicants, the effects would be disastrous. Even worse, if the humans alerted the galactic powers of the invasion, all their plans would fail. Past experience of failure told them what would happen then. Wholesale slaughter. A massacre of their kind. No opportunity to return to the void. No chance of life within the physical realm or the ethereal place that was their home.

All resources were to be devoted to eliminating these humans. Already, devices newly acquired had been used to shut down external communication to galactic and intraplanetary receivers. Now, all new weapons obtained were to be targeted at the trapped humans. It was vital that they were eradicated.

To add to the difficulties, as well as the persistent threat of the six renegade humans, an old enemy had emerged within the void. A never-ending battle had resumed. Beings who chose to thwart their attempts to infiltrate the physical realm had discovered their schemes and, once again, risen up against them.

Through an infinity of nothingness, the two sides tussled. Never tiring and unable to die, the fighters fought without respite, whirling in patterns of ether and light, fleeing only to be recaptured, and securing their opponents only to have to eventually release them.

Two escapes were open: Earth and other planets of the galaxy, where they could live on within replicants, or a final defeat of their enemy within the void. If they could achieve both, victory would be sweet. They could live on forever within their corporeal and ethereal forms. They could enjoy physical pleasures and the freedom of the void, and move between the realms without restraint.

They had only to destroy the trapped humans and vanquish their ancient foe. Then, eternity and infinite space could be theirs.

# TEN

Carl passed a hand over his eyes. Jas stopped the playback of what she'd witnessed inside the Shadow trap. They were alone in the basement of the Lees' home. Sayen had refused to watch the replay of the vid. Seeing the events through the spy fox's eyes as it had happened was plenty, she'd said, before going upstairs to talk to her parents. Carl was wishing he'd followed her lead.

Though the recording had been a confusion of figures and movement, he had seen enough detail to understand the terrible events. He didn't think he would ever be able to forget the images of the men and women sinking—*dissolving*—into the floor, or erase from his memory their cries of terror and agony.

Jas had been able to view the scene first hand because she'd watched it through the surveillance device's visual sensors. She'd estimated that if she'd been watching with human eyes, she wouldn't have seen a thing in the darkness. The Shadows had retreated to another chamber, and the dim beams from their distant flashlights were the only illumination. The victims had acted as though they were blind.

"Krat," Carl said. "I never even imagined what they went through. Margret, the officers on the *Galathea*, the governor on

Dawn, and the soldiers...Jas, do you think *that's* what happened to my parents?"

Jas reached out and took his hand. "I said I didn't think you should watch. If you hadn't insisted on seeing what the Shadows did, I wouldn't have shown you. It's probably best not to think about it."

He placed his other hand over hers. "I get that you wanted to protect me, but I suppose it's better that I know. We've got to *destroy* these misborns, Jas. We've got to take them out—forever."

"I know. And we will. We will. But wait a moment. Watch the next part."

She restarted the vid. The human victims had entirely disappeared, absorbed by the Shadow trap floor, but the Shadows returned and stood as if waiting for something. They pointed their flashlights at one wall of the chamber.

After a short time, a bulge appeared in the wall. A lump of dark gray material protruded. A little farther down the wall, a similar bulge appeared.

"Look," Jas said, pointing at the first gray lump.

Carl leaned forward to peer at the screen more closely. The surface was changing, melting like ice cream on a sunny day. The material shifted around, and lines and irregular shapes appeared. "It's a face," he exclaimed. "So, this is...?"

Jas nodded. "This is how the victims' Shadows emerge. Watch."

When the lump had changed into a recognizably human, dark gray head, it began to struggle, as if it were trying to fight its way out of the wall. A smaller lump appeared below the head, and another below that. The struggling head moved forward, dragging out a torso behind it. As the body appeared, it grew more defined. It moved out into the room, pulling its legs and arms free, until finally a human form stood unsteadily in the chamber.

While this was going on, more human-like figures were pushing through the wall and struggling free. Soon, a group of new Shadows were standing together, the same number as the victims who had been murdered. The aliens were breathing, taking on color, and moving about uncertainly. The original Shadows went forward to help them. It was like witnessing a set of bizarre, horrifying births.

After some time, when the new Shadows had gotten used to their bodies, all of them left the chamber. Jas turned off the recording.

Carl exhaled as tension left him. "What did you do then?" he asked.

"I had to follow them—at a distance," Jas replied. "Even the visual sensors Sayen's dad installed in the fox needed *some* light to operate, and it was pitch black in there. Without light, I would never have found my way out of the place. As well as the darkness, it's a maze. I remember the same from the LIVs I conducted when we were aboard the *Galathea*. I needed my helmet's navigation function to find my way out again. I guess that's part of the trap. If you wander in, or you're tempted or forced inside, I don't know how anyone would ever find their way out. I don't know how Haggardy did it."

"Do you still think he's a Shadow?"

"I don't know. Maybe he is, or maybe he's just the same misborn he's always been. It doesn't matter anymore. There were Shadows here on Earth before we returned. One more or less isn't going to make a difference. But, Carl, we don't know for sure if that's what's happened to your parents. No Shadows of them were waiting for you when you got home."

"That's right. I wouldn't have stood a chance against two Shadows catching me by surprise."

"I wonder what did happen to them."

Carl smiled ruefully. "Knowing my folks, they wouldn't have let themselves become victims of the Shadows. They'd rather have died."

The significance of his words hit him, and he reached out to Jas and drew her close, burying his face in the crook of her neck. She wrapped her arms around him. They stayed that way for a while, until his emotions were spent.

Carl was exhausted. The last time he'd slept had been on the mountainside where Ozment had taken them. It seemed an age ago, and there would be no opportunity for rest that night. The bombardment from the Shadows was continuing, a dazzling display of power. They could break through at any moment. He and Makey had to take out the suppressor as soon as possible.

After that, who knew what would happen? It seemed likely that Carl's next sleep would be his last, but now that he'd finally accepted that his parents were gone, maybe that didn't matter so much anymore.

On the far side of the basement, the elevator chimed, and the doors opened. Sayen stepped out. "Have you two finished watching that vid yet? I came to tell you that the Shadow attack has stopped for the moment. The skies are clear."

"Yeah, all done," Jas replied. She turned off the screen.

"What do you think?" Sayen asked as she walked over. "Enough evidence to show the Council? Or do we need a real live Shadow too?"

"I guess the Council might be persuaded the vid's been faked," Jas replied, "but it's enough to raise their suspicions, especially if your parents send it. Even so, I still think we should catch a Shadow and send them the positive result from the scanner. No one could argue with that, and it gives us something to do until the truck's ready."

"Great," Sayen said. "I was getting bored just sitting around. Ha, it's weird. I would never have wanted to do anything like this before. Now I can't wait. I wish my brother were here. He always used to tease me for being a little mouse. I think he'd be proud of me."

"We're all proud of you," Jas said.

"That's right," Carl said. "How are your parents doing with their alterations to the truck?"

"About another hour they said. You should see Makey. He's in heaven. I don't think I've ever seen him happier."

"Do we have enough time for a short expedition?" Jas asked.

"Yeah, I think so. I'll ask Daddy if he can turn off the defenses for a moment so we can go through the secret gate and arrange a time for him to turn them off again so we can get in. What do you think?"

"Sounds good" Jas said. "I didn't tell you," she said to Carl. "After I came out of the trap, I found one of the Shadows asleep alone in a room. It shouldn't take more than fifteen to twenty minutes to slip out, grab her, and slip back in again."

"It's a woman?" Carl asked.

"No, it's that little girl you wanted me to grab when we arrived. For some reason, she's sleeping apart from the adults. The others seem to be sticking in groups."

# Eleven

Sayen waited as Jas checked the time. They were in a wooded section of the estate, but near the house this time, at the secret gate.

"Thirty seconds," Jas said.

They were wearing dark clothes, and Sayen's father had given them something to wear over their heads that covered their faces and necks. The material allowed them to breathe easily, but prevented light from reflecting off their faces and revealing them in the darkness. Both also carried two weapons strapped to their hips in case something went wrong and they had to protect themselves. Sayen was bringing a sedative to inject into the sleeping Shadow so that she wouldn't wake up and raise the alarm.

"Fifteen seconds," said Jas.

Sayen got ready to open the secret gate. Her father had pointed out the barely visible outline of it in the fence. Beyond that point, all was dark. The sky had clouded over and the moon and stars weren't visible. Sayen blinked and used her night vision. She saw no forms other than the sparse desert plants. There was no sign of any movement.

They had to get the timing right. Touching the gate at the wrong moment would mean certain death. They had only five seconds to go through and close it behind them. They couldn't risk turning off the defenses for longer. The aerial attack could recommence at any time. Once they were through, they had twenty minutes to find and bring back the Shadow. If they missed the time scheduled for their return, they would be locked out.

"Five, four, three, two—" Jas said.

Sayen reached out.

"One."

She opened the gate. They stepped through, and she pulled it closed.

"Let's go," Jas said.

"Wait," said Sayen. The gate had disappeared into the fence. Once they left it, they would have a hard time finding it again. "Get some rocks," she said to Jas.

"I see what you mean. Good idea."

She waited while Jas gathered a few rocks. After stacking them in a small pile in front of the gate, they set off to catch their Shadow.

Sayen was glad she had something to do while they waited for her parents to prepare the truck for its assault on the Shadow's suppressor. She knew she should really have gone to check on Erielle—the woman was unwell and alone in a strange house—but she couldn't bring herself to. Not after their argument. She didn't know what to make of what they'd both said. Her mother had told her that Erielle was spending most of the time asleep anyway.

The truth was, though she didn't agree with the underworlder, she could see why she thought as she did. Though the arguments Sayen had used to defend her parents were all true, and she loved them deeply, she wasn't sure she could excuse their lifestyle now that she'd heard Erielle's opinion, not even to herself. Why were they so highly paid? Did they really deserve everything they had? What had they meant when they said they helped the work against 'enemies of the Government'? How were the devices they made used? Were they used for good? Could her parents even tell?

On the other hand, Sayen was sure that all the money in the world couldn't fix what was wrong with their society, nor improve the lives of the worst off, like the underworlders, over the long term.

So, in a way, both she and Erielle were right. She just didn't think she would ever get the woman to see it that way. The underworlder was passionate about the inequalities and injustices she saw.

It seemed inevitable that they would have to part ways. There could be no future for two people with such different backgrounds and who held such different views. Sayen just didn't feel ready to have that conversation with Erielle yet.

They were nearing the road. "Crossing that is going to be the toughest part," said Jas. "Lights from the Shadows' building reveal everything for quite a distance. We'll have to go far out of our way to cross in darkness. That's why I told your father we needed twenty minutes."

"Okay," Sayen replied, though it seemed they would be cutting it very fine. She supposed Jas knew what she was doing.

They moved through the desert until the light from the Shadow's building was faint, then crossed over the road in little more than a heartbeat. Even with her enhanced hearing, Sayen detected no sounds coming from the aliens' building. They began their approach.

In another few minutes, they were squatting below an open window. According to what Jas had seen, the Shadow girl was asleep in this room, alone. The plan was that Sayen would go inside, sedate the sleeping girl, then lift her and pass her out to Jas. When Sayen was outside again, they would take the Shadow back to the estate.

She stood to peer over the windowsill. Inside, all was dark. She heard breathing. Using her night vision, all she could see was bare floor and walls.

Jas touched her leg. When she looked down, the hunkered-down woman spread her hands wide in a questioning gesture. Sayen raised flat palm. *Wait.* She listened again. Someone was definitely in the room. No. She could hear two people breathing. She lifted two fingers to Jas, who grimaced in response.

Sayen frowned as she listened again. There were definitely two sets of breathing sounds. One was soft and light. That could be the Shadow girl. The other, though, was even softer, lighter, and faster. If Sayen had been forced to guess, she would have said there was a baby in the room. Had the Shadows taken a baby? The thought sent a shudder down her spine.

Jas pointed at her timer. Sayen had to act now or it would be too late.

She grabbed the windowsill and pulled herself up and over in one smooth motion. She checked her momentum as she landed right next to the Shadow, who was sleeping under the window. The girl's eyes opened at the sound of Sayen's arrival. Her mouth also opened to shout or scream. Sayen quickly pressed down on the child's face with one hand, muffling her voice, and with the other hand, she delivered the sedative into her bare neck.

As the girl's eyes closed and her body went limp, Sayen glanced around. Where was the second breather she'd heard? The room was empty. The girl was alone as she'd been when Jas had last seen her. There was no time to figure out the mystery. She had to pass the Shadow out of the window, and they had to get back home in time for the momentary defense shutdown.

The Shadow girl was lying on a pile of clothes and blankets beneath an adult woman's coat. Sayen reached under the coat to grab her around her waist and pull her out. As she did so, her hand encountered something soft, warm, and furry. She pulled back in surprise and lifted the coat to see what it was. A cat was curled up next to the girl. After Sayen exposed it, the animal took fright. It jumped onto the girl and out of the window. It must have landed on the waiting Jas, because Sayen heard her gasp from outside.

The Shadow had been cuddling a cat. Or had the cat only approached her for warmth and she'd let it stay? There was no time to figure it out.

Sayen lifted the girl's limp body and lowered her into Jas's waiting arms. She vaulted out the window and down onto the desert sand. Jas was already running, carrying the Shadow child. Sayen quickly caught up to her.

"Pass her to me," she said to Jas. "I won't feel her weight at all."

Jas handed over the Shadow, and Sayen put her over her shoulder.

The aliens in the building didn't seem to notice the missing girl, because no sight or sound of pursuit came from behind. They ran from the revealing lights and into the darkness, to the point where they could cross the road unseen.

As they approached her home, Sayen saw movement at the front. The truck was pulling around from the back onto the driveway, with Makey at the wheel. Her parents must have finished the modifications. They were nearly ready to destroy the suppressor.

She and Jas had their Shadow. With the information they would be able to send, the Transgalactic Council couldn't ignore the Shadow invasion. They had to dispatch the Unity forces to drive them out. Earth would be saved, even if she, her parents, and her friends might not live to see it.

# TWELVE

"You all right, mate?" Carl called down to Makey from his position behind the weapon on the roof of the truck. They had less than two minutes before Sayen's dad would drop the force field and they would set out on their mission.

"Yeah, I'm fine," the kid replied. "All set. And you?"

"I'm all set, too."

"We have time to swap places if you want. You know I'm a better shot than you."

Carl laughed. He liked the kid's spark. "In your dreams. I was shooting rumpabugs before you were born. Now shut up and concentrate on driving this thing straight. Have you got the shields up?"

"'Course."

"Then let's wait for the signal."

Carl settled himself back in his seat, his palms resting on the controls of the weapon Sayen's mother had modified. Above him was the shield Mr. Lee had constructed. It was a smooth rotating dome, open only a slit where the barrel of the weapon ended. He wasn't totally blind to what was happening outside, however: a visual of the sky was provided by an interface screen between his controls.

He hardly recognized the weapon as Ozment's out-of-date

missile launcher. His brief instructions from Mrs. Lee had been basically to tell him to let the weapon do its thing—that its capabilities far exceeded human powers. His presence was only required in case the automatic targeting got taken out by a hit. Then, it would operate manually, but only to the extent of Carl's ability.

In case he lost targeting *and* visual on the interface, Mr. Lee had fitted an explosive eject system for the dome. It was a desperate measure, but Carl would be able to continue firing by sight. He hoped his skills would be sufficient to protect the truck until Makey had done his job. If they survived *and* made it back, that would be a bonus.

The truck began to vibrate. Makey had started the engine and was driving. It was time.

As the truck started toward the gate, Carl flipped the switch to activate the weapon. The display lit up, and the barrel swiveled right, taking Carl in his seat with it. On the screen, a large heli was revealed. The Shadows had seen the truck begin to move and had launched their response. Concentric lines moved down the screen to the heli's center. The weapon had identified its first target before they were even outside the gates.

The screen flashed repeatedly, as if the weapon were begging Carl to fire. He had to wait. If he fired, the charge wouldn't penetrate the force field.

"Nearly there," Makey called, aware of the fact that Carl could see nothing but sky.

He heard a rumble as the estate gates opened.

———

Makey had argued so hard to be allowed to do this, and tried so hard to get the adults to stop treating him like a kid. Yet when it came to it, he still felt like a kid inside. Maybe he'd been wrong to push so hard. Now, everyone was relying on him, and he wasn't sure he was up to it. Maybe he should have let someone else drive the truck.

His palms were sweaty on the steering wheel. Through the slit in the cab's shields, he could see Mr. Lee standing at his front door, holding a small control device. He held one hand up in the air, its fingers spread. Five. Five seconds until Makey had to begin the drive down to the gate.

It was too late to back out now.

He gripped the steering wheel hard. He could do it. He *would* do it. He wouldn't let everyone down.

One finger on Mr. Lee's hand dropped. Four. Another finger. Three. Two. One.

Makey pressed the gas, and the truck approached the gates. He was counting in his head. He had ten seconds until Mr. Lee would open the gates and drop the force field long enough for him to drive through.

He had one job. Get to the correct side of the building and drive right into it as fast as he could. It was vital that he destroy the suppressor. Otherwise everyone's effort would be wasted. No message would get through to the Transgalactic Council, and Earth would fall to the Shadows.

His stomach clenched. It was all on him. Everything they'd done up to that point, everything that everyone had gone through, was so that he—a kid—could do this.

"Nearly there," he called to Carl.

Almost as he was upon them, the gates parted. In another moment, he was through. Immediately, the truck rocked with the force of an explosion on the roof, and another explosion to the right caused it to buck violently. Makey wrenched the steering wheel to bring the swerving vehicle back under his control. He was veering too far to the left. Now he was too far to the right. He couldn't seem to keep it straight. The truck was heading off the road and into the desert on either side, almost out of control.

Flames erupted to his right as a heli hit the ground. Carl had got one. The truck shuddered again as they took another direct hit. On the left was another that sent deep vibrations through the cab and into his bones and teeth.

Something was wrong. The truck wasn't driving like it should. It was leaning and juddering hard. The Shadows had succeeded in shooting out tires on one side. Carl had told him this might happen, but he'd said the truck would still go, only it would be harder to control her.

Makey brought the vehicle around. The building appeared in his sight. He only had to keep the truck straight and get her to top speed before impact. If he could only do that, it would be enough.

———

They were barely through the gates before Carl fired the weapon. The heli that the gun held in its sights exploded and toppled from the sky, but before it hit the ground, the weapon was already swiveling around to another target. Carl fired again and caught a glimpse of a missile just before it dissolved in midair. *Missiles?* The Shadows weren't only attacking from the air, they were firing at them from a base far away from the estate. *Krat.* He had no chance of finding and destroying the base using the weapon in the truck. They were vulnerable to every missile launched at them, and so was Sayen's parents' estate.

He had no time to think about that. The weapon was swiveling rapidly once more. A shuttle was passing overhead, and both its guns were firing. Streaks of fire streamed down toward the truck, but on their way an answering bolt crossed them, traveling in the opposite direction into the heart of the shuttle's engine. The space vehicle split apart like a massive exploding firework. Flaming debris was scattered across the sky.

The truck took another hit from the missile launcher. It nearly turned the vehicle on its side. Carl was amazed at Makey's skills at reacting to the deluge of hits, keeping the truck going. He guessed that they were driving toward the building.

With a deafening crack, the dome above him blew away. A hit had triggered the eject device. The cold desert wind chilled his skin, and he saw the predawn sky with its clearing clouds and fading stars. The sky held more than stars, however. Carl was being carried around in his seat again as the automatic targeting system locked onto another aircraft.

The gun roared, and Carl's seat kicked back as it fired. The weapon was better than any he'd ever known, but would it be enough? The top of the building rose up at the edge of his vision. They were nearly there. They'd nearly made it. A stream of fire ran across the truck's roof, searing the weapon. Flames flickered from Carl's clothes, and for several seconds he battled to prevent the fire from enveloping him, scorching his hands as he extinguished the flames.

As his panic eased, he became aware that he and the weapon were no longer moving. The hit had taken out the automatic targeting. If he were to defend the truck and Makey, it was now entirely down to him. He grabbed the controls and spun the weapon around, searching the skies for a target.

A massive boom sounded to his right, and the truck began to topple. It leaned so far, Carl knew it would never recover. The power of the blast and the speed of their falling meant Makey would never right the vehicle. They hadn't reached the Shadows' building or the suppressor inside. It was over. As Carl was thrown to the side in the falling truck, more of the building became visible. They were only a few tens of meters from it. They'd almost made it. Almost.

A heli appeared overhead. Was this the aircraft that had defeated them? Had the Shadow pilot come to gloat over his victory? With an enormous effort, Carl wrenched the weapon around and fired a final shot as the truck hit the rocky desert floor. He was thrown from the vehicle. Momentum carried both he and the truck forward. Carl tumbled along the dry dirt; the truck slid along on its side with a dreadful screeching and showers of sparks.

As Carl finished rolling, he leapt to his feet to run after the vehicle. He had to reach Makey and get him out of the cab before Shadows emerged from the building. They might have failed to destroy the suppressor, but that didn't mean they would give up. They would fight to the last.

The sound of roaring came from overhead, and the ground lit up with reflected light. Carl looked up to see that the heli he'd fired at—the one that had delivered the decisive blow—was falling from the sky.

With his last effort, he'd hit it. Carl smiled in grim satisfaction, but his expression turned to one of joyous disbelief as he realized the trajectory of the doomed vehicle. It was heading straight for the Shadow building. It was going to hit it on the corner they'd been aiming at.

The truck finally slid to a halt only meters from the building. Carl sped up. The heli hit and crashed through the brick wall. As shattered fragments of brick sprayed out, the inferno that had once been the heli exploded.

Carl was at the truck's cab. The heat from the downed heli was almost unbearable. The cab's shields were still up. He peered through the slit and just made out an unconscious Makey inside. He had only seconds before the metal of the shields heated up and fried the kid. But how could he get to him? He tugged at the door handles, burning his hands. They were jammed. He hammered on the steel shields, but Makey didn't stir.

Despair gnawed at Carl. He couldn't let the kid die. He screamed at him through the window slit, and as he did, he saw the dark hole of the tunnel entrance behind the seats. Of course. In a moment, he was at the roof of the truck where it lay on the ground. He grabbed the edge of the tunnel and pulled himself up. Feet first, he climbed down into the chokingly hot cab.

Makey was out cold from a blow to the head. Carl undid his seat belt. Somehow, he managed to maneuver the kid out of his seat and pull him up through the tunnel. He gulped the cool desert air as he emerged onto the roof with the unconscious young man and tumbled with him to the ground.

Movement caught his eye. He looked up. They were surrounded by Shadows.

# Thirteen

Jas and Sayen had made it back to the fence surrounding the Lees' estate just in time. They carried the unconscious Shadow child inside and to the elevator to take her down to the basement. The Lee Family androids had put the scanner there after removing it from the back of the truck. The Shadow girl was about ten years old—the human victim had been about ten, Jas corrected herself.

Like all the aliens, the Shadow was indistinguishable from the child whose place she had taken. Her hair was shoulder length and loose, and long bangs hung down as her head lolled. She had freckles across her nose, and two of her front teeth were missing.

"Where was the cat when you went into the room?" Jas asked Sayen as they neared the scanner. The androids had connected it to a power supply. It was a simple, flat-bottomed tube on a waist-high base. Jas noted it was similar to the one she'd been scanned in when she'd first arrived on Dawn. An interface at one end displayed one word: Ready.

"It was sleeping with her. They were both under a coat. I frightened it, I think, when I lifted the coat. That was why it took off."

"It was cuddled up with her? She was cuddling a cat?"

"That was how it looked. It could've crept in there by itself after she was asleep, I guess."

"It must have, don't you think?" Jas asked. "Kinda weird if it didn't. I mean, I never thought of the Shadows liking other creatures. They don't even seem to like each other that much."

"It's hard to tell what they like or dislike. They're aliens. They might not even have likes and dislikes. But I agree, it does seem weird. I don't think I've ever been more surprised in my life than when I took that coat off of her and found a cat there. I was expecting a baby or something."

Jas tried not to contemplate the idea of a baby experiencing what she'd seen happen to the humans in the Shadow trap.

"Come on," Sayen went on. "Let's do this. My parents said they have the packet ready to send the minute the guys destroy the suppressor. We just need to upload the readings from the scanner."

They laid the girl out on the belt. Sayen touched the interface, and it started up, moving the Shadow into the tube. Soon, they were looking at the soles of her bare, dirty feet. The scanner hummed quietly.

To her surprise, Jas found she was holding her breath. She had this sudden, irrational hope that the child wasn't a Shadow, even though it would mean that their plans to alert the Transgalactic Council might fail. She didn't want to think about the victim's death, or the Shadow's strange affection for an Earth animal. She couldn't reconcile her understanding of the aliens with the image of this little girl sleeping with her arms wrapped around a cat.

"Look," Sayen said. She was gazing at the interface screen.

Jas joined her at the display. It showed a 3D graphic of the child's body, split into sections. A faint glow emanated from all parts of the girl. As Jas watched it, the graphic disappeared and was replaced by the words, Shadow Confirmed.

Her heart sank.

Sayen was already swiping the screen, capturing the results and sending them onward to the message packet her parents had prepared.

"We did it, Jas," she said as she touched the icon to close the display. "After all this time, we finally did it."

"Yeah," Jas replied half-heartedly.

"What's wrong?"

"I don't know. I guess I can't quite believe that she's a Shadow." Jas sighed. "So, what now? When will the sedative wear off? And what do we do with her then?" She realized she hadn't thought about what they would do with the captured alien.

"She should start coming around in another ten minutes or so. Then—"

Behind them, the elevator pinged. They turned to see Mrs. Lee step out. "We got the results, honey. And Daddy's sending the packet now to the nearest deep space link. When the Council receives it, it shouldn't take them more than a few days to get to Earth and begin investigating."

"He's sending the packet?" Jas asked. "You mean you have deep space comm? Carl and Makey destroyed the suppressor?"

"Yes, just a few moments ago. The waves blinked out to nothing."

"But what about the guys?" asked Jas. "Are they back?"

"Not yet. The truck turned over before it hit the building. But one of the helis Carl downed smashed into it instead. That must have been what destroyed the suppressor."

Sayen and Jas shared a look. "Let's go," Sayen said.

"You're going out there?" said Mrs. Lee. "Oh, Sayen, do you have to?"

They were already running for the elevator. "Yes, Mama, I do. They're my friends."

———

It took Sayen several minutes to persuade her father to turn off the force field so they could go out to rescue Carl and Makey. He repeated that he would go himself rather than let her risk her life. But she pointed out that he had to stay home. He couldn't leave her mother and their sick guest, Erielle, alone.

"Be careful out there," were his final words as he turned off the force field. He had a look on his face like he thought he would never see his daughter again.

Jas had armed them both with extra blasters before leaving the house. She held one in each hand as, together, they ran across the road toward the burning building. No time for precautionary measures now. If Carl and Makey were still alive, every second would count in keeping them that way.

The Shadows' building was rapidly turning into an inferno. Flames rose twice as high as the walls, and a dull roaring filled the air. They were still far away when Jas felt the heat of the fire on her face.

The sun was rising, but the light from the fire was brighter. Jas could only just make out the end of the truck. It was also on fire, and the dark shapes of men and women were outlined in the light. She could vaguely see some kind of struggle going on.

"Krat. Sayen, the Shadows have them."

"You tackle them from this side," Sayen said. "I'm going around the back."

"But—"

Sayen was already leaving, running at her impossibly fast speed toward the rear of the building.

At the fight with the Shadows, someone was lifting a large rock as if they were getting ready to bring it down heavily on an opponent's head.

Raising her weapon and aiming as she ran, Jas fired. She got the Shadow holding the rock in the back. It looked down, incredulous, at the smoking hole that appeared in its chest before dropping limply to the ground. The rest of them turned. She fired again, and another Shadow fell.

They were armed. As one raised its weapon to return fire, Carl plowed into its side, sending it flying into some of the others. Makey was sitting on the sand, looking barely conscious.

More Shadows raised their weapons. There were too many of them. Jas could never shoot them all, and Carl had been disarmed.

Just as Jas was accepting this was her last fight, a cry of rage rose above the crackle of the flames. The cry had come from the burning truck. The Shadows turned toward the sound in puzzlement.

Sayen was on top of the vehicle, standing within the blaze. She leapt down. She was firing, and she was on fire. Shadows fell at each blast of her weapon, and Jas shot down more of them. They only stopped firing when the rest of the aliens fled.

Suddenly, Carl had Sayen on the ground. He was rolling her in the dirt, putting out the flames. Her clothes were little more than blackened shreds.

Makey staggered to his feet, shaking his head.

"You did it," Jas exclaimed to Carl. "The suppressor's destroyed. Sayen's parents have sent the packet."

"*We* did it," Carl said. "We all did."

The Shadows seemed to have retreated. Sayen and Carl were burned, and Makey had taken a severe blow to the head, but they'd survived. Carl and Jas hugged. They held the kid's arms to support him, and all four of them turned toward Sayen's home.

It was at that moment that the mansion took a direct hit.

# Fourteen

"Krat," Sayen exclaimed. One side of the front of the beautiful house was ruined, and smoke was already pouring from the windows nearby. The next second, she was gone. She was running toward her home, her raggedy clothes trailing behind her.

Jas, Carl, and especially Makey, struggled to keep up with their friend.

"What's firing at the house?" Jas asked Carl, scanning the early morning sky. "I thought you shot everything down?"

"They've got a missile launcher somewhere out in the desert," he replied. "It almost destroyed the truck too. The automatic targeting was taking out the missiles, but it couldn't zero in on the launcher."

Another missile screamed overhead, and as they watched, it tore through the electrified fence. The house took another hit.

"Look at that," Carl said, looking behind. The Shadows had reappeared and were running toward the estate. "Do you think they're after us or Sayen's parents?"

"I don't know," Jas replied. "Whatever it is they want to do, it isn't going to be good. We have to catch up to Sayen. She can't take them all on by herself."

But it wasn't easy to catch up. Makey could barely run. Carl and Jas were partly supporting him and partly dragging him along.

Sayen had reached the gate. She leapt over its ruins and went speeding up the driveway. The other three struggled after her. Jas saw her swing open the front door and disappear inside.

By the time the other three reached the same spot, Makey was nearly unconscious again. He collapsed onto the front steps.

"Take him upstairs, Carl," Jas said, glancing over her shoulder. The remaining Shadows were clambering over the ruins of the gate. "Take him to Erielle's room, so I know where you all are. I'm going to find Sayen and her parents. We might escape the Shadows yet."

Carl put his hands under Makey's arms and hauled the kid to his feet. Like a drunken couple, the two made their way up the staircase. Jas followed, helping to support the unconscious Makey. At the top, they parted ways.

Carl said. "After I get him to Erielle's room, I'm going to give Erielle a gun and lock them in together. Then I'm going to come and find you. Take care, Jas."

"I will," she replied and gave him a fleeting smile.

As she ran to Mr. Lee's room, another explosion rocked the house. She grabbed a desk to steady herself. It would only be a matter of minutes before the place was rubble. The elevator was at the basement. She called it and, too slowly, it rose.

As the doors opened, Jas's heart missed a beat. The interior was splattered with blood. Whose blood, she didn't dare to think. She stepped inside. As the elevator went down, she readied her weapon. Whatever was waiting for her at the bottom would see the elevator was descending. She pressed her back against the corner to the right and aimed the muzzle of her gun at the crack between the doors. She aimed low.

The elevator chimed. Before the doors had opened more than a slit, Jas fired. A laser beam returned her fire, scoring a deep burn in the wall opposite the door. The doors opened wide. No more laser beams were discharged. Jas peeked out. She'd hit the Shadow girl. She was on the floor, and Sayen and her parents were behind her. Mr. Lee's head was streaming with blood.

"Thanks, Jas," Sayen said as she saw her. "The Shadow was about to kill me. Daddy had forced her down back here when she tried to escape, but she'd gotten the upper hand."

"No problem," Jas replied. "But hurry. We have to get out. There are Shadows in the house. We have to collect Erielle, Makey, and Carl, and leave. Now."

At the end of her sentence, the lights flickered and went out. The basement was suddenly pitch black.

"The power supply's been hit," Mrs. Lee exclaimed.

"Oh no," came Sayen's voice in the darkness. "How are we going to get out? The elevator won't operate without power."

"It's okay," said Mr. Lee. "There are stairs for just such an emergency. We only have to get to them. Everybody, join hands. Follow me."

"Be careful," Jas said. "The Shadow girl will be coming around soon."

"What? You didn't kill her?" asked Sayen.

"No. I didn't know who I might be shooting at. It could have been one of you three. I set my weapon to stun."

"Krat," Sayen said.

"Sayen, that isn't very polite," said Mrs. Lee.

Sayen sighed. "Sorry, Mama."

They went farther across the workroom, Mr. Lee slowly guiding them around the workbenches and machinery. After a short while, he bumped into something. "Ah. I believe we're nearly at the wall. Yes, here it is. Now we just follow it to the left. If we're lucky, I should be able to locate the door handle."

"Hey," said a voice in the distance. A little girl's voice. "Where are you? Where are y'all going?"

Jas's stomach clenched. The Shadow sounded exactly like a sad, lost child.

"Don't answer," whispered Sayen.

"I heard you," said the girl. "I know where you are. I'm coming over. Wait for me."

Jas could see nothing but darkness. She could feel nothing but Sayen's hand and the smooth wall they were following.

"Are you here?" asked the Shadow. Already, it sounded like she was nearby. "Please answer. I want to find you. I have to find you. I have to get out. Please take me with you. Don't leave me down here all alone."

A quiet expression of satisfaction came from in front. Mr. Lee had found the entrance to the staircase.

"I can hear you," said the girl. "Wait for me. I'm coming."

There was a rustle and a creak as Mr. Lee opened the door. Jas felt Sayen's tug, signaling her to follow. She felt the door's edge. Sayen let go of her as she went through.

A soft, small child's hand plucked at Jas's arm. She froze.

"There you are," said the Shadow, excitement in her voice.

Horror and dread overcame Jas. She kicked out. Her foot met its mark and sank into something soft and warm before sending the thing flying. There was a shriek. Jas bolted through the door and slammed it closed. She was in the stairwell, but she was still in darkness.

"Here, Jas," called Sayen. Following the sound of her friend's voice, she tripped over a step. Scrabbling sounded from the other side of the door. The Shadow was trying to find the door handle. Jas hadn't been able to lock it. The girl would be through the door and after them at any moment.

She raced upstairs. Somewhere above, light appeared, casting a faint illumination down the steps. Mr. Lee had reached the top and opened the door into an upper level room with a window.

From below came the sound of creaking as the door opened followed by light footsteps running up. Jas broke into a cold sweat. She felt a special horror about the cat-loving Shadow girl. Something about her was especially fearful, and yet Jas wasn't sure she could kill her.

Jas emerged into the room at the top of the stairs. She slammed the door shut. "That *thing's* coming up after us," she panted.

"Don't worry, sugar," Mrs. Lee said. "Not a problem." She jammed a chair under the doorknob.

"Which way to Erielle's room?" Jas asked.

"Follow me," Sayen replied.

"Have you noticed something?" Mr Lee asked as they left the bedroom. "The bombardment has stopped."

"Probably because Shadows are in the building," Jas said. "They don't want to kill their own kind. They must be planning to capture us, or pick us off one by one."

# FIFTEEN

"Erielle," Sayen called through the door. She didn't want to take the woman by surprise. If she was armed, opening the door without announcing herself could be disastrous.

"Thank krat," came Erielle's reply. "Get in here."

Sayen went inside to find Erielle in bed with Makey lying unconscious next to her. Carl was sitting down with his arms folded. The two android servants were standing over him as if on guard duty.

"What's going on?" Jas asked.

"They wouldn't let me leave," Carl replied in an exasperated tone.

"Sir, Ma'am," said the female android, Florence. "It appears that the estate is under attack. We took the initiative to keep our guests safe while we awaited your further instructions."

"And you did a wonderful job," Sayen's mother replied. "Now I have another job for you. First—Jas, Carl, please give our servants a weapon."

Jas held her blaster protectively to her chest. "What? Why?"

"Because they're going to defend us. I've reprogrammed them with military skills, as far as I was able. Their primary function now is to save our lives. That's why they wouldn't let Carl leave the room."

"Oh, I see." Jas handed over a gun.

Mrs. Lee addressed the androids. "Now, I want you both to understand that the creatures that are roaming this house and looking for us are not human. They may look, sound, and act human, but they are not. Do you understand that? Do you believe me?"

"Yes, we do, Ma'am," chorused the two androids.

"That means you are not breaking any fundamental law by shooting at them, right?" she continued. "In fact, you would be doing us an enormous favor. Do you think you'll be able to do that? If you kill the invaders, it would help us. It would give us a chance to escape."

"We can do that, Ma'am."

"Wonderful," said Sayen's father, looking out the window. "I think it's high time we got the krat out of here."

"Craven," exclaimed Sayen's mother.

Erielle pushed down her covers and pulled herself out of bed and onto her crutches. She refused all offers of help. Sayen picked up Makey, and they went out into the corridor.

"Where now?" Jas asked.

"To the helis on the roof," Mrs. Lee said. "We'll never get out with Shadows all over the house looking for us. Now that the force field's down, we might as well take our chances in the sky. Was that your plan, Craven?"

"Exactly, my dear," her husband replied.

The android servants went one way to head off the Shadows, and the humans went the other. Sayen's father led them away from the main staircase and into the smaller corridors. A Shadow wandered into view, and Carl shot it. Sayen hoped the alien died before it had a chance to tell the others where they were.

She knew this part of the house well. She'd often played hide and seek with her brother there when they were children. It was also the quickest route to the roof. She'd walked it during her short-lived stint at the Global Government Security Headquarters.

Wisps of smoke were following them down the corridor, and the air was filled with the smell of burning. They would have to leave soon if they didn't want to go up in flames with the rest of the place. Sayen's heart sank at the knowledge that the only home she'd ever known would soon be gone. But they'd sent the packet to the Transgalactic Council, and with a little luck, they could escape the Shadows pursuing them and find some place to hide out while waiting for the Council to come to Earth's aid.

A cry echoed out. Someone had been shot not far away. The androids had their backs. She hoped they would last out a while longer.

They redoubled their pace. Soon, they were running. Poor Erielle was hobbling along as fast as she could on her crutches.

"Here we are at last," Sayen's father said. He opened the door to the stairway that led to the roof. The corridor echoed with footsteps. Sayen turned to see several Shadows running toward them. They'd broken through the androids' defenses. Jas fired, killing the leader, but the others only jumped over him and came on.

"Hurry up," said Sayen's mother as she guided Erielle up the stairs.

When they were all inside the stairwell, Sayen locked the door. They stepped out onto the windswept roof. Smoke was rising up all around them into the early morning sky.

To one side, where the helis had stood, was a pile of smoking ruins. A missile had destroyed the helis. They weren't much more than lumps of charred, twisted, reeking metal. "Krat," exclaimed Sayen's mother. They walked slowly over to what was left of their only means of escape.

"What now?" Carl asked.

Sayen's father turned to him with a stricken expression. "I'm all out of answers to that question, son."

Sayen swallowed. "Daddy, Mama, it's okay. We did what had to. We've done all we could." She put Makey down so that she could embrace them both. Then she turned and hugged Erielle, holding onto the stubborn, pigheaded, dogmatic woman as if she were life itself.

Jas and Carl looked at each other and smiled briefly. They

turned, raised their weapons, and aimed them at the door on the other side of the roof, waiting for the Shadows to emerge.

A blast of hot air swept down from above, and over the roar of the burning house came the whine of a shuttle engine.

"Krat," shouted Jas. "They're coming at us from above too." She turned and aimed at the floor of the shuttle that hung over them. A tiny escape hatch opened, and the head and shoulders of a man appeared in the space.

As Jas sighted her gun, Sayen ran at her and knocked her down.

"What the...?" she exclaimed from the floor.

"Phelan," yelled Sayen. "Mama, Daddy, it's Phelan. Back up, everyone, so they can land."

"They can't land on the roof. It'll only burn the place down faster," Carl shouted over the engine's whine.

"Not our roof," Mrs. Lee called in reply. "But we'll have to take shelter from the heat of the engines. I think Phelan was trying to warn us."

"Over here," Mr. Lee said, and he led them to a raised section. Sayen picked up Makey and carried him over. They hid on the side facing away from the descending shuttle. Nevertheless, the air turned very hot as the aircraft fired its landing jets.

When the shuttle's noise was quiet, they ventured out. A couple of Shadows must have tried to emerge onto the roof as the shuttle was landing. Their lobster-red, blistered remains were contorted into tortured shapes. They made their way across the roof. The shuttle door opened, and Sayen's brother, Phelan, came out.

"Hurry," he called, gesturing at them. "This place is going up in flames. We don't have long before it collapses."

Sayen ran to her brother, who took Makey from her before disappearing inside the shuttle. Jas and Carl helped Erielle as she shuffled along on her crutches. Mr. and Mrs. Lee brought up the rear. Crashes and explosions came from the disintegrating mansion beneath them. Suddenly, a portion of the roof collapsed, a jet of flame leapt up, and the shuttle began to slide toward the hole.

"Come on," yelled Phelan, gripping the door edge for support in the angled, moving shuttle. He waved frantically at them with his other hand and moved aside as Jas and Carl arrived at the door and helped Erielle through. Sayen stepped aboard, then turned to check on her parents.

Her mother was right behind her, but with horror she saw that Shadows were pouring onto the roof, and that her father had stopped to fire at them, trying to hold them off so the others could get away. Her mother noticed Sayen's expression and turned back to see her husband's plight.

"Craven," she screamed.

"Go," he shouted over his shoulder.

The shuttle was sliding inexorably toward the hole. "Inside, Sayen, Mama," yelled Phelan. "Now."

He pushed Sayen in and tried to pull his mother aboard the shuttle, but the woman shook him off. "I've been with that man for forty years. I'm not abandoning him now." She gave her son a mighty push, sending him through the shuttle doors. The aircraft was at a precarious angle, and everyone was slipping down the floor.

Sayen had fallen down in the entranceway and was staring at her brother in shock. Phelan slammed the doors shut. The engines fired, and they were airborne.

# Sixteen

J as went to comfort Sayen, but she was inconsolable. She sat on the floor, sobbing and rocking in almost animal-like despair. Her brother was white-faced and trembling. He was shaking his head, as if trying to rid himself of the memory of the last few minutes. After a while, he sat with his sister, and they held each other.

No one spoke. Everyone but Makey was in the entranceway of the shuttle. Away from the heated air and the roar of the burning mansion, the quiet, cool interior of the spacecraft seemed almost surreal. Its flight was easy and smooth.

Finally, Phelan composed himself a little. He held his sister's shoulders and looked into her face. "When I got the packet from Mama saying you'd gone missing," he said, "I came as fast as I could, but I was on the other side of the galaxy."

Sayen nodded and wiped her eyes.

"I'm glad you're safe," said Phelan.

Jas, Carl, and Erielle went into the passenger cabin to give them some time together. There were only eight passenger seats in the small craft. Jas sat down and wondered what it was that Sayen's brother did that took him across the galaxy. She hadn't noticed a company logo on the side of the shuttle.

Makey had been deposited in a seat. He was awake but disoriented. Jas inspected the already deep purple, large bruise on his forehead. She hoped there were medical facilities wherever it was that the shuttle was taking them.

"Are you okay?" Carl asked her. When she nodded, he said, "I'm gonna talk to the pilot." He left her with Erielle and the kid.

The underworlder was looking better after her short stint of care at Sayen's home. She was clearly troubled, however. She glanced repeatedly at the doorway to the shuttle's entrance, obviously concerned about Sayen.

Jas sat back in her seat and stared unseeing in front of her. Mr. and Mrs. Lee didn't stand a chance, of course. Even if they survived the searing heat of the shuttle's engines and they defeated the attacking aliens, there was no way they would make it out of the burning building alive.

They were such wonderful people. So smart and wise, and they loved their family so deeply. The world would feel their loss. *She* felt their loss, and she'd hardly known them. She wanted to weep for them, but as usual, the tears wouldn't come.

Yet the ache in her heart had to be nothing compared to how Sayen and her brother must be feeling. It was at times like these the fact that Jas had no family that she knew of brought her some small comfort. She missed out on the warmth, closeness, and love that most families seemed to experience, but she also missed out on losing them.

Carl reappeared from the pilot's cabin. He sat next to Jas and fastened his seat belt.

"How's the kid?" he asked.

"He needs medical care."

Carl nodded. "He should get it soon. I talked to the pilot. It turns out Sayen's brother owns a deep space mining company. His starship's in orbit, and we're going to it now."

"They've been in deep space for the last few months?" Jas asked.

"Looks like it."

"So it's unlikely they have any Shadows aboard?"

"I think so. The pilot had no idea what I was talking about. Never heard of Shadows. Never seen a trap."

For the first time in what seemed like forever, Jas relaxed. For the immediate future, she wouldn't have to worry about encountering one of the hostile aliens. She wouldn't have to wonder if the person she was speaking to really was who they appeared to be.

What was more, they'd done what they set out to do: they'd alerted the Transgalactic Council. Yet somehow, she couldn't take any pleasure in the achievement. So many lives had been lost. The Shadows were even abducting children and replacing them with weird, animal-loving dopplegangers.

Carl reached out and took her hand. He folded his fingers over hers.

"After we get to Phelan's ship?" she asked him. "What then? What do we do next?"

"I don't know. I have to go and get Flux, for one thing. The little fella probably thinks I'm dead. After that, I'm not sure. I don't want to abandon the farm, especially if the Shadows have plans for it, but Earth isn't safe anymore."

"No, it isn't. When the Transgalactic Council receives the packet, what do you think they'll do?"

"They'll have to react. If they don't stop the Shadows from taking over Earth, the rest of the galaxy will be next."

They lapsed into silence. The shuttle flew on, taking them farther from their alien-infested world and closer to their temporary safe haven.

Carl's fingers loosened their grasp on hers. Jas looked at him and found that he'd fallen asleep. She was glad to see that peace had settled on his face.

But then, despite their miraculous escape, and despite the fact that they were on their way to the first safe place they'd known since the *Galathea* had landed on K. 67092d, a chill settled over her heart. There was only one way the Transgalactic Council could react. They would have to go on the offensive to decisively rid the galaxy of the Shadows' menace.

War was coming, and somehow Jas knew that she, Carl, and their companions would find themselves caught up in it.


JAS'S STORY CONCLUDES IN ...

*THE GALACTIC CHRONICLES*

Sign up to my reader group for a free copy of *Starbound*, the Shadows of the Void prequel that tells the story of what happened to Jas Harrington in Antarctica, and for exclusive notice of new releases, advanced reader opportunities and other interesting stuff:

https://jjgreenauthor.com/free-books/

# ALSO BY J.J. GREEN

STAR LEGEND

STAR MAGE SAGA

SPACE COLONY ONE

CARRIE HATCHETT, SPACE ADVENTURER

INTERSTELLAR FLEET